Diversion Books
A Division of Diversion Publishing Corp.
443 Park Avenue South, Suite 1008
New York, New York 10016
www.DiversionBooks.com

For more information, email info@diversionbooks.com

First Diversion Books edition October 2014.
Print ISBN: 978-1-62681-425-7
eBook ISBN: 978-1-62681-311-3

THE
ELEMENTALISTS

THE TIPPING POINT PROPHECY
BOOK ONE

C . S H A R P

DIVERSIONBOOKS

THE LORD OF FIRE

Far below the surface of the earth, buried in a river of magma beneath the tectonic plates, the Old One slept. Once he had been called Nagapenthe by the little men who worshipped him as a god and looked on the volcano where he lived with reverence and fear. A thousand years later, the city builders of the eastern empire had named him Chien-Tang, and they'd honored his presence in the river that crossed their land with a sacrifice of ten bulls and a virgin at the dawning of every spring.

He had been a muse to artists and an icon to leaders of men, but those times had been forgotten by the scribes of history. That had been before the age of mankind's rule, before they had spread with their creative spark and viral ability to adapt. The era of his kind had ended, and the elemental powers of the earth had slipped into obscurity, becoming the stuff of myth, buried beneath mountains and oceans.

He had slumbered for another two thousand years and had only recently grown restless of his dreams and this endless pondering of the cosmos. Even from miles below the crust, he could hear the buzz, click, and whir of the machines that coated the earth. He could smell the smoke and poison that billowed into the air and sank into the soil. Now all the waste and fury of the humans marred his dreams with fearful visions of a dead and spent world. They goaded him with their arrogance and cruelty, challenging him to rise up from the furnace of the land and remind them of those who came before.

He huffed two fountains of boiling rock from his nostrils and lashed his tail against the ceiling of stone as the earth trembled around him. The ripple from his movement traveled up through the ground, and the plates shifted and groaned against his might. He settled again, taking a deep breath as he blocked out the infernal noise, and tried to dream of more pleasant things.

Soon he would wake and climb from this prison to join his brethren above. He would find his queen and become again a king of his kind. They would come with the breaking of the earth and fire in the sky. Tidal waves would swallow the cities of metal and glass, and the spiraling wind would carry away their rickety towns. They would wash clean the pestilence of humanity from the surface of the planet and reclaim her beauty for the natural cycles of life and death once more.

Soon, but not yet.

CHAPTER 1
BEES AND THE BIRDS

Chloe lay in the grass on the side of a gentle hill, unmoving, as a honeybee hummed through the air only a few inches from her face. It landed on the yellow crown of a buttercup, and the thin stem bowed toward the grass with its weight. Its legs were already dusted yellow with pollen as its head busied about the stamen, the tiny flower bobbing with every movement it made. Her eyes tracked as it rose again into the air with the blurry triangles of its wings returned.

It hovered in place a moment, as if deciding which direction to go, and then came closer, landing on her elbow. She watched from the corner of her eye with her chin perched on her steepled knuckles. Her heart lurched as the tickle of its legs navigated the hairs of her arm, stepping closer to her cheek in a zigzag pattern. But she kept her cool, remaining stone still, knowing that there was nothing to fear if she didn't give it reason to sting.

Chloe's favorite teacher last year, Mrs. Greenwald, had told them that a disturbingly large percentage of the honeybee population had been dying off over the last few years and that the death of the bees had a domino effect that could disrupt the balance of nature. With no bees, there was no pollination of the flowers, and that meant far less of the fruits and vegetables that humans and animals rely on to survive. And of course, no more honey. Chloe loved honey.

Some of her classmates, like Kendra Roberts, the Queen Bee herself, had made a joke out of it, saying, "Whatever, less bugs is less bugs, right? My dad runs like a massive bioengineering company that totally knows how to pollinate flowers without bees. And I use Splenda anyway." Her drones had all giggled in compliance before returning their fleeting attentions to the latest texting exchange. But Chloe couldn't stop thinking about what Mrs. Greenwald had said then, noting that "some scientists and theorists speculate that the death of the bees is an early sign of the decline of Mother Earth itself," the beginning of the end.

A breeze kicked up and the bee let go of its hold, carried away toward the pond at the bottom of the hill. Chloe watched it until she lost the receding speck among the dance of dandelion parachutes that pinwheeled through the air to land gently on the sheen of the water. Just then, a small fish jumped, no doubt investigating the slight disturbance on the pond's surface, hoping to find a tasty gnat rather than the wayward seed tuft. From high up she heard the cry of a hawk, and her eyes found its red-tailed form circling beneath the gathering clouds as it watched the flop of the fish far below...All of life's little movements, flowing in their natural cycles of cause and effect.

She loved this place—alone with her thoughts, at peace in a way she could not find at home or among her peers. Here it didn't matter that her mom was overworked and unlucky in love, or that Chloe had worn the same pair of running shoes every day for months and they smelled like something had died in them.

Another fish jumped, and her gaze returned to the concentric circles that rippled out from that spot. Then another? Soon sunfish and perch were taking to the air with frantic tail-flapping leaps all across the pond before splashing down to the unremarkable looking water.

Chloe sat up to get a better look, amazed that so many fish could even live in this pond, let alone all decide to try to escape it at once. Over the summer, she'd spent most of her free time on this hillside, hiding from her mom and Brent and the struggle to be cool. She came here to read and watch the animals. To listen to the wind in the leaves and fantasize about all the places she would escape to when she was older. But she had never seen the fish act this way.

Maybe they could sense her anguish, offering their joined protest over her need to report to school again tomorrow. The tenth grade—the first day at Charlottesville High School.

A blustery wind whipped through the trees, and her unkempt, brown hair lashed her cheek. Being in the accelerated program had always seemed like a blessing throughout her three years at Buford Middle school. But now, as the other girls in her class laid out their competitively slutty outfits for the big day while gossiping over the phone about which boys they hoped to find in homeroom, Chloe was left wondering if her bookish ways and latest Walmart fashion wouldn't prove a horrible curse. She was not ready to face the morning.

She tracked the red-tailed hawk as it sailed into the clearing above the pond and fluttered to a graceful, wing-tucked perch on a branch overhanging the water. Still the fish were jumping, but the raptor only watched with jerky ticks of its head rather than going for the easy meal. Something about the scene didn't seem right. Then the mad squawking of a murder of crows raced overhead, and twenty or so of the black birds landed in the surrounding trees opposite the hawk.

Their chatter continued as they also seemed to watch the riled water. Smaller birds joined the odd vigil as well: sparrows and robins, chickadees and blue jays, more and more flapping to join the ring around the pond every second.

Chloe stood, blue eyes squinting in the wind as she put her hair in a ponytail with callused hands. Her nails were bitten short with nervous attention. The rain started a few moments later, tapping the leaves above her with a building rhythm. She looked up at the dark clouds above the branches as heavy drops spattered across her forehead.

"Where did you come from?" she asked the storm, as a jagged claw of lightning flashed across the sky. She counted, "One Mississippi, two Mississippi, three—" and the thunder roll followed. She wanted to continue her observation of the strange avian gathering, but a soaking sheet of rain descended, blocking her view.

Chloe ran, sprinting toward home, as lightning fell again with a deafening crack. Her feet carried her deftly through the woods without need of a path to guide her. She let out a merry yelp as the cold wet clung to her shoulders, but she didn't stop the liberating run until she'd reached her back door a mile away.

She did not see the muddy fountain of bubbles that rose in the center of the pond, nor did she glimpse the silvery form that stirred beneath the surface and then was gone.

As quickly as it started, the fish stopped leaping, the birds scattered, and the storm moved on. In moments, the water settled again into a glassy sheen.

·   ·   ·

"Chloe McClellan, stop right there and step back to the door! How many times do I need to ask you to take your shoes off when you come in?" Audrey McClellan noticed that her daughter was soaked and shivering as well. "You're dripping wet! Stay there while I get a towel."

Chloe hopped on one foot and then the other as she peeled off the soiled running shoes. She spied her cat, Shipwreck, watching from across the room. She'd found him bleeding in the gutter from a hit-and-run four years ago and had nursed him back to health. He'd been her constant shadow around the house ever since. His green eyes betrayed no emotion as his tattered ears swiveled to track the return of Chloe's mother. Then a fresh towel that smelled like her childhood was thrust in Chloe's face. "Thanks, Mom."

"Didn't you see that there was a storm coming?"

"No, actually. It kind of came out of nowhere," Chloe answered while toweling off her head.

"I'd almost believe you if you hadn't come home drenched in pond water every other day for the last three months," Audrey retorted with the hint of a smile.

"I wasn't swimming this time, I swear! And the birds were acting really weird!"

Audrey returned to ironing her uniform from Positive Pete's Diner as the cable news prattled on in an endless cycle of nothing, but Chloe could tell that her mom wasn't finished... "Well, if *I* were you, *I'd* stop acting so weird; you're starting high school tomorrow. You could use a few more friends that don't have four legs or wings."

There it was—it only took an instant for the high dam that Chloe had built to block out the failure of her social life to buckle and crack. For three months, she had neglected the friendships she'd worked to gain last year, avoiding plans that would have kept her informed of the youth politics of greater Charlottesville, Virginia, and drifting further from the ability to participate in normal teen conversation. She blamed it on the fact that she'd always been one of the nerdiest and least developed girls in her class, but still, none of it interested her... or at least that's what she'd told herself.

"Thanks, Mom," she muttered again while toweling off her skinny legs. "Where's Brent?" she said in an attempt to redirect.

"He'll be here tomorrow night, and I'd really appreciate it if you could try to say his name without wincing."

"Ah, let's see: Brent. Brrrrent. Good ol' Brent," she tossed the towel on the floor and shook her head. "Nope, sorry Mom, he's still a bit of an ass—"

"Chloe!"

"Okay, a bit of a jerk then."

Audrey turned on her with a wounded scowl. "Yeah, well, he's a bit sweet too. And I'm not sure if you'd noticed, but your dad's not coming back, and I'm not getting any younger here."

Shipwreck wisely chose that moment to saunter from the room.

Chloe felt sorry for her comment, but mentioning Dad was a forbidden topic! She could feel her face getting red. It was the last night before the start of Chloe's nine-month prison sentence, and in typical fashion, the McClellan women were gearing up for another shouting match...

> *We interrupt this Labor Day broadcast with Breaking News: Reports have just come in from the Associated Press and our affiliates in Asia that a massive 9.2 earthquake has rocked the Quinghai Province in central China. The epicenter was located beneath Quinghai Lake, the largest lake in China, only*

thirty-five kilometers west of the provincial capital of Xining. Initial reports describe massive devastation throughout the city and surrounding townships, and early casualty estimates are as high as two hundred thousand dead.

The cable news anchor shuffled his papers and put on a look of grave concern.

I'm being told that this is only the eleventh earthquake of such high magnitude since 1900, but that five of those have occurred in only the last three years.

He paused as someone continued talking into his ear-bud.

We will be back with continued coverage of this story throughout the night, and of course our thoughts and prayers go with the people of China.

And just like that, the McClellan fight was forgotten and Chloe was reminded that her problems were very small. "Wow, another big one: Haiti, Yoshu, Chile, Alaska, Siberia, and now this. They're coming more frequently, like the planet is getting angry," she said. "Maybe the world really is ending?"

"Well, unless it ends tonight, you're still going to school tomorrow," interrupted her mother. "Now go wash your hands and put on some dry clothes for dinner."

"Mom, hundreds of thousands of people are dying in China and you're worried about wet clothes and dirty hands?"

"Go!"

Chloe clicked her wet-socked heels and saluted crisply. "Oh captain, my captain."

"I wouldn't have to boss you if you didn't show up with dirt caked under your nails every night. Now hop to it, I want to have a nice sit down meal with you before my shift starts; we need to celebrate the big day tomorrow!"

"Honestly, Mom, except for how bad it's gonna suck, what's so big about starting high school? Everybody does it."

"Daughter, trust me here, high school can be one of the

best times of your life. You've got the brains and grades to go to college, and a good one, and that will be even more fun. But I didn't get to go to college; all I had was high school, and I lived it large." Audrey unplugged the iron and left it to cool on the board, lost for a moment in a memory of youth.

Yeah, until I came along and ruined everything, Chloe thought with a pang of guilt.

Audrey snapped out of it and started to change into the uniform right there. Once again, Chloe couldn't help but admire her mom's thirty-four-year-old body, wondering if her dad's genes would ever relinquish dominance of her looks.

"While you're young and free, you should live every day you have as large as you can, 'cause whether it's bills or bad luck, when it's gone, it's hard to get back...That's what you owe to those poor people in China. Live big every day, starting with tomorrow."

CHAPTER 2
THE WORST FIRST DAY

Chloe took a seat in the back row of her homeroom class, American Civics, resolute in her decision to keep her hand down and her answers to herself unless she was called on. She had carried the whispered title of "brownnoser" through all the grades that brought her here, and she did not intend to foster its return for these final three years of adolescent purgatory. She recognized some of the faces that filled in the empty desks, but many others were new to her, coming from the other junior high or private school programs that fed into Charlottesville High School's three hundred-plus sophomore class. She hoped she could remain fairly anonymous.

Liz Legrand walked into the room with a designer handbag instead of the backpack she and Chloe had used to carry their butterfly jars only two summers back. Liz had traded her muddy sandals for high heels and her friendship with Chloe for a spot in the Kendra Roberts fan club. Chloe had seen it all coming, but couldn't help but stare at her old friend's over-applied makeup and new, curve-flaunting clothing. Liz waved at one of her new cohorts across the room with a pearly smile before her eyes settled on the last of the empty seats—directly in front of or beside Chloe. The smile faltered.

Chloe had been dreading this moment. "Hey, Liz, how was your summer?" she offered as her old friend came closer.

Liz took the seat in front of her, looking a little pinched. "It was great, yours?"

"Too short, as always…" and the awkward pause stretched.

"You still collect butterflies?" asked Liz with a hint of derision.

"No, I've moved on to birds and squirrels, but the killing jar is huge," she answered with a smirk.

Liz laughed as the tension was dispelled between them. Chloe gave an internal sigh of relief.

Liz turned toward her with a conspiratorial whisper. "I'm kind of dating Paul Markson now."

It was said as if the ground might break open with the delivery of the news, but Chloe couldn't remember who Paul Markson even was. "Which one is he?"

"He's a junior on the varsity soccer team. They're state champions!"

This, too, was meant to shake the earth, but again Chloe failed to register the significance. She tried feebly to mask her total lack of excitement. "That is so awesome!" she said, though it came out stilted. Liz's face hardened again. She might have been turning to the dark side, but she wasn't stupid.

"Yeah, it's kind of a big deal for me." She spun back around to answer a text from her new friend across the room.

Chloe's heart sank, and she looked longingly out the window. It was sunny and beautiful outside, but already she could tell that this day was going to suck. She turned when the teacher ambled into the room, somehow already disheveled and winded by the effort just to get here. His button-down shirt was sporting yellow pit stains as he began to write his name on the board with a shaky hand. The waft of cigarette smoke was evident all the way across the classroom.

MR. JACOBSO-

It was only then that Chloe noticed the hunched figure in the seat beside her. He was draped over the desk with his face buried in his crossed arms. Chloe had never seen him before. He glanced out from behind the shield of fingers to catch Chloe's stare. He was Asian and looked older than fifteen, with chiseled cheek bones and sad, beautiful eyes. His red, glassy gaze met Chloe's for only a moment, and then he hid his face again.

Chloe faced forward, embarrassed, as if she'd intruded. And though she felt even worse for thinking it: *At least someone in this school is having a worse day than me.*

. . .

She stood at the front of a bustling cafeteria with her tray of semi-edible, mass-produced food steaming in her hands. A third of the school shared her lunch period—a mix of almost four hundred students from all three grades—sorting themselves into messy little groups that would shift and tighten in the weeks to come. Chloe was in a financial assistance program and qualified for subsidized lunches, but looking down at her near-sauceless pizza wedge, clump of browning iceberg lettuce, and green banana, she made a mental note to remember to brown-bag it from now on. The prospect of the walk before her was no more appetizing.

She advanced through the long hall of tables, trying and failing not to notice those she passed. There was, of course, the obligatory table of football players and their cheerleader girlfriends in a prime location by the windows. And nearby was the better part of the state champion soccer squad. Liz sat among them. On one side was the boy who must be Paul Markson, grinning with a deliberately gross amount of brownie wedged in his teeth; on the other sat a screeching Kendra Roberts.

God, she sounds like a hyena in heat! Though Chloe had to admit, Paul was pretty cute in a preppy, privileged way. She walked faster, averting her eyes.

Drama nerds, band geeks, skaters, math league, and Goths; she didn't belong with any of them, and she was running out of tables. At the back of the cafeteria, there was a smaller side room with lower ceilings, dim fluorescent lights, and no windows. This was the infamous Cave, filled with all the kids that didn't want to be noticed. This was the place for her.

She scanned for a lonely seat just as a flailing boy stumbled into her and sent her tray flying. Both he and her lunch clattered to the ground with a shower of lettuce as all eyes in the immediate radius swiveled their way. Chloe could already feel her face getting red.

"Oh shit! I'm sorry," said the boy on his butt. "That total douchebag pushed me," he pointed at a laughing boy nearby.

"Brian, you destroyed this girl's lunch, dude!" Now he was laughing too. "That is not cool!"

Echoes of "not cool, Brian," broke out from the nearest table as Chloe knelt to salvage what she could.

The pizza had landed cheese down. She'd peeled most of it from the linoleum floor before the fallen boy scrambled over to help pick up the lettuce.

"Hey, I'm really sorry; you can have my tuna-fish sandwich if you want." He had bloodshot eyes and clothes that reeked of patchouli.

"No, thanks. I'm all right." She picked up the banana. "I wasn't that hungry anyway," she lied.

"Oh man, you're a cool chick. You could have been totally bitchy just now. What are you, a sophomore? What's your name?"

"Yeah, I'm a sophomore. Uh, Chloe."

"I'm Stan Strakowski. Nice to meet you, Cool Chloe," he said, offering his hand. Stan had an oily hat head and a horsey grin. His palm was warm and sticky as he helped her to her feet.

"You too." She smiled weakly. "Well, see ya."

"Yes, you will, Cool Chloe," Stan declared.

As she walked away, she wiped her hand on her T-shirt and tried to block out the chatter behind her.

"Dude, she was totally hot…in a boyish way!" Stan announced to his table with a chorus of sniggers in response.

She lowered her head and walked faster, finally coming to a stop at the last table in the corner. She dropped her empty tray and fell into a chair with a tight hold on her banana. This day was not getting better.

She looked up to find the sad boy from homeroom only a few seats down on the far side of the table, watching. The red rim around his eyes highlighted the striking honey brown of his irises, and his jet-black hair was artfully messy. He nodded, "Do you want half my sandwich? I'm not going to eat it." His gaze was intense, but disarming.

"It's all right—"

"Really," he cut in, "I'll throw it away if you don't want it." He had barely touched his lunch and was fidgeting with a cell phone.

She smiled, "All right, thanks." She reached across the table to accept the offer. "You saw that, huh?" She motioned back to the scattered remnants of her lunch.

He nodded again, this time with the beginning of a smirk, though his eyes were still sad. "Good first day?"

"Yeah, not so much," she mumbled, taking a tentative bite of the sandwich. It was grilled chicken and avocado and far better than the pizza-like product she would have otherwise choked down. "Only a hundred ninety two and a half days to go."

"A hundred eighty two and a half," he corrected. "We get ten sick days, and I plan to use every one."

Chloe smiled with a nod of agreement. She'd gotten the perfect attendance record the last three years in a row, but wasn't about to admit it. She was very conscious of trying not to look at him for too long and even more conscious of the fact that he hadn't stopped looking at her since she'd sat down. He'd taken off the button-down he'd had on that morning to reveal tanned arms and a frayed T-shirt that said "Costa Rica," and then "Pura Vida" beneath.

He was way too easy to look at and looked way too old to be in the tenth grade. She turned away to fetch her Nalgene water bottle from her bag and took a deep, unintentionally audible gulp.

"Are you a sophomore?" she finally blurted.

"Senior, but this is my first day, too."

She raised an eyebrow.

"I just moved here from Santa Cruz a couple months ago. My dad got a job here, so...now I'm here, too."

"Santa Cruz, that's pretty cool," she said. "Are you a surfer?" she asked with a little too much excitement. *Oh God, I sound like a yipping puppy dog!*

"Yeah, I was a pretty goddamned good surfer, actually," he admitted.

"And now you've traded the waves for the woods?" *Did I really just say that?*

"Not by choice."

"...But if you're a senior, why are you in my homeroom?" she asked, only then remembering that he had been upset in class this morning. Her breath froze.

"Yeah...I already have enough credits in science and math to graduate, but need to make up a couple school requirements, like American Civics," he answered, now more guarded.

Chloe tried to conceal her nervousness with another bite of sandwich. He didn't look it, but maybe he was a bit of a closeted nerd, too?

"So what's your deal? Are you some crunchy hiker girl, or something?" he asked without any discernible scorn.

"Yeah, I guess I'm kind of a loner bio-geek. But I was thinking of going for aloof and mysterious this year," she said, immediately wishing she could learn to self-edit.

"Sorry, I already claimed aloof and mysterious," he responded without hesitation. "You're going to have to find something else."

She stifled her grin and thinned her eyes—playing at aloof and mysterious. "I know this is the first day for both of us and all, but technically I've been in town a lot longer, so I kind of have dibs."

"I don't know, Cool Chloe, you already have a pretty unmysterious nickname and a fan club." He motioned to the table of party kids, where Stan was jumping on a chair and hooting like an ape.

Despite the wound behind his gaze, his humor was natural and effortless. And Chloe was fairly certain that he was flirting with her. So far, it was an alien and awesome feeling, and she didn't want it to stop. "So let's hear your mysterious name," she challenged.

"Kirin Liou."

"Kirin...really?" she asked.

He nodded.

"For Charlottesville, Virginia, that's pretty good," she admitted. "Kirin Liou—what is that, Japanese and Chinese?"

Kirin looked impressed. "You're good. Dad is from China and Mom was Japanese." The sadness sunk into his eyes once more.

Chloe kicked herself internally; she needed to keep this going. "Did you hear about that earthquake in China yesterday?" she flailed. "They say it was one of the biggest recorded quakes in history."

Now his smile dropped, and his gaze went glassy and distant. It was as if he looked right through her. The silence stretched on, save for the thundering in Chloe's chest.

"My grandmother lives in Xining, China," he answered stonily, his emotions starting to crack. "We still haven't heard anything."

"God, I'm so sorry. I was just—"

"It was nice to meet you, Chloe," he stood abruptly and gathered his things. "I have to make a phone call." And with that, he walked briskly away and out of the cafeteria.

Chloe exhaled slowly and dropped her head to the table with a painful thud. Now the universe was just being mean.

·   ·   ·

And then there was gym.

Chloe stood on the football field among a diverse cluster of girls, all wearing bright orange gym shorts and shirts with their first initial and last names written on the chest. Her shorts were too short for her thin legs, and the shirt hung like a dress. It was mortifying.

They were spread out to stretch, led in the endeavor by Ms. Anita Barnes, a scowling, boxy woman who always carried a Ping-Pong paddle and a whistle. Chloe's eyes glanced to the cluster of boys as they ran around the track. They wore the same outfit, but in unobtrusive black, which seemed a little unfair to Chloe as she was forced to squint from the sun's reflection off her day-glow tangerine chest. Some of the boys watched the girls intently from afar, no doubt hoping to catch good angles for the most compromising of stretches...Kirin Liou was not among them.

"Touch your toes and hold it for fifteen seconds!" shouted

Ms. Barnes. The whistle chirped, and Chloe leaned over and touched her head to her knees. Her mom had always said she should be a dancer, but she'd never been able to tolerate all that practice. She counted slowly to ten, glancing upside down at the girls around her. The whistle sounded again and she straightened.

Kendra Roberts righted with an impressive flip of her fire-red mane. Somehow her body still looked amazing in the neon polyester. Chloe couldn't help but stare. *Fifteen is way too young to handle that kind of power. She looks like some sort of supernaturally nubile succubus out of mythology.*

Mrs. Greenwald had often talked about all the hormones and chemicals that had filtered into the world's drinking water, causing periods and puberty to come earlier and earlier. "Boobs and hips are showing up on some eight- and nine-year-olds," she'd warned.

Chloe still hadn't seen much of that in the mirror. Her period had arrived at lucky thirteen, accompanied only by all the glorious benefits of monthly mood swings, manic irritability, and clockwork migraines that ruined at least one full day of every month. She'd already done the math: her sixteenth birthday on December 21st—still four months off—would be especially sweet.

"Twenty jumping jacks on my whistle!" barked Ms. Barnes. The whistle blew, and arms and legs began to fly in a disjointed mockery of group rhythm. Chloe's jumping jacks were smooth and precise, her mind already slipping into the quiet place it found during exercise, able, if only then, to fully shut out the cascade of anxious thoughts.

Most of the girls around her flopped and sweated in the punishing September heat—still pushing ninety degrees and brutally humid, though the summer had supposedly come to an end. Chloe had spent much hotter days outside these last few months, and if the air was moving at all, her mom opted for open windows over air conditioning bills, no matter the heat.

It had been the hottest summer she could remember, and it was headed toward being the hottest year on record for the fourth year in a row. To the average kid of Charlottesville High

School, it was only a statistic that meant more time at the mall or inside and online, but to the millions who'd been caught up in the drought and famine riots across Africa and parts of Asia, it was a life-changing, and often life-ending, reality.

The whistle chirped for the twentieth time. "Nicely done, Ms. McClellan!"

Chloe didn't even register what Ms. Barnes had said until some of the other girls turned to look at her with judgmental glares. She looked back, confused, wondering if maybe a bird had pooped on her or something. Kendra looked her up and down before spinning away with a snort.

"That's just great," Chloe mumbled to herself. *I don't even have to open my mouth to make everyone dislike me.*

"Line up on the track for the one mile run, girls!" yelled Ms. Barnes as she marched across the field with a wave of her Ping-Pong paddle. "Four laps, and I will be timing this! I want to see everyone try to finish in less than ten minutes!"

Groans and protests erupted from all around, but Chloe followed silently. The boys were just approaching the finish; two clearly athletic kids sprinted toward the line as the others trailed at an ungraceful distance.

"Five minutes: thirty-three, thirty-four, thirty-five, thirty-six!" called out the male gym teacher, Mr. Johnson, as the two boys passed him with competitive flourish. "Good work!" announced Mr. Johnson as the boys slapped each other five and slowed to a rubbery-legged stroll.

Chloe recognized Paul Markson as one of them, breathing heavily and puffing out his chest for the watching girls. Kendra took that moment to put her signature hair back in a ponytail, making sure to arch enough to show some skin at her midriff. Paul's eyes lingered there before they exchanged little waves. *Does Liz know just how cool her new friend, Kendra, really is?* Chloe wondered as she lined up on the track beside her. Visible waves of heat rose from the lanes.

Other boys decided to finally exert themselves for the finish, crossing the line in eight or nine minutes, with gasping stumbles and a lot of sweat. Still others ambled on, more than willing to miss the ten-minute time limit that had been assigned.

The whistle screeched again. "Eyes front, girls!" yelled Barnes. "I want your best efforts here! You will be marked on your improvement throughout the year!"

"Then why would we try to go fast now?" muttered Kendra under her breath, followed by snickers of approval from the girls around her.

"Those of you who plan on joining the indoor track team this winter might want to consider this as an introduction, Ms. Roberts!" announced Barnes in response. "I've heard through the grapevine that you could have some real talent, so let's see what you've got."

Her? Talent! Chloe rolled her neck with a crack.

"Good luck," offered Paul Markson with a smile to Kendra.

"No sweat," she answered, sliding into an overdone runner's stance. Some of the boys chuckled and whispered behind her.

"At the sound of my whistle!" yelled Barnes as tension spread down the line.

Sunlight reflected off the white sheen of Kendra's running shoes and flashed Chloe in the eye. She turned her head away just as the whistle blew.

The boys rose in a chorus of encouragement, and Kendra took off like a bolt. Chloe reacted a step later, fumbling the first few strides until her skinny legs found their rhythm. A cluster of other girls were ahead of her as well, jockeying for position as they stretched out along the inside lane, but Chloe's eyes were fixed on the annoying bob of the red ponytail in the lead. She settled her breathing and found the quiet zone within once more, knowing that the others had started too fast and would soon wilt in the heat.

One by one, Chloe passed them, all left blotchy and gasping in her wake by the end of the first lap—all but Kendra, whose perfect legs continued to move in long, elegant strides ahead.

"Looking good, Kendra!" shouted Paul Markson as they passed the cluster of boys.

Chloe pushed harder, erasing the distance between them until she came up on Kendra's heel. Kendra glanced over her shoulder, and without thinking, Chloe challenged her gaze. At this, Kendra accelerated, but Chloe hung with her, moving up just behind her shoulder.

At the end of the second lap, the boys' cheers had acquired a more spirited edge. Chloe tuned out the shouts of "Come on, Kendra!" and "Dig deep!" and focused instead on the growing flush of Kendra's cheeks and the wheeze of her breath. Already they had lapped most of the other girls. Halfway through the third lap, Chloe moved up directly beside her, their long strides matching for twenty-some paces as the pain and defeat sunk into Kendra's face. Then Chloe pulled ahead in a quickening burst that left no room for comparison.

When she flew past the boys for the third time, all the shouting had been silenced. "Goddamn, she's fast," she heard someone mutter.

In the back of her mind, Chloe was vaguely aware of the little voice screaming: *Don't do this, idiot!* But it felt too good to let loose and show what she could do, too liberating to sit back and let perfect Kendra claim all the eyes and praise yet again. Chloe might not have been the prettiest, wealthiest, or most popular girl in her class, but she was pretty sure that she was the fastest. Today she was going to prove it.

She didn't have to run as fast as she did; she had clearly won. But she had been running from the pond to her door almost every evening for three months now and wondered just how fast she could go. She rounded the last bend toward the finish line and caught sight of the ecstatic look on Ms. Barnes's face.

"Come on, McClellan! Five minutes: fourteen, fifteen, sixteen, seventeen, eighteen!" cried Ms. Barnes with a giddy hop as Chloe lunged across the line.

She gradually slowed with a series of hard exhales and her hands on her hips. Her legs felt like Silly Putty, and she ran in place for a moment as the endorphin glaze started to clear. Her heartbeat was pounding in her temples, and she cleared her throat and spit a foamy glob to the grass.

Only then did she turn around and become aware that all the boys had started clapping for her. She made eye contact with

Paul Markson as he and the boy next to him bowed with big grins. Chloe was glad that she was already beet red from the run.

She looked back to see Kendra bent over and dry heaving on the other side of the track. Her run had disintegrated into a disjointed hobble as she tried to hide her face from the waiting spectators. Other girls passed her as she added an overdone limp to her finish, stumbling across the line with mock heroics at a still respectable six minutes, twenty seconds. She all but fell into the arms of Ms. Barnes as Chloe approached, hoping to do some damage control.

"Chloe McClellan!" Ms. Barnes shouted unnecessarily while still holding on to Kendra. "You absolutely must join the cross-country team!"

Kendra was a sweaty, overheated mess, looking like she might dry heave again.

"With some coaching and practice, you could win a state championship before you graduate." She turned back to mark the times of the others.

"Wow, okay. Thanks," Chloe said, feeling neither aloof nor mysterious. Kendra glared at her with open disdain as she hobbled to a rough seat in the grass. "Hey, Kendra, that was a really good race," she offered.

"It wasn't supposed to be a race, you brownnosing freak," Kendra hissed in response as some of her underlings came to rest beside her.

That stung, but Chloe couldn't think of a pithy response. "I was just going as fast as I could, I didn't mean to—"

"Whatever, you're probably just a twelve-year-old boy anyway," she interrupted, having gained strength in numbers. "They should probably do a DNA test just to make sure you're the real thing."

Chloe had nothing left to fight them. Luckily she didn't have the water left for tears either as she turned away from their chorus of cruel laughter.

CHAPTER 3
FREAK STORM

So there it was, in just under seven hours of high school, Chloe had already solidified her identity as a "brownnosing freak." There would be no shaking it now, not after she'd run a mile faster than the boys. Not after she'd run Kendra into a quivering husk of her former beauty—dry heaving and drenched before a bleacher full of potential suitors. This was not "aloof and mysterious;" this was social suicide!

She stormed through the back door, tossed her backpack toward the living room, and charged the kitchen. "Mom!" she yelled to announce her arrival. "You lied! High school is almost completely terrible!"

"Your mom's not here," interrupted Officer Brent Meeks from the kitchen table. He sat in front of a laptop with his hands on the keys. Its bluish glow glinted off his badge. "She got called in last minute to cover Loraine's shift, 'cause of an emergency situation. She asked me to stick around and make sure you're okay."

Chloe just stood there, glaring at his freshly trimmed crew cut and self-important brow, trying to contain her scream. Clearly Brent was not on duty, but of course he was still wearing his uniform. It was as if he didn't want anyone to forget that he was a cop. *What a jackass!*

There was something about him that Chloe didn't trust. And he sure as hell wasn't good enough for her mom.

"Anything you want to talk about?" he asked, trying too hard.

"What was the emergency situation?" she asked, ice water

in her veins.

"What?"

"Loraine—what was the situation?"

"Why would I know what the situation was?" he challenged with an oddly defensive edge.

"Well, because you're a cop, right? Don't people call you when they have an emergency?" she knew she was baiting him, but couldn't stop herself.

He chuckled without humor and straightened in the chair. "I guess this was one of those situations where they called an ambulance, not the police."

"Right," she said, fetching the Brita from the fridge. "Do you know when she'll be back?" She reached for a glass from a high counter. She could feel him watching her from across the room.

"Who? Loraine?"

"No, my mom." She poured and gulped, hiding her burning glare behind water and glass. He looked like a distorted pink-and-blue blob.

"Oh. I think she was going to try and get a replacement to cover her shift later, but I haven't heard anything more on it. I'll let you know if she calls."

"Gee, thanks, Officer Meeks," she said, refilling the glass with an empty smile.

"I'm off duty, you can call me Brent."

"Okay, thanks, Officer Brent," she said, returning the Brita to the fridge.

"No problem, Chloe," he responded with disingenuous cool. He gave her a quick toe-to-head appraisal, the way Kendra had, before returning his attention to the screen. The hint of a smirk crept across his face.

Chloe stood there for a little too long, just staring at him in disbelief. After this day of full-blown adolescent hell, all she really needed was to vent…Something told her Liz wouldn't be accepting her calls. Mom was, once again, MIA. Opening up to Brent would be about as rewarding as talking to the STOP sign on the corner. She held her breath, feeling her face turning red and shaky, and forced herself out of the kitchen before she voiced something she'd regret.

Now what? Assigned reading? Homework? Was she really going to sink back into her old routine of hiding behind the quest for good grades? For Chloe, sacrificing her social life on the altar of study came a little too easily. She snatched her backpack from the sofa and began the sluggish retreat to her room—mopey and defeated.

Luckily her pocket started ringing just as she rounded the banister to the stairs.

She tossed the backpack again and yanked the cell phone from her shorts with a shower of loose change. The screen said "**MOM CELL**" above a picture of her mom's face with cheeks filled to capacity and a smile that spilled half-chewed Cheerios down her chin. *About time!* With a victorious glance toward the kitchen, she barreled out of the screen door before answering.

"Mom, can you please come home?" she implored.

"Honey, I'm on my break; I'm sorry I can't be there. Loraine's husband was in a car accident and she had to go to the hospital. I'd planned on the three of us having a nice dinner, but it looks like I'm going to be stuck here until ten," Audrey replied with the sounds of a busy kitchen behind her.

"Ten?" *Another night of reheated food and only a cat to talk to.*

"I'm really sorry. Believe me; I'm not happy about it either."

Chloe could hear the sound of an opening door and then the clatter of the kitchen was replaced by the whir of street traffic.

"Are you home now?" Audrey asked.

"Yep, just me and Brent, getting some good quality time in." Chloe rounded the house, glancing through the open windows to see if Brent was still at the kitchen table. She didn't see him. "Mom, did you ask him to babysit me?" she whispered.

"I asked him to stick around and make sure you got home okay. What's wrong with that, Chloe?"

"Well, I'm home, so you can call him and tell him to leave now. I don't want him here."

Audrey sighed heavily. "If that's really what you want?"

"It is," Chloe cut in. "I'm telling you, Mom, there's

something off about him."

"Chloe, can we please not do this right now?" Audrey pleaded. "Let's not make this about Brent...Tell me about your day. What happened at school?"

"Oh yeah, school; I lived big all right." She kicked an acorn as hard as she could. It sailed into the unkempt grass at the edge of the yard. "Let's see, I managed to piss off Liz, dump my lunch on the cafeteria floor, make a cute senior sad, and publicly embarrass the most popular girl in my class." She felt tears welling up and fought to swallow the impulse. "I'd say it was a banner first day."

"Honey, I'm sure it wasn't that bad."

"No, I'm pretty sure it was. I might as well transfer now, or maybe we should consider homeschooling?"

"Chloe, don't you think you're being a little dramatic?"

"Mom, Kendra Roberts said I was a freak and a boy!"

"So what? Kendra Roberts is a mean-hearted jerk with mean-hearted jerk parents. She'll have to live with that the rest of her mean-hearted, jerk life. Why don't you focus on the positive things; didn't anything good happen today?"

As Chloe rounded the house, Shipwreck emerged from the forsythia bushes and took a lazy, playful swipe at her passing heel. It seemed that even he was conspiring against her.

Audrey sensed something in her daughter's silence and pushed deeper. "This cute senior sounds promising."

"Yeah, until I brought up his missing grandmother." Chloe peered through the bay windows into the kitchen nook, but Brent had left his seat. The computer still sat on the table, facing her. It was open to his e-mail.

Shipwreck slinked by, rubbing against Chloe's shin. She knelt and kneaded his battered ear as he purred in ecstasy.

"He sounds sensitive, and he loves his grandmother, what's wrong with that?" asked Audrey. "Just give him a little time and talk to him again."

"Mom, he hates Charlottesville, is two years older than me, and he runs away every time I'm near him."

"So, do you like him?" Audrey asked with a smile in

her voice.

"What? I don't know him." Chloe couldn't help but glance back to the e-mail. "I mean, yeah, he was pretty interesting, but there's just no way." She leaned in closer toward the open window. Her eyes squinted through the screen and worked fast.

> The car is totaled, but Andy isn't hurt too bad. They say he's got a broken leg, some bruises, and a minor concussion. Still, they're gonna keep him in the hospital overnight for observations and tests and things.
>
> So, it looks like I'm alone at the house tonight. I'll be there at around 8:30, and I definitely think I'll need some protective custody, don't you, Officer Meeks?
>
> You want to wait all night for Mama Bear to get home or come do your duty and help a poor woman in distress?
>
> Hmmmmmmmm?
>
> L.

Chloe wasn't sure at first what she'd read. She read it again. "Mom, what's Loraine's husband's name?"

"What? Don't change the subject."

"No, really Mom, is it Andy?"

"Yes, it's Andy. But Loraine just called to let us know he's okay. He's got a broken leg and was pretty banged up, but he'll be all right. She's staying with him at the hospital until visiting hours are over at ten, so she can't switch shifts with me and none of the other girls are available." A loud truck rattled by and she sighed, "I'm stuck here until closing."

That bastard! I knew he was a sleaze! "Mom, I think that Brent is having an affair with Loraine!" she whispered.

"What? Why would you say that, Chloe?" Her mom sounded hurt.

"I'm reading it in his e-mail. He's going to meet her tonight at 8:30."

"Chloe McClellan! You read Brent's e-mail?" Now she was angry.

"No, it's just, I'm looking at it right now through the

window and there's a message from Loraine—"

"Chloe, you are unbelievable! Why do you insist on trying to sabotage any chance I might have to like a guy?" Her mom was getting to that upset place of no return.

"No, Mom, I'm not making this up—"

"I'm really trying to hold everything together right now, and you know what, I'm doing a pretty damn good job of it! But I deserve a little ME time, too, once in a while, don't you think? I need to be allowed to have relationships, whether you approve of them or not, and you need to be okay with that!"

"Mom, you're doing a great job. But I'm really sorry, I know what I read. He's cheating on you with Loraine!"

"Chloe!" She was shouting now. "I don't want to hear it!"

Shipwreck cocked his ears and stiffened, hearing the familiar tone and heavy breathing through the phone. He skittered into the bushes.

Now her mom was cold and final: "There's a pot of potato-leek soup in the fridge and some frozen French bread in the freezer. Heat some up for dinner and do your homework before I get back." There was an unspoken threat there.

"Mom—"

"Not another word, Chloe. I mean it…I have to go back to work."

Chloe's hand was shaking and the tears were on the way. "Mom," she pleaded.

"I'm very upset with you right now," Audrey's voice quivered. "We'll talk when I get home."

"Mom?" she begged again with no response. She looked at the phone, reading the word "**Disconnected**" on the little screen. *This day can't be happening!*

She looked back to the e-mail, but the computer was closed. Brent stood at the window, watching her. The window was open. She met his gaze.

"Chloe, I think you're a little confused. Could you please come inside so we can talk about it?" he asked through the screen.

Chloe wanted to tear him apart for hurting her mom, but she was too upset to find the words. *What if she gets depressed again? What if it all comes apart? I don't have the strength for this, now...* She just shook her head, terrified, disbelieving, and mute. All at once, the dam came crashing down and the old flood of anxiety washed over her. She gasped like a barking seal, and the first wave of sobs spilled out. Before she knew it, she was sprinting away, trailing tears through the back yard, across the street, and into the woods.

.   .   .

Her legs were clunky and sore from the timed run earlier that day, but Chloe dug deep, still covering the distance from house to pond at a pace that would have sent Ms. Barnes into a giggling spasm of joy. She did not stop as she came out of the woods to the clearing, but continued to barrel down the hill toward the glassy sheen of the water.

The fish had stopped jumping and the birds had gone. Only Chloe broke the utter stillness of the scene with flailing arms and a stumbling stride that brought her toward the bank without slowing. She launched herself from the rocks and arched into a sloppy dive, destroying the tranquil surface with a belly flop. She kicked furiously toward the center of the pond, releasing the last reserve of frustrated energy before succumbing to total physical and emotional fatigue.

For good measure, Chloe let out one last furious shriek, and the sound of it traveled through the surrounding woods and echoed back with primal rage. She treaded water, and her body ached. A part of her wondered if it wouldn't be better just to stop fighting and let herself sink beneath the surface. Just to be dramatic, she stopped kicking for a moment, shut her eyes, and dropped below. She waved her arms to propel herself down through the darkness, expecting to touch the bottom, but she had to turn back with burning lungs before she did.

She surfaced with a loud inhale and a lot of sputtering, and bitter laughter spilled out of her where the crying had been. It echoed back.

"My life is a joke!" she announced, to test the echo again.

She wondered how she'd never noticed the reverberating sounds here before.

"What do you want from me?" she asked the universe, wondering if the echo might actually contain an answer. It only repeated again, and again.

Chloe flipped to her back with gentle waves of her arms to keep afloat. Eyes closed, she listened to the silence and tried to settle the fury in her veins. At first, the quiet was marred only by her strokes of the water and steadying breaths, but then a current gathered in the air. Before long, a breeze arrived, drifting along the tops of the trees and rustling the canopy around the clearing. Then a wind whistled through the upper limbs, and the branches began to sway and creak with vigor...

Chloe opened her eyes to dark clouds gathering overhead. The billowing grey cover seemed to swirl above the clearing, ominous and angry. Thunder sounded from a few miles off. *This isn't possible. What, am I cursed?*

Then she felt the whole pond lurch below her as a massive, mud-filled bubble gurgled up to toss her into the air with a burst of thick, brown water. She sucked in a dirty mouthful and splashed back to the riled surface with a yelp. Earthen grit was in her mouth and eyes as she struggled to reclaim her bearings. But as lightning struck nearby, lighting her blurry vision with a blinding flash and leaving her ears ringing, she lunged desperately toward the shore.

She reached the bank and pulled her way up, coughing and blind, onto the rocks just as the pond shifted again. A wave rushed past her, dumping her further onto the grass in a flopping heap before sucking her, clawing and frantic, back into the pond. Panic set in with a pounding rain and howling wind.

Chloe climbed frantically, scraping her knees and palms as she escaped over the pond's edge again. She crawled over wet earth as fast as she could, her body wracked and constricting as her lungs fought to expel the layer of silt. Somehow she found her feet and ran, rubbing her eyes and stumbling as lightning cracked into the woods somewhere behind her—too close.

She slipped on the wet grass and found herself on hands

and knees once more. Climbing the hill as fast as she could, she was terrifyingly aware that she was now the tallest point for a hundred feet in every direction. All she could think of was the relative safety of the dense woods ahead. She worked her arms and legs with borrowed strength, fueled by adrenaline.

Lightning struck again and again around the water, and the earth shook with every impact. Then behind her, a monstrous roar rose up from the depths. She looked back, wide-eyed and cringing.

Through the stinging rain, she saw a massive, silvery form emerge from the waterfall that had been a pond. A hulking, shining beast climbed into the air, its crocodilian jaws open to the sky at the end of a long, sinewy neck. Huge, membranous wings unfurled on either side and beat to hold it aloft, each flap sending little tornadoes across the clearing. Its roar sent a shiver through her bones. Chloe covered her ears, fearing they might burst from the punishing vibration.

The hairs stood on end across her body as an odd tingling gathered in her feet. She was only vaguely aware that she was screaming as the impossible thing from the pond turned its piercing blue gaze toward her and set its primordial, hooked claws to the ground with a force that trembled the hillside.

She started to feel light-headed just before another bolt of lightning slammed into the tree above her and all went white and then black.

CHAPTER 4
THE GIRL WHO WAS STRUCK BY LIGHTNING

Before she could see, Chloe heard the same methodical beeping that was so prevalent on all the doctor shows on television. Someone was clutching her hand with a tight, sweaty grip. She lifted her lids with fluttering effort. At first, everything looked grey and blurry, but then her mom materialized out of the haze, leaning in close with worried eyes.

"I'm right here, baby. Can you hear me?" Audrey asked.

Chloe's throat felt raw, and her mouth was incredibly dry. "Hi, Mom," she rasped.

Audrey rushed in with a hug and kiss, failing to hold her tears at bay any longer. "Oh, thank God, thank God," she whispered again and again.

"Mom, it's okay. I think I'm okay," Chloe reassured, glancing around at the uninspired painting of flowers on the wall beside her and then the little TV suspended above her bed. An oversized clock on the wall read 6:34p.m. She hadn't been inside a hospital since her father had been admitted that one time by the police eight years prior. She could still picture the sickening purple of his shattered hand, and the far away gaze that seemed to see right through her as the cops conferred with her mom in the hallway—but she had no idea how she had come to find herself in the hospital now.

"Chloe, what happened? How did you get here?" Audrey asked.

Chloe had been about to ask the same question. She

remembered only vague snippets of what had transpired at the pond: the fast spiraling clouds, a mad rain, the fountain of mud that rose below her, and lightning. And there had been something else, too. Something from just before the electricity had reached into her and claimed her consciousness…the sound of a roar, born out of the storm.

"I don't know. I was at the pond. Lightning hit the tree beside me, and…I don't remember anything else."

"You were in shock, and your blood pressure was really low when you got here. Apparently you were covered in mud; it was all down your throat and in your eyes. They had to give you oxygen just to get your heart back to normal," Audrey rattled, starting to get herself all worked up. "Honey, the nurse said a man carried you into the emergency room—just dropped you off and left without a word. They said you didn't have on any shoes…" She looked like she might explode. "Honey, if something happened out there, I want you to know that you can tell me anything. If he—"

Chloe hadn't seen that frantic edge in her mom's eyes since dad had started slipping either. She would do anything she could to calm that rising squall. "No one touched me," Chloe reassured. "I don't remember anyone being there, and I'm fine now. I was just swimming in the pond, and all of a sudden there was a storm. The water was shifting and bubbling, and I ran. There was lightning everywhere, and then…?"

Audrey watched her daughter closely.

"Mom, I'm telling the truth!"

"I know, honey. I was just so worried. Do you have any pain? The doctor said you could have some lingering effects from the jolt."

Just then, a portly, young nurse bustled in with flushed cheeks and a practiced but warm smile. She wore a nametag that said "Nurse Shiflet," and she handed Chloe a cup filled with water and a straw. "Hello there, Chloe," she said with a little Virginia twang. "I bet your mouth is pretty dry. We had to flush out your throat and eyes there 'cause of all the dirt."

Chloe drank and winced.

"Your throat is gonna be sore for a couple days. And your hands and knees had some nasty scrapes that are gonna take some healing as well," she trilled cheerily. "But other than that, you seem to be just fine. You gave us a little scare in the beginning with your blood pressure, but we usually see between three and seven lightning strikes a year. Trust me, you're one of the lucky ones."

Nurse Shiflet glanced at the printouts from Chloe's heart monitor. "Everything looks good now. How do you feel?"

"Confused, but okay," admitted Chloe.

"And what about the possible lingering effects: memory loss and headaches and stuff like that?" asked Audrey, still clinging to Chloe's hand.

"Yeah, those are commonplace after such a serious shock to the system. Short-term memory loss should be expected, and some other complications can creep up on you and last for a good while, too. But you should cross that bridge if and when you come to it. For now, just count your blessings, go home, and get ready for school tomorrow," Nurse Shiflet answered a bit too merrily for Chloe's liking.

"School?" Chloe croaked. "I can't go to school after being struck by lightning."

"I don't see why not," answered Shiflet with a quick mark on Chloe's chart. "You check out fine, and you said yourself that you feel okay, right? Why not go home for a good night's sleep?" She turned to Audrey with a whisper. "And you might want to start the checkout procedure pretty soon. It's best to clear out if you can before the shift change at seven or you could get stuck here all night." She winked and bustled back toward the door.

"Nurse," Chloe called, wincing with the attempt at an elevated tone, "the man who brought me in…who was he?"

Nurse Shiflet stood in the door smiling. "I didn't see him, but from what the other nurses say, he was sure worth looking at—amazing blue eyes." She winked again.

"Do you know what time I got here?" Chloe asked, trying to piece it together.

"Your chart says you came in just a bit after five."

Audrey looked at her cell phone history. "The hospital called home, and Brent called me at 5:22."

Chloe thought about it—she'd gotten home from school after 4:00, had her run-in with Brent and started toward the pond no earlier than 4:45, and had swam for at least ten minutes before the storm came. "That's impossible; the lightning must have struck around 5:00 at the earliest, and that was more than ten miles away and in the middle of the woods."

"Well, then, whoever he was, he probably saved your life." Nurse Shiflet marched away with a rubbery squeak at every step.

Chloe and her mom sat in silence for a long, loaded moment.

"It seems you have a guardian angel," said Audrey.

"This is all so weird."

"And you're really all right?" Audrey asked.

Chloe sensed trouble and nodded reluctantly.

"Then what the hell were you doing out at the pond in the middle of a storm again? You could have been killed, Chloe!"

"Mom, it's Brent—"

"Brent was worried sick about you!" Audrey cut in. "He was out scouring the woods and luckily came back to the house just in time to answer the call from the hospital. He beat me here and has been by your side right up until you woke up, so let's not start that again," she said with a shaky voice and wet eyes.

Chloe could only nod in agreement. "I...I really need to pee," she said, realizing the uncomfortable pressure on her bladder.

Audrey cleared her throat. "There's a bathroom just down the hall. Maybe you could clean yourself up a little bit, too. I'll start the paperwork and meet you back here in ten."

Chloe swiveled from the bed and noticed the cool breeze through the back of her open gown. Beneath she wasn't wearing anything but her underwear and some light blue, hospital-issue polyester booties. The public nudity was disconcerting at best. "Do you have to go back to work?" Chloe asked.

"Are you kidding? My daughter was struck by lightning on her first day of high school. They can manage without me." Audrey placed a gentle hand on Chloe's cheek. "I love you,

Chloe. You're all I've got."

Chloe felt a familiar weight press on her chest. "Me too, Mom. I'm really sorry."

Audrey stood and exhaled slowly. "You think you can stay out of trouble for ten minutes?" she asked with a smirk.

Chloe shrugged. "I'll try."

.   .   .

Chloe really wished she'd thought to change into her regular clothes before leaving for the bathroom—if she'd known what waited for her down the hall, she would have held it in and skipped the little journey altogether. Instead, she found herself shuffling along in the slippery booties while holding the gown at the small of her back to keep her underwear-covered butt from hanging out for all to see.

She glanced into the various rooms as she passed, seeing less fortunate people in all states of distress. An older man was moaning and thrashing in his bed while a male nurse moved about the room, completely ignoring him. In another room, a woman lay motionless with a tube down her throat and a steady, wheezing hiss from an attached machine. In the next, Chloe saw a sleeping man with his leg suspended above the bed and locked in place.

She turned back to focus on the hallway, not wanting to see any more of these snippets of other people's misery. Instead, she saw Brent and a familiar woman sequestered in the shadows by a vending machine at the end of the hall. They leaned close to each other and whispered emphatically. Officer Brent was clearly trying to contain the woman's emotional state as she trembled on the verge of an outburst. Chloe knew this woman; it was Loraine, from Positive Pete's Diner. *Oh, come on!*

Chloe put her head down and shuffled faster. The unisex restroom sign was just ahead; she needed only to get inside and wait for the clandestine meeting to break apart at the end of the hall. She prayed that the room wasn't occupied, her heartbeat rising as her hand found the handle and yanked.

She opened the door, slid inside, and locked it in one quick motion. The smell was atrocious! Her hand shot to the collar of her gown, and she yanked the polyester weave across her nose. It didn't help. Her selected hiding place had been recently abused. She raised the lid with a wad of paper between her fingers and the porcelain. As she hovered above the seat, she felt the burn in her twice-abused legs.

Somewhat relieved, she washed her hands thoroughly, working to dislodge the mud that was caked under her nails. The skinny girl with matted hair and bloodshot eyes that stared back from the mirror did not impress. Dirt was caked behind her ears and under her chin, and she picked a strand of freshwater weed from her clumpy locks with a sad shake of her head. She looked like someone who'd been stranded on a desert island for a few years, or maybe someone who'd...been beat up by an angry pond and struck by lightning. She would need a hot shower, a big bowl of soup, and about ten hours of sleep to be human again.

She returned to the door, pressing her ear to the cool surface and listening for some indication of Brent's whereabouts. She figured the coast would be clear after another few minutes...Just then, someone tried the handle and Chloe stepped back, biting her lip. They knocked a second later.

"Occupied," Chloe called. *What if it's Brent, or Loraine, or both?* She looked around for another escape, but of course, that was stupid.

The knock came again, this time more forceful. "What, is somebody dying in there?" a female voice muttered.

Well, it wasn't Brent, and she sounded younger than Loraine—maybe it was her lucky day after all. Hopefully her luck would hold out long enough for her to make it back to her room, get changed, and get out of the hospital without confronting the love triangle that would break her Mom's heart.

Chloe unlocked the door and swung it open. Her jaw dropped.

"You!" spat Kendra, back to her perfectly beautiful, bitchy self.

"Kendra, what are you doing here?" Chloe stammered.

"Oh, like you didn't hear," Kendra challenged with a pinched sneer.

Chloe felt like she was going to pass out again. She shook her head.

"Heat stroke, thanks to you. I've been here since sixth period on an IV drip."

"Kendra, I'm really sorry," Chloe offered. "If it's any consolation, I guarantee I had a worse day than you."

Kendra looked Chloe up and down again, taking in her wild appearance. "Yeah, what happened? You look like a freakin' crazy person!"

"I got struck by lightning," Chloe said with a shrug.

Kendra burst out laughing, the high pitch of her cackle echoed down the hall. "For serious? That's classic!" She immediately wiggled her iPhone from her too-tight back pocket, snapped a picture of Chloe, and started texting. "Kelly and Mags are gonna totally shit when they see this."

Though it didn't seem possible, Chloe's heart sank a little further. "Cool, well, I'm glad you're okay now."

"You too," answered Kendra before returning her eyes to the little screen. "If you'd died, it would have totally ruined my chance to hate you."

As Chloe stopped to ponder the intricacies of that statement, the gruff voice of an older man cut in.

"Kendra, you are supposed to be using the bathroom, not texting! We've already lost four hours to this place," barked a jowly, red-faced man in a very fine grey suit.

"Sorry, Dad," mumbled Kendra, suddenly seeming sheepish and meek. "The bathroom was *occupied*." She said the last word with an accusatory glare at Chloe.

"Well, it seems to be free now, doesn't it?" As Mr. Roberts came closer, he let his eyes focus on the disheveled girl beside his daughter and actually took a step back. "Oh, who is this?"

"Dad, this is Chloe McClellan, the girl from school I was telling you about," muttered Kendra.

"Ah, yes, McClellan, I know the name. I hear you're quite

the speed demon. You beat Kendra so badly she couldn't hold her lunch or her bowels. Well done." He glanced at her still-dirty hands and decided against offering his own to shake. "I would hope my daughter can give you some further competition later this year," he said with an expectant look to Kendra. Her mortified gaze flashed to Chloe and then fell to the floor. "And what brings you to the hospital today?" he asked Chloe with a raised eyebrow and subtle wrinkle of his nose.

"I got struck by lightning," Chloe muttered, wishing she could say something else.

"Really?" Now Mr. Roberts leaned in closer, oddly interested. "I wasn't aware of any storms in the area today. Where was this? You know my company has started tracking inclement weather patterns across central Virginia as part of a new project that we've been working on?" He smiled with artificially white teeth.

"In the woods, about a mile or so from the top of Red Hill Road," she answered, pretty sure that he wasn't really listening.

"I'll have my man look into it," he added. "If I can keep the R and D team on schedule, by early next year, no one in this whole region should ever be struck by lightning again…What do you think of that?"

Chloe wasn't sure if she was actually supposed to come up with an answer. "Yeah, wow. That would be something."

"It *will* be something, Chloe. And that's just the tip of the iceberg for what the Daedalus Group is going to offer the world in the coming months." He placed a controlling hand on the back of Kendra's neck.

Again, Chloe felt like some acknowledgment of gratitude was expected. "Cool. Thanks," she offered.

Mr. Roberts nodded and his smile faded. "Let's go, Kendra, we've spent quite enough time here."

"Dad, I still have to use the bathroom," Kendra whined.

"Stop being a child; you can go at home." He steered her away without any room for dissent. "Nice to meet you, Chloe," he said without looking back, though Kendra glanced over her shoulder with fire in her eyes and a look that said: *THIS NEVER HAPPENED!*

"Nice to meet you, too," Chloe muttered, only then remembering to look out for Brent and Loraine. The shadows beside the vending machines were empty, and she let go of an exhausted sigh.

She shuffled back down the hall in the opposite direction with her eyes averted from her surroundings, looking up only after she'd reached the familiar sight of her mom's comfortable waitressing shoes. Audrey was hunched over a clipboard of paperwork, filling out pages of little boxes. She whipped the pen in the air in an effort to gather the ink in its ballpoint tip and glanced to Chloe.

"Go get dressed, honey."

"I ran into Kendra Roberts," Chloe stated without emotion.

"Yeah, I saw her dad," Audrey sympathized. "He's a real piece of work—told me all about the great things his company is doing for Charlottesville when, in fact, they're pushing out all the local farmers to develop fake food while dumping all their chemical byproducts a few towns over and poisoning the river water that flows right back to Charlottesville. He wants a key to the town for driving up real estate prices and taking away jobs and land from the families that have lived here for generations. And the saddest thing is that the local politicians will probably give it to him."

Chloe recognized that heated tone—her mom wasn't one to back away from presumed injustice. Audrey noticed her daughter's solemn stare and cut herself off.

"I'm sorry you had to run into Kendra, honey. But if you're gonna have to start off this school year with an enemy, for what it's worth, I think you picked the right one."

"Loraine's here," Chloe said, meeting her mom's eyes for a brief moment of understanding.

"Yeah, I saw that too," Audrey admitted with the barest hint of a nod.

"I'm really sorry," Chloe said.

Audrey put down the pen and held Chloe's chin for a gentle moment. "Me too," she said with glassy eyes. "Now go get dressed; it's a school night after all."

. . .

The tired, little horn honked twice as Audrey puttered away from the school parking lot with a few unwelcome lurches of the transmission in the twelve-year-old Honda CR-V. As if linked to the bottomless reservoir of Audrey's energy, the car simply refused to stop—now 210,000 miles and three fender benders since Chloe's dad had purchased it. Audrey always joked that, aside from Chloe, that car was the best thing that Ray McClellan had left her.

Chloe watched it idling at the stoplight a hundred yards down the road and considered taking off after it at a dead sprint. If she was going to be the future state champion of distance running, shouldn't she start practicing now? The light changed and the car disappeared around the corner as Chloe sighed and turned to face the long gauntlet of cars and kids that stood before her and the entrance to Day 2 of high school... *Crap.*

Heat waves radiated off the blacktop of the senior parking lot. The first bell wouldn't ring for another fifteen minutes, but the 150 prime spots reserved for students, mostly seniors, were just a couple cars shy of filled to capacity. Three times as many kids clustered and milled about: laughing, posturing, and blaring music. Chloe clutched her brown-bag lunch tightly, despite the bandaged cuts across her hands, and she made a mental note to have her Mom drop her off at the side entrance from now on. She rolled her neck and stepped from the sidewalk to the blacktop, wearing last year's running shoes, now brought out of retirement. She'd survived lightning; she could survive this.

A huge boy nearly took her out as he lunged past her to catch a football that torpedoed in from across the lot.

"Sorry," said Ezra Richardson without much more than a glance before he wound up and rocketed the ball back over the swarm of cars in a perfect spiral.

Ezra had been the starting quarterback of the football team for the last two years and was expected in this, his senior year, to lead the team to a state championship. He stood about six foot four and was a perfect specimen of African-American male physical beauty: perfect skin, chiseled cheek bones, statuesque muscles, and a Hollywood smile. He had his pick of colleges, made everything look effortless, and was completely self-absorbed. Chloe was mesmerized for a moment by the definition in his throwing arm and decided then and there that she hated him. She shuffled on quickly.

She passed an old, busted van with a slapdash industrial orange paint job and caught a whiff of illicit smoke mingled with tobacco plumes wafting from the cracked windows. Jam band music and laughter rose from within just before the side door banged open and Stan tumbled out in a guffawing heap.

"Brian, you total A-hole, this is my van, dude!" he declared while regaining his feet. He looked around at the handful of other students who snickered and stared. "And once again, you are totally making an ill-advised scene on school property!" He flashed a toothy smile before catching sight of Chloe walking by.

"Hey, Cool Chloe!" he shouted with a point and a wave. He took his cell phone from his pocket and hit a couple buttons before holding it up with the hospital bathroom pic that Kendra had taken the night before on the screen. "Lightning Girl! Awesome!"

Chloe put her head down and kept moving, but now a few other students were glancing in her direction as well. More than once, she glimpsed her picture displayed on the phones of random strangers. *You've got to be joking!* Kendra had been busy.

Chloe spotted her new enemy surrounded by the soccer posse the next aisle over. Kendra was holding court beside Paul Markson's silver BMW, draped across the hood as she let out one of her shiver-inducing cackles. Chloe just stared, willing the car to explode and silence Kendra with a jagged shard of metal through her skull and a brilliant fireball to finish off her friends...But her pyrokinetic powers failed her once again.

Liz moved between cars to intercept her.

"Chloe, are you all right?" asked Liz with a worried glance to the bandages on her hands. She, too, held a portable phone with Chloe's picture on the screen.

Chloe reached out for the phone, and Liz reluctantly

handed it over with a grave look. Sure enough, there was Chloe in her hospital gown, covered in dirt, with matted hair and bug-eyed surprise. The text below read: **Beware crazy person in our school! STAY BACK, you might get shocked! Approach LIGHTNING GIRL at your own risk!**

At first, Chloe was too pissed off to answer. "Why don't you ask your new friend?" she seethed.

"I'm sorry about the picture, Chloe. That was a really bitchy thing to do." Liz looked down at her shoes. "I just heard about it this morning; I would have called. I was worried about you."

Chloe handed the phone back. "Yeah, I'm sure you've been dying for an excuse to call me again all summer, and now you've missed your chance, is that it?" Chloe wished she could take the words back or silence those that would follow, but she was just too far gone to stop. "No worries, Liz, I'll probably either get run over by a bus or be attacked by a pack of dogs later today, and then you'll already have credit for caring for old times' sake, and you and your cool friends can have enough fodder to make my life hell for the next three years."

Liz looked like she was about to cry. "Chloe, that's not fair," she whispered.

"Yeah, well, I've come to realize that life is pretty freaking unfair in general, so I guess we can all look at this as a learning experience," Chloe spat. "And you can tell Kendra that I was the most unassuming kid in her class. I was gonna keep my head down and stay out of everyone's way. But if she wants an enemy so badly, then so be it—she's got one." She was shaking.

Chloe stormed past Liz without another glance, only half-aware that she was gripping her lunch so tightly that she'd mashed her peanut butter and honey sandwich into a pulpy ball. She felt the cuts on her fingers opening again, but she was too angry to care. Other kids saw her coming and got out of her way. She silenced both the laughter and their whispers with every shift of her furious eyes.

Day 2, and already she'd gone from "brownnosing freak" to crazy and dangerous. For a moment, she imagined the entire school leveled to a pile of indistinct rock with the parking lot turned into a broken field of twisted metal and scorched bodies. She envisioned herself walking over the shattered remains, calling deadly claws of lightning down upon anything that moved around her. She was destruction—the fury of the elements at her grasp, returning the earth to its wild and natural state.

She caught the partially detached sole of her shoe on a speed bump and fumbled to keep her feet. Nope, she was still just Chloe: skinny, friendless, sophomore girl, without a hope or a clue. She wrestled back the flood of tears that threatened to break free from her thundering skull, eyes locked on the entrance to school, the last place she wanted to go.

"Lightning Girl," someone called.

Don't look; don't even give them the satisfaction of a response.

"Hey, Chloe!" he persisted.

She turned, ready to bite. "What!" she snapped, seeing Kirin getting out of a dark blue, classic, woody-sided Grand Wagoneer.

He walked toward her, casual and smiling. "You look pretty good for being a victim of the elements," he offered, taking her off guard.

"Oh, thanks. Just lucky, I guess," she mumbled.

"Lucky? I think it's one of the coolest things I've ever heard." There was no noticeable mockery as he held up his phone with the picture blazoned across the screen.

"I'm dangerous, you know; you might not want to get too close."

"I like living on the edge."

"How did you even get that text? You don't even know anyone at this school yet," she challenged, feeling her anger dissipating.

He smirked, "I told you, I'm aloof and mysterious; I have my ways."

"Yeah, well, I'm glad it's going so well for you." She remembered then the missing grandmother. "No, I'm sorry. Have you heard any news about your grandmother?"

Kirin smiled sadly. "Not yet, but thanks for asking. My uncle is going to try and get to Xining to see if he can find her, but for now we all just have to wait. It's pretty bad over there;

the whole city was leveled to dust and debris."

Chloe thought about her angry fantasy for the school and felt stupid.

"I don't think I can deal with this place today," Kirin admitted. "I'm thinking about taking one of those ten sick days…if maybe you wanted to come along?"

Chloe's heart was racing again, but this time for a different reason. "It's only the second day," she answered feebly.

"So what? The first day sucked." He got back into the driver's seat, having clearly made up his mind. He shut the door and leaned out the open window. "Come on. You got struck by lightning yesterday, and I don't know anyone else in town." He nodded his head toward the passenger door. "Get in, you can show me around."

Chloe stood in silence with her thoughts racing. Against all intentions, she'd already become the most famous person in school, and for none of the right reasons. Despite it all, in that moment, she couldn't contain the grin that blossomed across her face.

CHAPTER 5
THE LOST SHOES

For seven years, Chloe had tried to do everything right: perfect grades, an unflagging dedication to her chores, and an acute sensitivity to the needs of her mother. She'd led a contained, squeaky clean existence—ditching class, let alone on the second day of high school, made her feel a little like a criminal. It felt pretty good, too, and around Kirin, her usual cascade of minor anxieties and racing thoughts was blissfully stilled.

There was something about his presence that had the same calming effect on Chloe as the few times that she'd stood before the ocean. She was inclined to say things she had intended to keep bottled away. "I've never skipped school before."

"Really?"

"Yeah, I guess I'm kind of a nerd," she admitted before biting her lip in the hopes that it might make her stop talking.

Kirin glanced at her for a moment and then returned his eyes to the street. Like everything he did, his driving was fluid and effortless. "So where do you want to go?"

"I don't know. What do you want to see?" she shot back.

"Hmmmm," Kirin pondered. "What does this town have to offer?"

Chloe thought about it for a moment, looking out the window so he wouldn't see her barely contained excitement. They passed a sign for the UVA campus. "The university is really pretty? It was founded by Thomas Jefferson—"

"Seen it," he cut in. "What else?"

"Uh," she thought. "The downtown area has some pretty cool stores and a nice outdoor mall—"

"Skip it," he silenced her playfully. "Santa Cruz had cool stores and an outdoor mall. I want something I can't find everywhere else."

She looked out the window at a stoplight and hoped for inspiration. A couple of college kids lounged on an old stone wall and drank coffee by the side of the road... *What do the locals do?* "There's an abandoned quarry where a lot of kids go swimming," she suggested, unsure of herself.

"Is that where you go?" he asked.

"No, there's usually too many people in bathing suits, and I don't have a car to get there," she admitted.

"So where do you and your friends hang out?" he asked.

Chloe shrugged. "Maybe you noticed this morning, but I'm not exactly swarming with friends right now."

"Right, the dangerous Lightning Girl," he remembered with a chuckle. "So then, where's the Lightning Girl's secret lair?" It would have sounded mean coming from anyone else, but Kirin seemed genuinely interested. He was one of those people who made whoever he was with feel as if they were the center of the universe.

"I guess that would be the pond in the woods up in the hills near my house," Chloe offered. She'd never brought anyone to the pond but Liz. It seemed almost sacrilegious to speak of it now, but she couldn't contain the giddy roll in her gut.

"That's where we're going!" Kirin declared.

Chloe winced. "I'm not so sure. It's about a mile walk from the road, and my Mom kind of forbade me to go there again after the whole lightning incident."

"Yeah, my dad forbade me from skipping school," Kirin countered with a challenging glance. "But I want to see the spot where Lightning Girl got her special powers," he ribbed.

"So far, my only powers seem to be human repulsion and extreme embarrassment."

"You're stalling," he sang.

She tried to shoot him a disapproving look, but her smile couldn't hide for long. "You're kind of a pain in the ass, huh?"

"That's *my* special power," he pumped his eyebrows.

Chloe laughed. "Make a U-turn."

.   .   .

They parked at the side of the road a few miles from Chloe's house. Getting caught sneaking back from the one place she was forbidden to go during second period was not on her list of ways to turn the first calamitous week of high school around.

Kirin had picked up a walking stick a couple hundred yards from the road and strode through the woods as if there was nowhere else in the world he'd rather be. Chloe was in awe of him—watching as he marched ahead and whacked the stick against trees as he passed. How could anyone be so comfortable in their own skin? For a prolonged moment, her eyes held on the ripple of definition that outlined his tanned calves with his every assured step.

Out of the car, the quieting effects of his presence on her inner monologue had begun to dissipate. Though this had long been her terrain, she now moved under branches and around the rocks with a growing disquiet in her gut, and only partly because of the impromptu rule-breaking journey with the freakishly cute senior.

Why did violent storms come the last two times I was at the pond? What bubbled up beneath me as I swam yesterday? Who was the blue-eyed man that saved me? Where are my shoes? The questions had returned in a constant cycle. She walked faster to catch up with Kirin's latest charge up a hill.

"There's no path at all?" he observed, glancing over his shoulder.

"The pond doesn't even show up on surveyors' maps of the region," she answered.

"Cool," he offered. "How do you know about it?"

"I found it running in the woods a few years ago."

"Ah, yes, the wild Lightning Girl, sprinting through the hills on her secret missions." He was clearly pleased with himself.

This time, Chloe gave him a glare when he glanced over his shoulder. He grinned and turned back to the steady advance through bush and branch, whacking a shrub with his stick as he passed.

"Are you gonna attack all the plants until we get there?" she challenged, looking to distract herself from the cascade of doubt.

"Nope, just the ones that get in my way."

What a boy thing to say, though she noticed that he peacefully strode around the next sapling that stood in his path.

"So, if you're such a runner, are you going to join the cross-country team or something?" He scaled a rocky jut with only a few well-placed bounds.

"I'm not really much of a joiner, but I guess I was thinking about it," she admitted for the first time out loud. "What about you? You seem like one of the few who is still capable of interaction with the real world, rather than just video games and online chats."

"My dad wants me to join the swim team, but I don't think so. It's one thing swimming in the ocean, but what's the point of going back and forth in a little segmented box?" He leapt off the rock and landed out of sight on the other side.

Chloe circled around but didn't see him anywhere. She advanced hesitantly, searching the trees. She couldn't let him get the better of her and kept talking like he was right beside her. "I guess just to prove that you're the fastest."

He appeared at her shoulder from behind, no sound, same cocky smirk. Chloe's heart jumped.

"I was born for the water; I already know I'm the fastest. Why should I have to prove it to anyone?" he said.

The pond was just over the next ridge, and her fear of what she might find there returned in a drenching wave. She glanced at the cuts on her hands and remembered the roar of thunder and the quake of the earth. *Maybe this isn't such a good idea.*

But Kirin charged past her and stopped at the top of the ridge with a growing smile. "Now we're talking! No wonder you've kept this to yourself!" he declared with his eyes locked on the perfect sheen of water below, glittering in the sunlight and reflecting the blue cloudless sky above. "This place is awesome!" he yelled before taking off at a run.

"Wait!" cried Chloe without effect. "It's not safe!"

Kirin dropped the stick and shed his shirt and shoes without stopping, carelessly discarding them in the grass as he approached the pond. Chloe could hear his laughter, and she was momentarily distracted from her worry by the look of the sunlight on the golden-brown muscles across his back and shoulders.

She knew she should be chasing after him with her arms and voice raised in warning, but she could only watch with dumbfounded admiration as he reached the edge of the pond and launched himself into a graceful, arching dive. He slipped into the water with barely any splash and disappeared beneath the surface.

Chloe was moving again, watching the water for the fountain of mud and glancing to the sky for the gathering clouds while she counted the long seconds that Kirin stayed under. *One, two, three, four, five, six, seven—something is wrong!* She started to run.

But then he surfaced in the middle with a joyous yelp, and she found her breath again. Nothing had changed about the clearing—it was just as beautiful and inviting as it had been all summer long—and Kirin fit effortlessly against the backdrop.

"The water is perfect!" he yelled. "You have to come in!"

Chloe stepped tentatively toward the edge, picturing the way the whole surface had shifted with the unlikely rush of the powerful wave the day before. "The last time I got in, things got less perfect real fast." She shoved her hands in her pockets and looked again to the decidedly unthreatening sky.

She knelt on the rocks, wondering if the water level across the whole pond didn't seem about a foot lower than it had been. Kirin was watching her as he swam closer. He climbed out on the rocks a few feet away and wrung the dripping water from his cargo shorts before flopping to the grass without any sign of self-consciousness. He had clearly spent a lot of time hanging around without a shirt on, and Chloe could definitely see why. Charlottesville didn't have too many guys like him, or at least none that she'd encountered. She tried not to stare.

"I didn't mean to be pushy, making you come here," he offered. "I didn't really think about it before, but I suppose getting struck by lightning was probably pretty traumatic, huh?"

Chloe shrugged. "Yeah, I guess so," she mumbled, wondering if he would think she was even more of a freak if she told him what really happened here. "I don't remember anything after the lightning hit, but the stuff I remember from just before was pretty...weird."

"Tell me," he suggested.

She glanced over, and her focus flashed from abs to eyes. He smiled. She blushed and cleared her throat. "I was here on Monday night, too, Labor Day, and all the fish were jumping across the pond. Then all these birds started to gather in the trees," she motioned to the branches hanging above them. "Crows and sparrows and blue jays and a hawk: hundreds of birds that wouldn't be together, just sitting there, watching the water."

Kirin raised an eyebrow, but it was too late to stop now.

"And then after school yesterday, I was swimming, like you just were, and a storm came out of nowhere. The whole pond moved and a giant bubble of mud came up from below. And then there was a wave that carried me onto the shore, and rain, and lightning everywhere, and a huge fountain of water, and a...roar."

Kirin thinned his eyes to look at her. His smile had gone.

"I don't know; I can't explain it. I just felt really small and helpless," she stammered. "Whatever. Maybe Kendra's right; maybe I'm just crazy and dangerous."

"That's how I feel," Kirin said, cutting her off before her defensive pity party could reach full bloom. "All these millions of people, trapped and dying in China—my grandmother, this eighty-year-old woman living by herself—and I can't do anything to help, nothing to even contact her, just to let her know that I love her." He glanced back to the pond and hugged his knees to his chest. "I feel useless...inconsequential. We go through all the motions and drama at school, or at home, and in the big scheme of things, none of it matters, you know?"

Exactly! Chloe looked over and found him looking back, both of them just staring at each other as the breeze rustled the leaves above…

"Is this where it happened, the lightning?" he asked, breaking the moment of pregnant silence.

She motioned to the top of the hill. "No, it was up there. I was trying to make it home."

He looked over his shoulder at the slope and squinted into the sun. "Show me."

Minutes later, they were poking about the roots at the top of the hill, Kirin using his walking stick and Chloe her tattered old running shoes. He had, unfortunately, reclaimed his shirt as well, though Chloe now found it easier to focus on the mystery at hand. She wasn't sure, but looking back down at the pond, she thought this was around where it had happened.

"Look at this," said Kirin, pointing to a deep crack of scorched wood in the tree above them. A major limb dangled to the ground, broken and burned, and the trunk was split almost to the base. He probed the wound with the end of his stick, and charred bark flaked off with every jab. "Good thing it hit this first, huh?"

It was a sobering observation. The big oak had probably grown here for a hundred years, but it didn't look long for the world now. Chloe stepped closer with her eyes set and mouth open, and tripped, stumbling straight into Kirin.

He spun, dropped the staff, and caught her in one swift motion. Chloe scrambled to regain her feet, keenly aware of the feel of his supporting hands on her waist. She noticed her own hand pressed to his chest for balance. Their eyes met for a quick moment, and she stepped away with the tickle of goose bumps.

"Sorry," she swallowed.

"What is that?" asked Kirin, looking over her shoulder.

She turned back to see two indistinct lumps among the roots. They stepped closer and knelt down on either side of the find. The fabric and mesh were blackened and brittle, and the rubber of the soles had melted in places and fused together in a little puddle. The laces had burned away completely. The two shapes faced the pond, with the shiny "N" of New Balance still discernible on the right lump.

Chloe must have somehow been blown clear out of them when the lightning had climbed up from the wet ground below. Looking at them and the tree, she could not fathom how she could have possibly survived.

"My shoes."

. . .

Ancient, sad eyes watched the two young humans as they moved back into the woods in the direction from which they'd come. The irises were the color of glacial ice and flickered with an internal spark. By contrast, the black pits in the center threatened to draw in and consume anything that looked too close. The unblinking gaze registered every subtle movement in the trees: each ant that scurried back and forth in its food-gathering line, every flutter of wing and shake of a tail, but they held focus on the inexplicable girl until she passed from sight beyond the ridge.

The lids closed over. The watcher needed no eyes to follow. He could hear her thoughts of confusion and excitement from a great distance, having heard her even through water and earth and from beyond the wall of sleep. He did not understand it, but somehow *she* had drawn him out from the depths, capturing his far-drifting attention with the endless flow of her questioning mind and the hungry rhythm of her heart. She had startled him awake with her fury and strength, summoned him up to the world above with all of its beauty and sorrow. A human.

He had not let her die as he knew he should when the lightning had come to claim her. He did not know why he had done it—healed her burns and breathed life back into her heart—allowing himself to be seen to take her to the human house of medicine. Though he had stripped her mind of the memory, it was forbidden to interfere on their behalf; it was against the laws of nature and the prophecy of those who had come before…But he could not allow her death, not yet.

Long ago, other people had occupied this land, and their wise folk, with their smoke and drums, had looked on the mist-covered mountains where he dwelled with bowed heads and prayers. They wove stories of him around their cooking fires and passed them down to the young boys before they underwent the trials of manhood. They had treated the world with respect and honored the mighty Horned Serpents that protected it in their songs. But now, it seemed, he was to be a herald of doom and bringer of war. For the first time in centuries, unease crept into his thoughts.

It was not in his nature to be afraid, but the world was not as his kind had left it. Beyond the woods, the land and air had become alien and sickly. Grumbling down the tar-stinking snake ways nearby or soaring through the sky overhead, the machines of men always encroached and threatened. He could smell the toxins in the soil and hear the constant buzz of the wires that crisscrossed the globe. It was as the prophecy had stated: the humans would pay for their indiscretion.

But something had gone terribly wrong. It was still way too hot; the air did not yet smell of frost and death as was foretold. He opened his lids and stared into the blazing sun through the branches—the alignment was wrong; it was still many days away from the Ascension, which would break the earth and blot the sky. The others remained asleep in their distant prisons, and until they woke, he would be vulnerable and alone.

The girl had done this. He had to find out how. It was all that he had.

CHAPTER 6
HEAD DOWN AND
MOUTH SHUT?

Kirin had neglected to warn Chloe that their new school might have an automated service that would call to notify her mother of her absence. But after seeing the shoes and grasping what could have been her fate, neither her two-week grounding nor Kendra's continued smear campaign was enough to dampen the realization that Chloe was very lucky. In the weeks that followed, she kept her eyes on the floor as she walked the hallways by day, and she kept her nose in the books at night.

She read every page of the assigned reading and then researched further on topics that seemed poignant or sparked her interest. She aced her first battery of quizzes, and her short papers in American Civics and English were "*INSIGHTFUL*" and "*CONCISELY ARGUED, A+ WORK*." Without being showy and rarely raising her hand, Chloe made sure that the teachers took notice.

She and Kirin continued their playful banter in the back of homeroom and then again deep in the recess of The Cave at lunch, but he, too, had been punished for ditching, and his father turned out to be a lot stricter than Audrey. In addition to the perfect attendance and good grades that Chloe had been tasked with, Kirin was also stripped of phone and car privileges and locked away at home by 4:00 p.m. every day.

His argument for leniency was not aided by his continued refusal to join the swim team, whereas Chloe had negotiated her willingness to start cross-country practice as a means of two more hours of relative freedom per day. In truth, Audrey was so thrilled that her daughter had skipped school with the "cute senior" and had now joined a bona fide after-school elective that Chloe was pretty sure that she would have been granted a full furlough from her sentence if she'd only asked.

Though she'd never admit it to Kirin, Chloe was glad for the two-week, semi-forced return to her old ways. The escape into books was reassuring after so much chaos. But thanks to the continued ill-timed exclamations by Stan and his stoner friends and the regular assault of bitchy comments from Kendra, the Lightning Girl nickname had stuck at school. A week after Chloe's rash declaration of war to Liz, she found the words "*FOR A GOOD TIME, CALL LIGHTNING GIRL–SHE'S FAST*," along with her home number, scrawled in permanent marker inside the third stall of the girls' first floor bathroom. Kirin confirmed that it had been repeated in every stall of the boys' room just down the hall. She'd never even really kissed a boy, and yet now, only two weeks into high school, her name had become synonymous with slut... *Awesome!*

At home, she could just be nerdy, overachieving Chloe again. But home had its own set of problems. Chloe had only seen Brent once since the hospital—through her bedroom window, engaged in a heated discussion with her mom in the front seat of his spit-shined cop car. Audrey had been quiet and mopey since, unwilling to talk about it, except to tell Chloe that she and Brent were "taking a break." Despite the continued hot weather, the mood and feel of the house tended toward frosty.

Chloe couldn't help but feel partly responsible for the return of Audrey's sadness. The same melancholy that had surfaced four times in the last six years at the end of each failed attempt at love—all stemming from the debilitating, year-long pit of depression that had claimed Audrey after Chloe's dad had left.

Chloe feared the woman that had taken over her mother then—bitter, distant, crying far more than laughing—and she still carried the anger of that eight-year-old girl, who had been forced to hold on for the emotional roller coaster that followed...

But despite the minor blips here and there, things had been

great between Chloe and her mom for years. *This is nothing. There's no way that Brent could be more than just another blip.*

She figured that as long as she stayed away from the pond, kept up the 4.0, and continued to excel in cross-country, Audrey would be okay. Brent would become nothing but the butt of an inside joke, as he deserved. *I survived lightning! I can handle this.*

. . .

It was two weeks from the day of her and Kirin's mutual grounding. The solitary confinement would end that night, and Chloe wasn't sure she was ready for freedom's return in the morning. Of course, she would also be getting her monthly migraine any day now. *Perfectly bad timing, yet again.*

Chloe had spent the better part of those two weeks fantasizing about whether Kirin would ask her to do something again, hoping he might call her as soon as his phone was returned to him. It was bordering on the obsessive. She spotted him at the usual table in the back of The Cave, but slowed her approach around the ferns as she noticed someone else occupying her chair.

Cynthia Decareaux was a senior, Queen of the Stoners, and one of the few students at Charlottesville High, like Ezra Richardson, who was known to everyone. *Why is she sitting across from Kirin?*

She was beautiful, and she used it well. Tall, laid-back, and blonde, she had a long history of storied relationships with now-graduated, older men. She always wore her hair in a loose ponytail, and the tips were dyed blue. Somehow, she actually made it look cool. She laughed as Kirin finished one of his stories and gave her his disarming smile.

Uh-oh! Chloe's heart started beating faster. She slowed her approach as she emerged from behind the potted foliage. Kirin waved her over, but Chloe noticed his smile change before she reached the table.

"Hey, Chloe, this is Cynthia," he offered as Chloe sat in the chair beside her. She reached out and met Cynthia's hand for the shake. Her fingers were long and delicate, but her grip was strong. Cynthia eyed her appraisingly.

"Chloe," she said, as if testing the name. "Are you the sophomore who was struck by lightning?" she asked, still holding Chloe's hand.

Chloe nodded. "Yeah, that's me."

The senior released Chloe's hand. Her green eyes were piercing and betrayed no emotion. "Is it true that your shoes melted together?"

Chloe shot Kirin a glance. He responded with a guilty shrug. Cynthia was still waiting for more.

"Yeah, I guess that when the electricity rose up from the wet ground, I was blown out of my shoes. I got lucky, but they didn't fare so well."

"And you're totally okay?"

"Pretty much," answered Chloe. "I don't remember it too well, and my fingers and toes still get a little tingly when it rains, but other than that…"

"That's one of the coolest things I've ever heard!" Cynthia's unflappable demeanor split into a gorgeous smile.

"Thanks." Chloe felt a little giddy, suddenly wanting this fabled girl to like her.

"You know, when I was a sophomore, people wrote that I was a slut in the bathrooms, too," Cynthia admitted. "Only difference is that with me it was true." She gave Kirin a sly glance that Chloe would think about for days.

I don't stand a chance.

"How do you know Kirin?" Chloe asked, trying to appear uninterested as she unpacked her peanut butter and honey sandwich.

"AP Biology, we're lab partners," Cynthia answered with a casual smirk.

"Next week we're dissecting a cat," added Kirin.

"And I'm not amped about it," continued Cynthia.

"Which is why I'll handle the surgery, and you'll have to memorize the names of every stinking muscle and bone in its formaldehyde-soaked body," finished Kirin with a chuckle.

The two of them played off each other with an easy repartee that Chloe didn't like. She nodded and hid behind her sandwich, deciding maybe she didn't like Cynthia Decareaux after all.

"Ugh!" Cynthia banged her head gently on the table for dramatic effect. "I'm gonna puke on that cat, I know it!" She turned to Chloe. "Honestly, Chloe, could you cut open a cat?"

"I don't know; I have a pet cat. But yeah, I guess I'd be kind of interested to see what it looks like inside, you know?" *That came out wrong!* She was getting flustered. "I mean, if it was already dead, and not my cat, obviously...just a cat in general for school."

Kirin was laughing at her.

"Jeez, that's kind of twisted," Cynthia said, joining in the mirth. "I like her," she declared to Kirin. "What are you two doing tomorrow after school, or are you still grounded?"

Chloe tried to exchange a conspiratorial glance with Kirin, but he was looking at Cynthia.

"Nope, the two weeks are over tonight," he announced.

"Me and some friends are going to go hang out at this cool retro diner called Positive Pete's, if you want to come?" She unbound the elastic on her ponytail and let the blue tips drop forward across her face before flipping her head back with expert grace. She eyed Kirin as she retied it tighter.

Kirin glanced at Chloe and then back, "Yeah, that could be good."

"What about you?" Cynthia asked Chloe. "It's got a great jukebox and amazing milk shakes...and Stan is going to be there. I think he likes you," she whispered.

Chloe felt the heat of a blush bloom across her face. *Great!*

"I can't," she admitted. "I have cross-country practice until five thirty. We're running ten miles tomorrow."

"Well, you should come by afterward. We usually hang out there for a while," Cynthia finished, standing from her chair. "It was nice to finally meet you, Chloe—good to put a face to the legendary Lightning Girl." She smiled again, and the gleam of her teeth could fry an egg. The smile shifted to Kirin. "And I'll see you tomorrow, Cat Killer."

She walked away, and Chloe was pretty sure that she caught Kirin staring at her ass as she left.

"What happened to aloof and mysterious?" she asked, trying not to sound the way she felt.

He shrugged, unabashed and unfazed as always. "I guess it's working."

. . .

All of Chloe's anger, frustration, and fear had been sweated out by the eighth mile of the run—one and a half blissful, punishing miles to go. It was the farthest they had gone in the first two weeks of endurance conditioning, and while many others had fallen back with complaints of shin splints and the persistent heat, Chloe gobbled up every step along the hilly path through the woods. She was fast becoming addicted to the solitary focus of running, as if locked in a trance by her heavy breaths and the cadence of her stride.

She did not think about Kirin, no doubt flirting with Cynthia at that very moment, or her mom waiting on them at Positive Pete's while trying to mask her melancholy with a fake smile. She did not picture a massive bolt of lightning picking off Kendra during her field hockey tryouts or Officer Brent Meeks and his pristine uniform, caught in a hail of bird crap from a passing flock of geese...

None of that mattered while her lungs and legs ached and her heart thundered away. She was at home in the woods, an animal in her natural state. There were a few seasoned juniors and seniors ahead of her—some who were faster or in better shape—but none were more at ease with the leaves and wind whipping by and the promise of exhaustion at hand.

Chloe was only half-aware of the large form that came from behind and fell in step with her steady gait. Instinctively, she reacted by picking up the pace a bit, but the long, dark, muscular legs stayed with her. She glanced up from the corner of her eye and was surprised to see Ezra Richardson beside her in all his chiseled glory. He was breathing hard and dripping sweat, but looked comfortable and focused despite it.

"You're fast…for a girl," he said in two bursts between breaths.

She surfaced from the deepest pools of the trance, remembering that Coach Barnes had mentioned that a couple members of the varsity football squad might join them for a few select practices. "You're fast for a football player," she answered.

He flashed his beautiful smile, and she nearly lost her footing down a little slope. *How does someone so big and pretty move so well?*

"You set a good pace…s'cool if I run with you?" he asked.

She nodded and focused back on the path. *How is this even happening?* The only possible explanation was that Ezra Richardson, quarterback Adonis, was so egotistical that he might have been the only person left in school who didn't know who she was.

"As long as…I won't get…struck by lightning," he added with a little chuckle.

She snapped her head around and eyed him close. "I make no promises," she challenged before returning her full attention to the run. *Okay, let's see what he's got.*

Chloe dug deep and picked up the tempo. The initial distraction of the unlikely presence beside her fell away. Her long strides carried her down and then back up the winding path through the trees, and Ezra's far longer stride held with her. Their journey had wound throughout the streets and pathways of Charlottesville proper, but they were in the familiar territory of the woods behind school now, and the final approach toward the track was not far ahead.

Chloe's legs were still sore from the 400-meter interval run they'd been made to do on Wednesday, but she had come to relish the feel of the muscle burn and even delighted in the rubber-legged wobble that immediately followed every practice. She was not as conditioned as most of the upperclassman and was probably the third or fourth fastest girl on the team, but she was pretty sure that she pushed herself harder than anyone. The gap between her and the front would not last long.

She navigated through a web of roots and then leapt a

dried-out creek bed, handling the terrain as assuredly as she moved through the woods behind her house. Ezra fumbled while climbing back out of the creek, but he kept on her heels with the sound of his heavy breath rising. Chloe kept pushing.

She shot out from the woods into a gently sloped field and counted the seven runners ahead of her: five of the boys' varsity squad and the two girls vying for regional dominance. Further ahead she saw the practice field for the soccer team and the stick drills and wind sprints of the girls' field hockey hopefuls spread across it. Chloe's lips took on a slightly sinister curl.

Her thighs screamed as she brought her arms up tighter for the final few hundred yards, but the vacillating movement of Ezra's defined triceps held in the corner of her eye. Chloe started gaining on one of the boys who was lagging behind the others, and she felt like a pursuing beast, coming to gobble him up. She dug deeper, looking for more speed than her legs could muster, wanting more from herself than what she could produce. Ezra ran beside her, and their long footfalls fell into a joint rhythm. She could smell the sweat that dripped off him: earthy and oddly appealing, like the mixture of hay and the freshly tilled soil of a farm. His beaming smile had been replaced by the joyless grin of full exertion.

They passed by the soccer field without slowing, though Chloe couldn't help but glance at the cluster of prancing girls in the center just long enough to lock eyes with Kendra. Even from forty yards Chloe could see the shock and confusion on Kendra's pretty little face as she and Ezra's matching strides flew by.

They came out of the fields and turned onto the sidewalk leading toward the track behind the school, and already Chloe could hear the encouraging bellows from Coach Barnes's bullhorn. Ezra was not letting up and neither was she, both trying now to dislodge the other in a duel of equally matched talent. The harder they tried to break free of each other, the more simpatico their joint effort became. They covered that last stretch of ground to the track faster than all those who finished in front of them.

"Come on, Chloe!" shouted Coach Barnes with distorted amplification. "Leave that football jock in your dust!"

But there was no ditching Ezra Richardson. They crossed the line in what would have had to be a photo finish, and the two came to a floppy, stumbling halt among the other runners.

"Nice job, Chloe" and "All right, McClellan" were offered by a couple of her teammates, but she was too light-headed to tell who. Her heart thundered in her temples, and she felt a little like she was swimming through the air, only vaguely aware that Ezra's towering form stumbled beside her. She looked up at him and caught his eyes trained on her. He was still breathing hard.

"Goddamn," he gasped. "You're an animal!" He reached out and slapped her five and did his best to smile again.

Their hands were covered in sweat and spit, but it didn't matter—it was awesome! "You're pretty quick for a dumb quarterback, too," she answered with a mischievous grin.

Laughing took more energy than either one of them had left, but they gave it a pitiful try nonetheless.

"My girl!" he exclaimed with a haggard chuckle. "Nobody messes with the Lightning Girl."

Chloe could only emit a croaking hack in response. Perhaps Ezra Richardson wasn't so bad after all.

. . .

Kendra stood in the hallway, jumping up and down with her hockey stick thrust in the air with provocative abandon. An appreciative cluster of varsity soccer players passed by on their way to the men's locker room, but the show was intended for Paul Markson, who lingered a moment with his eyes scanning the unsubtle offering. He tried to play it off with a cool 'sup nod, but he was clearly a bit flustered.

Chloe watched from around the corner of the ladies' locker room, waiting for the shameful display to cease so that she could begin her laborious forty-five minute trek on bus and foot to get home. She had no patience for Kendra's games today, but had resolved to keep her opinions to herself after the miserable outcome of her attempt to intervene on her mother's behalf in that adulterous relationship. *Is Liz even still my friend anyway?*

Paul stopped and turned back toward Kendra as she released a barrage of cutesy giggles that sounded to Chloe like a baboon's impersonation of a donkey.

"So, you think you're gonna make the squad?" Paul asked.

"Come on," Kendra answered with a deft twirl of her hockey stick. "They'd be fools not to take me with the way I handle the stick."

Paul actually blushed. "Cool, but I hope you still have time to come to some of our games; the team could really use some more motivation on the sidelines," he said with a cocky grin before gulping from a bottle of water.

Kendra batted her long lashes and pretended to be demure. "Of course, but you know that you can use my motivations anytime, if you wanted."

Paul choked and sputtered as a group of the other cross-country girls passed Chloe on their way out of the locker room. Chloe fell in behind them, intent on making her escape. She walked swiftly and focused on her feet.

"Lightning!" shouted Ezra Richardson as he emerged from the men's side at the same time.

Chloe winced and turned, scanning past Kendra's piercing glare as she did.

"Hey," Ezra continued, strolling right between the traitorous flirtations. "A bunch of us were talking about going out for a bite to eat—you're coming!" he declared as the entire cluster of cross-country girls gathered around him, vying for his attention.

For some reason, his confident gaze held on Chloe. Kendra bristled beside her. "Uh, okay. Where are you guys going?"

"Not sure yet, any ideas?" asked Ezra with his gleaming smile returned.

Kendra's mouth was agape now. Chloe smiled back. Actually, she did have an idea. "How about Positive Pete's Diner? They have great shakes."

"Yes!" he shouted. "Positive Pete's in twenty minutes!" He leveled a commanding point at Chloe. "Do you have a car?"

She shook her head.

"You're riding with me," he announced before heading off down the hall with a 'follow me' wave.

The other girls and a number of the cross-country guys chased after him, but Chloe paused for a moment to catch her breath, feeling oddly emboldened by Ezra's public recognition. She ignored Kendra's scorching stare and turned to Paul as she strolled by. "Hey, Paul, have you seen LIZ around?" she asked, overemphasizing her old friend's name.

"Uh, no…not for a few hours," he answered, taken off guard.

"Oh, okay. Could you tell her I was looking for her when you see her?" she asked without waiting for an answer.

"Uh, sure," he said in her wake.

She strolled after her team with an extra little saunter to her step.

CHAPTER 7
FREE AT LAST

Chloe had always sat at the last stool at the counter and had always eaten for free. Over the summer, she had come to Positive Pete's at least once a week when her mother was on the dinner shift and watched the groups that occupied the booths behind her in the mirror that hung on the wall over the coffeemakers. She liked her special seat and relished the insider looks and gossip she exchanged with her mom, but she had always been jealous of the camaraderie and conversation she spied in the reflection.

Now Chloe sat in the coveted corner booth, surrounded by older kids while local sports king, Ezra Richardson, sat beside her telling jokes and holding court. He hadn't paid any attention to her since they'd gotten there, but his huge arm was draped casually on the rim of the booth behind her. She felt oddly protected by its hovering presence.

She'd greeted Kirin and Cynthia on entry—scrunched a little too close to each other a few booths down—but had excused herself to sit with the team, despite their invitations to join them. She'd walked away with Stan's bloodshot stare tracking her from the other side of their table.

She tried to focus on any one of the conversations around her, but found herself glancing over to Kirin with annoying regularity instead.

Ezra looked up from an intense search through the menu. "So what's your deal, Lightning?" he asked, commanding her attention again.

She wasn't sure how to answer that. "I was trying for aloof and mysterious, but now that's failed miserably, so I'm going with misunderstood genius."

"You're the youngest chick here, but the only one who isn't hanging on my every word," he whispered. "W'sup with that?"

"Oh, I didn't mean to offend, Your Highness."

Ezra narrowed his eyes, looking through her. "Is that Asian dude your boyfriend or something?"

"What? No!" She was flustered. "He's a friend of mine."

"Uh-huh," he said doubtfully as he leaned out of the booth to get a better look at Kirin. "I've never seen him before."

"Don't stare," Chloe hissed as she sunk lower and hid her face behind a menu. Ezra caught Cynthia's eye and waved.

"Well, if you like him, you're gonna want to get him away from Sin Decareaux, I'll tell you that," He righted himself again. "That girl has an appetite," he added knowingly.

Chloe swallowed her embarrassment. "Sin, huh? I guess you speak from experience?"

"We've been in the same class since seventh grade," he answered somewhat cryptically.

Chloe watched her mom bring a tray of milk shakes to the stoner table—Kirin got a black and white. *Of course, my favorite.* She turned back to meet Ezra's expectant gaze.

"Okay, so what's your story?" she shot back. "Famous sports god with the whole world groveling at your feet: women, awards, and riches, just yours for the taking?"

Ezra glanced down at his callused hands and lost the curl of his smile. "I've never been handed anything in this life. I work my ass off every day to get where I'm going," he said. "I might play big and act like it's easy, but I'll always remember where I came from and why I'm working to get somewhere else."

That caught Chloe off guard. "I didn't mean to imply—"

"It's cool," he cut in with a now more sheepish smile. "It's just that people are always telling me how lucky I am. Sometimes I want them to know that luck had nothing to do with it…"

She reached out and shook his hand. "I'm a Straight-A nerd with no friends, a falsely tarnished reputation, and an attraction for bad weather," said Chloe.

"I'm good at football because I work at it every day all year long. I get okay grades, but football is my ticket to becoming the first person in my family to go to college. If one day I can make money by playing this game, maybe I won't be the last."

This guy is full of surprises! "My mom had me when she was nineteen and raised me more or less on her own in a little house that's falling apart at the top of Red Hill Road. Unless this running thing pans out, all I've got is my grades. She didn't go to college either, and it's like her dream for me to be able to go, so she works two and a half jobs to try to afford it, and it's still iffy."

"Me and my little sister live with my grandparents on a run-down farm on the other side of Walcott Avenue, and I've had to balance my work in the field with a construction job for the past five summers just to get enough money to buy that piece of junk car," he countered.

"My dad abandoned us when I was eight. You've probably heard the rumors. A lot of people think he had some sort of psychotic break or something. I guess he used to go off on these intense apocalyptic rants in public, and a couple times he got picked up by the cops…One night, my mom asked him to go out for a quart of milk, a red pepper, and some toilet paper as she was making us dinner, and he never came back.

Turned out he'd packed his bags and put them in the pickup earlier. He left me a hundred dollars and a message on a Post-it note, but he never said a word…My life is a white-trash cliché."

"I've never even met my dad, and my mom died of a drug overdose when I was ten," he said, still holding her hand with a triumphant smirk and a lot of pain behind it. "Just another young black man left behind with a chip on his shoulder and something to prove."

"Really?"

"Yup."

"I'm really sorry; that must have been awful," she blurted, realizing how much she had misjudged Ezra Richardson.

"I guess we're just a couple of sad stereotypes, huh?" he chuckled, still holding her hand tightly.

Then Chloe's mom cleared her throat beside them.

"Can I take your order?" asked Audrey with a pen and pad

in hand and a sly smile on her face.

Chloe let go of Ezra's grip, blushing and flustered. "Hey, Mom."

Ezra flashed his teeth and swung his liberated hand over to Audrey without a moment of hesitation. "I'm Ezra," he stated. "I'm very pleased to meet you."

"I'm Audrey," she answered with a firm shake and a corresponding pencil point to her name tag. "I'm happy to meet you, too," she grinned. "Are you on the cross-country team?"

"Football, ma'am," he said, subtly flexing his arms. "But Lightning here is going to be my endurance trainer, twice a week until game season starts."

"I am?" asked Chloe.

"Yup, Tuesdays and Fridays for the next three weeks," answered Ezra. "Congratulations—it's an important job," he added as the little twinkle in his eye danced between Chloe and her mother.

Are you flirting with my mom? This was the Ezra Richardson she had expected, but now she saw past his cocky veneer with a newfound respect. She was oddly excited about the proposed schedule, but couldn't let him win so easily. "Wow, I feel really blessed. Can I hold your shoes and help put them on your feet?" she barbed.

"Yes, you can!" he declared jovially.

Audrey smiled. "What can I get for you all today?" she asked as the rest of the table starting barking out orders of burgers, fries, and shakes. She scribbled fast and worked her way around to Ezra with an expectant look.

"Just a large water and the bread basket," he answered.

Audrey shot Chloe a look, and Chloe reopened the menu on the table in front of him. "What do you really want?"

Audrey nodded, and he ordered again without needing to look at the menu. "Grilled chicken penne in vodka sauce and a large banana health shake."

Audrey scribbled and glanced to Chloe with a playful smile. "Enjoying freedom?"

"I'll have the usual," Chloe muttered with a furrowed brow

as Audrey spun away.

"I'll be right back with those drinks," she sang over her shoulder.

In the silence that followed, Chloe took the opportunity to glance again to Kirin. He was listening with rapt attention to whatever Sin Decareaux was saying. Chloe looked back to Ezra, who held his eyes on the kitchen door.

"I think I'm in love with your mother," he stated.

Chloe winced. "Oh, come on, man! That's gross, and she's thirty-four!"

"Well, then there ain't nothing wrong with thirty-four, is there?"

Chloe was not having it.

"She's hot!" he argued.

Chloe crossed her arms and stared out the window. It looked like it was going to rain.

"Don't worry, Lightning, you're hot, too! I mean, look at you, sitting there all hunched and pouty—you're just about the cutest person I've ever seen."

Chloe couldn't give him the satisfaction of a smile.

"But you're too young for me, and you know it." Ezra smiled enough for both of them and glanced back to the kitchen. "But Audrey there is ALL woman…I bet she could teach me things."

"You're really gonna have to shut up now, or I'll tell her to make you pay for the penne and shake!"

He immediately surrendered. "I'm done." He pretended to zip his mouth shut.

Chloe rolled her eyes as rain started pattering against the windows. She looked out, searching for something ominous in the sky. It was an unexceptional grey ceiling of clouds, but the rain started to pick up.

"Uh-oh, here comes the rain," taunted Ezra. "I must have made Lightning Girl mad."

"Trust me, you'd know it if I was mad: thunder, flooding, tornadoes, the works!" she joked just as the tinges of a migraine pulsed from the base of her skull. *Not now!*

She'd hoped that maybe the routine physical exertion would

cure her of the headaches, but she could already tell that the throbbing pain and waves of nausea were coming. Soon the idea of food would be repulsive. Tonight she'd be curled in the fetal position with the lights dimmed, her eyes shut, and a hot towel draped over her forehead. Tomorrow—*of course, a Saturday*—would be a total wash, but her real concern now was trying to get through the next hour without making a complete whimpering spectacle of herself.

Audrey returned with a tray laden with shakes, soda, and water, expertly balancing the precarious load as she doled out drinks from memory.

"Thank you, Audrey," said Ezra a little too sweetly as he took his health shake.

Audrey only needed a glance to recognize the abrupt onset of her daughter's waxy pallor and dark rimmed eyes. Chloe managed a meek smile in response.

"It's almost the twenty-first, isn't it?" Audrey realized.

Chloe nodded. "Naturally."

"You want this to go?" Audrey asked, holding up the Black and White shake. "I can take a fifteen-minute break and drive you home," she whispered.

"No, I'll take it. It might be my last chance to eat something for a little while," Chloe answered as the rain started pelting the window. She closed her eyes and sucked on the straw, trying to will herself to enjoy the perfect flavors that reached her mouth before it was rejected by her stomach.

"You feeling all right, Lightning?" asked Ezra. "Your whole cutesy-sulky thing is starting to look more sickly-pitiful."

"Sorry," she muttered, squinting into the near-blinding brightness of the window despite the clouds and rain. "I get pretty bad headaches sometimes, is all."

"Ah, say no more," Ezra said with a knowing wink. "I have a sister."

This guy is a smartass!

"If you need to go or something, I can give you a ride home," he offered.

A really nice smartass, though.

"If you want, I could even stay there for a while and make sure you're okay…You know, until your mom gets home." He flashed his teeth again.

Chloe had to laugh, even though it hurt like hell. She glanced over to the stoner table and noticed Kirin looking back at her during one of the brief lulls in his fervent exchange with Sin D. Chloe quickly looked to Ezra. "No, I think I'll stick around."

But now Ezra was looking out the window.

At first, it sounded like someone was throwing acorns at the glass, and then it started to sound more like golf balls. One of the girls across from Chloe yelped. From a few tables away, Stan shouted the obvious. "Dude! Hail!"

Quarter-sized chunks began to fall across the parking lot, clanging off street signs and trash cans and shattering against cars. Outside, traffic stopped as pedestrians screamed and ran for cover, shielding their heads with whatever they could find. Everything from trees to stoplights swayed and jostled violently. The windshield on Ezra's already battered Ford Focus took a particularly large smack that left a spiderweb crack around the impact. Everyone backed away from the windows.

Ezra leaned closer to Chloe. "Is this what you mean by *the works?*"

"Yeah, something like this," Chloe whispered as her gaze picked out a figure standing at the edge of the woods across the street.

It was a man, partially hidden by the trunk of a tree, unmoving, and making no effort to protect himself. It was hard to see through the cascade of ice, but he seemed to wear nondescript clothes that matched the shadows of the woods. His hair was long and silvery white, his face chiseled and pale. Despite the distance and obscurity, his crystal blue eyes bore into Chloe with alarming intensity.

Immediately the migraine reached up from her spine and slammed against her skull as if with an echo of the lightning strike. Her senses caved in and faded to black, save for the bone-quivering sound of a bestial roar that rose out of her memory along with a spike of terror. She tasted the coppery tang of blood in her mouth, unaware that she'd bit her tongue until the sting of it registered.

She clenched her eyes so tightly that her lids shook as the initial wave crested. Then, as quickly as they had come, the headache and violent weather subsided. Breathing slowly, she opened her eyes again and looked for the figure across the street. He was gone.

Positive Pete's Diner was completely silent. Ezra turned to her with a quizzical look. He opened his mouth as if he wanted to ask a question, but didn't. Chloe held her pale and sweaty head in her hands, barely able to keep her eyes open.

"How 'bout we get the food to go and I give you that ride home," he suggested.

Chloe glanced at Kirin once more, but this time he was staring out the window as Cynthia clung to his shoulder for protection. She turned back to Ezra as the next ripple of migraine swelled on the horizon. "Yeah, thank you, Ezra. That'd be good."

.   .   .

Chloe lay on her back in the dark with clenched lids. She couldn't sleep, wracked with tides of nausea and pain. Occasionally the onslaught ebbed into five- to twenty-minute windows of respite, but even then she could not distract herself with books, television, or music. Eye strain, bright lights, and noises were crippling, and the idea of food was abhorrent. For now, all she could do was press the hot cloth to her forehead, breathe deeply, and hold on for the latest wave to break.

Shipwreck leaned against her hip and purred gently, his contented presence both comforting and goading.

Chloe moaned and pressed the cloth down harder over her eyes with a tickle of warm water dripping past her ear. The hot stabs through her skull had unearthed hazy images buried in her subconscious: the bone-shuddering roar and then a glimpse of an impossible creature rising from the water...

She tried to think of something else, anything, but could

not escape the nightmarish picture of a blue, reptilian gaze or the sense of utter helplessness as its dinosaur-like claws shook the earth.

A tremble of cold passed through her, and the throbbing in her temples began to abate. Slowly, Chloe opened her strained eyes to the dark ceiling. She took a series of long breaths while charting the familiar patterns of cracked paint and mildew stains above. A tiny moth hung beside the light, as if waiting hopefully for someone to turn it on.

Chloe sat up and glanced to her computer, asleep on the desk at the other side of the room. With a slow exhale, she swiveled to the edge of the bed and placed her sweaty feet on the floor. It made no sense. This memory from the pond couldn't be real. But it seemed as true an experience as any other from her first two freakishly unpredictable weeks of high school. *Maybe I really am going crazy!*

But then she remembered the strange man who was watching from beneath the trees outside the diner. Something about his piercing gaze reminded her of…the other. *Was he the one who carried me into the hospital?* The hospital staff had seen the man that had brought her in; if he was the same man from the hail storm…*then I'm not crazy?*

Chloe stood on wobbly feet and shut her eyes again until the dizziness settled. Shipwreck let out a little yowl of protest from the bed, but she glanced past him to the alarm clock on her nightstand: 12:21 a.m.

The first step toward the computer sent an unpleasant shock to her temples, magnified into a pounding drum inside her head. But she forced her feet forward with the knowledge that she had only about five or ten minutes left of this comparatively manageable state. She slumped into the desk chair with a whimper and let another stirring of dizziness settle before bringing her hand to the mouse.

She closed her eyes again before her fingers moved to wake the screen, but even through clenched lids, she was assaulted by the bright glow. She squinted into the LCD onslaught and sent a hand fumbling for the brightness button on the monitor, only to be attacked by a series of grating beeps instead.

Her fingers hovered over the keys. She was a devoted student of evolution and biology, unable to bring herself to type the word that haunted her addled mind. The little black cursor blinked expectantly.

Slowly her fingers pushed the keys: "D, R, A, G, O, N, S," and with a resolute sigh, she pushed "ENTER." In less than a second, more than 35,000,000 distinct results were listed before her, topped by a collage of colorful, artistic renderings of the giant winged lizards of myth, often shown dueling in the air, leering over a corny depiction of a wizard, or readying for takeoff with some half-clad woman mounted on its back. Without thinking, Chloe rolled her eyes with another jolt of pain that brought her palm to her head.

In that instant, she saw again the beast from the pond staring back at her. She peered at the screen from between her fingers. She had to admit that some of the pictures did look pretty close. At her bidding, the cursor drifted down and clicked on the Wikipedia entry below. Pages and pages of text about the etymology, history, and many faceted myths of dragons appeared, all discussing legendary creatures of abnormal size and power with serpentine and/or otherwise reptilian features. The dragon myth, it seemed, had been prevalent in every ancient culture across the globe, some seeing them as horrible monsters and others regarding them with reverence and great honor.

Her weary eyes skipped through comparisons of the European and Asian dragon and passed over the Greek roots of the word, settling finally on the section concerning the still culturally significant Chinese dragon. The ancient Chinese had viewed dragons as symbols of great wisdom and importance, linking the image of the five-clawed dragon with the position of the Emperor himself. They viewed dragons as the physical and spiritual incarnations of natural elements, the guardians of Earth, both capable and responsible for bringing great advancements to humanity and causing vast natural disasters that had erased entire cities from history.

Chloe was a little embarrassed that her heart had started

beating faster, but she couldn't help it. She scanned on.

According to the nameless "experts" of the Wikipedia dragon page, a bronze cauldron that dated back almost three thousand years to the early Zhou Dynasty was said to contain the earliest engraved scripture detailing the Tipping Point Prophecy, which concerned the preordained return of the dragons.

There was nothing more on the subject there, and no further reference to it in the bibliography listed below. She clicked back to the Google homepage and searched for "Tipping Point Prophecy," but the results were underwhelming at best. She scanned down a list of sites with close matches, all discussing outdated Mayan doomsday scenarios, new age conferences, and other assorted scientifically unsupported alarmist hokum. But halfway down, she spotted a long-since-updated mention of the Chinese Tipping Point Prophecy at: www.ancientchinese-legends.blogspot.com.

She opened the site to a splash page ringed by a poorly drawn cartoon dragon, and she raised a skeptical eyebrow. At the bottom of a list of page titles she saw "Tipping Point Prophecy" and clicked on it with the sound of a synthesized gong.

She raised the other eyebrow too and started reading the oversized aqua green letters on a background of star-speckled black:

> *The Tipping Point Prophecy was inscribed in bronze on the Tianlong Cauldron, dating back to the ancient Zhou Dynasty of Western China. The prophecy states that when the rule of man reaches its zenith and the world begins its decline at the hands of human arrogance and neglect, the elemental powers of the earth will rise from their prisons, deep beneath the water and rock, and wipe clean the pestilence of mankind.*

"Riiiiight," Chloe chuckled with a buzzing reverb in her head.

Then the screen and timer went blank, and she heard her mom swear from downstairs. Thunder rolled gently in the distance. "Are you kidding me?" Chloe whispered to the darkness.

Slowly her ears adjusted to the complete lack of electrical hum. The symphony of crickets through the open window seemed louder against the hushed quiet of the house. Shipwreck mewed plaintively as if in an attempt to add to their song. Chloe swiveled to find him perched on the windowsill between the green drapes that had been part of the summer redecoration project. He stared into the woods with rigid intensity.

She stood, instinctively glancing back to the dead clock before stepping to the window. The streetlights were out down the road in both directions, and the cloud-covered moon offered no light to cut though the layers of shadow at the edge of the yard. Chloe leaned down with her hands on the sill beside the cat and followed Shipwreck's gaze to the trees. She held her breath, half expecting to see the blue eyes emerge from the gloom, but there was nothing but the darker outline of the branches.

She watched and listened, feeling the heavy pulse of her blood in her temples. The crickets raged, and she heard the faint hoot of an owl...When she'd been a little girl, the now-silent call of the tree frogs had blanketed all the other night sounds through the warm months. Like with the bees, Mrs. Greenwald had talked of how the death of the frogs was a sign of widespread ecological decay.

She rubbed Shipwreck's head, and he added a purr to their somber vigil. "Any dragons out there, buddy?" Chloe asked as they peered into the woods across the road. She heard her mother's footsteps creaking up the stairs behind her. Moments later, her mom knocked softly and peered in with a flashlight.

"You okay, honey?" Audrey asked, spotting Chloe at the window.

"Yeah, I'm in a lull," she answered as the sky flashed again, with another unhurried rumble to follow.

Audrey stepped in and put a fresh bowl of steaming water beside Chloe's bed. "You need anything else? A candle or flashlight?"

"No, I'm covered. I'll be lying down with my eyes shut again soon."

"You going to be able to sleep?"

Chloe shrugged.

"Well, I'm going to bed, but if you need anything at all…" Audrey was upset as always that she couldn't somehow fix Chloe's pain.

"I'll be all right," Chloe reassured, though she felt the familiar ripples of unease traveling up her spine, which always preceded the next wave of migraine. "Mom, do you remember the sound of the tree frogs when I was little?"

"Of course, but that was nothing. When I was your age, the frogs were so loud that I had trouble sleeping at night." Even through the darkness Chloe could see the smile that bloomed across her mother's face. "Every year, when you first heard them, you knew that summer was coming. Cicadas all day and the tree frogs all night; it was great."

Chloe started to feel dizzy again. With a last look to the dark trees beyond, she turned back toward the bed. "Do you think it means something that they're gone?" She sat on the edge of the mattress and closed her eyes as the next wave came on. "Do you think it could be a sign that something…bad is coming?"

Chloe felt her mom's hands helping her to ease back into the pillow and then heard her mom dip and wring out the washcloth in the bowl.

"Things change, honey. The world goes through cycles, just like we do. Maybe right now Earth is getting her migraine, only it takes a lot longer to pass."

Chloe felt the hot, damp cloth pressed across her brow and the pressure of her mom's hand, as if holding back the throbbing torment. "It's just, all the famine and flooding and earthquakes and war—it seems like it's all going downhill fast, like we're headed for a tipping point or something," said Chloe.

"I know things were bad for us in the past, but I'm better now, we're better. We're going to be fine—I need you to know that, Chloe." Audrey lifted the washcloth and planted a gentle kiss on Chloe's forehead. "A lot of people have it pretty hard right now, a whole lot harder than we can imagine. But it's just like it was with me, and is with you now; the pain recedes and the world keeps on going. That's what humans do; we adapt and keep going—it's just a part of life."

"I just wish I could do something," Chloe mumbled.

"You know what I always say, honey? The same thing your grandmother always said to me—you can do anything you set your mind to."

But when Chloe shut her eyes again, she found only those frightening reptilian eyes staring back from the darkness behind her lids.

.   .   .

Shipwreck's eyes were wide open, however, as he continued to stare into the murk. They held on the dark figure that stood just beyond the tree line. The cat had been drawn to the presence there, just as the insects and birds that gathered in ever greater numbers from across the woods. They came to offer their voices in reverence, to herald the coming of the lord of beasts.

Shipwreck was powerless to tear his gaze away from the shadowy form. It was like a man but not, motionless except for the sapphire eyes that followed closely. And the cat could not resist the overpowering will that had slipped into his mind to hold him in this trance. He could tell that something was coming, like the feeling he got before the arrival of a storm or the sense that came to him when Chloe was angry—only this was much, much bigger.

He was afraid of what waited in the woods and mewed again, long and filled with sorrow. His instincts told him to run, but he was frozen. There was nowhere to escape to and nowhere to hide.

CHAPTER 8
A DAY OF FIRSTS

Chloe was subdued in the aftermath of the headaches, like a mental patient coming off an electroshock marathon. She shuffled around the house in slippers and pajamas and ate large quantities of ice cream. With the lights back on and the pain subsided, thoughts of winged monsters and absurd prophecies began to fade from her mind. On Saturday, it seemed like a bad dream. By Sunday afternoon, it was gone altogether, and she retreated into her normal studies, happy to be distracted from the rapidly growing complexities of her life with books and homework.

In junior high, she'd been prone to a constant flux of random fascinations, and once again, she found that they could easily be directed toward the creation of reliably Grade-A papers for any number of her classes. On Sunday night, it was a seven-page paper on the aerial hunting techniques of raptors, complete with strike position diagrams and a two-page glossary. On Monday, it was an in-depth analysis of the character and motivations of Simon in *The Lord of the Flies*.

Math was her weakest subject, but with a little extra work she could consistently get A's there, too. A sick part of her was actually looking forward to calculus her junior year. But science was her real passion, and after one month of entry-level "natural science," she was seriously contemplating an attempt to leapfrog a few classes up to AP Biology as early as next semester. For the basics, she could probably have done a better job of instruction than her teacher, and she already understood the complexities of what Kirin and Cynthia discussed over the lunch table better than they did.

But the science of interpersonal relationships was a different story. Outside of the classroom, Chloe would give herself a C- in social chemistry. Lunch and homeroom remained the only times she saw Kirin, and her store of witty comments had seemingly dried up around him. Every day after school she was booked until dinner with running, and he had yet to pursue another opportunity for just the two of them to hang out. In The Cave, she was forced to feign indifference to the little glances that passed between the "lab partners." Despite Sin Decareaux's casual grace and welcoming demeanor, Chloe found herself resenting the daily sight of her beautiful face.

It was better just to maintain her schedule from the grounding—pretend that her return to freedom had never happened. It was easier just to remain a bookish, friendless, unattached nerd. The only sticking point was the elevated heart rate and increasing anxiety that overcame her whenever Kirin was nearby and, of course, the persistent and inexplicable attention from Ezra Richardson. True to his declaration, Ezra did indeed keep running and bantering with her during practice on Tuesdays and Fridays for the following two weeks; and for reasons she could not fully grasp and her peers could hardly believe, he went out of his way to talk to her in the hall and genuinely seemed to like her whenever he did.

Their relationship wasn't romantic—though Ezra did flirt with her constantly. He flirted with everyone, but with Chloe, his attentions seemed more in line with a big brother taking a youngster under his wing. After their unguarded repartee at the diner, Chloe found it difficult to take people's opinions and expectations of him too seriously, and he seemed to like that she was in on the joke. He remained obnoxious and incorrigible, but he always gave Chloe the inclusive wink that made her smirk while everyone around her swooned.

That's why on the second Friday night of October, after she had commanded her place on the varsity girls' cross-country team in the first official race of the season, Chloe found herself, against all better judgment, sitting in the bleachers among the sold-out crowd at the first football home game.

Ezra had made her promise that she would come, but she was more and more seriously considering making a run for it with every passing minute. She sat among a cluster of her teammates, but found that she had little to say to them outside of the runner's arena. She was a necessary part of the team and universally accepted by all, but as they gossiped about boys they liked and girls they hated, while regaling on the strengths and weaknesses of various products, Chloe remained largely mute and entirely uncomfortable.

She scanned the throng of spectators for Kirin and the stoners, but caught the miserable stare of Liz from a few rows down instead. *Oh, crap!* Liz sat on the outskirts of Kendra's hive of "it girls" as they buzzed at the fringes of a raucous gathering of soccer players. Kendra tossed her hair and placed a playful hand on Paul Markson's shoulder, and all her little drones laughed with her—all except Liz, who sat a few bodies further removed from her supposed boyfriend.

Even from the distance, Chloe could tell that Liz had recently been crying. Not knowing what else to do, she gave her a little wave. Liz waved back and then started shuffling past the line of knees to come closer.

The nights had finally started to get a little chilly, but still Liz was wearing a short skirt and a top with too much skin showing. She looked cold and miserable as she stumbled into the aisle, and her high heels kept getting caught in the slats of the bleacher stairs as she awkwardly climbed up to Chloe's row.

"Can I sit for a moment?" she asked meekly, with a mix of shame and desperation worn on her face.

"Of course," answered Chloe as she nudged the girl next to her to slide down.

Liz sat with a pitiful sniffle and wiped her eyes with the back of her hand. "I bet you think I look like a real idiot."

"No, I think you look cold and unhappy," answered Chloe. "I'm sorry about what I said to you in the parking lot; I know it wasn't you—"

"No, you were right," Liz interrupted. "Right about Kendra."

They both glanced over and found the bob of Kendra's red mane amid the sea of bodies and banners. She was standing with her arms in the air and screaming like a banshee. Below, Ezra ducked a tackle, rolled out, and threw a bullet of a pass for a clean catch halfway down the field.

In an instant, the crowd roared up around Chloe and Liz as the game disappeared from view behind a wall of people.

"I think maybe we're supposed to stand at this part," yelled Chloe amid the din. Liz laughed with a little stream of snot firing out of her nostril, and that made her laugh harder. This was the Liz that Chloe had been best friends with: a little dorky and unsure of herself, but game for anything and always ready with a laugh.

Liz got control of herself with a last battery of desperate heaves. "Chloe, I'm really sorry we didn't hang out over the summer…I just wanted to try—"

"I understand," Chloe cut in. "It's just that all the outfits and makeup aren't really my thing. I'd look stupid if I even tried," she admitted. "And I think you're better than those girls."

"Yeah, maybe," answered Liz with a blank look that went beyond the crowds. "Believe it or not, Kendra can be really funny sometimes. And when you're with her, you feel kind of like you're at the center of the universe."

Chloe gave her a skeptical glare.

"But she's a serious bitch, too," Liz added with a shrug. "She was kind of my ticket to the cool crowd, you know?" Liz stared at her feet. "I don't like what she did to you, but she's the one who set me up with Paul. And now I really like him."

Chloe saw the vulnerability in her old friend's eyes. "Did you…?"

Liz nodded and bit her lip, "Yeah, over the summer…"

Chloe wasn't sure what to say. *That* still seemed like light years away to her. The crowd settled back into their seats, and Chloe watched Kendra lean provocatively over Paul to take a handful of popcorn.

"Let me guess, now Kendra's decided that she likes him too?"

"They grew up together and have known each other since they were babies," Liz added in defeat. "Dr. Markson is the cofounder of Kendra's dad's company, and Kendra and Paul were always supposed to get married or something."

"That's kind of creepy," observed Chloe.

"Kendra always said that he was like her brother!" Liz was getting worked up again. "I mean, she was the one who set us up and kept urging me to go all the way with him!"

"That's even creepier," Chloe muttered.

"I thought Paul really liked me. We talk all the time, and he actually listens, you know? But now I don't have a chance...I mean, look at her," Liz pointed back at Kendra as she dropped pieces of popcorn into her mouth one by one. "She looks like a porn star, and I can't even walk straight in these stupid shoes!"

"She's a vapid asshole with daddy issues, and you're smart, cool, and hot," Chloe cut in. "If Paul Markson doesn't see that, then forget him and move on."

Liz emerged from the pool of self-pity and turned to look at Chloe for the first time. "You're probably the only real friend I have, and I've been treating you like total shit."

"It's okay," said Chloe as she watched Ezra break from a sack attempt and advance the ball up the field before ducking out of bounds. She turned back to Liz. "I'm still here if you ever need anything."

Liz's face brightened as if with a grand idea. "You're coming with me to the party tonight!"

"What?"

"Paul's parents are out of town, and he's having a huge party after the game! Everyone is going! You have to come with me and help me get him back!"

"What? No, I don't. That's not what I meant at all," Chloe stammered. "That would be a terrible idea for both of us...they hate me!"

"No, that's just Kendra. Paul thinks you're awesome! Whenever you come up, he talks about how fast you are and how cool it is that you don't give a crap what anyone thinks about you," offered Liz. "And everyone is talking about how you're so tight with Ezra Richardson and Cynthia Decareaux. I'm sure they'll be at the party tonight."

The hamsters in Chloe's mind started fighting over the wheel. *People are talking about me? Jocks I've never met think I'm cool? Cynthia's going to be at the party…with Kirin?*

"I can't let Kendra win without a fight," Liz declared. "What is it you always used to say to me? You can do anything you set your mind to." She sat up straighter. "Well, you've inspired me. You always see things so clearly. I need to do this tonight, and I need your help."

Chloe winced.

"You said you were going to get Kendra back for what she did to you. Well, if I can get Paul to choose me over her, it'll get her where it hurts." Liz thinned her eyes as a smirk crept across her face. "Chloe, you need to help me beat her at her own game."

Below, Ezra Richardson rocketed the ball across the field for a leaping catch in the end zone. The crowd shot up from their seats again, blocking Chloe's view and drowning out the sound of her groan with their cheer.

CHAPTER 9
THE BEST NIGHT OF YOUR LIFE?

I've got to be the dumbest person on the planet! And yet Chloe forced herself to open the car door and step out to the edge of the perfectly manicured lawn. Lush grass covered a gentle hill that climbed to the sort of house that might grace the cover of *Architectural Digest Magazine*. There were kids everywhere, yelling, laughing, drinking beer—totally uninhibited with the multi-acre estate around them that acted as insulation from neighbors and the law.

Chloe had tried to back out of her part in Liz's plan after the game, but they'd run into Ezra on his way to the locker room, where he and Liz had met for the first time and immediately ganged up on her. They'd made her promise to go to Paul's party under threat of kidnapping if she tried to escape.

Still, she'd thought to test their resolve, demanding to be dropped off at home for a shower and a change before the festivities started. She'd had little intention of leaving her house again, but Ezra didn't even call before showing up at her door with his victorious smile. He promptly started flirting with her mom, and Chloe relented soon after.

Despite Audrey's protests, Chloe left the house still wearing jeans and Chuck Taylors, having only traded her sweatshirt for a grey, military-cut jacket in her grand effort to dress up. When they'd stopped to pick up Liz, she was, by contrast, wearing a skintight miniskirt and a push-up bra, though she'd at least had the sense to trade the awkward high heels for some bejeweled flats.

Chloe and Ezra had sat in the idling car and observed as Liz approached with a tentative smile.

"Wow, she looks kind of like a prostitute on her first day," Ezra had observed.

"I'm sure you would know," Chloe mumbled. "But remember, she's fragile, be nice," she'd commanded.

"Don't get me wrong; it's a good look," Ezra had added with a grin before the back door had opened...

...Now three car doors slammed in quick succession, and the odd trio came together in the middle of the driveway. Bass-heavy music blared from the house, and somewhere a girl screamed her indecipherable approval. Liz looked like she was about to explode with nervous energy. Chloe looked like she was about to throw up.

Ezra draped a heavy arm over each of their shoulders. "Damn, I'm gonna walk into this party like royalty—two *fine* sophomore ladies at my side!"

Liz beamed while Chloe coughed out a laugh. Ezra chuckled with her, but pulled her a little tighter as he nudged the procession toward the house. "Come on, Lightning, if you let down your guard and live a little, this might be the best night of your life."

"If this is the best night of my life, then I'm not sure I deserve to go on living."

Ezra pointed across to Stan's orange van parked on the other side of the looping driveway. "I don't know, I think your boyfriend might be here," Ezra prodded.

"What boyfriend? Who's your boyfriend?" chirped Liz.

Chloe punched Ezra in the stomach and actually hurt her hand a little bit.

Ezra chuckled. "She's sweet on that Asian surfer dude who transferred in."

Liz brightened. "For real? That guy is hot!" she trilled. "He's so quiet and mysterious." Her brow furrowed. "But isn't he with Cynthia Decareaux?"

Chloe was not enjoying this. "I'm not sweet on him; he's just a friend. And no, he's not with Cynthia; they're just lab partners,"

Chloe shot back in a feeble attempt to silence them both.

Ezra kept chuckling. "Riiight." He marched them up the driveway with a kingly saunter and nodded his head coolly in response to a series of shouted greetings.

"Good game, Ezra," offered some girl with batting eyelashes who Chloe had never seen before.

"I can't believe these people actually take you seriously," Chloe whispered.

"Neither can I; that's why it's so damn fun," he retorted under his breath.

Liz couldn't stop grinning, both confused and fascinated by the odd dynamic between her antisocial friend and the legendary star quarterback of the varsity football team. As they got close to the front steps, everyone hanging around out front seemed to be looking at them…and looking at her. More than anything, she prayed that Paul would see her before Ezra took his arm from around her shoulder.

If Chloe could have lifted Ezra's other arm, she would have taken off at a dead sprint. A cluster of students was gathered in a backlog at the door, and she could see countless people beyond them. It seemed like the whole school was there as she scanned the sprawling party that filled many of the fifty or so windows that were visible across this side of the massive house. It was quite possibly the finest home she had ever seen. It made her feel inadequate, but the prospect of facing the crowd inside filled her with outright dread.

Ezra whistled. "You see, I could get used to a place like this."

"It's nice, right?" added Liz just before a group of Ezra's teammates noticed his approach and started whooping and cheering.

"Mr. Richardson, arriving in style as always!" one of them called out.

"Tapping the young talent early this year!" hollered another with a Neanderthal laugh.

Chloe was too mortified to look up as the crowd parted to make room for Ezra's approach. He raised his hands to give sporadic high fives as they neared the open door. Paul Markson waited on the other side with a beer in hand. Ezra detached from "his ladies" and shook Paul's hand.

"Hey, man, great game tonight! I'm glad you could come." Paul shot Liz a quizzical look.

"You're a lucky man, Mr. Markson. You've got yourself a great house and a fine woman here," said Ezra, nudging Liz forward. "You best keep her happy and close, but let me know if it doesn't work out." He actually winked.

Liz was practically vibrating with excitement. Chloe bit her lip to stifle a cackle.

"Thanks?" Paul said, temporarily shaken from his 'cool host' presentation. "Beer's in the kitchen and on the back patio, and the liquor's in the basement," he recovered. "My house is yours."

Ezra left Paul with a final 'peace out' nod and steered Chloe deeper into the party. She looked back over her shoulder to catch Liz mouth the words "THANK YOU" as she was sidling up to Paul, and Chloe responded with a little 'peace out' nod of her own.

"Thanks for that," she shouted up to Ezra in an attempt to be heard over the increasing noise. He smiled and nudged her on past the living room.

The music was piped through surround-sound speakers mounted in the walls, and an intensely focused DJ bobbed to the beat as he stared into his computer in the corner of what had become a makeshift dance hall. The sofas and coffee tables had been pushed to the side, and a mass of inebriated kids was grinding and flailing along with the mix. Ezra moved with the music and forced Chloe to shimmy with him as they went.

She tried uselessly to squirm away. "My work here is done; I think maybe I'll go now," she shouted.

"No chance, Lightning, you're here to party!" he shouted back while leading her down a packed hallway and into the kitchen. The fridge door was open to a wall of canned beer, and two kegs sat in ice-lined trashcans nearby with meatheads manning all stations. The floor was already slippery with spill, and the room was packed with bodies, all jostling to get to or away from the source.

Chloe could only cringe as Ezra muscled his way into the room with her as his battering ram. With his hands on her shoulders, he smashed her into anyone in his path.

"Sorry! Excuse me. It's not my fault!" protested Chloe as she caught elbows and angry stares in response to her forced progression. But most everyone fumbled to make way when they saw it was Ezra behind her. Before long, she was disheveled, but at the front of the throng beside a keg.

"Three beers," ordered Ezra after exchanging nods with the nearest meathead.

"I'm not really much of a drinker," Chloe protested just before Ezra thrust the first beer into her hand.

"Start with that," he said as he took the other two beers in hand and nudged Chloe toward the fridge. There he took two cans and put them in his back pockets, and then took two more and slipped them into the pockets of Chloe's jacket. "That's for later."

He took Chloe by the shoulder and turned her toward the exit. She shook her head and tried feebly to resist. "Don't."

"Keep your shoulders down and protect the drink," he said at her ear.

She could feel his smile hanging there. She sighed and switched the cup to her left hand with a sharp glance back. His unrelenting gaze held to the crowd. "You suck," she muttered as she turned to the right and put her shoulder down.

"On the count of one...ONE!" Ezra started pushing and Chloe's shoulder clipped someone in the ribs. But Ezra kept on ramming her deeper into the herd. "Sorry," he said to the swaying lad, "she's very clumsy and terribly rude."

"Oh God! Excuse me! It's not my fault!" yelped Chloe in quick succession as she bumped all those in her way. She tried not to spill the beer, but left a trail of wet, foamy splashes across numerous elbows, butts, and backs.

They pushed through the crowd to a large back den, equipped with a pool table and a floor-to-ceiling library. Music blared through the wall speakers: a mash-up of hip-hop and an old seventies funk track. A sprawl of hipsters occupied the leather sofa and chairs that commanded the center of the library, and a varied collection of wannabe players surrounded the pool table, waiting to call, "Next!"

Ezra eyed the table hungrily. "I'm gonna run this table," he announced to himself as he scoped the competition and decided it came up lacking. "You want to be my partner?" he asked Chloe.

"No, I've never played before. If you want to win, find someone else." She was still trying to catch her breath.

"Come on, we'll still win. I can carry you as you learn," he offered with a cocky smile.

"No, really, it's cool; I'll go look at the books," she said, staring at the stacks of leather-bound first editions.

"Okay, but make sure to drink that beer while you're at it. After this, we're gonna hit the dance floor," he declared.

"That is definitely not going to happen," she answered as he turned away with a knowing chuckle.

Chloe immediately began to second-guess her decision to venture off on her own. She eyed the walls of books, but the other inhabitants of the space awoke the social butterflies that Ezra's sturdy presence had helped to quiet.

Stan occupied one of the reading thrones, staring a little too intently at his own hand. His accomplice, Brian, was sloppily making out with a hipster girl at the edge of the sofa. Chloe didn't know the others…Kirin and Cynthia were nowhere to be seen.

Against all better judgment, she sipped the beer and tried to quell the initial impulse to gag. She kept her head down, but couldn't help but glance over at Stan as she rounded the outskirts of the room. He tried and failed to hide his wounded interest in Brian's lascivious display.

Stan's gaze flicked up and met hers for half a second.

Damn! She buried her face in the cup and took a gulp without thinking. Her mom never drank beer, but Chloe remembered how her dad had always said that beer was "an acquired taste." She shuddered and coughed—not there yet.

Her hurried step brought her to the stacks, where she deliberately turned her back to the group sitting nearby. She imagined for a long hushed moment that Stan's eyes were locked on her, and she waited with a ready wince for the embarrassing bellow that was sure to come...but didn't. The tension in her shoulders eased and she let her eyes take in some of the titles that lined the shelves before her.

Her jaw actually dropped as her fingers found the leather spine of what appeared to be a first edition of *Treasure Island*. Then her fingertips drifted, passing over equally pristine copies of *Watership Down* and *The Wind in the Willows*.

The shelf was marked with a little golden placard labeled "CHILDREN'S BOOKS."

Chloe had loved her tattered and stained copies of all those books and many of the others beside them, though she didn't really see all of them as books solely meant for children. She thought it a little sad that these treasures were so neatly arranged and seemingly untouched here. She was more of a random pile-in-the-corner sort of organizer, and found herself oddly disconcerted with the rigid and unloved collection before her.

Still, she was also keenly aware that a few of them could probably have paid for an entire year of her college tuition. Just one of the shelves was worth more than the yearly take-home from her mom's two and a half jobs combined. Her gaze climbed the stacks...There were hundreds of them, maybe a thousand.

She had a strange urge to smell the pages, but feared that an alarm might sound, bringing the party to a screeching halt with only her to blame. Instead, she sipped the beer again and glanced back to the pool table, where Ezra had claimed one of the sticks, chalking it with a focused study of the layout of balls before him. He cracked his neck and lined up his first shot.

Chloe turned back to another shelf that carried priceless copies of Brontë, Dickens, and Faulkner and shook her head in bewilderment that so much wealth could be displayed so casually. She wondered if Paul had an inkling of how amazing this small corner of his house was, let alone the vast grandeur and privilege of all the rest. She leaned in to examine a string of silver-framed photos on the next shelf.

The first picture showed an attractive older man in his best golf attire with one arm around a ten-year-old Paul Markson and the other draped across the back of Mr. Roberts as he gripped the shoulders of a smaller, less developed Kendra. Both Paul and Kendra wore T-shirts that said "Daedalus Group Family Field Day: 2010."

The next photo showed the same two men, twenty years earlier, standing in full mountaineering garb at the top of a snowcapped peak. Another little gold-engraved placard was fastened at the base of the frame: "Captains of the World, 1992."

Chloe snorted and rolled her eyes until they landed on a crystal statue prominently positioned on the next shelf. It was in the shape of a swooping angel's wing that emerged from an engraved base that said:

DAEDALUS GROUP
VISIONARY'S AWARD
(For Outstanding Achievement in the
Field of Bioengineering)
Dr. WILLIAM "Wilkie" MARKSON

The "ENGINEERING" section was cleverly positioned on the shelf above, and the extensive "BIOLOGY" section was on the shelf below. This time, she couldn't stop her hand from shooting out and snatching a book: a reprint of John James Audubon's, *Birds of America*. She put her beer down by the award and opened the creaking leather-bound edition with reverence. Every page held a beautiful full-color painting of a different bird, and Chloe absorbed each of them, turning the pages with a growing smile.

She'd seen one of the prints before at a museum in Washington, D.C., where a much larger first edition of the book was displayed beneath a thick glass box. The freedom to casually flip through the almost five hundred pictures seemed almost dreamlike. A flutter of butterflies climbed in her gut as she flipped the heavy paper, scanning over paintings of owls, loons, marsh hens, and herons.

She froze on a painting of two peregrine falcons tearing into a couple of bloody ducks, but started to feel like she was being watched. She glanced up toward a blinking red light in the corner. A small security camera was pointed right at her. Her smile faded, and she gently closed the book.

"Don't worry about it," cut in Stan as he stepped beside her. "The real one is downstairs in a vault."

"Sorry! I, I was just…" she stammered while fumbling the book back on the shelf.

Stan reached out and gently took the book back out, opening it up to a picture of a red-breasted woodpecker. His lids were half-closed over bloodshot eyes, and he wore a little smile. "No, really, it's cool. I've known Paul since like the first grade; his dad loves to show off this collection. He keeps the really valuable ones in the basement."

Chloe breathed again, eyeing Stan carefully. "Some of these books would be worth thousands of dollars."

"Yeah, but the first-edition copy of *Birds of America* is worth like ten million," said Stan with a little laugh.

"Seriously—and it's downstairs?" Chloe whispered.

"Yup," answered Stan as he slid the book back on the shelf with unexpected respect.

Chloe retrieved her beer and took another drink. "Are you into books?" she asked, a little surprised.

Stan laughed again. "No, not really; I just like birds. My mom's an ornithologist."

Stan's eyes flashed back over to Brian. Chloe could see the muscles tighten in his jaw as his smirk faded. He looked back at her, trying to play it off.

"I think I'm gonna take a walk," he declared. "You want to go see it, the original?" he asked with his mischievous smile returning.

"In the vault?" Chloe asked. "That doesn't seem like such a good idea." She looked back to the pool table, where Ezra was beginning to dismantle his opponents. "Plus, I'm kind of waiting for a friend."

Stan laughed. "Dude, Ezra will run that table for an hour, and I promise to bring you back safe and sound before then." He pointed toward another exit and nodded. "Trust me, Cool Chloe, there's stuff down there that's worth seeing!"

"How?"

"Paul likes to show off by leaving the vault open at parties. There are so many cameras that no one could steal anything anyway." He reached his hand out toward her expectantly.

Chloe hesitated and sipped her beer.

"I promise to take good care of you, under penalty of a severe beating by Ezra Richardson." Stan put up his other hand, as if taking an oath. "Scout's honor."

"You were a Boy Scout?" she asked skeptically.

"Eagle Scout, actually, so you know you'll be safe with me," he winked, grinning like the Cheshire Cat. "And your boy, Kirin, is downstairs, too."

"Oh yeah?" she asked, failing to hide the sharp rise in her voice and the sudden flush in her cheeks. She tried to look uninterested and hid behind her cup.

"Yup, he's totally wasted," Stan answered with a sad glance back at Brian.

Chloe coughed with the last unnecessarily large gulp of beer and smiled.

.   .   .

From the top of the stairs, Chloe could smell the distinct reek of pot smoke rising from below. She paused on a step midway down and considered turning back, but the warm buzz of the alcohol had kicked in. She needed to see Kirin, needed to see how he would act when he saw her. Her curiosity would not be denied.

Stan clomped ungracefully down the stairs ahead of her. "Come on," he called back with an encouraging wave, followed by a discouraging chuckle.

The overhead lights in the basement were set to a dimmed orange haze, and strings of Christmas bulbs ringed the wood-paneled walls. The room was thick with smoke, and an assortment of random kids were sunk into the sofas or splayed across the plush carpets. A senior boy who she recognized from the soccer posse was manning a fully stocked bar; he sported sunglasses and had an unlit joint behind his ear. He passed a shot of something brown to a girl who looked like she was already having trouble standing. The dance beats from upstairs were piped through speakers here too, though thankfully not quite so loud as above.

"You want a drink?" asked Stan at her ear.

She felt like she was supposed to say yes, but the beer she'd drunk had already taken her well past her comfort zone. Coolness was probably not in the cards. "No, I've got a beer," she said, taking one of the cans from her pocket and opening it with a foamy spurt. She slurped at the suds and pretended to like it. "You want one?"

Stan shook his head. "No, thanks; I don't really do well with alcohol. Plus, I'm driving."

Chloe hadn't expected that.

"The vault's back here," he said, continuing to move through the maze of hunting-lodge furniture and inebriated bodies.

Chloe followed and sipped at her second beer, hiding behind the can in the hopes that the others wouldn't see her for the faker she was. She scanned the crowd for Kirin's jet-black hair and casual posture, trying hard to avoid eye contact with all the non-Kirin faces she passed. She barely recognized any of them. *Do all of these people go to my school?*

Stan led her into another room where a long leather sofa faced a beautifully lit tropical aquarium that was set into the length of the wall across from it. The crystal-blue water was stocked with a wide array of multicolored fish, darting about in little schools or sliding casually through the coral maze. Chloe was temporarily mesmerized by the sense that she was underwater with them as the ripples of light shimmied across the walls and ceiling all around her. She saw little lobsters crawling along the rocky floor and sinuous eels slipping among the slowly dancing weeds. A cluster of brilliant blue fish moved as if with one mind as a larger red-tinged fish with jutting teeth followed in lazy pursuit.

"Cool, right?" Stan said with a nod of appreciation. "It's like Dr. Markson's meditation room, designed so that if you sit in the center of the sofa, you can only see water and fish in your peripheral vision...It's a totally awesome place to get high," he added as he lit a joint beside Chloe and took a long inhale. He held it in with his mischievous grin returned and offered the joint her way.

She tensed as the white, musky smoke spilled out of his nose and his chest slowly deflated. "You want some?" he asked with a pinched voice.

"I thought you said you were driving?" she challenged.

"Yeah, no alcohol; weed is fine, though."

"I see...I'm gonna stick with beer for now," she answered with another nervous gulp of the nasty-tasting stuff. She turned away to hide the latest shudder and saw a watery ripple of light dance across a familiar blonde ponytail with blue-dyed tips at the far edge of the sofa. Chloe's heart started pounding in her chest.

Cynthia Decareaux was straddling someone, making out furiously while enveloping the unidentifiable figure with a heavy onslaught of her considerable sexual attention. The unknown participant's tanned fingers held tightly to Cynthia's jean-covered butt, though to Chloe it didn't look like the clothes would impede them for long.

Chloe's mouth was suddenly very dry. She wanted to turn and run the other way, but found herself taking a step forward.

Stan followed her shell-shocked gaze to the compromised twosome on the sofa. "Ah, yes, we all saw this one coming," he chuckled with a roll of his eyes. "Another hapless victim of Sin-D."

Cynthia shifted as she kissed down his neck, and Kirin's bright red face came into view as his heavy head lolled back against the headrest of the sofa. His eyes were shut, and he looked disheveled and hopelessly drunk, but then her lips found his again, and he joined her willingly in the hungry pursuit. Chloe's breath caught in her throat as she imagined the aquarium glass exploding and thousands of gallons of water and sea life flooding into the room. She wanted to scream and rage, to grab the blue-tipped ponytail and yank. Instead, she stormed away with a last ravenous gulp of beer.

She pelted the empty can at the floor and opened the third beer without thinking.

She was chugging it by the time Stan caught up to her at the foot of the stairs. He touched her wrist gently. "You like him. I'm sorry, I didn't know," he stammered. "If it's any consolation, I know how it feels."

The room shimmered oddly, and Chloe's scalp was tingling. She was drunk, and she wanted to get drunker. She reached out and swiped the joint from Stan's hand, holding it before her face as the destructive urge took control.

"I'm not sure that's such a good idea. If you've never smoked before, this is kind of—"

Chloe took a long, hard pull and felt the smoke go deep into her lungs.

"—strong for beginners," Stan finished, as Chloe's ill-advised foray into drug use devolved into a barrage of hacking coughs.

"Dude, you've got an impressive lung capacity."

After a few moments, Chloe righted and wiped her mouth on her sleeve. She had no idea what to expect, but was happy enough just to have something to distract her from what was going on in the other room. "I don't get it; nothing is happening."

"Yeah, I think it'll probably kick in any moment now. That was kind of a big hit," muttered Stan with a sympathetic wince as he took back the joint and tamped it out on the lip of an empty bottle.

Chloe waited…"I think maybe I need more or something."

"No, I don't think so."

Chloe started to feel a little strange, but it might have just been the alcohol. She noticed the way that Stan was staring at her expectantly. "Really, I'm cool. I think maybe I feel it now… I'm not sure what the big deal is, though?"

She started to feel light-headed as a giddy wave bubbled up from her gut. She wasn't sure why she was smiling, but

Stan's toothy expression and bloodshot eyes suddenly seemed very funny. "Honestly, the whole thing seems really overrated," she giggled.

Now the room seemed to vibrate, and the music sounded muffled. She wasn't sure, but she felt like all the other kids in the basement were looking at her out of the corners of their eyes.

She swallowed, but her mouth was extraordinarily dry, so she swigged the beer as her body began to feel oddly weightless.

"You might want to slow down on the beer. This can be pretty surprising the first few times."

"Any advice?" she asked, beginning to question her decision, though she was uncertain if her words had made any sense or perhaps if she'd actually spoken at all.

"You know, be like a bird; just go with the wind at your back, and see where it takes you," he suggested.

"Oh," she whispered. Suddenly she felt like she might float away, as if the gravitational force that held her feet to the floor was beginning to weaken. She needed grounding. "I've got to go find Ezra," she blurted with an inexplicable belt of a laugh. "Will you help me?" she begged, trying not to completely lose it at the sight of Stan's horsey grin.

He nodded and took her hand in his sweaty palm, leading her back up the stairs. "Follow me."

*   *   *

Ezra was no longer by the pool table, where he was supposed to be. Chloe scanned the den for his commanding presence, but felt as if there were eyes following her every move. The room seemed much smaller than it had before, and the walls pressed in from all sides. She glanced to the camera in the corner and then to another blinking red light on the opposite wall. *Are they pointed at me?* It didn't seem safe, as if the whole party was a trap, set up to lure her in and take her in this vulnerable state. Her mouth was so dry. She sipped at the beer again.

She turned to Stan beside her and had trouble focusing on his face. "Ezra said he was going to hit the dance floor next."

Stan's gaze had returned to where Brian and the girl had been on the sofa. They, too, were nowhere to be seen.

Chloe was wasted, and any sense of tact or restraint was lost to her. "You like him, don't you? As more than just a friend... I'm sorry, too."

Stan suddenly looked like a trapped bird. "What? No. What are you talking about? You're totally high!" he laughed nervously.

For a moment, Chloe tried to think how she might diffuse the awkward bomb she'd already set off between them, but the room was swimming and she couldn't shake the image of Kirin's heart-wrenching exploits below.

"Whatever!" Chloe blurted, grabbing Stan's wrist and heading toward the dance floor. "Come with me."

The dance floor had now spilled out of the living room and consumed much of the back patio as well. There were what seemed to Chloe like thousands of students crammed around her and gyrating to the thumping beat. She half wanted to move with them and half wanted to drop into a fetal ball and wait for it all to go away.

Even with his size and stature, finding Ezra amid this crowd seemed like a near impossible task. But only he could anchor her now, only he could get her to truly forget the horrors she had witnessed in the basement. "Do you see him?" she shouted to an oblivious Stan, still holding on to his wrist with white-knuckled pressure in her grip.

It was too loud to hear much of anything past the music, and Stan looked just as shell-shocked and out of place as she felt. He shook his head. "We need to get out of here," he mouthed with a dazed look.

"Ezra first!" she yelled, positioning herself behind Stan with an eye toward the open patio door. "Keep your shoulder down and don't stop moving!" she bellowed before pushing Stan forward into the crowd.

"Wait! What?" he yelped as his gangly elbow clipped the ribs of a flailing rave kid. Chloe kept her head down and kept pushing, enveloped on all sides by the sea of movement, and laughing uncontrollably as she powered through. Stan, true to his own advice, stopped fighting against the wind at his back and went with it, ducking and weaving his way through the throng until they stumbled over the threshold and breathed the fresh air of the night. By then Stan was laughing too.

Outside, the crowd thinned out, though there were still too many people to see far, and Chloe was too short to see over any of them. "Do you see him?" she repeated, now approaching the onset of her first bout of chemically induced spins.

"Nope," answered Stan, balanced on his tippie-toes. "There are people going all the way back to the fire pit."

"Fire pit!" barked Chloe, starting to push Stan again as the press of faceless bodies moved past in streaks of muted color.

After tripping a few more times and a lot more unhinged laughter, Chloe stopped pushing as the hot glow of a raging fire caught her eye through the maze of torsos and arms. "Come on!" she shouted as she weaseled her way through the last line of people. She finally stopped to catch her breath with the surprisingly intense heat of the open flame on her face.

The bonfire was taller than she was, with a pyramid inferno of stacked logs ringed by a stone ledge. A bulk supply of largely untouched fixings for s'mores lay on the patio beside it. Chloe eyed the faces around her, searching hopefully for Ezra's reassuring smile…Instead, she glimpsed electric-blue eyes in the crowd, and a tingle of recognition traveled across her scalp. She craned her neck and took a step forward just as the flaring heat of the fire drove everyone else back in a reverential circle—everyone except Kendra, who pranced around the stone ledge with a graham cracker and chocolate wedge in one hand and a long stick with a skewered, burning marshmallow in the other.

With her flame-red hair, burning torch, and form-hugging clothing, she looked like some sort of elemental creature that had crawled from the fiery pit to tempt men to their destruction. Nearby, Liz nuzzled contentedly against Paul Markson's chest, though he continued to watch Kendra's added heat with a casual eye.

Chloe grimaced and tried to back away into the obscurity of the crowd, but Stan pushed her forward with the stale breath of his Cheshire grin in her face.

"No way, dude! You forced me here; I'm getting a damn s'more for the trouble!" he declared, pressing her toward the heat.

"Abort! Retreat! Let go!" Chloe stammered, but it was too late.

"You've got to be kidding! What is SHE doing here?" Kendra screeched.

Chloe shrank as her paranoia of being the center of attention came to fruition. The eyes of the crowd turned to her with a sudden flaring of tension in the air. She stopped struggling and faced Kendra, but couldn't think of anything to say.

Stan munched on a piece of swiped chocolate and stood obliviously to the side.

"You really must be crazy, showing up at my party!" Kendra spat with the dance of the fire reflected in her pupils.

Kendra was clearly buzzing and fired up, but for the first time in her life, so was Chloe. She sipped her beer and tried to contain the destructive acid rage that gurgled up from her belly. She glanced to Liz's horror-stricken face and then back to Kendra. "I came with friends," Chloe said through clenched teeth. "Didn't mean to disturb your show."

Kendra's eyes flared as she stepped closer. "What did you say, bitch?"

That does it! "I said this isn't your party—and you might want to step away from the fire before you overheat again." Chloe locked her gaze on Kendra like a hunting animal sizing up its prey. "I wouldn't want you to have to go back to the hospital covered in your own filth in front of all these people...What would Daddy say then?"

Now it was Kendra who was rendered speechless. Her face turned red as her eyes widened. She started to shake oddly as a feral shriek climbed from her gaping mouth. Time seemed to stand still...and then she charged, raising the burning marshmallow stick over her head to strike.

Chloe stood dumbfounded, unable to believe the words that had just come out of her. Everything seemed to slow as

Paul's hand reached out to catch Kendra's attack and Stan's patchouli-smelling arms enveloped Chloe.

"Get me out of here," she croaked as she let herself be hustled away through the crowd.

CHAPTER 10
OVER THE EDGE

Chloe wanted to die. She was curled on the filthy floor of Stan's stoner van as he lurched down the winding streets of Charlottesville. She had already thrown up twice in Paul's front yard, and she was pretty sure that she would do it again if either the van or her spinning mind kept moving for long.

Her pocket had vibrated twice with incoming text messages since she'd fled the party, but she hadn't yet found the strength or courage to see who it was. It took great effort to fumble the phone from her jeans before she tried to focus on the spinning glow of the little screen.

The first text was from Ezra: Lightning! Where the hell R U?

The second was a follow-up: U better not have left this party!

She was only vaguely aware of the gentle patter of rain on the roof of the car and the ominous rumble of thunder in the distance.

"Where do you live?" asked Stan over his shoulder as the van careened around another twisting bend in the road.

"I can't go home like this," mumbled Chloe as she held her temples in a feeble attempt to steady the violent movement in her mind. "This is awful."

"Sorry, I tried to warn you," Stan defended guiltily. "It might help if you sit up and try to focus on the road or something."

But Chloe was too scared to open her eyes and face reality. She could only focus on that last image of the crowd of faces around the fire—now twisted and distorted as they laughed and pointed while the final nail was driven into the coffin of her social life.

There was something else there, too—blue eyes that burned through her…But then she pictured Kirin and Cynthia in the basement and could almost hear their awkward, horny moans. She let out a pathetic groan and tried to block out the relentless, haunting imagery. Chloe was done at Charlottesville High School; there was no going back now.

"Where should I go?" asked Stan as the rain picked up and the streets started to get slick.

"Someplace without people," Chloe whimpered as she tried to respond to Ezra's messages but found that she couldn't figure out how to work the keypad. "Ezta I'm sppery. I left with Stern. Geeeling very sic!" She tried to read it back and gave up, dropping the phone amid the fast food containers and dirty laundry.

Soon enough, she felt the bump of the tires as Stan turned off the street and continued with a rumbling clatter down an unpaved road. She groaned again with the additional vibration, vaguely aware that they were headed downhill and that the vehicle had no shocks to speak of. Just as she was about to protest, the van came to a slanted stop, and an empty soda can and some discarded AA batteries rolled past her head. The engine finally came to a heaving rest and Stan yanked on the emergency break. Chloe was left to wallow in the loud silence that followed as a steadier rain began to clatter against the roof.

"Where are we?" she mumbled as she sat up with her arms braced against the seat, as if she might float away at any moment.

"The old quarry," Stan answered as a match flared up in his hand and he relit the joint with a plume of the noxious smoke.

"Please, no more of that poison!" implored Chloe as the queasy roll in her gut threatened again.

"Sorry," coughed Stan as he rolled down his window and tamped the joint out on the side of the van.

"How long is this gonna last?"

"I don't know, a few hours."

Chloe choked back a sob before climbing slowly up to the passenger seat and hunkering against the door. She hugged her knees to her chest as the wind blew cold through the open window and the rain came down a little harder. The van was angled, facing the fifty-foot drop into the quarry, but it was too dark to see the wide hole beyond the rocky lip. She shivered and shut her eyes again.

"So I guess you and Kendra Roberts have some sort of history," observed Stan as he rolled his window back up.

"Not much of one, but what we've had wasn't any good," Chloe mumbled. "I'm sorry I dragged you into it." She wiped a tear on the jeans over her bony knee.

"It's cool, dude. Sorry I brought you down to where Cynthia and Kirin were…you know." He clicked the keys in the ignition partway and turned on some classic rock. "You really like him, huh?"

Chloe sniffled. "What was I expecting? I'm such a moron."

"Hey," Stan cut in with a sad chuckle. "At least you're not gay and in love with your best friend," he blurted.

Chloe looked up at him, noticing the look of shock on his face. Despite her own internal torture, she reached out and took his sweaty hand in hers with a tight grip.

"I can't believe I just said that," he confessed.

"I guess we're both hopeless," she offered with a weak smile.

The rain started pouring so hard against the windshield that they couldn't see much beyond it. Stan raised Chloe's hand and kissed the back of her knuckles with chapped, scratchy lips. "I know this night wasn't quite what you expected and isn't ending how you would like, but I'm really glad I ran into you, Cool Chloe."

"Yeah, it's kind of been one big disaster after another since I saw you, but I know what you mean." Lightning flashed across the sky, illuminating the quarry and surrounding woods for a brief moment. She felt the press of paranoia closing in again, and the pull of the incline they were on suddenly seemed precarious.

"If it's cool with you, I'd really appreciate it if you kept what I said to yourself, you know?" Stan stated nervously.

"Of course," Chloe answered without hesitation. "Though in truth, after tonight, I wouldn't have anyone to tell anyway," she admitted. "Don't tell anyone about the whole Kirin thing either," she added. "We can be secret collaborators in unrequited romance."

"Deal," said Stan with his signature grin, just as lightning fell again in the woods across the quarry. They both jumped, and in the instant of the flash, Chloe thought she saw silvery movement disappear behind the edge of the cliff.

"Maybe we should get out of here," she suggested. "Not sure if you've heard, but me and bad weather seem to have a way of finding each other."

"Yeah," said Stan, turning the ignition, "I have heard that." The engine shook to life, and he switched the ineffective windshield wipers to high speed. As the headlights turned on, they could see the fast-moving rivulets of muddy water that rushed down the hill around them to cascade over the cliff.

Stan furrowed his brow. "You might want to put on your seatbelt," he suggested.

"Why, is something wrong?" Chloe asked as she fumbled with the strap.

"No, it's just a lot of rain is all," he said, buckling up himself. "This van isn't exactly great for off-roading." He put it in reverse and pressed the accelerator with a grinding screech before breaking again abruptly.

"What was that?" blurted Chloe just as Stan reached over and undid the emergency brake.

"Whoops," he said with a sheepish chuckle.

"You sure you're okay to drive?" Chloe asked.

"Do you have a better idea?" he challenged as the van started to back up again, this time without the grinding of metal on metal. "Just hang on."

In that moment, it started to rain even harder. Chloe cringed in her seat as she watched the fast growing river of runoff shoot out into the empty space before them. She gripped the handrest tightly enough to leave a permanent mark as the van backed slowly up the hill.

"See, nice and steady…No problem," announced Stan just before the front tires spun in the mud and the van drifted a little to the side. He braked fast and exhaled slowly.

"What was that?" Chloe said again with a wide-eyed look

out the back windshield that showed nothing but wet darkness.

"Chill out, dude. It's a little slippery; nothing to worry about," Stan reassured. He took his foot off the break and accelerated gently as the van started to back up the steepest section of the little hill.

The rain pummeled the roof so hard that Chloe was worried it might actually cave in. She cringed into an even tighter ball on the seat and buried her face in her knees. But with her eyes closed, she saw again the mocking faces of her peers and began to hear Kirin's passionate moans hidden amid the falling water. She told herself that this was all just some horrible drug-induced nightmare that would soon pass...But instead, she remembered the image of enormous, unfurling wings of an impossible beast and then the skewering look of its reptilian eyes.

The wheels slipped again, and as they spun uselessly with a high-pitched whirring, the van turned to the side and began to lose ground.

"Stan!" Chloe looked up to see the river that rushed around them and the alarm on Stan's face.

He tried to brake, but it didn't slow them at all as the growing mud current swung them around and pushed them back down the hill. For a moment, the van was sideways, and it felt like they might tip over as both Stan and Chloe started screaming in earnest. Then the rear tires swung around and the headlights were facing uphill as they continued to slide backward.

Chloe peered back over the headrest, searching for some indication of the distance to the cliff's edge, but she saw nothing in the blackness.

"Unlock the door and jump!" shouted Stan. "You have to jump!" he repeated as he unbuckled his seatbelt and managed to lift the lock on his own door.

Chloe heard his words, but didn't know how to make sense of them. She fumbled at the door, but couldn't get it open, frantically clawing at the handle without any result. "It won't open!"

And then the van crawled to a halt on the even ground at the bottom of the slope. Chloe and Stan froze in place, too scared to breathe...

All of a sudden, the rain's onslaught relented and then came to a stop. In the relative silence that followed, Chloe heard again the cheesy classic rock that was still playing on the radio and let go of the breath that had lodged in her throat.

Stan was the first to chuckle, and a moment later, they were both heaving with the outpouring of shaky relief. Chloe wasn't sure if she was laughing, crying, or both, but she knew, without a doubt, that she'd never been so happy to be alive and would never do drugs again.

But Stan was also the first to stop laughing, and Chloe followed his curious gaze up the path of the headlights to the large shadowy object that crested the hill and headed toward them in the rushing washout. Chloe's laugh faded, too, as a wide, uprooted tree reached the furthest edge of the light and barreled downhill with a claw of jagged limbs. She was unable to register what she was seeing as it accelerated toward them.

"Hold on!" screamed Stan just before a thick branch tore through the windshield with a spray of glass, and the trunk slammed into the front bumper, plowing the van back toward the cliff with violent force.

Chloe didn't even have time to shriek before the van tipped backward and lost contact with the ground. For a moment, she watched the tree as it snagged on the edge and wrenched free, tilting and plummeting away as the headlights passed over the rock wall of the cliff. Then there was only dark sky above. She instinctively lunged toward the shattered windshield, hoping to smash through and instantly learn to fly, only to be held helplessly in place by her seatbelt. *This is it! This is how I die! How lame!*

She closed her eyes with the horrific sound of tearing metal, followed by a violent lurch as her stomach rose into her throat and the van swung in what felt like a dipping arc through the air. Her head and shoulder slammed into the door with disorienting force and then she was flung back in the other direction over the gearshift. She opened her eyes to see Stan's unconscious form, crumpled and bleeding against the driver's side door. *Why am*

I still alive?

Then the van swung back again with the screech of wrenched steel, and she looked up at the cab's ceiling, where five giant black hooks had torn through the roof. Out of her window, she saw the dark woods of Charlottesville passing by a hundred feet below, but the van was no longer falling. Looking up, her mind took a moment to accept the sight of the wide, undulating flaps of what looked like a giant batwing.

It was then that the long sinuous neck of the thing that carried her looped back, and its massive, shining blue eye stopped to regard her through the window. Chloe finally and blissfully slipped from consciousness.

• • •

Chloe lunged awake with a scream, cut short when the shoulder strap of her seat belt jerked the frantic breath out of her. Her eyes darted about the glass-covered cab of the van, taking in the long strips of gouged bark and a scattering of leaves that had been left behind from the violent run-in with the wayward tree. Stan was still crumpled against the driver's side door with a thin trickle of blood down his temple. He was snoring loudly and drooling from his open mouth, but he wore an oddly peaceful look on his face.

"Stan," she whispered, gently shaking his shoulder. "Stan!" she repeated more emphatically. He smacked his lips and smiled in his sleep.

The engine was still running, but the front headlights had been smashed beyond use. Chloe turned with a sharp jab of pain in her neck and saw that they were backed against a tree, illuminated by the red glow of the taillights. Charlottesville's classic rock station continued to spit out a string of spacey electric riffs on the radio, but Chloe could hear the trilling song of a whippoorwill through the shattered windshield. She reached over and turned the key in the ignition until the engine and radio were stilled, and she listened for a hushed moment to the bird's dipping melody.

She was disoriented, nauseous, and utterly confused as she tried to piece together the events that had somehow brought her…where? She rubbed the heels of her palms in her eyes, hoping that it might somehow bring greater clarity. Instead, her head still hummed from the abuse she'd inflicted at the party, though thankfully the full brunt of the disorienting chemical assault had been flushed out by the rush of adrenaline. Now she felt profoundly tired and psychically stripped bare—unsure which of the night's hazy string of calamities had really happened.

She undid the belt buckle and leaned forward to get a better view through the hole in the windshield. Past the dark canopy of leaves and limbs above, she could see the bright band of the Milky Way cutting across the sky. There were no other lights around to give her any sense of where she was or how much time had passed. Her phone wasn't in her pocket as expected, but then she vaguely remembered trying to text someone before the accident. She reached back and groped around through Stan's garbage, now sprinkled with sticks and jagged little glass cubes that cut her thumb and forefinger before she found the phone.

Opening the screen, she was temporarily blinded by the bright blue light, but was pleased to discover that it was only 11:14 p.m.—about a half hour past her estimated arrival at the quarry and a full forty-five minutes before her curfew.

She unlocked her door and shouldered it open with a loud creak as it wrenched away from the bent frame. Her Chucks found the firm security of pavement. Out from behind the distorted lens of the wet and cracked glass, Chloe recognized the shadowed bend in the road as a spot only a few hundred yards from her house. The Red Hill Loop trailhead began here and intersected with the white blazes of the Appalachian Trail only a few miles further down the ridge.

She'd walked this stretch of road to the Loop a thousand times in the day, but didn't remember this bend in the street being so dark at night. She glanced up at the nearby streetlamp, now hanging loosely by a sparking wire as it swung gently in the stilled air. A little further down the bend, the next light was torn down completely; it lay smashed by the side of the road. Her heart started thundering in her chest.

All at once, Chloe remembered—she'd seen a *monster*! She could picture the way the lights from below had reflected off the sheen of its wet scales as it carried the van over Charlottesville with the heavy beats of its enormous wings. And she'd seen it before. It had been there when the lightning struck…a dragon, rising up from the water. Surely this was all some freakish imagining of her drugged state. Or perhaps her mind had finally fractured completely? *Next stop: the nut house?*

But then something large moved through her peripheral vision. Her neck snapped painfully around as her eyes widened. The whippoorwill went quiet. An expectant hush fell over the woods. Chloe could hear the beating of her heart in her inner ears as the heavy shadows seemed to gather, taking shape in a colossal form. She blinked, trying to focus, and then it moved again, a long sinuous shape, sliding through the trees.

She turned to run toward home, but in that instant, two ice-blue eyes the size of car tires flashed from the gloom as an alien will enveloped her mind to lock her feet in place. She could not budge or scream as the thing crept closer. It brushed against tree trunks with enough force to strip large chunks of bark and shake the upper canopy. Its head emerged from the shadows and approached at the end of a long, serpentine neck. It looked like a giant bearded crocodile. The overlay of its plate-sized scales reflected the silvery-blue moonlight, and a set of curving horns as long as the van sprouted from the top of its head. It hovered before her like a cobra, readying to strike.

Chloe couldn't look away, mesmerized by the electric ripples of light that swam across the blue irises before her and the vacuum draw of the black slits in the center. She felt like she might fall forward and be sucked in at any moment. Still, it kept coming with powerful, clawed arms and legs, which gouged deep grooves into the road with every clacking step. Its body stretched back into the shadows for a hundred feet or more. The hooked and membranous wings that she'd seen unfurled before were folded neatly across its ridged spine. Terror coursed through her. She started to tremble as its head shifted to examine her more closely with one giant shining eye.

This isn't possible! It's not real!

As if in reply, it huffed a jet of hot, fetid air from its nostrils, blowing Chloe's hair back like a giant hairdryer. She winced and blinked as her hair settled and the trickle of some unfathomable liquid slid down her cheek. *That felt pretty real!*

She had the sense, through the link in her thoughts, that it was toying with her, testing her response to its presence and studying her reactions. In that instant, it let go of its hold, and she stumbled. She was immediately aware again of her own two feet and the overwhelming urge to run. But somehow, either through disbelief or perhaps the lingering sway of the drugs and alcohol, she stood her ground.

The thing bristled with a deep whistling inhale as the terrible jaws creaked open before her, revealing long rows of dagger-like teeth and the threatening flit of a forked tongue. What looked like sparks gathered in the back of its throat, and Chloe became keenly aware that another, even more potent threat of attack loomed from deeper down its savage maw. But her gaze was directed instead to the diamond-shaped plate between the thick, bony ridges that framed its watching eyes. There, a faint glow began to pulse from within.

Chloe was drawn toward it, inexplicably wanting to reach out, almost like a child's urge to touch the hot stove, despite her mother's warnings. Her blood fired through her veins with an overload of adrenaline, but she did not budge from that spot.

She exhaled slowly and reached up with a shaking hand. The tingle and spark of static electricity passed between them just as she touched the bony jut of its snout. Its scales were warm and smooth and surprisingly supple to the touch, like the surface of a snake. Her fingers buzzed as the tickle of the charge climbed down her arm to her elbow and the diamond in its forehead started to grow brighter.

This is nothing but a drug-induced hallucination, she reminded herself, though she couldn't help but admire the raw power and beauty of the creature before her. It seemed like she should probably bow, or at least show some respect. "Thank you for saving me," she croaked with a quivering voice.

It shut its jaws with a loud snap and reared up, its head suddenly high among the branches of the trees. The shadowed canopy was bathed in light as the diamond plate burned hotter still, now almost too bright to look at, though Chloe couldn't turn her head away. Through the residual presence of its will in her mind, she could sense its curiosity and confusion.

Then Stan let loose with a wet cough in the van, and instantly the link was broken. The beast hunched low to the street and launched straight up through the air with a force that shook the ground and whipped the overhanging trees into a frenzy. Chloe fell back against the van as a rain of leaves, branches, and acorns fell around her. She looked up to see the huge, silvery wings unfurl in the moonlight before the thing soared away into the dark.

From inside the van, Stan snuffled and opened his eyes with a pained groan.

"Did you see that?" asked Chloe in shell-shocked awe.

"Holy crap, dude," mumbled Stan, with his hand coming away from his scalp with a smear of blood. "My van!" He scanned the damage, taking in the liberal clutter of foliage left behind. "What happened?"

He didn't see it! Chloe tried to think of some way to explain, but she couldn't find her way to the truth…"You saved us; it was amazing," she blurted. "When the tree hit us, you smashed your head against the window, but somehow you managed to steer us clear and drive back up the hill." She glanced to the holes in the roof, trying to figure if her story made any sense. "I was totally freaking out, and I think I passed out at some point…We were just so lucky those branches didn't get us when they came through the roof and windshield," she offered.

Stan looked confused. "I think I remember flying over the cliff, or something?"

Chloe reached over and hugged him in an effort to hide her unconvincing expression. "Thank God, no! But it was so close!" He smelled like patchouli and sweat. "You're a hero! You even tried to drive me home, but I guess you passed out before we could get there. You probably have a concussion." She brought her hand to his head tenderly. "Does it hurt?"

"Yeah," he admitted, clearly liking the heroic story he'd been given. "But how am I gonna explain this to my parents?"

"Tell them the truth," Chloe counseled. "You were hanging out with a girl by the quarry, and a freak storm would have killed us both if not for your quick action and levelheaded thinking."

Stan grinned. "Yeah, that's good. I like that." He turned the key in the ignition, and the van sputtered to life along with the return of the classic rock. "It still runs."

"Are you okay to drive?" she asked skeptically.

"Yeah, dude, I actually feel kinda good," admitted Stan, sitting up straighter in the seat.

"Well, you really might have a concussion, so you should check your pupils for irregular dilation and you might not want to go to sleep tonight."

Stan chuckled, "Thanks, Doc. At least I won't have to use Visine to hide the red-eye, right?"

Chloe leaned in and kissed him on the cheek. "Thanks for one of the weirdest nights of my life."

"Yeah, well, thanks for being so cool, Cool Chloe," he returned as Chloe got out of the van and stood beside the door. "Wait, don't you want a ride the rest of the way home?"

"No, I'm just around the bend, and I could use the walk to clear my head...No more drugs for me, thanks."

Stan chuckled guiltily.

"Your headlights are smashed, so you need to throw out the pot, put on your hazards, and drive straight home," she added with a quick glance to the suspicious holes in the pavement.

"Smart," Stan said as he put on his blinkers without any indication that he'd heard the rest. "Wanna have lunch on Monday?"

"I'll see you there." She smiled and shut the door with a wave.

Stan gave her a thumbs-up and rolled away slowly. The tires bumped over the gouges in the street before he picked up a little speed and honked the nasally horn.

Chloe watched the red, blinking taillights as they receded around the bend before exhaling. *I think that actually worked.* She checked the time on her cell phone—thirty minutes left until her curfew—and then scanned the skies for movement.

A moment later, she was sprinting toward home.

.   .   .

Chloe shut the back door as quietly as she could before locking it and throwing the deadbolt for the first time in years. She stood on her tippy-toes and scanned the yard through the little oval window, half expecting to see a hundred-foot-long mythological creature lurking beside the untended barn. Her heart was still going a mile a minute as she turned away, trying to reconcile the seeming absurdity of her fears with the inconceivable interaction she'd just had with…either a very convincing figment of her imagination or the unknown super species that would call into question the entire timetable of evolutionary biology. *What if I really am going crazy, like Dad?*

Shipwreck sat at the foot of the stairs, watching her intently. It was uncharacteristic of him not to have come immediately to mark his territory by rubbing his face along her shins. Chloe knelt down and made the clicking sound with her tongue that she used to call him. "Here, buddy," she whispered, brushing her wild hair from her cheek. "Ooh," she blurted, looking down at the gooey strand of mucous that had smeared on her fingers.

Shipwreck's ears pinned back as he produced a feral hiss and bolted up the stairs.

Chloe raised an eyebrow and wiped the slime on her jeans with a shudder. *Okay, that's kind of freaky!*

She emerged from the foyer to see her mom splayed out on the sofa with a now-cold cup of hot chocolate resting precariously on her stomach between her hands. Audrey was asleep, breathing heavily with a little sigh at every exhale. Chloe crept closer, not wanting to wake her. The television news was still on in hushed tones, with the seemingly perpetual "**BREAKING NEWS**" logo highlighted across the screen—this time, accompanying shaky-cam footage of a picturesque, snowcapped, conical mountain spitting a heavy plume of smoke and ash into a blue sky.

Chloe stepped closer and rescued the tilting cup from her mother's grasp before draping a blanket over her. She took the remote from the coffee table and turned off the latest disaster in progress, not having the energy for yet another indication of the impending end of days.

"Mount Kilimanjaro is erupting," mumbled Audrey with her eyes half open. "They think it might really blow for the first time in like 350,000 years or something."

"Sorry, I didn't want to wake you," whispered Chloe, hoping her lack of interest wouldn't be a telltale indication that something was up.

"Did you have fun with Ezra?" Audrey asked with a tired smile.

"Yeah, I suppose," answered Chloe unconvincingly. "I'm not sure parties are really my thing."

"Did you see that other boy you like?" Audrey prodded.

Chloe could instantly feel the flush of emotion in her cheeks, and was horrified that just thinking about Kirin could make her feel this way, despite everything else that had happened that night. "Yeah, but I kind of want to try to forget the whole thing right now."

"Okay," Audrey said, backing off, "but you know you can talk to me about anything."

Yeah, wanna bet? "I know it, Mom. I love you."

"Good night, honey," said Audrey as she snuggled back into the cushions and shut her eyes again.

Chloe dropped off the mug in the sink and downed a big glass of water before retreating to her room as quickly as she could. Though she wanted to block out that last heartbreaking image of Kirin and pretend that the disastrous party had never happened, she was equally determined to hold on to every subtle detail of her dreamy encounter with the...dragon? For some reason, in that moment, she felt like her life depended on it.

THE IRON KING

A solid ball of iron the size of the moon spins at the center of the world. Over time, iron crystals form and melt at its edges, pulled from and returning to the molten ring of metal that surrounds it. Swimming in that ring, in an eternal spiral dance that helps to govern the magnetic fields above, is mighty Ogun.

He had carried many names and visages throughout his eleven thousand years, but some of the people of West Africa and the islands of the Caribbean still called him Ogun and made offerings in his honor. This was the name he liked best. Even from miles below he heard them chant; he smelled the cigars they lit for him and could almost taste the rum they spit over the clay and shell statues they'd made. It pleased him to know their continued respect, and sometimes he still blessed them with the power of his will in their bodies, making them invulnerable to pain as long as they danced and writhed to the thundering beat of his heart.

He almost felt bad that they, too, had to die, but he longed to climb up from this elemental prison and reclaim the iron that their kind had leached from the land. He would collect all that rightly belonged to him, take back from their buildings and bridges so that he might finally build a nest worthy of his presence above. For centuries, he'd been designing it in his dreams.

Perhaps he'd keep some of the devoted to work in his mines and sing his songs. Perhaps he would make all those who stood in his path slave in the smiths of the Master of Metal. He would claim their greatest city and build a house the likes of which the world had never seen, and no dragon, man, or beast would dare pass through the domain of mighty Ogun without his consent or wrath.

A deep, rolling laugh billowed out from his gut as bubbles of boiling metal rose toward the mineral ceiling, working their heat and pressure through the cracks and fissures that fed the pools of magma above. Soon all the people of the land would know his name, and all would cower before the coming of his fury.

CHAPTER 11
GETTING SCHOOLED

Chloe felt like death the next morning, but managed to play it off until Audrey left for her first of two back-to-back shifts at Positive Pete's. For once, Chloe was glad that her mom wasn't around. After popping three Advil and chugging two glasses of water, Chloe rattled off a quick text apology to Ezra, and another checking in to make sure that Stan was neither dead nor in jail. Then she tossed her phone in the laundry basket with the intent to shut herself off completely from the outside world. She claimed her mom's vacated spot on the sofa, got a huge bowl of Honey Nut Cheerios, and settled in for a day of vapid channel surfing. It didn't work.

What little sleep she'd finally found in the early morning hours had offered some distance from the previous night's trial. Again, the whole thing was beginning to seem increasingly foggy and dreamlike, and she reminded herself that drugs and alcohol had been at the heart of the freak events that had occurred... But this time, real or not, the terror and exhilaration of facing off with a legendary creature had left a mark that did not so easily fade. She couldn't shake the last image of its towering, perfected form, the touch of its surprisingly smooth scales, or the disturbing sensation of its presence in her mind. She felt privileged and violated at the same time.

And she remembered now that she'd seen it before, had even researched the surprisingly universal mythology that fit the beast's description. She recalled the bone-quivering sound of its roar, the absurdity of the Tipping Point Prophecy, and the strange man that had been watching through the hail storm. It didn't make sense. *How could I have forgotten any of it?*

Later that afternoon, she would give up on television and pace the house like a caged animal, glancing out the windows at every chance and trying not to read some paranoid connection between the coming of the dragon and the constant string of world atrocities that occupied every news channel she flipped by. Kilimanjaro was about to erupt, threatening the lives of hundreds of thousands of already starving refugees along the border of Tanzania. The floods across the American Midwest had begun to reach epic proportions as day seventeen of active "Disaster Zone" status was blazoned across the screen with dramatic red highlights. And the ongoing relief efforts in Xining, China had taken a further hit when a powerful aftershock leveled the makeshift hospital that had been set up by the Red Cross in city center.

And those were just the new, big, and sexy stories; there was no more mention of the chronic mudslides in Brazil, the ongoing toxic leak in the Gulf of Mexico, or the water riots that had consumed large swaths of Africa and Southern Asia. War and tragedy had become so commonplace that after a week or so, no one bothered to talk about it any more. Someplace, far away from here, people are fighting and dying—the end...In other news: NATURE WANTS TO KILL YOU!

But Chloe couldn't accept that. Try as she might, she couldn't bury her head in MTV, video games, or online like she was supposed to. She couldn't make herself feel better by shopping or eating something fattening, and she sure as hell wasn't going to be drinking or trying drugs again anytime soon.

Against all reason or understanding, she'd seen a dragon, and it had saved her life—twice. If this wasn't the end of the world, it was at least the end of the world as she knew it. She needed to know more.

.   .   .

The libraries at the University of Virginia comprise one of the oldest and most comprehensive collections of research material held by any state institution in the nation. In addition to active students, faculty, and alumni, the stacks are available to a select group of community representatives from greater Charlottesville. Only a lucky few have been awarded a magnetic-coded picture ID after demonstrating a consistent devotion to scholarly pursuit. Community reps have full access to reading materials seven days a week before 7:30 p.m., if older than the age of sixteen or accompanied by a qualified adult. Throughout the history of the university, there have been only a few exceptions to this rule.

Chloe McClellan had been given her own unaccompanied full-access pass at the age of thirteen. On the Sunday after the party, she took two buses and then walked the rest of the way to the main library branch with a hurried step. She had made this journey at least once a week for two years and had only been awarded the privilege after the countless times she had written pleading letters and then stubbornly shown up without permission in the years prior. All the library staff and security personnel, as well as a handful of deans and the school president, knew her name.

"Hey, Chloe, having a good Sunday?" called Maurice, the security guard, as she swung open the front door of the main branch.

"Pretty good, I've got some reading to do." She unzipped the pocket of her backpack to retrieve her pass.

"Haven't seen you as much since you started high school." He put down his Sudoku book and pen.

"Yeah, I joined the cross-country team, but term paper season is coming up," she answered with a hint of genuine glee.

Maurice chuckled as Chloe swiped the card over the scanner and the little plastic gate swung open. "How's Shipwreck doing?" he asked, as always, since the initial consultation on the cat's rehab.

"He's getting fat, but he's still a terror."

"Well, you tell him I said hi," he said with a nod. "And remember, don't take any wooden nickels."

"I'll never forget," she said over her shoulder.

Chloe beelined it to the information desk. Yvette was staring at a computer screen behind the counter while typing at a breakneck pace. Chloe stepped up to the desk. "How's the book coming?"

Yvette looked over while her fingers finished banging out a last few words. "Page 262; this stuff writes itself."

"Getting good?" asked Chloe.

"Oh, yeah, it's hot, getting real steamy now."

"What title did you decide on?" asked Chloe.

"I got a new one. What do you think of, *Sux in the City*?" she asked with big eyes and a sheepish smile. "It says it all, right? Exclusive coven of four sexy vampire girls living in an after-hours world of high fashion and hot blood in the big city… What's not to like?"

"It'll be a scorcher," Chloe said with a smile.

Yvette swiveled over to face another monitor. "What'll it be today?"

Chloe swallowed. "Chinese mythology, actually."

Yvette started typing. A second later, she said, "There's a lot. Do you just want all the general anthologies or do you have anything more specific?"

Chloe thought for a moment, nervous to proceed. "Dragons," she mumbled. "How about Chinese dragons… and prophecies."

"Interesting." Yvette's fingers flew across the keys again. "Okay, that's better. There're still a lot of titles here, but only a few really specialize." She clicked the mouse and her brow furrowed. "Oh, but it looks like those are pretty much all checked out," she noticed. "Sorry about that." She clicked again. "A few of them are also available online if you want to wait for a computer," she suggested, motioning to the crowded bank of computers in the center of the room. Every station was occupied by a student, and there was a waiting line beside the sign-up sheet already seven students long.

Chloe's face sank.

Yvette leaned across the desk. "I'm not supposed to tell you, but they're all checked out by the same guy," she whispered.

"He's an adjunct professor here—Dr. Edward Liou."

"What does he teach?"

"Asian Studies or something; he's in the anthropology department. Nice guy. I hear he's really good." She glanced back at the computer with a conspiratorial little smirk. "And he's got office hours right now, if you're interested?"

. . .

Chloe knew the way to the anthropology department without needing to ask. She'd spent the better part of the previous spring lingering around the Brooks Hall building during her stint as an amateur collector of Native American arrowheads and pottery shards, which she'd had an uncanny ability to uncover in her explorations of the local woods.

Liz had been along for part of that adventure, though she'd never shown a real knack for the pursuit so much as being caught up in Chloe's contagious enthusiasm. Of course, by the end of that May, Liz had begun to distance herself from Chloe's shifting passions altogether, and by June, their failed anthropological quest had, for Chloe, become the symbol of their dying friendship.

Chloe allowed herself only a moment of nostalgic regret before she bounded up the front stairs and entered the Victorian Gothic structure. A skinny guy with a lazy beard and glasses sat behind a little counter, reading a book. His eyes flitted up and tracked her as Chloe waved and tried to keep going. "Can I help you?" he asked with more authority than necessary.

Chloe stopped and turned back with her best smile. She flashed her ID. "Sorry, I used to come here a lot and I forgot..."

The pinch-faced grad student just looked at her.

"Is Ms. Shaw here?" Chloe asked hopefully, knowing that Ms. Shaw would vouch for her presence.

"I don't know who Ms. Shaw is," he said unhelpfully. "Are you a student here?"

"No, I go to Charlottesville High School." She pointed in the general direction of school. "I just come here sometimes to use the libraries and do research. I have a community access pass."

He kept looking at her but seemed to be too bored to respond.

"I'm here to see one of the professors?" she suggested.

"Which one?" he barked.

"Dr. Edward Liou?"

"Yeah, he's here; I'm one of his TAs," he declared proudly.

"Cool," she said…"Does that mean I can go see him?"

"Is he expecting you?" he challenged.

"Uh, no, I was just hoping to stop by for his office hours…"

"Okay. But you're going have to sign in," he finally said as he swung around a ledger and clicked a ballpoint pen.

Chloe stepped back to the counter and reached her hand out for the pen, half afraid that he might snap at her fingers like an unpredictable little dog. She signed her name in the book and scribbled the coded number of her ID beside it, taking note of the other two names in the ledger above hers.

CHET SWANBURG: #123637 9:14 A.M.

DR. EDWARD LIOU +1: #288362 10:02 A.M.

"Thanks, Chet," she said as politely as she could before turning away and heading for the stairs.

"Sure," he looked at the ledger, "Chloe." He said her name with a nasally whine while wondering why he had to waste his precious time and intellect dealing with immature little girls. "Up the stairs, end of the hallway, fourth door on the left."

Chloe walked up the stairs, rolling her eyes. She wondered if all the students at college were so rude, or if the world would even be around long enough for her to find out. She crested the stairs and strolled down the hallway, trying to plan her approach to the next conversation. She stopped at the fourth open door on the left and peeked in.

An attractive Chinese man in his forties sat behind a desk laden with books. He wore black-framed glasses that made him look smart and stylish at once. The beginning of distinguished grey was peppered through his hair. Chloe's eye immediately fell on a gold dragon banner that hung on the wall behind him. He did not look up from his book until she rapped gently on the door.

"Hello there," he said with an instant smile. "Sorry, I didn't see you. Usually no one stops by for my office hours, especially on Sunday morning." He sat up and closed the book. "Let me guess, either you didn't like the grade I gave you on the midterm, or you have to drop the class due to an unforeseen scheduling conflict?"

Chloe gripped the straps of her backpack tightly and stepped into the room, unsure how to begin. "No, I just wanted to ask you a couple questions about…ancient Chinese mythology?"

His brow furrowed. "Are you in my class?"

"No, I don't actually go to school here yet. I'm still in high school. I'm just interested in the topic and wanted to find out some things I hadn't been able to find in the books or online," Chloe offered hesitantly.

"That has got to be the most refreshing thing I've heard in a long time!" His easy smile returned, and for a moment, something about it seemed oddly familiar. "I'm Edward," he offered, along with his hand.

"Nice to meet you. I'm Chloe," she responded with a curt little handshake.

"Take a seat," he suggested, motioning to the chair across from him. "Ask away, Chloe, and we'll see if I'm worth my salt as a professor here."

Chloe sat and swallowed, afraid he was going to think she was a crackpot. "Well, have you ever heard of something called the Tipping Point Prophecy?"

His eyes bulged in surprise, and then he burst into a raucous laugh.

Chloe sank lower in the chair as he pounded his fist on the desk with an echoing hoot. She wondered if she should get up and go.

"Who put you up to this? Professor Jones? Or was it Amanda Freed?" he demanded, still laughing. "Very well-played."

Chloe was profoundly uncomfortable. "No, I just read a

brief mention about it online and wondered if you might know more," she said meekly. "I tried to look it up at the library, but all the books were checked out."

He stopped laughing gradually and wiped his eyes. "Oh… You're serious? Really, you're here on your own?"

Chloe nodded.

"That's remarkable! I'm sorry; it's just that the Tipping Point Prophecy is a fairly obscure Chinese text that I happen to be writing an article on for *Anthropological Quarterly*—maybe even a book. A number of my colleagues have already offered some rather harsh criticism of my efforts," he admitted. "I'm not laughing at you at all. In fact, I'm a little bit amazed that you're here. I haven't been able to find anyone else who actually cares."

"So it's a real thing?" Chloe persisted, realizing then how much she wished that it wasn't. "The bronze cauldron where the prophecy was inscribed is an actual artifact?"

Dr. Liou looked impressed. "You've come to the right place. Oh, yes, it's very real," he said excitedly before scrambling through the papers on his desk and uncovering a series of photographic scans that showed a round-bellied, three-legged cauldron. He spread them out across his desk for Chloe to see. The bronze had turned a sickly green/black with age and was covered with complex Chinese calligraphy interwoven with sinuous engravings of spiraling, interconnected dragons. The cauldron legs ended in savage, clawed feet that reminded Chloe of what she'd seen tearing through the street only a couple nights before.

"These photos were taken in 1978, but the cauldron still exists in a private collection today," Dr. Liou said. "It's called the Tianlong Cauldron, or Cauldron of the Celestial Dragons, and it carbon dates back to around 850 BCE, which would place it in early Western Zhou Dynasty. It's a fairly typical example of a bronze Ding cauldron for that period, but there is nothing typical about what it says." Dr. Liou glanced at the photos the way a father might stare at his newborn baby. "No one knows who made it, but it was found in a sealed cave by a Belgian Archaeologist in 1956."

Chloe swallowed hard. "So they know what it says?"

"There've been a few translations over the years," he said as he produced a folder from his desk and almost reverently removed the single piece of paper within. "Of course, I've done my own translation, which differs a bit from those that were done before," he added with a hint of defensive pride. "But I think my interpretation hits a few insights that my predecessors missed."

He put the paper in front of her. A series of lines were scrawled out in ancient Chinese calligraphy with a direct, stilted translation in English beside it and then a more fluid, anglicized version below that. Without looking, he began to recite his translation by heart.

> *"The age of spirits soon fades to loss,*
> *Old powers hidden away by water, rock, and cloud.*
> *Time forgets those that came before,*
> *Replaced by man's dominion over the land.*
> *The cities will grow as the forests fall,*
> *Rivers will be drained and mountains moved,*
> *And the people will know no wisdom but their own.*
> *The spread of their mark will consume like a weed,*
> *As the earth chokes and cries out to deaf ears.*
> *Until the Old Ones hear from deep within their prisons,*
> *Hidden beneath the soil and under the oceans,*
> *Called back from the stars and the land of sleep.*
> *When the spirit of the land withers and dies,*
> *They will return with the breaking of the world.*
> *The ground will open and the wind will howl;*
> *Waters will rise and fire will blot the sun.*
> *The Five Claws will claim dominion once more,*
> *And the age of man's rule will shatter into oblivion."*

Dr. Liou finished with a nod and cleared his throat. He smiled expectantly.

Chloe felt light-headed. "That's kind of bleak," she mumbled.

"Yes, but it's amazing, too!" he said excitedly. "No other ancient Chinese text talks of the future. They're all concerned, especially in that time period, with ancestral worship and historical record. But this one cauldron is foretelling the end of mankind thousands of years from the time of its inscription. It's unique!"

"How many thousand years?" Chloe asked.

"Who knows, that kind of speculation is irrelevant to my research," answered Dr. Liou with a dismissive wave. "Cultures have predicted the end of days since the beginning of recorded history, but we're still here. Some of the Ancient Mayans thought the end would come just a few years ago, and I'd say that whoever made this cauldron had something like our modern times in mind, wouldn't you?" he added with a playful wink.

Chloe was having trouble seeing the humor that came so easily to him, hearing instead Mrs. Greenwald's words of warning echoing again in her mind. "What are The Five Claws?"

Dr. Liou grinned bigger still. "Good question. That is where I differ most clearly with my predecessors in interpretation." He pointed to a couple of the Chinese symbols in the photographs. "The Chinese word 'Tianlong' means heavenly or celestial dragon. They were the wisest and most powerful dragons, having ascended to some form of higher consciousness. In China, the five-clawed dragons, like those depicted here on the cauldron, were the Tianlong, equated with the emperor and divine province."

"Most scholars think that 'The Five Claws' is just another way of saying Tianlong—so that the cauldron's text speaks of the celestial dragons returning to destroy mankind. But if you notice in the series of photographs, there are five interlocking five-clawed dragons depicted here." He pointed to each dragon as he laid out his own variance on the doomsday theory. "One that looks as if it is made of rock, another covered in feathers like a bird, a third that looks like a hooded eel or sea serpent, a forth that trails fire and smoke, and the fifth surrounded by lightning…Earth, air, water, fire, and spirit, just like it says in the prophecy!" He paused for dramatic effect.

"I believe that 'The Five Claws,' shown on the cauldron, refers to five *specific* dragons, each representing an elemental force of nature, the kings and queens of dragonkind, if you will." He sat up in his chair and adjusted his glasses. "This is where my theory gets a little controversial. You see, the myth and iconography of dragons existed in almost every ancient culture—Chinese, Greek, African, Islamic, Aboriginal, Aztec, Native American, and on." He pointed back to the photos. "I'm not sure how, but not all of the dragons shown here are from Chinese legend. I think they come from various traditions from all over the world."

"But that wouldn't be possible in 850 BCE," Chloe observed.

"No, it wouldn't," he agreed, "but there it is." He placed the photo showing the feathered dragon on top of the pile. "The Aztecs and Mayans worshipped a feathered serpent god called Quetzalcoatl across Mesoamerica for almost two thousand years. He was the god of the sky and wind, and a bringer of knowledge and craft to the people who honored him."

He replaced it with the photo of the cobra-hooded sea dragon. "In a number of Hindu and Buddhist cultures throughout much of Southeast Asia, the Nāgas are an elemental race of water-based spirits that most often took the shape of giant snakes. According to Hindu mythology, their mother was a massive, black, hooded sea serpent called Kadru...Some Comparative Religion scholars think that Kadru was the same as the Baylonion sea goddess, Tiamat."

Chloe began to feel a pit growing in her stomach.

He replaced the top picture with that showing the roaring dragon wreathed in fire. "I believe that this one is Chien-Tang, one of the many names for a giant fire-breathing dragon that plagued ancient China. According to legend, he lived for a few hundred years in the Chien-Tang River and collected yearly payment of sacrifice in bulls and virgins from the locals."

Dr. Liou placed the last two cauldron photos on the desk: one showing a wingless beast, almost like a giant armadillo, covered in stony armored plates, and the other depicting a horned, winged, and four-legged dragon circled in lightning... Chloe leaned her face closer, looking at the vague diamond shape on its forehead beneath the thick layers of tarnish.

"These two I don't have a tested theory on yet, but this one," he pointed to the same dragon Chloe was focused on, "this one I may be getting close."

Chloe looked up, trying to steady her breathing. "Close to what?"

Dr. Liou was enjoying this. "Horned serpents were venerated across many Native American tribes. The Eastern Cherokee talked of an ancient beast they called Uktena, whose legend lived in the Smoky Mountains and later moved up the Shenandoah Valley toward central Virginia." He took a quick sip of water. "It was supposed to be a terrible creature that caused lightning storms when anyone approached it. They also said it had a shining diamond in its forehead, which was the source of vast wisdom but capable also of burning so brightly that it could blind those who saw it."

He shrugged. "My theory is still a little loose, but I think that maybe this Uktena could be the spirit dragon on the cauldron?"

Chloe fought to get what little saliva she could generate down her throat. "It's supposed to live in central Virginia?" she croaked.

Dr. Liou smiled. "It's part of the reason why I took the job here."

Maybe it'd be better if I was crazy? Chloe's heart was pounding so hard that she thought she might pass out. She had to tell him. Surely she wouldn't have accidentally run into the one man who actually knew something about the insanity she was experiencing if she wasn't also meant to bring him into her madness. "Dr. Liou, what if somehow the Tipping Point Prophecy is tru—"

It was then that Kirin waltzed around the corner, holding a couple cans of Dr. Pepper. "I had to go to three machines, but I found the Dr. Pepper!" he announced triumphantly just before he noticed Chloe sitting in front of his dad. "Chloe?"

Chloe lost her train of thought as her cheeks turned scarlet. "Oh! Liou…right." *I'm such an idiot!*

Kirin's face brightened with his disarming grin. "I would have gotten you a drink if I'd known you were coming."

"You two know each other?" Dr. Liou asked.

Kirin stepped in and handed his dad a can but didn't take his eyes off Chloe. "Yeah, Dad, this is my friend I've been telling you about—the girl who was struck by lightning."

"Really! You're *that* Chloe? I've heard a lot about you," Dr. Liou said with an unreadable expression.

Oh crap! He knows about skipping at the pond.

"Kirin said you were one of the most innately curious people he's ever met, and I can see now that your topics of interest are right up my alley." He smiled that same charming smile that ran in the family. The smile faded as he turned back to regard his son. "Now *you* can sit back down and return to your reading. Don't think I wasn't paying attention to how long it took for you to buy a couple sodas."

Kirin lowered his head and adopted an overdone hangdog expression as he shuffled to his chair in the corner. "Grounded again," he exhaled as he passed Chloe.

"Yes, Kirin decided it was a good idea to come home three hours past his curfew and blacked-out drunk on Friday night! So he'll be missing another three weeks of friends and phone calls until he can hopefully learn to focus and grow up a little bit," snapped Dr. Liou with a hard stare at his son.

"Gee, Dad, no Homecoming Dance for me. Major bummer," Kirin challenged.

Chloe felt immeasurably uncomfortable on so many levels. She couldn't bear to look at Kirin.

"Maybe you could take a page out of Chloe's book on proper ways to behave in high school," Dr. Liou suggested as Chloe furrowed her brow and winced. "At this rate, you're not going to get a chance to meet anyone else this year."

Yeah, except Cynthia 'Goddamned' Decareaux! Chloe suddenly found herself standing. She tightened the straps on her backpack until they dug painfully into her shoulders. "Thank you very much for talking to me, Dr. Liou!" she blurted.

"Really, call me Edward, and please stay. I could talk about this for hours if you were willing," said Dr. Liou, pretending Kirin wasn't in the corner.

"Sorry, I wish I could. I just realized what time it is." Chloe's eyes flitted about the room with no clocks in sight. "I have to get home to help my mom...bake a cake."

Both of the Lious stood at once.

"I hope we can talk again sometime soon," said Dr. Liou. "I'll let you know if this Uktena angle pans out for the fifth dragon."

"Thank you, and yes, please let me know what you find out," she said before forcing herself to turn and face Kirin behind her. She wanted to scream at him but smiled meekly instead. "See you at school tomorrow?"

"*Sorry*," Kirin mouthed before she turned and bolted out the door.

She stopped a few doors further down the hallway, panting hard, while trying to quell the multiple emotional tornadoes building within. She had not planned on still being in earshot of Dr. Liou's office.

"Thanks for making me look like an idiot in front of her, Dad!" shot Kirin in an emphatic whisper.

"Well, I can at least see why you like her," said Dr. Liou. "It's nice to know you haven't lost all sense of judgment since coming here!"

Chloe's heart lurched, and she took off toward the stairs. She did not bother to stop as Chet yelled for her to sign out. Despite her building fear that either she was heading toward a psychotic break or the world was heading toward its end, she couldn't help but feel the excited flutter of hope in her gut as she started the long journey home.

·   ·   ·

Ripples of electricity danced across the blue eyes that watched the girl from the shadows. The Fifth Claw of Typhon's Talon could smell the tension in her nerves and hear the flit of questions that played through her mind. She glanced back at the building she'd come from and then took off at a run. He would let her go for now.

He had already wiped her memory of his presence twice, but again she had unearthed his image from her subconscious. Now she'd found her way to this clever scholar who knew of the prophecy and the old names of the Five Claws. Tonight as the girl slept, the Lord of Lightning would cleanse her mind of her troublesome curiosity once more.

He shifted his piercing focus to the father and son arguing within. The boy did not belong here—this one was governed by the tides. He was at home only among the waves, yet he was drawn to the girl like a moth to flame, bound to her spark. And the father already knew too much, though he was not a believer. Perhaps if he came closer still, the Lightning Lord would need to make a meal out of him...For the meat he had been eating did not sit well in his belly. Fat, juicy cows that were too tempting to ignore, but once downed, something in the blood was making him weary and slow. These harvested beasts of men had become unnatural.

He turned his attention to the sky, blanketed with thick clouds above the trees, and listened to the dreams of his undying brethren. It would not be long now until the Ascension, when the others would rise and his power would bloom in full...He needed hold on for only that long.

CHAPTER 12
CHLOE'S BOYS

Chloe woke on Monday morning unable to fully remember much of what had happened at UVA, outside of the awkward meeting with Kirin's father, followed by the outright embarrassing run-in with Kirin himself. Oddly, she'd found it increasingly difficult to recall why she'd even gone there in the first place—something concerning mythology, the specifics of which she couldn't quite grasp. "Chinese...BLANK...and prophecies," she recalled asking Yvette, but for no discernible paper on her immediate academic horizon.

She assumed these memory gaps were the lingering result of the lightning strike, as Nurse Shiflet had warned, but she didn't want to burden her mom with that just yet. *Mom has enough on her plate; she doesn't need anything else to worry about—not when she's doing so well after the Brent incident.*

But what Chloe was really afraid of was that she might be slipping from reality, just like her father had... *Harvard scientists have now isolated and mapped a genetic link to schizophrenia.* That wasn't something Audrey would ever be able to take.

Instead, Chloe chose to focus on the last overheard exchange between the Lious. She played their hushed words over in her mind again and again; and for a few days, she'd convinced herself that, despite the age difference, maybe there really was a romantic possibility there. But after a week of building self-doubt, she had to acknowledge that they could have just as easily been talking about friendship. *I don't know what to believe anymore...*

Before high school, all of the drama and excitement that

surrounded Homecoming Dance had always seemed like an absurd cliché to Chloe. That being said, she was not surprised to find that most of her peers fell victim to the hullabaloo of expectation in the weeks that led up to the big night. What shocked her was how easily she herself fell into the trap.

Her idle thoughts hovered on tortured visions of Kirin making out with Cynthia on the dance floor. And she knew that the crimson demon, as Chloe had come to think of Kendra, wouldn't pass up a chance to seek her revenge at the upcoming public forum. But despite it all, and against everything Chloe had ever believed, she found herself imagining a storybook scenario in which Kirin would ask her to accompany him and then the various dresses she might wear.

She knew how pathetic this was, as she was reminded every day in homeroom that he was strictly grounded for the two weeks that led up to the dance as well as the one that followed. And at lunch, she was made painfully aware that even if he were allowed his freedom, he would quite possibly skip the public charade to go somewhere private with Cynthia instead.

Though Kirin seemed a bit more standoffish around Cynthia since the party, Chloe could not help but spy the heated glances she still cast his way, or the reddening of his cheeks and embarrassed aversion of his eyes when he felt those looks upon him. He'd become more reserved with Chloe as well, and now that Cynthia and/or Stan often joined them in the back of The Cave, she felt wholly deprived of the authentic connection she'd previously felt between them.

And so Chloe continued her routine: paying attention in school, running as fast as she could after her classes, and studying with laser-like focus at night. Ezra had forgiven her for disappearing at the party, but he'd also stopped training with her twice a week since the football season had kicked in. Other than their occasional greetings in the hallway or parking lot, she didn't see him at all anymore, and she missed the confident edge he gave her and the sense of grounding he brought to her foolish internal ramblings.

Now all she had to rely on was the devoted but flighty

attention from Stan and a renewed and relentless interest in her perpetually stalled love life from Liz.

· · ·

Chloe sat at the back corner desk of her homeroom class, doodling over a diamond shape in the margin of her notebook. Beside it was a handwritten date: *Thursday, October 16th*, and beneath that, the chicken-scratch words: *Homecoming Dance this weekend. Headaches coming soon ... Something not right?*

She looked up to catch a smile from Liz as she waltzed in wearing what had to be the tightest and skinniest jeans that would still allow movement. Liz lowered herself into the desk in front of Chloe, beaming, like there was nowhere in the world she'd rather be. Chloe didn't understand how she did it—day after day of bubbly cheer, though it was clearly tied directly to her relationship status with Paul Markson. Things had been good now for "almost two whole weeks!"

Chloe watched as Liz busied with her backpack and put her iPad on her desk. No books, pen, or paper, just the iPad, and Liz's was one of about twelve that Chloe counted around the room. Chloe drummed her fingers on her textbook.

Try unplugging once in a while to read a damn book, people! In truth, Chloe would have loved an iPad of her own; only there was no way she could afford one.

Liz spun around and hunkered down with a twinkle in her eye. "You should ask," she motioned with her head toward Kirin's empty desk, "to the dance today," she said.

"Not gonna happen. He's still grounded," Chloe whispered in an effort to silence her. It didn't work.

"Ask him anyway," Liz shot back with a mischievous smile. "At least then he'll know that you're thinking about him."

Chloe tried to shush her and glanced around to see if anyone was listening. "That's weird! Now drop it!" she hissed, which only made Liz giggle like an imp.

"The fearless Chloe McClellan, crippled with fear," she teased.

The lead on Chloe's mechanical pencil snapped off on the fifty-seventh trace of the diamond. "I never claimed to be fearless," she muttered, just as Kirin sauntered in with a head of hair unaltered from the pillow. Chloe found it annoyingly cute and averted her eyes, focusing on her diamond-doodle like it was a puzzle that demanded utmost concentration.

Kirin slid into the seat beside her with a sly sideways glance. He pretended to ignore her as he unpacked his things and then leaned over to get a better view of her scribble. "That's some impressive design work you've got going there."

"Pipe down; I'm trying to focus," she retorted without ever looking up.

Liz slowly turned back toward the front with a goofy grin.

"My dad was asking about you last night," said Kirin. "I guess you made an impression. He wants to talk to you some more about his old cauldron."

"Oh, yeah?" Chloe asked, realizing only then that she wasn't really sure what he was talking about. Mr. Jacobson shuffled in with a waft of cigarette stink and his trademark pit stains.

"Something about the fifth dragon; he said you'd know what that means."

Do I know what that means? It sounded familiar, but just out of reach. Was it something important? Chloe's hand froze halfway around another pass at the diamond, and she put the pencil down. "Maybe I could stop by his office hours again on Sunday?"

"Yes, please!" blurted Kirin. "I could use the company; I mean, how many more books can I read before I go batshit?"

I wonder if we like the same books... And just like that, thoughts of the fifth dragon had vanished again.

"Sunday morning, though?" Kirin probed. "Aren't you going to be all tuckered out from the big dance?"

"Do I really seem like the big dance type?" Chloe challenged with a little smirk.

Kirin shrugged with a curious glance. "I don't know, I thought maybe you'd go if Stan or maybe Ezra Richardson asked?"

Is he fishing for something? Chloe felt a little flushed but forced herself to laugh. "Stan and I are just buddies, and Ezra Richardson will probably arrive in a chariot carried by his adoring fan club. It's not really my thing," she stated as Mr. Jacobson started to scroll notes about the Louisiana Purchase across the board.

"Oh...good." Kirin turned sideways to face her. "I tried to convince my dad to let me go if you'd go with me. He almost caved, but still said no...I'm kind of glad that you wouldn't have gone anyway."

Liz visibly tensed in front of them.

"You wanted to go to Homecoming?" she asked, deciding to leave the more-to-the-point *"with me"* off the end.

"We've been in school for seven weeks, and I've been on house arrest for five of them—I would love to go to Homecoming!" he answered.

Chloe tried to stop her brain from sending the message to speak, but by the time she got the message, her mouth was already talking. "What about Cynthia?" she asked, realizing in that moment that Kirin had never mentioned what had happened at the party and she had never admitted that she had been there to see it firsthand.

"What about her?" he countered a little defensively.

Chloe was flustered. "I don't know; it just seemed like you guys might kind of...I don't know?"

Kirin recovered. "I'm pretty sure my dad wouldn't have approved of Cynthia," he said before turning toward Mr. Jacobson and leaving Chloe to mull over the meaning of that one.

The bell rang and the conversations petered out across the room. Chloe could feel Liz listening, and she wanted desperately to say the thing that her old friend was waiting to hear. She wanted to tell him that she would have loved to go to the dance with him. She wanted to say that she wanted to ask him herself. She wanted to say a lot of things in that moment...but she didn't.

· · ·

Chloe scooted down the hallway, trying to avoid eye contact with everybody she passed. Most were happy to ignore her; others looked closely, trying to place where they'd seen her before. But with her hair back in a ponytail and her face out from beneath the mud, she hardly looked anything like the increasingly infamous Lightning Girl.

Word about her public dressing down of Kendra had spread among certain crowds, and she walked from point to point on school grounds with the perpetual feeling that she had a big target on her back. She dropped her eyes to the floor as a trio of junior jocks came hooting down the hallway. They kicked a ball made of crumpled paper and masking tape between them with little regard to anyone in their way. Chloe dodged a wild pass and narrowly avoided the pursuing charge of a square-jawed boy with a white baseball hat on backward. In her internal ramblings, she'd begun to refer to the whole extended soccer and football family as the White Hats.

Kendra herself had taken to wearing a white cap blazoned with the Charlottesville High Black Knights logo to tamp down the wavy plume of her red locks. Chloe's keen eye, trained to pick out any warning flutter of red from a distance, now had to readjust to the possible dangers of white-crowned movement in her peripheral vision.

She walked the halls like some sort of prey animal, trying to appear calm and at home in her surroundings while her eyes darted this way and that with the smallest provocation. In gym class, Kendra hadn't even looked at her in almost two weeks, but Chloe could feel the smoldering heat of her presence at all times. Just making it through the school day without incident was kind of like juggling balloons of gunpowder and gasoline over a bed of coals.

Despite her vigilance, she failed to notice as Stan moved to intercept her path. She stepped into a face full of stale jean jacket and patchouli oil. "Hey, dude!" alerted Stan too late.

Chloe stumbled back with a yelp. "You might want to wash that jacket," she muttered with a pinched face. "Smells like it hasn't been washed since the sixties."

Stan grinned with a large piece of lettuce stuck in his teeth. "It was my dad's," he admitted proudly. "It probably hasn't."

Chloe looked at his eyes and shook her head—bloodshot as always. "Are you high in school?" she whispered.

He shrugged. "Isn't that why they call it high school?"

"That's kind of sad," Chloe admonished. "You're pretty smart, but at this rate, you're gonna stunt your growth and be rendered a clinical idiot before you graduate."

Stan only chuckled. "So, you going to Homecoming on Saturday?" He flared his red eyes with mock enthusiasm.

"Why does everyone keep asking me that?" she blurted defensively. "No, I'm not going! It's a totally stupid event, designed to reinforce stereotypes of social hierarchy among an already insecure and vulnerable populace. Even if I had someone to go with, I would boycott on general principle!"

"You want to go with me?" Stan asked, undeterred by her impromptu rant. "We could get dressed up and go make fun of everyone. I went last year with Brian, and it was actually really fun."

They started walking together through the throng, Chloe toward her next class and Stan away from his.

Chloe sensed the unspoken hurt behind Stan's momentary silence. "What's Brian doing this year?" she asked.

"He's going with that girl Rosalie, you know, from the party." Stan shrugged. "But I'd rather go with you anyway, and I'm sure it would thrill my mom to no end."

"Who's Cynthia going with?" Chloe asked.

Now it was Stan who sensed the question behind Chloe's question. "She's skipping it to go to a UVA party with some dude she's seeing there. Apparently Kirin hasn't been all that receptive to her advances since the party. Cynthia likes a sure thing, and Kirin was moving too slow for her." He winked.

"You mean they didn't...you know?" Chloe's voice had involuntarily gone up a few octaves.

Stan shook his head. "Nope."

Chloe couldn't help it; she was red-faced and even a little teary with relief. *How embarrassing!*

"So, what do you say, dude?" Stan stopped to face her. "Would you do me the honor of helping me convince my parents that I'm *normal* while having a kick-ass good time in the process?"

Chloe couldn't help but smile. "The honor would be all mine," she surrendered, "but under one condition."

"Name it, Lightning Girl!"

"No weed smoking," she challenged.

Stan winced with a big exhale of stale air. "Dude, you play mean...but okay, I'm in. No smoking." He offered his sweaty hand with the big grin returned, and they shook on it.

"And clean that lettuce out of your teeth," Chloe added with a sly smirk. "That'll be totally rancid by Saturday night."

. . .

It wasn't until after cross-country practice that day that Chloe finally ran into Ezra, freshly showered and looking magnificent as always as he exited the men's locker room. He cupped a hand to his mouth to make sure his ensuing bellows would be heard.

"LG in the house!" His words echoed down the hallway, and a number of people turned to look, much to Chloe's dismay. "My girl's looking primed and hungry to tear up the field in that district championship tomorrow!" He met Chloe in a half-awkward fist bump, which he embellished with an explosion noise. "I'm thinking it's time you quit holding back and take first place; show these crusty old biddies what a fresh young speed demon really looks like."

Chloe shot him a pipe-down look. "You're in rare form today. Not even a little nervous about facing the dreaded Monticello Dragons on your home turf Saturday?"

"No, ma'am, I'm gonna own that field!" Ezra declared for all in earshot to hear. "When I was a sophomore, our team sucked plenty, but not anymore! Now I'm king! I figure the worst thing that might happen is we don't beat those fools bad enough that they feel embarrassed to wake up on Sunday!" He closed his eyes, tilted his head back, and opened his arms in victory.

For a moment, Chloe could almost hear the screams of the adoring crowd. She laughed as Ezra opened one eye, checked both ways, and leaned in close. "Actually, I'm nervous as hell, but if I get a couple good nights' rest, eat right, and keep my focus, I think we can take 'em," he whispered.

"I have total faith in you, King Ezra the First," she said with a mock bow. "And what lucky lady will have the honor of being your queen Saturday night?"

"Homecoming Queen? We'll just have to wait and see," he answered. "Probably whoever's been campaigning the hardest for votes—Charlene or Samantha?" He hooked a thumb toward a couple of makeshift posters on the wall, advertising various junior and senior girls whose popularity score was publicly on the line. Chloe read the closest banner—complete with multicolored, stenciled letters and half a tub of glitter: *BRING IT HOME FOR SAMANTHA BROWN, SHES GOT IT ALL BUT THAT GOLDEN CROWN.*

Chloe could only hide her face in her hands and shake her head.

"Or maybe some dark horse candidate with a groundswell of support behind her," he added cryptically with a sly smile. "You never know…As for my Homecoming concubine, however," Ezra continued, "I had to dip into your class to find someone new."

Chloe tensed and peered up at him from between her fingers. "No."

"This year I've found me a red-haired vixen who would not be denied!"

"No," she repeated at a whisper.

"I know what you're thinking, but trust me: my girl Kendra is on FIRE!"

"You didn't." Chloe felt like she might throw up.

"I didn't do anything yet," he defended.

"Don't do this," begged Chloe. "You could go with anybody; ask someone your own age."

"I've already been through everyone my own age, and plus, she asked me!" Ezra was smiling, but was clearly a little taken off guard by the vehemence of Chloe's horror. "What's the big deal? I'll be a gentleman."

"She's only fifteen, and she's a complete asshole!" Chloe whispered.

"Actually, she turns sixteen tomorrow, and have you seen her?" He was nodding. "There is nothing too young about that; she looks like a Victoria's Secret model!"

"You're disgusting!" Chloe snapped.

Ezra looked a little hurt. "You're jealous."

Chloe couldn't even look him in the eye. "No, it's just that most guys act nice but are secretly jerks, whereas you act like a jerk but are secretly nice...Except when you do stupid, stereotypical jock things like ask the biggest underage bitch in school to boost your already out-of-control reputation," she hissed.

"Jesus, Lightning, what's crawled up your butt?"

"Whatever," she said, marching past him toward the long bus ride and walk home. "Good luck with your STD-laden future."

"Come on, Lightning, don't run away again," he called after her. "I can give you a ride home."

She kept on walking.

"Chloe!" he tried one last time behind her, but she was deaf to all but the buzz of anger that filled her ears. Finally she understood why Kendra hadn't retaliated before now...Though she didn't want to admit it, Ezra was right—she was jealous.

CHAPTER 13
THE PREAMBLE SCRAMBLE

Ezra was right about another thing, too—fueled by all her rage and confusion, Chloe was a monster at the district championships on Saturday morning. She didn't win the race, coming in second place to Angela, the fastest senior girl on her own team. But with her "gutsy and bold" performance, Chloe had proven that she was one of the most important girls on the varsity squad and that she could have a real shot at one day becoming the fastest long distance girl in the state.

To her knowledge, Chloe was one of only six incoming tenth graders who had made it onto varsity sports teams in the first semester, though she was loathe to qualify Kendra's coup at making the varsity field hockey squad—after her father's generous donation to the booster's program—as equivalent to achievement in sport. Regardless, despite Chloe's designs on quiet anonymity, she'd once again done something newsworthy that would spread fast and only increase the notoriety of the elusive Lightning Girl. For some annoying reason, she just couldn't stop herself from living loud and large at every turn. And now she was preparing to go back into the belly of the beast.

She looked at herself in the full-length mirror on her mom's closet door and sighed heavily.

"What's wrong with this one?" challenged Audrey. "You look adorable!"

Chloe stared at the purple satin and chiffon dress, trying not to make eye contact with the spindly little girl who was wearing it. "I look like a flower girl at an eighties-themed wedding."

"You're incorrigible, you know that?" said Audrey before

delving back into her overstuffed closet. "You've looked good in every one of these."

Chloe glanced over to the three discarded dresses already tossed recklessly on the bed and grimaced at the memory of the way she looked in each. The first was a yellow floral-patterned assault on the senses, the second an ultra low-cut evening gown monstrosity, and the third an oversized smock dress that made her look like she was wearing a Snuggie.

"I'm not even going with a real date," she reminded her mom. "Can't I just wear some nice pants and a button-down or something?"

"No," Audrey's muffled voice carried from deep within the closet. "I've got something for you in here."

"Seriously, Mom, what's the point?" Chloe protested. "I don't have anyone to look good for. I would've skipped the whole stupid thing if Stan hadn't needed my support." She yanked off the purple dress and tossed it toward the bed. Beneath she had on her typically underwhelming underwear that Audrey had picked up in a four-pack from Target. This time, the reflection in the mirror stared back with open disdain.

Audrey emerged from the closet with a dusty dress box and lint in her hair. "This is the one I was looking for," she declared with a knowing smile. "This is what you're wearing tonight."

"You sound pretty sure of yourself," Chloe muttered as she hunched her shoulders.

"Yes, I am," answered Audrey as she placed the box on the bed and reverently opened the lid. She smiled as she removed a vintage, though understated, A-line, dyed a rich, dark green. "I wore this when I was just a little younger than you are now," she said.

She stepped over to Chloe and held the dress up to her back. "It was a Junior Assembly dance in the eighth grade, and for the first time in my life, I felt beautiful." She reached over Chloe's shoulders and held the dress up in front of the mirror.

Chloe had to admit the dress was gorgeous and exactly her size.

"I didn't wear it for anybody else but myself that night. I

looked good just for me," said Audrey. "But you know what? It was only once *I* realized that I could be beautiful that anyone else took notice."

"News flash, Mom: I don't look like you. Believe me, I wish I did, but I'm not the girl who gets noticed that way."

Audrey ignored her as she pulled the dress over Chloe's head without asking. "I'm telling you, honey, you've got everything going for you, and the only one who isn't impressed yet is yourself. Why else do you think you have a cute surfer from California, the star quarterback with a killer smile, and now this new hippie kid all circling for your attention?"

"One of them is grounded so often that he can't make any other friends, one is fawned over so much that he has no one else to see through his BS, and Stan is too confused and terrified to let anyone else in on his secret."

Audrey threaded Chloe's arms through the holes and pulled the dress into place, tying the waistline into a thin bow at her back and tugging out a couple of kinks in the skirt. It reminded them both of the way that Audrey had dressed Chloe as a child and filled them both with unspoken contentedness. Next Audrey grabbed a brush and started in on Chloe's tangle of hair. Something about the methodical working of the teeth through her locks robbed Chloe of her intent to protest further.

The dress fit perfectly, and Chloe turned her head slightly to get a better look, noticing the little victorious smirk on her mom's face. The satin band cinched at Chloe's slim waist made her well-defined shoulder line pop, and the high bust line was countered by a sexy crisscross of straps that ran down the back. The skirt flared perfectly in delicate, overlapping layers of silk that masked Chloe's spindly legs, but not so much that it looked overdone or impeded her easy movement.

With her hair brushed out and the intricate silver bracelet that had been her grandmother's clasped at her wrist, Chloe had to admit that she looked pretty good.

"See," said Audrey, going for her long-unused makeup kit.

For once, Chloe had no ready retort, unable to suppress the stir of excitement that the image in the mirror brought out of her. Audrey returned with a dab of rouge for both cheeks, which she worked in gently with her finger. Chloe shut her eyes and relished the feel of her mom's calloused, capable hands. She stood at silent attention as Audrey moved in with a little eyeliner and a few gentle strokes of mascara and lipstick.

"Now open your eyes and take notice of the gorgeous young woman in the mirror," Audrey commanded from behind her.

Chloe did as she was told and added a little more natural red to the makeup on her cheeks. She doubted she had ever looked so good in her life, and the long imprisoned girly girl inside her blinked into the sunlight.

"I guarantee that when you walk into that dance tonight, every guy there is going to notice you, too," added Audrey with an impromptu kiss at Chloe's ear. Chloe caught her mother's proud gaze in the mirror, and both were glassy-eyed and swelling with emotion in an instant.

"I'm sorry I couldn't get you a new dress, honey. That's what you deserve," said Audrey with a tear spilling down her cheek.

"No, Mom. It's perfect," Chloe said, trying not to unleash a flow that would ruin her makeup. She stared at the ceiling and exhaled dramatically.

As Audrey delved back into the closet for matching shoes, Chloe turned to admire her back in the mirror, standing on her toes and looking at the curve of her butt through the fabric. Once Audrey was completely buried in the closet, Chloe even allowed herself a quick spin, just to see how the skirt flared midtwirl.

I'm making this too easy on her. "Hey, Mom, don't bother," she said. "I'm just gonna wear my Chucks."

Audrey emerged from the closet with wide eyes and flaring nostrils before Chloe broke into a giggle.

.   .   .

Despite the peep-toe heels, Chloe bounded down the stairs two at a time.

"You're going to twist an ankle!" Audrey warned from her bedroom.

Chloe ignored her, leaping to the foyer with a little wobble and a smile. She was feeling less apprehensive about the costumed role she'd agreed to play that night and had even consented to getting dropped off at Stan's house so that she might do her part to sell his false heterosexuality to his parents before the mortifying main-stage event.

Shipwreck was watching from the back of the sofa with a look that said, *and what are you supposed to be?* The cat had kept an uncharacteristic distance for several weeks.

Chloe gave him a spin. "Hey, buddy, how do I look?"

He just stared, then yawned.

"Who asked you, anyway?" she challenged before heading out the back door. Audrey had to get ready for the night shift at Pete's, and Chloe wanted to take a quick head-clearing walk around the bend before it was time to begin the torture.

It felt oddly liberating to be walking out in the sunlight for anyone to see her in the fancy getup. It was almost like Halloween, her favorite holiday.

She looked back to see Shipwreck slink out of his cat door and start following in feline stealth mode. Ever since she'd nursed him back to health, he'd been a little less graceful than he thought he was. He hunkered among some spindly weeds by the barn and tracked her movement as if he were stalking her from a point of total concealment.

Chloe rolled her eyes and headed for the street, wanting to get a better feel for the uncomfortable footwear before she'd have to make a public show of it. She brushed a wayward strand of hair from her face as she stared along the pavement with a little extra sway to her step. Ahead, the streetlight came into view from around the curve in the road—something about it drew her forward.

She stopped beneath the pole and stared up at the pristine metal of the arching lamp arm—not a speck of bird crap or graffiti in sight. Littered in the grass around the base, she found shards of plastic from what might have been a shattered bulb cover, but she couldn't be sure. She glanced around to catch Shipwreck's question mark tail following through the tall grass by the storm drain, but her attention was drawn across the street toward the little pull-off beside the trailhead.

There, beneath the dappled shadows, the pavement was gouged and cracked. She crossed and knelt to examine a series of marks that tore at least six inches deep into the concrete. They looked like puncture holes...Chloe moved to a large rock by the side of the road and climbed up to get a better vantage. Her heels wobbled on the uneven surface, but from above, the pattern was instantly recognizable as animal footprints.

She'd once spent an autumn tracking and sketching various animal prints throughout the woods along the trail. But then she had been following raccoon and deer tracks over muddy and moss-covered ground and not what appeared to be some giant thing across pavement.

Each print had five thick, hooking claws. The last set, closest to the center of the street, was surrounded by spiderweb impact cracks in the pavement. Recognition stirred from deep within her subconscious. *Five claws, just like Dr. Liou said...*

Curiosity took control. She hastily jumped down and followed the prints back toward the woods. The same pattern of deep gouges in the gravel ran along the side of the road and then again through the leaves and dirt at the edge of the trees. A large patch of bark was shorn from the trunk of an oak about ten feet up and then again on an elm, where scrapes of blonde, sap-covered wood had been exposed.

Chloe stepped to the rough terrain at the forest's edge and grabbed a tree branch to keep from toppling over. She was reaching down to unbuckle her shoes, when she sensed a large form in the street behind her. She spun quickly with a feral yell, only to snap her mouth shut as Kirin's eyes went wide from within his familiar Grand Wagoneer.

Chloe righted herself awkwardly and smoothed back her hair as Kirin lowered the passenger side window and raised a quizzical eyebrow.

"Sorry, I didn't mean to startle you. I was just driving by and...what are you doing?" he asked with a smile tugging at the corners of his mouth.

What am I doing? "I was just...looking for my cat?" she offered with more of a question than she'd intended.

Kirin looked across the street and pointed to where Shipwreck was sniffing around the base of the streetlight. "Is that him?" he asked as Shipwreck stiffened and met Chloe's gaze from across the street. The cat took off like a bolt back toward the house before Chloe could respond.

Typical. "Yeah, that's him," she responded, stepping closer to the Jeep and suddenly starting to feel self-conscious about the outfit.

"I think he's getting away," he joked, though he was staring at her intently.

She swallowed. "It's okay, he's headed home; I live right around the corner."

Kirin's eyes drifted down her body in a way that sent a tickle up Chloe's spine. "I thought you didn't believe in going to Homecoming?" he added quietly.

"I don't," she blurted, "It's just that I'm doing Stan a favor by going."

"Oh, wow, to what does the lucky Stan owe this great honor of your presence?"

"I didn't mean it like that!" Chloe was flustered. "It's just that he likes someone else and wants to go to save face or something, and he asked if we could go as friends."

Kirin laughed and put up his hand to silence her. He reached across the seats and opened the passenger door for her. "Get in, I'll drive you home."

"I live right there," she said.

"I know, but it looks like you're having trouble in those heels, and I came here hoping to find you, though I wasn't expecting...this." His cheeks turned a little red and he looked back at the road.

Chloe climbed in and slammed the door a little too hard, hearing Liz's voice in her head, counseling her to flaunt the natural curve of her back and accentuate her butt. Instead, she shifted uncomfortably in the seat and felt the exposed skin between crisscrossing straps stick to the faux leather of the seatback. She, too, stared straight ahead.

Kirin glanced over, like he was going to say something, but then he switched gears into 'DRIVE' and started to roll.

"Wait!" blurted Chloe, bringing them to an abrupt stop.

"What?"

Chloe pointed at one of the giant five-clawed prints in the road before them, needing a final confirmation that what she saw was really there. "What does that look like to you?"

Kirin stared at the pavement for a long moment as Chloe held her breath. "What, you mean the holes in the road?"

"Yes."

"I don't know." Kirin seemed genuinely baffled. "A dinosaur crossing?" he suggested.

Chloe exhaled slowly. "That's what I thought, too…kind of weird, right?"

Kirin chuckled. "Hey, maybe it's one of my dad's dragons?"

A shudder passed through Chloe, and she started to laugh nervously. Kirin was looking right at her, and she immediately lost the nerve to delve any further into that subject. "How are you out and about anyway?" she diverted. "I thought you were under house arrest for another week."

The Jeep started to roll again, and in moments, Chloe's house came into view. She could see Audrey bustling about the back of the Honda CR-V, now wearing the dress whites of Positive Pete's.

"My dad let me out to buy groceries for a mandatory father/son barbecue tonight, and I'm taking the long way around." He snuck another glance at Chloe out of the corner of his eye. "How are you getting to the dance anyway? Is Stan picking you up? I heard his van got pretty messed up a couple weeks ago."

Chloe wondered how much of that story Kirin might have heard. "He's going to borrow his dad's car, but my mom is dropping me off at his house first. He wants me to play it up a bit in front of his parents or something."

Without needing direction, Kirin steered the Grand Wagoneer into the leisurely turn from the road and bumped down into the gravel driveway toward Audrey and the CR-

V. Chloe met her mother's gaze through the windshield and watched as her initial confusion at the Jeep's arrival gave way to a little smile.

"That must be your mom," he said as he turned off the ignition. "She looks just like you." He got out without prompting and walked toward Audrey, extending his hand for a shake.

Yeah, right! I wish. Chloe scrambled to catch up.

"Sorry to barge in, Ms. McClellan. I just found Chloe walking through the woods in a cocktail dress and thought I'd bring her home." He and Audrey shook hands. "I'm Kirin Liou, a friend of Chloe's from school."

"Oh, I know who you are, Mr. Liou," Audrey said playfully. "You're the one who got my daughter to cut class for the first time in her life."

Chloe shot her mom a look of warning. Audrey laughed.

Kirin responded with a guilty but charming shrug. "Yes, that was me. But I want you to know that after countless hours of grounding, I have seen the error of my ways and reapplied myself to my studies," he declared with a mischievous smirk.

"I hope not," said Audrey. "Chloe could use a little more reckless fun in her schedule," she added with a conspiratorial whisper.

Kirin broke into his disarming laugh, and Chloe could see that he'd won over her mom then and there. "I'll see what I can do."

"Well, it was very nice to finally meet you, Kirin. I've certainly heard a lot about you." She turned to see Chloe wince—already aware what her mother was about to say. "And I really hate to cut this short, but unfortunately, I have to get to work soon. Honey, you about ready to go face the music?"

Kirin spoke up. "I could drop her off at Stan's if that would be any help. I'm headed that way, and this is probably the only nonfamilial human interaction I'll get all weekend."

Audrey glanced back to Chloe with big eyes and registered her daughter's faint nod. "Yes, that would be very helpful," she said. "You see, honey, maybe you should dress up more often?"

. . .

They drove down the winding street above Charlottesville in relative silence. Chloe held the Googled directions to Stan's house, and her voice called out the first turn with focused purpose, but her stomach was buzzing with a nervous spark.

Kirin's fingers thrummed an anxious rhythm against the top rim of the steering wheel. He tried to focus on the twisting road, but Chloe could feel his glances out of the corner of his eye. The air between them seemed to vibrate as the Jeep came to a trembling stop at the first traffic light. There were no other cars in sight, and the first few seconds ticked by like minutes.

"I'm really glad I found you," Kirin said, breaking the expectant silence. "My uncle located my grandmother—just today, in a makeshift shelter in Xining." His smile was genuine and full of relief. "She's banged up and hungry, but otherwise okay."

"Oh my god, Kirin, that's amazing." Before she knew it, Chloe found her arms wrapped around him and her face pressed into his shoulder. He smelled like the beach in summertime, and the little spark in her gut instantly spread throughout her extremities.

Thankfully, he let go of the wheel and hugged her back, with his cheek tucked in to the top of her head, and his hands pressed to the spaces between the straps at her back. She was keenly aware of her own skin, appreciative of its existence in a way she'd not known before. The delicate tickle of a static charge gathered in his jacket and her hair.

The curt blast of a car horn ruined the moment, and they disengaged with matching self-conscious looks. Together they glanced to the impatient man in the pick-up truck behind them, and then to the waiting green light ahead.

Kirin straightened with a chuckle and drove through the intersection into a more residential neighborhood. "My father is trying to work it out so that she can come here and live with us for a while until the region stabilizes a bit."

"I'm so happy for you," Chloe said. "It must be such a relief."

"Yeah, we're celebrating tonight, but you were the first person I wanted to tell…I feel like we haven't gotten a chance to really talk in a while."

"Me too," she said. "I've missed talking to you."

"Me too." His eyes met hers for just a second before returning to the road, but there was a lot of look in that moment.

Chloe focused back on the directions. "Take a left at Vanderbilt."

"I was wondering, have you been back to the pond since we went?" he asked mid-turn.

"No," Chloe answered, feeling the loss of her favorite place more acutely by acknowledging it. "Ever since cross-country started, I haven't been able to find the time to do much of anything, let alone extra running in the woods."

"It's too bad," said Kirin. "I only went there that once, but for some reason I find myself thinking about it sometimes. I even tried to find it once on my own, but got turned around in the trees and had to backtrack my way out of there," he admitted.

"Really? You should have called me; I would have shown you."

"No, I mean it's too bad that *you* haven't been back," he amended. "I feel like that's *your* spot, you know—your secret place where the weather changes and the animals gather just for you…I kind of had a spot like that in Santa Cruz, a certain wave break that only I and a couple others knew about, where things just seemed to happen for me, you know?"

He looked at her for a moment and then back to the road. "It's what I miss most about California. I kind of feel like I betrayed that spot in the ocean, or maybe I betrayed myself by leaving." He smiled, trying to diffuse the seriousness of his words in case she thought it was weird. "I just feel like you shouldn't make that same mistake, just because it's scary or because strange things happen when you're there. Maybe that's the land trying to talk to you?"

Chloe was quiet for a long moment, trying to wrap her head around the perfection of what he'd said. "Thanks, Kirin."

"I still dream about that spot in the ocean almost every

157

night, but the last time I went surfing there I was bumped by a pretty big shark, and I totally lost my nerve to go back for the last couple months we were there. It's my biggest regret."

"I'm not sure I would ever go into the ocean again after that," Chloe admitted with wide eyes before looking back at the directions. "Turn right at the stop sign. It'll be the third house from the corner."

Kirin turned. "Why not? The shark was at home, more at home than I was there, and it came up to say hello. I feel like it was just acknowledging my presence, maybe even welcoming me, and yet I reacted with fear. Now in my dreams, I think it's trying to talk to me, and I can almost understand what it's saying, right up until I wake up."

He pulled up in front of a modest ranch house in need of a paint job and put the Jeep into 'PARK' behind Stan's battered van. A Volvo station wagon with a Charlottesville High School sticker occupied the driveway.

"Thanks for the ride," said Chloe. "I'm so happy that your grandmother is okay."

"Thanks," said Kirin, clearly wanting to say something more. He turned toward her with a noticeable swallow. "My uncle finally made it to her street the night of that party at Paul Markson's house a couple weeks ago—her whole block was completely destroyed, and things didn't look good…I was pretty upset, and I went overboard with the drinking and stuff. I'm not sure what you heard about all that, but I kind of got myself into a stupid situation…with Cynthia…that I'm not too proud of."

Chloe shrugged and feigned ignorance, though her face felt like it was throbbing. "Oh," she whispered.

"I just wanted you to know that, in case Stan or someone told you something about it," he added nervously, looking away.

Chloe's heart felt like it might explode out of her chest. She glanced at Stan's house and wished she could tell Kirin to keep on driving.

"And you know, I'm serious about what I said earlier. Stan is really lucky; you look amazing."

They stared at each other with hushed expectation, and

Chloe felt a building swell of courage. Before she knew what she was doing, she reached over and put her hand on top of his. His skin was cool as he moved to entwine her fingers with his own.

Bold, alien words started spilling out of Chloe's mouth. "You always look amazing," she mumbled to herself, but out loud. "I think you're probably the coolest person I've ever met, and just so you know, if your dad had allowed it, I would have much rather gone to this stupid dance with you."

This time it was Kirin's turn to get a little red in the cheeks, but then, as always, he broke the tension perfectly with a smile. "I would have liked that," he said. "How about next time?"

"I don't know; you think you can stay out of trouble that long?" she challenged.

He raised her hand and brushed his lips over the back of her knuckles, and somehow it wasn't cheesy or forced—it was perfect. "I make no promises, but I'm sure as hell gonna try." He released her hand, just as Stan came to the front door of his house in a seventies-style light blue tuxedo and waved.

"Oh, boy," said Chloe as she saw him. Reluctantly she opened the car door.

"I'm living vicariously through you, so have fun tonight," said Kirin with a gentle nudge at her back. "Call me tomorrow if you get a chance. I want all the gruesome details."

Chloe looked back, swallowing the urge to cry, cackle, and scream all at once. "Bye."

He nodded as she closed the door, and he honked the horn as he pulled away from the curb and proceeded up the road. Chloe turned back to face Stan, who pumped his eyebrows in acknowledgment of what he thought he'd seen. His huge, horsey grin followed an instant later.

Without thinking, she raised her hand to her face. It tingled as if mentholated. *Oh my God, I think I just told Kirin that I like him!* Chloe was practically bouncing as she headed toward the event she'd been dreading all day.

CHAPTER 14
THE KING AND THE FOOL

The smile that Chloe had been wearing naturally for more than an hour faded as she stepped into the strobe-lit school gym. She'd even managed to maintain the natural grin, without too much effort, through a prolonged picture-taking session by Stan's father—posed in front of the azalea bushes in the front yard with Stan's arm entwined in hers and an absurd corsage pinned to the strap of her dress.

Any other day and she would have had the same pinched, uncomfortable expression that found its way to her face in most every other photo ever taken of her, but the timing of Mr. Strakowski's digital assault could not have been better. Chloe left Stan's parents believing that their goofy son had landed the most radiant young girl they'd ever met.

Now the flame of Chloe's cheer was quickly suffocating as her eyes drifted across the sea of entwined couples that covered the basketball court in some sort of slow jam nightmare. "Stan, let's go see a movie or something," she suggested.

Stan's toothy smirk kept on gleaming in the dark. "No way, dude, this is gonna be fuuun!"

Chloe couldn't tell if he was actually being serious or if he somehow reveled in the misery of adolescence.

He nodded his chin in the direction of the bleachers. "Come on, let's get something to drink and then get a good seat." He offered his arm to Chloe, and she took it with a theatrical roll of her eyes. "My date is hawt!" he proclaimed for no one but her to hear. She couldn't help but smile along with his absurd glee in the face of such horrors.

Still, Chloe kept her head down as they skirted along the sidelines of the basketball court. They wound their way through the mass of milling bodies that stood on the shore while the sea of slow-dancing couples clustered beneath the giant, dangling disco ball at center court. Kids were dressed to the nines: suits and even some tuxedos for the boys and the full array of cocktail dresses, from slutty to classy, for the girls.

Chloe glimpsed Liz and Paul locked in a slowly rocking embrace near the three-point line. Liz looked beautiful in a long, black dress that showed a lot of back and just enough cleavage to keep Paul's attention and attract the occasional glances from a number of the other boys around them. Chloe was strangely happy to see her old friend nestled so contentedly into the crook of Paul's shoulder.

At the other end of the gym, a cheesy deejay with overdone sideburns and a well-trimmed mullet grooved his big head to the tune on a stage set up beneath the basket. Chloe's eyes were drawn for a moment to the gold plastic Homecoming crowns, positioned on a red felt pedestal beneath a spotlight. "Oh, boy, this is going to be painful," she whispered.

Stan pulled her hand toward a long table draped in a white cloth that was already stained with numerous pink spills. A sign read *"EXOTIC PUNCH."* Getting closer to the three big bowls of sugary goodness, Chloe could see a caterer replenishing the contents with two gallon jugs of ginger ale and fruit punch, and an entire carton of rainbow sherbet—the "exotic" special ingredient.

Undaunted, Stan slid right up to the table and held up two fingers with a nod and a grin. He made certain to point out that each cup needed a healthy scooping of the sherbet before he walked away contented. He handed Chloe a cup like he was giving her some sort of life-giving chalice.

"Here's to making light of serious situations and making serious fun of stupid situations," he raised his own cup of now muddy colored brew for a toast. "And to good friends to join us for both."

Chloe had to admit, sometimes Stan had a real way with

words. She raised her cup, and they clacked the plastic together before drinking. Right off, she got a cold lump of undissolved sherbet in her mouth, followed by a semicarbonated rush of sugar. After years of her Mom's conscientious support of local farmers, the sheer amount of artificial flavoring that Chloe ingested in that one gulp was enough to make her shudder. She actually gasped with her tongue sticking out, already dyed an unnatural red.

Stan downed his entire cup without coming up for air. He finished with a satisfied "Yes,", capped with a foamy moustache. "That tastes awesome!" he declared with enough volume to turn a few heads around him. "I'm gonna get some more," he bellowed before heading back into the increasingly large throng around the table.

Chloe could only shake her head as she turned away to scan the room, but was cut short as she came face to belt with Ezra Richardson's looming form.

He also held a couple cups of punch, looking down on her with a furrowed brow. "Are you here with *him*?" he asked, letting his disapproving eyes glance to Stan's receding head.

"I'm pretty sure you don't need to be lecturing me on the quality of our dates," Chloe said coolly.

"Listen, Lightning, I didn't know that you and Kendra had some sort of problem with each other when she asked me to the dance. I wouldn't have said yes if I'd known it would bother you so much. But I got to tell you, other than the fact that she seems to want to find out everything I can tell her about you all the time, she's a pretty cool girl," Ezra insisted. "But that dude, Stan, is no good for you."

"Leave Stan out of it!" Chloe snapped. "He's a friend, and he's been there when I've needed him," she added. "What did you tell Kendra about me?"

Now Ezra looked a little stung. "I didn't tell her anything except that you were my people and that she's wrong about you. Just like I've been trying to tell you about her! Damn, you two are a lot alike—hot tempers and cruel wits—I think maybe you two are made for each other."

"Not likely," Chloe muttered.

"Whatever," Ezra shot back. "But your boy Stan is a drug fiend, and I don't want to see you messing with that road."

"Oh, Mr. High and Mighty, now you're going to tell me who I should be hanging out with?" Chloe said. "Stan smokes pot, and trust me, I can handle being around him without falling victim."

"Yeah, that's how it starts," said Ezra with surprising force in his voice. "And you can trust me, I know where it leads! I've seen what that shit does, and I won't sit back and watch it happen to you!" His cups of punch were shaking in his grip.

Chloe was silenced beneath the force of his conviction, feeling the press of his will towering over her…"Okay," she said meekly. "I won't get caught up in that, I promise."

Ezra's fury deflated, and he was left looking surprisingly vulnerable. He avoided eye contact with Chloe as he gathered himself and cleared his throat.

"I'm sorry," mumbled Chloe, wishing she could somehow let him know that she understood why he was upset and how flattered she was that he cared so much about her. Against all better judgment, and despite the unprecedented moment of victory she had achieved earlier with Kirin, she felt the urge in that moment to reach up and meet his beautiful face with her own, just to let him know that she cared for him too.

Instead, Kendra slid her hand around Ezra's waist from behind as she slinked under his arm and pressed herself against him with a deep kiss that he did not have time to see coming or the will to resist. At first, he looked surprised, but then he closed his eyes and leaned in for more.

Kendra looked stunning. Her hair fell in a wave over her shoulder, matching the floor-length, blood-red dress that clung to her figure like the ephemeral covering over some ancient Greek goddess of love. She looked like she belonged on the red carpet at the Oscars, and she would have been a best-dressed contender even there. She made every other kid on the floor, besides Ezra, look like they were playing dress-up in their parents' closet—which of course Chloe actually was.

She disengaged from Ezra, leaving him befuddled and silent before turning her fiery gaze on Chloe with a victorious sneer. "Well, well, look who it is," she sang with fake cheer. "Don't you look adorable!" She looked Chloe up and down. "I was so hoping you would come to the dance. Ezra has been telling me good things about you, and I wanted to bury the hatchet and let bygones be bygones." She reached her perfectly manicured hand out to Chloe as the edges of her plump red lips curled dangerously.

Chloe's instincts told her to back away from the hand like it was an open flame, but with an encouraging nod from Ezra, she forced herself to accept the smooth, heavily lotioned palm. Kendra's grip was firm, on the verge of painful, and Chloe clenched back with all the force she could muster as she nodded with an oily smile of her own. "You look beautiful as always, Kendra."

"You're sweet," Kendra said, releasing the shake before slithering back against Ezra. "I just hope it's enough to keep Mr. Richardson's attention," she said with her vicious smile blooming in full.

Chloe struggled to keep down the shudder that threatened to spasm up her spine. "I'm sure you'll figure something out," she said through clenched teeth as Stan stepped up beside her with a refilled cup and his punch-stained grin flashing between the gathered parties.

"Hey, dudes," he said innocently as Ezra's hard glare fell upon him and Kendra's wicked glee became complete. The slow jam ended, and the deejay mixed it up with a hot dance number that made the crowd cheer and brought many of the kids in the bleachers to their feet.

"Come on, Ezra, let's hit the floor," said Kendra with a playful tug on his arm.

Ezra held his gaze on Stan, however, and there was a threat there that even Stan couldn't miss. "You better be good to her," he commanded as Kendra kept tugging.

Stan was a little flustered. "Yeah, no problem, dude," he offered with a nervous chuckle.

Ezra turned back to Chloe, looking like he wanted to reach out and grab her hand but for the cup of punch in his grip. "Don't leave yet, Chloe; don't run away again. There's something I want you to see tonight before you go," he said cryptically with a flash of mischief in his eye and something more behind it. Kendra kept pulling as Ezra was slowly carried away from Chloe's look of confusion. "Promise me you'll stay this time, for just a little longer," he called back.

"Yeah, whatever, I promise," said Chloe with a dismissive wave as Ezra and Kendra were swallowed by the swell of people onto the floor.

"What the hell was that?" asked Stan before gulping at his second cup of punch.

"I have no idea," admitted Chloe before taking a second sip of her own appropriately oversweetened poison.

.   .   .

Chloe leaned back against the top row of bleachers and stared down at the sea of dancing kids that moved in jerky flashes beneath the strobes. Stan lazed beside her with a face-splitting grin. Three empty cups of punch were discarded on the seat in front of him. Despite herself and her surroundings, Chloe couldn't help but be caught up in his unending mirth.

"So let me get this straight," Stan said as a fresh wave of chuckles spilled out of him. "The super-jock quarterback guy is your special friend and protective keeper. The new-kid-surfer-dude and you have a budding…thing," he made air quotes. "And you're archenemies with the hottest, richest, and bitchiest chick in the school?"

Chloe was nodding her head. "Yup, that's about right." She was amazed at how absurd it all seemed when listed together.

"Who is the mysterious Lightning Girl?" he asked with the mock voice of a sensationalist newscaster. "Faster than a speeding bully, bringer of nature's fury, and YES, she even looks good in her mom's eighth grade dress."

Chloe snorted. "Okay, you're going to have to shut up now."

Stan kept going. "You may not see her coming or know what's happened until it's too late, but BEWARE: if you get too close to her, you WILL be shocked."

Chloe punched him in the thigh, and he doubled over whimpering and laughing at the same time. "Don't underestimate the Lightning Girl! She may be small, but she packs fists like THUNDERBOLTS!"

Chloe wound up to punch again, but he threw up his hands and cringed away. "Stop! No!" he blurted. "I'm done!"

As Chloe lowered the threat, Stan fluttered back beside her with a hangdog face. He rubbed the place on his leg where she'd hit him and winced. "Ouch, dude. That really hurt."

"Well, keep that in mind next time you want to push it, buddy."

"Man, you're mean," he joked…"If encountered, one should NEVER provoke the Lightning Girl!"

Chloe laughed as she scanned the dance floor for Ezra's head above the crowd. Instead, her gaze settled on Brian and Rosalie as they sloppily climbed the bleacher stairs toward them. Brian looked pretty good in a dark brown suit, having cleaned up to a hipster-chic that Chloe hadn't thought him capable of. Rosalie was equally cute in a little hippie dress that probably cost more than the full worth of Chloe's wardrobe. They also looked like they were out-of-their-minds wasted.

Chloe nudged Stan's leg with a warning look. When Stan noticed the approaching twosome, he straightened a bit, and a nervous chuckle spilled out of him.

"Oh boy, this is gonna be a blast," he said with a pained smile.

Brian gave the 'what's up' nod as he approached, holding on to Rosalie's wrist while her spacey attention trailed behind. Brian came at Stan with an intricate handshake before the two newcomers plopped down on the row of bleachers below. Rosalie's gauzy, canary-yellow-covered rear came down directly onto Stan's trio of cups with the clatter of breaking plastic and a cold, wet surprise from the "exotic" dregs.

Rosalie released a high-pitched yelp that sounded to Chloe like a hungry kitten, and then she stared oddly at the ceiling with her mouth locked in a bizarre rictus grin. She made no effort to move as the red stain climbed up her backside.

"Dude," said Brian with a zonkered gaze of his own. "Rosalie has never taken mushrooms before."

"How considerate of you to let her do so in such a safe and calm place," Stan said as the deejay moved into another dance number that brought a cheer from the crowd.

Chloe watched as hands shot into the air and the mob churned with renewed vigor. She spied Liz among the many, moving her hips and shaking her hair as Paul bounced beside her. Chloe tried to suppress the part of her that wanted to go down and join them.

Brian brought her back to the drama at hand with a sleazy nod toward Rosalie for Stan's benefit. It was like she and Rosalie weren't even there, which was looking more and more accurate in Rosalie's case. She was still staring at the ceiling, mesmerized by the play of lights across the rafters as Brian made an unsubtle 'blow-job' gesture.

"Seriously?" spat Chloe under her breath.

Stan looked like a deer caught in headlights as Brian hooked a thumb toward Chloe and gave his blow-job rendition again. Stan could only shake his head and grimace.

"Oh my God, you are like radiating an amazing golden aura right now," Rosalie slurred with her big, crazy eyes now fixed on Chloe.

Chloe wasn't sure if she'd heard that right. "What?"

"You have a golden aura!" Rosalie shouted above the music. Chloe raised her eyebrows. "Is that good?"

"Oh yeah," answered Rosalie with a drifting nod. "Very rare…It's like the second best next to pure white!" She watched Chloe with an expectant, almost reverent gaze.

"Good to know. Thank you," Chloe offered as Stan snickered beside her.

Brian suddenly stood, his attention having drifted back to the floor below. He took Rosalie's hand and pulled her back to her feet. "This is a great song…Rosalie, I was wrong! We should keep dancing!"

"Oh, okay," she said with a baffled smile.

Brian whirled back toward Stan. "Dude, I will catch you later."

"No doubt," answered Stan with a wave as the pending trainwreck moved away. Rosalie spun back toward Chloe with a wave. "I totally voted for you," she hollered as they stumbled back down the stairs.

"What did she say?" asked Chloe.

"I'm not sure," Stan admitted, watching them go with a blank expression.

"Are you all right?" she asked.

"Oh yeah, I'm great! I'm totally gonna get a blowie from a girl with a golden aura," he pumped his eyebrows. They both burst into laughter.

"Do you think Rosalie is going to be all right?" asked Chloe. "She seems pretty out of it." At the bottom of the bleachers, Rosalie was battling a sudden onset of noodle-leg syndrome as Brian bear-hugged her from behind in a fumbling effort to keep her from toppling over.

"Absolutely," joked Stan. "She's in good hands with a fine gentleman chaperone."

Chloe put her hand on his shoulder. "You know, I get that he's your friend and all, but I think in the romance department, you could do much better…and gayer."

For that, Stan had no ready quip. "Thanks, Chloe." Rosalie was now bent precariously over a trash can.

At first, Chloe thought that she was spewing punch and mushrooms, until she reemerged shock-straight with a discarded corsage held aloft in her hand like it was the Holy Grail. "I think they really might get in trouble," Chloe observed. "See, aren't you glad that you didn't smoke weed tonight?"

Stan's face went blank and he shrugged.

Chloe narrowed her eyes. "You didn't smoke weed, did you?"

"Nope…scout's honor," he said with his hand in the air. "I didn't SMOKE any weed at all."

"What does that mean?"

"Well, I may have ingested a stale pot brownie from a couple weeks ago," he admitted with a casual wave. "It doesn't even count, just a tiny, old thing."

Chloe was not impressed. "You're high right now?"

"I guess, technically," he answered sheepishly.

"You know, never mind what I said before; I think maybe you and Brian are perfect for each other."

"I'm sorry," he said, with the corners of his grin returning. "I'm a very weak-willed man."

Chloe could only shake her head. "You're going to owe me for this," she declared.

"Just name it," he offered as the deejay segued artfully into yet another radio hit and the crowd roared again.

Chloe spotted Ezra's smile above the rest as his perfect teeth glowed bright blue with the black light. He looked like he was having a lot of fun. Then her eye caught the red mane in the flash of a strobe light—Kendra circled her prey with sultry moves and dramatic flare. From afar, it looked like Kendra thought she was performing in a music video. Chloe had to admit, *the bitch is pretty convincing!*

But Chloe's death ray was broken by a sudden scurry of activity at the stage. Principal John Harlow mounted the stairs and shuffled through some papers beside the microphone stand. He stood just barely five feet tall, with a sincere but tired face and a rapidly receding hairline. Behind him, a group of three upperclassmen that looked like they'd dressed for a church retreat followed him up to the stage amid a frantic conference of whispers.

"Oh, goodie, here we go," said Stan as the music began to fade and the spotlights over the stage came on.

One of the girls handed a folded piece of paper to Principal Harlow, who read its contents with a furrowed brow. He turned back to the nervous committee and asked them something that brought a trio of exasperated shrugs in response. Soon the four of them were reengaged in another heated round of discussion as the student body below them began to take notice with hushed expectation.

All eyes drifted to the brightly lit crowns on the pedestal as whispers of prediction passed through the crowd. Even from the top row, Chloe heard the name Ezra Richardson bandied about more than once as Kendra bounced and clapped with glee before giving him an unsolicited peck on the cheek.

"I think your gallant protector is about to become royalty," suggested Stan a little too loudly amid the relative quiet.

A couple of goths sitting nearby turned around to see who'd spoken, but upon seeing Chloe, the doughy boy with dyed black hair gave her a thumbs-up. "Lightning Girl!" he announced with a nod. The heavily pierced girl with Buddy Holly glasses spoke up, almost as if not wanting to be outdone by her date, "Good job at districts today. I heard you totally kicked ass!"

"Uh, thanks," Chloe answered with an uneasy tinge along her spine.

"You're a legend in your own time," Stan whispered in her ear, just as Principal Harlow cleared his throat over the microphone.

"Good evening, Charlottesville High School. This is the moment you've been waiting for," he said while squinting through the spotlight.

Chloe heard the shrill spike of what sounded like Rosalie's high-pitched cackle rising from somewhere in the crowd.

"After much deliberation and a lot of time counting and recounting ballots, we are now ready to announce this year's Charlottesville High School Homecoming King and Queen," Principal Harlow announced in his nasally twang, clearly hoping for more of a response than the lackluster cheer that greeted him. He looked back to the Homecoming committee for morale support, but they all still looked a little stunned by the whole thing.

"Well, let's get right to it then," Harlow suggested as he was handed a gold-leaf envelope. He opened it with a ragged tear. "After leading our fighting Black Knights to an upset victory over the Monticello Dragons earlier today, it should come as no surprise that this year's Homecoming King, by a landslide, is none other than Mr. Ezra Richardson!"

The crowd went wild as Ezra bloomed with the biggest smile Chloe had ever seen. Kendra clung to him like some sort of parasite, hoping to be carried with him up to the stage, but Ezra managed to dislodge her as he met a wave of high fives coming at him from all directions. He moved through the masses with Kendra scooting behind in his wake as the horde started to chant his name.

Everyone went crazier still when Ezra mounted the stage in a single bound, suddenly coming to stand by the pedestal with his arms raised victoriously above him. Chloe had to smirk at Kendra's awkward shuffle at the front of the stage as Ezra turned away from her to shake the hands of all four presenters.

Principal Harlow handed Ezra a gold-painted cardboard sword and then removed the crown from the pedestal. He stepped to Ezra, who stood more than a foot taller than him, and for a moment, Ezra let Principal Harlow stretch up on his tiptoes with the crown raised to the utmost of his reach while the student body hollered in approval. Finally Ezra dropped to one knee and bent his head with theatrical flare as Harlow exhaled in relief and placed the too-small crown on the new king's head.

Ezra came to his feet again as the football team started chanting "Speech! Speech!" Principal Harlow motioned toward the microphone, and of course, Ezra couldn't pass up a chance to address his constituency. He leaned over to the mic with one hand on his head to keep the crown in place and paused for dramatic timing…"Thank you, Charlottesville High School!" he boomed with his sword jutting into the sky. The crowd erupted.

He waited for them to die down before he continued. "I am honored to stand before you tonight and to be the one who gets to tell you all that it is time for Charlottesville High School to start kicking some ass!"

The kids went nuts. Despite his disapproval of the public cursing, Principal Harlow found himself begrudgingly clapping along with Ezra's infectious charisma. Some of the other adult supervisors around the edges of the floor were among his loudest supporters.

Chloe gave a bark of a laugh, but even she couldn't help but be swept up in the enthusiasm.

Stan shouted over the din, "That dude is gonna be president someday."

"God help us," Chloe laughed.

Ezra waved the crowd back down to silence. "As your Homecoming King, I plan to do my part to help lead this school toward the greatness and respect that we deserve…And I know that my fellow queen will equally embody the strength, beauty, and conviction that we'll need to take this year to the next level." He stepped back from the mic with a rascally little tip of his crown and scanned the throng of his adoring people as if looking for someone in particular.

Chloe was brought to giggles, watching the way that Kendra stood at the foot of the stage, trying desperately and failing to catch her date's searching eye. Principal Harlow stepped back to the mic with a new envelope in hand and exhaled loudly as he waited for the hush to return.

He looked to Ezra, who gave him a supportive nod. "This year's race for Homecoming Queen comes with a bit of an upset," he admitted. "It was a very tight contest between three worthy candidates. But one name won out by only five votes, and with some key endorsements to back her up." He was sweating beneath the lights, and the three committee members behind him were fidgeting with nervous energy. "Traditionally we only accept the names of upperclassmen in the race, but this year an incoming student and surprise write-in candidate proved to have the most support…After a lot of debate, we've decided to let the vote stand."

Chloe could see the furious posturing of a couple of the senior front-runners near the stage, just as Kendra's little hive of sophomore girls buzzed up around her with a flurry of excited energy. Chloe suddenly found herself on the verge of shouting. "You've got to be kidding me! She's a stinking tenth grader!" She looked to Stan for backup.

He had nothing.

"What, did she sleep with the whole damn Homecoming

Committee?" Chloe challenged.

Harlow cleared his throat as the spark of outrage and anticipation receded to a quiet rumble. "This year's Homecoming Queen is…" he fumbled with the envelope and read the name on the card like he'd never seen it before, "…Chloe McClellan!"

Ezra leaned over him toward the mic. "Lightning Girl!" he shouted as the crowd exploded with a mixture of cheers, laughter and fury.

At first, Chloe wasn't sure what was happening, unable to make any sense of the words she'd just heard. But as the goths turned back around with huge smiles and loud hoots, she began to feel the swell of panic in her gut. She glanced to Stan, who was still wearing the nervous remnants of his signature grin as she looked for some sign of understanding or reference for the joke that was forming around her. Stan could only shrug as Chloe began to feel the press of more and more eyes.

"Queen Chloe 'Lightning Girl' McClellan!" Ezra's voice boomed again through the speakers, cutting through the encroaching haze of madness. It provided an anchor for Chloe's focus, though it came from the last place in the world she wanted to go. "Please report to your coronation!" he commanded from the stage.

What felt like an invisible fist buried into her stomach, and she totally lost the ability to breathe.

Stan leaned over and shouted into her ear, "I think you have to go down there, dude…You're the Homecoming Queen!"

Chloe's wide, terrified eyes turned on him. "Did you know about this?" she croaked.

He shook his head furiously. "No!" He stuck his hand in the air. "Scout's honor."

Chloe contemplated making a run for it, but too many eyes had already found her among the high shadows as Ezra began a quiet chant over the microphone below.

"Lightning, Lightning, Lightning," he said it over and over again in a building rhythm, and before the fifth "Lightning," many other voices had joined in.

The goth kids were shouting along with fists pumping in the

air. At the edge of the crowd, Chloe spied Liz jumping in glee as she rallied those around her to join in the infectious ovation. Most of the kids that yelled her unwanted nickname had no idea who she even was. Only a handful had ever actually spoken to her, and most had probably never even seen her before or since Kendra's e-mailed introduction.

Chloe's humiliation had officially become a spectator sport. She tried to will herself into an aneurysm or a massive coronary, anything to keep her from having to face the path ahead. Instead, she found herself rising to wobbly feet with the help of a supportive push from Stan.

Though she couldn't feel her legs, her feet started moving down the bleacher stairs as the cheer from the aisles around her swelled with her passing. She thought she might pitch forward and tumble to blissful silence, but she kept on coming with steady, almost automated steps.

At the bottom of the bleachers, she moved into the thicker crowd, and the sea of cheering, well-dressed bodies parted before her. Their group sound was muffled and distant in her ears as she advanced with only a vague notion of the direction toward the stage.

She passed Brian and Rosalie as they clung to each other amid the swarm.

"It's a golden light! It's so beautiful!" Rosalie's shrill voice sounded above the chant before she was swallowed again by the crowd.

Chloe glanced at Liz, who was pumping her fist toward the sky and doing her part to lead the hive mind in support of their new queen right along with Ezra. *How long have they been planning this?*

Liz looked like she was about to burst with joy as she pounced on Chloe and kissed her cheek. "This is awesome!" she squealed in Chloe's ear before bouncing back and waving her on. Paul Markson led the chant in his section with renewed vigor.

This is not my life. But Chloe kept moving, blind and deaf to the press of cheers and jeers all around her as the stairs to the stage came into view ahead. She tried not to openly tremble, though she'd begun to feel light-headed and cold. The stirrings of a migraine toyed at the base of her skull.

Beside the stairs, Kendra and her defeated drones watched Chloe's approach with silent hatred. Kendra stepped before her path with a gaze that left a heated trail across Chloe's skin. "I'm going to end you, little girl!" she snapped.

What Kendra didn't know was that she'd already won. Now Chloe wouldn't be able to escape the Lightning Girl nickname for the remainder of high school. She was officially a super hero, accept without anything super or heroic to show for it—just a foolish little girl in costume as everyone around her pointed and laughed. "Please do," she answered without stopping. She sidestepped Kendra and watched her own high-heeled feet as they climbed the stairs toward the harsh spotlight.

She looked up to see Ezra's self-satisfied smile as he broke away from the pounding chant and nodded toward the gilded dunce cap that awaited her. She wondered what it would do to her reputation if she decked the Homecoming King in front of the whole school. She actually would have considered it if she could have reached his perfect jaw or if doing so wouldn't have almost certainly led to a broken hand and suspension.

Principal Harlow stepped forward to grip her sweaty palm. "Congratulations, Ms. McClellan, I heard about your impressive showing in districts this afternoon, and I'm told your grades more than speak for themselves." He plucked the bulbous crown from its velvety perch and placed it on her head with a pat. "I'm sure you will be an exemplary model of excellence on both the field and in the classroom."

Unlike with Ezra, Chloe's crown was too big for her head and slipped toward her brow, causing a fresh wave of laughter from the watching horde. She didn't even bother to fix it.

Chloe barely registered that many of the meatheads at the front of the stage had started yelling "SPEECH!" again before Ezra gripped her by her shoulders and directed her toward the microphone.

She froze, squinting into the harsh light with only a ghost image of the many eyes that watched her expectantly. She felt a surge of panic, and for a second, the lights seemed to flicker and dim. She prayed that the power would go out altogether and she might escape in the darkness. Instead, she heard the wind of her breath against the microphone.

She tried to swallow, but there wasn't enough moisture in her mouth to get it down. She smacked her lips, trying to get something going, and the sound of it echoed about the room. *Holy shit, say something!*

"Uh…" she glanced up to the top of the bleachers and caught Stan's huge grin in the shadows. He gave her the thumbs-up…"I feel like this must be some sort of mistake," she admitted.

Ripples of laughter carried through the audience, and Chloe was painfully aware of Principal Harlow's nervous shuffling beside her.

"This isn't really my thing, and I didn't even know I was running for it…So I just want the people, you know, who actually care about this, to know that I'm sorry…And to all the people who voted for me…uh, thanks, I guess, but I kind of wish you hadn't." Chloe could hear a few isolated points of support as she spoke and decided to block out all the mockery and anger and speak just to them. "I wasn't even going to come tonight; to be honest, I think the whole thing is kind of stupid."

This time, the outburst of applause had gathered significantly in size and commitment. *If I'm going down, I might as well go down in flames!*

"It seems to me that this whole charade is set up to reinforce some antiquated notion of social hierarchy that doesn't really belong in high school in the first place," she announced to another wave of scattered cheers and laughter. "And if I had any real power as your newly elected symbolic queen, the first thing I'd do is abolish the whole idea of a Homecoming Court!"

With that, she'd officially won over the bleachers, but there was still a lot of laughter and hard looks directed her way from the dance floor. In the corner of her eye, it looked like Principal Harlow was preparing to step in and cut her off at any moment. "But I do want to say one thing about our new Homecoming King," she shot a deadly look back at Ezra and enjoyed the momentary chink in the armor of his smile. "You might know him as a ladies' man and football phenom, but who knew that he was such a humanitarian toward the disenfranchised underclassman?"

The whole crowd answered with a roar of laughter.

Chloe unexpectedly felt life stirring within again. "He's right about one thing, though: he is the champion we need and deserve to take this school into the future, and I for one will do my part to support and follow his inspired lead," she managed a playful smile, starting to get a little heady with the resonant sound of her own voice. She swept an arm back toward Ezra. "It is my honor, no, my duty to re-present Charlottesville High School's real Black Knight—King Ezra the First: Dragon Slayer!"

The crowd went bonkers. Chloe looked back again to meet Ezra's smirk. He answered with only the faint shake of his head before stepping forward again to jam the cardboard sword into the air and reclaim the attention he so enjoyed. Chloe tried to step back out of the spotlight just as Principal Harlow took back the microphone.

"And now it's my pleasure to introduce this year's Charlottesville High School Homecoming King and Queen for their first dance," he announced before briskly stepping away with a relieved exhale.

Chloe found herself facing Ezra again as the first few notes of an old Lionel Richie slow jam climbed out of the speakers. King Ezra offered his hand for the dance. Aware of Kendra's burning gaze of hatred upon her, Chloe took it and let him pull her close. His other arm reached down and wrapped around her waist, and his strong fingers pressed into the small of her back. She shivered a little and tried not to look out at the milling crowd. Some had broken off into dancing pairs again, but many continued to watch the stage. Chloe could not let them see that a part of her loved the way this felt—the hidden-away and disenfranchised girl that wanted to spin joyously across the stage for all to behold. She couldn't even afford to acknowledge the existence of that girl to herself. *God, Mom is going to be so happy!*

She looked almost straight up to find Ezra's waiting eyes. "I don't think I'll ever forgive you for this," she said.

"You will," he answered assuredly. "And one day, you'll thank me."

CHAPTER 15
THE UNEXPECTED TURN

Chloe did her stint dancing awkwardly on the stage. Then she had to pose for a photograph with Ezra, which would no doubt rekindle half the school's hatred for her on Monday morning when it appeared on the front page of the *Charlottesville High Herald*. After that, she returned the ceremonial crown to its velvet pillow, received a trio of pinch-faced smiles from the Homecoming Committee, and got the hell away from there as fast as possible.

She was waiting for the hot sting of Kendra's knife in her back as she fought her way through the crowd; instead she received supportive pats and sporadic bursts of applause the whole way. She did her best to smile when Liz blocked her retreat with an ecstatic dance that consisted of jumping up and down while spinning and squeaking in an octave that most people probably couldn't register. *God, why didn't she elect herself Queen?*

"I am so happy, I think I might explode!" shouted Liz.

"Please don't. That would be really messy, and I kind of like this dress," Chloe responded with as much joy as she had to give. "Was this your idea?"

"No, it was Ezra, but he recruited me a few weeks ago to help rally the soccer team and underclassman to the cause!" She started bouncing again. "I can't believe it actually worked!"

Chloe laughed without humor. "Yeah, me neither."

"Did you see Kendra's face? She looked like she was going to burst into flames!" Liz added triumphantly. "You're like the most popular girl in the school!"

"That's not really the role I'm trying out for here,"

Chloe muttered.

Liz trilled like a pixie, "I know, that's why you're so good at it." She was completely undaunted by Chloe's obvious discomfort. "I knew that if they made you give a speech, you'd say something awesome!"

Chloe could only glower.

Liz answered by bouncing toward her like a crazed rabbit and planting an almost dainty kiss on Chloe's cheek. "You're the queen," she whispered.

Liz smelled like honeysuckle and spring. Some of Chloe's happiest memories had been accompanied by that smell. Liz was impossible to stay mad at for long. "Thanks, Liz."

Liz bowed with a formal flourish and then bounced back toward Paul and a cluster of the other varsity soccer players. As Chloe started moving again, Paul turned to give her a salute.

The whole world has gone crazy!

She made a beeline back to the comparatively sane company of Stan. But by the time she'd climbed to the summit of the bleachers, the combination of Stan's illicit brownie and the absurd spectacle of the evening had sent him into a perpetual state of unnecessary giggles and overly happy feelings.

"You are now my hero, dude! This night is better than I would have ever thought possible!"

"I'm so glad," Chloe snapped. "But we're leaving now, and we've got to do it quickly and quietly, so stop laughing."

"What are you talking about? I don't ever want to leave," Stan admitted with a grin that showed little chunks of chocolate between his teeth. "I'm here with the Homecoming Queen!"

"Yeah, well, you owe me, remember? And you have the car," she reminded him with a hint of desperation. She swallowed the urge to scream and let her newly found noble blood do the talking. "And if I'm your queen, then you have to do as I say, and I say we're going right now!" she declared without any room for discussion.

This just made Stan laugh harder.

"Pull yourself together, make sure you have the car keys, and start moving toward the door," Chloe hissed…"Or I'll tell our new king that you're trying to get me to do drugs."

Stan stopped laughing and stood up straight. "Yes, my queen, as you command."

But Chloe was already moving, with her head down and her eyes locked on the red glow of the 'Exit' sign. "Follow me."

.   .   .

Chloe drove back up the winding hills above Charlottesville—where life made more sense. She hadn't bothered to get her learner's permit yet, but Audrey had let her try out the CR-V a few times already, and there was no way she was going to let a high Stan drive her home again. She cruised along the mountain roads that she knew so well in the Strakowski station wagon she didn't know at all.

Chloe had never driven at night before, but the power of the wheel behind the bright headlights was intoxicating. The big boat of a car hugged the road at exactly 30 miles per hour as Stan smiled in the seat beside her, occasionally scanning his iPod in pursuit of a better classic rock song to fit his flighty whim. Once she'd hustled him into the car and wrestled the keys from his grasp, he'd settled contentedly beside her, clearly not caring where she might take him or how qualified she was to operate heavy machinery.

It was only 10:30, and she was still buzzing on the adrenaline of the night—not ready for home just yet. Stan bobbed his head to a spacey guitar riff, and Chloe realized how much she enjoyed his mellow, unencumbered company. Just as Ezra tended to make her feel grounded and safe, and Kirin inspired her to be more fluid and open to new experiences, Stan had the ability to make her see the world as if from above, and he helped her to not take that world too seriously.

Chloe smirked as she remembered the tingling sensation of grabbing Kirin's hand and the odd sense that she had watched as it happened from somewhere outside herself. *I really like Kirin… and he might actually like me back!*

And I'm the Homecoming Queen! She still couldn't wrap her

head around that inexplicable fact. And she doubted that she'd ever fully accept that she had been the one responsible for that impromptu speech on the stage.

I really must be losing my mind, she realized as she tried and failed to swallow the giggle that spilled out of her. The hilarity only grew with her attempts to quell it, and before she knew it, she'd erupted into an all-out, stomach-clenching laugh.

"What's so funny?" asked Stan as the virus of her unhinged humor started to spread.

Chloe glanced over at his bug eyes and curling lips and started laughing so hard that tears ran down her cheeks. The rapid firing of her lungs left little room for a full breath. A moment later, Stan was roaring right along with her, even less aware of why he was doing so, but for the simple joy of letting go and floating away.

But her laughter stopped abruptly as she stomped on the brakes, pulling to the side of the road with a reckless skid through leaves and gravel. The car came to a halt amid a plume of dust. She peered across the street with laser intensity. She knew this stretch of the Ford's Loop Road by heart; it was the place where Kirin had parked before she had led him along her secret path through the woods to the pond.

A big, white sign that she'd never seen before was practically glowing in the light of her high beams. There was a dirt road beside it that hadn't been there a week earlier, stretching off into the darkness of the forest. Hundreds of healthy trees were gone. Chloe's heart started going a mile a minute as her eyes scanned the black words:

PROPERTY OF THE DAEDALUS GROUP
NO TRESSPASSING
VIOLATORS WILL BE PROSECUTED

Her mind took a moment to process what she was seeing. *Those bastards!*

Stan finally stopped laughing as he followed Chloe's hateful gaze to the sign. "Hey, that's Paul's dad's company," he noted.

"What does Paul's dad do?" Chloe hissed.

"I think he's like a nuclear engineer or a rocket scientist or something," Stan offered. "My dad always said that Dr. William Markson was the smartest man he'd ever met."

"And the Daedalus Group?" Chloe asked through clenched teeth.

"I don't know; they're into all kinds of stuff," Stan speculated. "Bioengineering, alternative fuel sources, government contract work. My dad also said that Dr. Markson had sold his brain to Richard Roberts and his soul to the devil."

Without any warning, Chloe switched her foot to the accelerator and jerked the wheel. The back tires fishtailed through the grass before the wagon shot across the street and raced down the new road. Stan watched the sign fly by his window as the high beams illuminated the otherwise lightless and bumpy path through the trees.

The way stretched into pitch darkness, and he felt the press of eerie shadows beyond the headlights' reach. He'd never seen Chloe like this: red-faced with the veins pulsing in her neck. He waved his hand, trying to draw her determined scowl and wondering if it was safe to speak.

"Uh, Chloe…what are you doing?"

"I have to see something," she muttered. The car was only doing about 25 mph along the hard-packed dirt, but it seemed like it was going much faster.

"I'm not so sure this is a good idea, dude."

"You owe me, remember?" Chloe said without breaking her focus. "We're doing this, so turn off the music and keep on the lookout."

Stan sat up straighter, switched off the music, and nodded. "Yes, my queen…but what exactly is it that we're doing?"

Chloe didn't answer as her foot pushed down harder and the little red hand in the dashboard climbed back up to 30 miles per hour. Stan glanced into the side mirror as the dust cloud rose behind them, and then he looked unsuccessfully for the glow of the moon through the branches above. The clouds flashed with the dance of electricity, but there was no thunderous report that followed. He buckled his seatbelt.

After another tense minute of violent vibration, the car began to slow and the tree line broke ahead. The road ended in a wide, grassy clearing that opened out of the woods. Chloe rolled to a stop and abruptly silenced the engine.

"You know where we are, don't you?" Stan observed as Chloe peered through the windshield with alarming intensity.

Her eyes climbed the hill to the place where the lightning-struck oak had been, but the tree lay in a sawed-up pile, and the hill was now capped with a massive metal tower that climbed high into the sky over the forest. Her mouth fell open as she took in the full scope of the abomination: thirty feet wide at the base and at least a hundred feet tall with a series of blinking red lights at its crown. The hill itself was crisscrossed and gouged with numerous deep tire tracks. A bulldozer, forklift, and crane were still parked on the level ground beside the pond.

Chloe's special place—which Kirin had been so right to claim as her own—had been destroyed. Again, the clouds above the clearing lit up with the hidden crawl of a noiseless electric charge.

"What the hell is that?" asked Stan with an open mouth as he craned his neck toward the heights.

"A lightning tower," whispered Chloe as she remembered the way that Mr. Roberts had grilled her about her incident here and his odd fascination with lightning in general. She tried to remember how much she'd told him as a swell of guilt bubbled up from her gut. She opened the door, deaf to Stan's halfhearted protests behind her.

She was already marching toward the defiled hill before he cracked his door to call after her. "Maybe we should get out of here?" he suggested to her back.

But Chloe was too mad for reason. Her heels got caught in the mud, and she yanked them off without thinking, gripping the delicate, soiled footwear tightly as she continued the furious ascent with the cold grass poking at her toes. Stan stepped from the car and slammed the door behind her as the clouds flared again. He doggedly started to follow.

Chloe could run ten miles with breath to spare, but she was so full of adrenaline and rage that she was breathing hard by the time she crested the rise. The wide, four-legged base of the tower covered the place where she'd been struck by lightning, and the closest steel girder tore through the spot where she'd spent the better part of the summer. Trying not to cry, she craned her neck back and looked straight up at the metal monstrosity. High above, the blinking red lights taunted her with their steady mechanical rhythm.

She actually snarled as she turned away and stormed to the nearby woodpile that had once been a tree. She scanned the various stacks of neatly cleaved limbs and claimed a halved branch that she brandished like a club.

Only halfway up and Stan was winded for real. "I need to get in shape!" he announced with his hands on his hips. He watched as Chloe set her unhinged gaze on the shiny new structure and came at it with the big stick cocked over her head.

She swung with everything she had, and the wet wood connected with the metal leg with a sharp CLANG that echoed about the clearing. The impact's vibration traveled unpleasantly up her arms, but she swung and connected again and again with building ferocity. The ringing took on an odd rhythm as the CLANGS and ECHOES became indiscernible from each other. The stick was coming apart with exposed gouges of blonde wood, but she persisted. Her hands were scraped and buzzing.

Stan came up behind her and claimed a quarter-sized rock from the grass. With a feral yell, he hurled his imposing weapon at the unresponsive enemy. "Stupid tower!" he yelled as the rock bounced harmlessly off an upper support and fell away into darkness. Chloe turned back to look at him with wild eyes. He gave her a big grin and a thumbs-up. "We totally kicked its ass, dude."

She couldn't help but burst out laughing, though the part of her that held to idealism, nostalgia, and all that she'd ever believed in wanted to weep. She dropped the stick and looked at the ineffectual smears of wood resin and bark across the steel.

Stan leaned in close to the offending girder. "Look at that," he pointed to what looked like a faint scratch on the surface of the metal. "I think you hurt it."

Chloe deflated. "This was my special place that no one else knew about." She scanned the view that had held her attention through warmer times, now littered with construction debris and garbage. "They've ruined it."

"This is where you got struck by lightning, isn't it?" asked Stan.

Chloe pointed to the now-barren earth at the center of the tower's footprint. "Over there," she said as the ripple of electricity danced through the clouds again, this time with a low grumble of thunder to accompany it.

Stan eyed the ominous sky and absently wondered about the decision to have this conversation beside a lightning tower. "You really do have a somewhat jarring effect on the weather, don't you?"

Chloe looked to the glassy sheen of the pond before she answered. "Yeah…things have been a little strange for a couple months now." She remembered the way the pond had lurched and thrown her to the shore, then the five clawed tracks through the street. She could picture the words, "*TIPPING POINT PROPHECY*," blazoned across her computer screen in a swirling aqua green font…and then the word spoken by Kirin earlier that evening: "*DRAGONS!*"

"Let's hear it, dude," Stan suggested. "I spend most of my time thinking strange thoughts."

"I don't know; this is stranger than most," she challenged.

He flashed his best Cheshire grin. "Try me," he said before plopping to the ground, already forgetting his intention to make a hasty retreat. He patted the earth beside him and looked up expectantly.

Chloe tossed her shoes and joined him in what was left of the tamped-down grass, facing the pond and the heavy construction vehicles beside it. Stan was high as a kite and already half-asleep with heavy lids over red-washed eyes, but Chloe was still hesitant to tell her story of preternatural weather and alarming memory gaps.

"The night before school started, I caught my mom's boyfriend in an affair with another woman," she said, hoping to build up to the weirdness. "My mom didn't believe me at first, and the boyfriend overheard me trying to tell her about it—so I ran away to here. You know, just until things cooled down."

Stan had closed his eyes, but he was still sitting up and listening. "That's some drama," he muttered with a sleepy drawl.

"It was still really hot then, so I jumped in the pond for a swim, just like I had a hundred times before, but this time—" Chloe lost her words as another more forceful crack of thunder descended from the clouds. She looked up warily, suddenly feeling the autumn chill. "Do you believe in...end-of-the-world prophecies...or supernatural stuff?" she mumbled before looking back to Stan, who was snoring blissfully with his mouth ajar.

"Stan?" she said, to no response. "Oh come on!" Chloe hollered just before a glint of movement caught her eye from down by the water's edge. She held her breath as ripples moved across the still surface of the pond.

A hazy figure emerged from below, climbing from the water to stand stock-still on the rocks along the bank. It looked like a man, visible only as a black silhouette against the reflection of the night sky behind him.

Slowly his shadowed form stepped toward the hill. He had long hair and wore dark clothing.

Chloe couldn't look away, but her hand shot out to grab Stan's shoulder with a forceful shake. "Stan, get up!" she commanded, though a part of her already knew that he wouldn't answer. She shook again, rocking him violently, with nothing more than a contented little murmur in response.

The man kept coming, steadily moving through the grass with unnaturally lithe steps. As a cold breeze whipped through the trees, he paused at the foot of the slope and cocked his head as if to listen. The sky rumbled angrily once more, and his hair reflected silvery-white through the darkness. He started up the hill toward her.

"Who are you?" she called out with an unsteady voice.

But he did not answer, drawing closer—now twenty feet away and closing.

"What do you want?" she demanded just as her fight-or-flight instincts took over and she scrambled to her feet.

Sit! His resonant voice lanced through her mind like another crack of lightning and brought her firmly back to the earth. The word hung, echoing in her temples with the same pulsing pain of the migraines. He stopped only a couple strides from Chloe, and she saw the bright flash of electricity ripple within his piercing blue gaze.

He was shoeless and his clothes seemed as if stitched from shadows. His face was somehow young and old at the same time, with smooth, alabaster skin stretched over the sculpted bone structure of a man that looked to be little older than a teen in motion, but perhaps middle-aged when still. The yawning pits of his ice-rimmed eyes bore into her, threatening to consume her with their attention.

The hair stood on the back of her neck, and she shuddered as his will infiltrated her mind. She felt cold and helpless as the tickle of electricity sparked through her body. She wanted to scream and run, but found herself frozen mute and unable to blink. All at once, the cascade of stolen memories flooded back into her—she felt like her mind might drown beneath the overlapping waves of understanding and horror.

Chloe ground her teeth and fought to resist his leaching on her thoughts. "What are you?" she croaked.

He turned his ear skyward again as if he were a dog hearing a high-pitched sound. "Your mind never stills," he observed with cold interest. His voice was deep and perfectly clear, and his words echoed within her skull. "Remarkable. So much curiosity and hunger from one so feeble and fleeting."

Chloe's eyes watered and sweat beads gathered at her brow. Her voice trembled as she fought to speak. "You're the dragon?" she croaked.

"Dragon," he repeated, as if testing the sound of it. "My kind has had so many names over the millennia...I last awoke in this land before the language of *that* word had come to it."

He knelt before her with feline grace and froze like a statue, watching her the same way that Shipwreck might watch an injured bird before the kill.

Chloe's head was throbbing as she struggled to wade through her newfound memories to find the names of the five dragons of legend that had circled the Tianlong Cauldron. Her heart was pounding in her chest, though she felt cold in a way that made it seem like she wasn't getting enough blood to her extremities. "You were called Uktena then, weren't you…by the people who lived here before?"

A glimpse of surprise flashed over his features. "Uktena," he repeated. "That is what the Cherokee people called me," he remembered.

"Uktena," she echoed, still frozen in place and unable to shake the disturbing notion that he would most likely kill her as soon as they stopped talking. "I'm Chloe," she offered, trying to keep her voice from faltering.

He leaned closer and his nostrils inhaled her scent. "You are the queen of your people," he said, though Chloe wasn't sure if it had been a question or a statement.

"Yes," she finally said, deciding it wasn't actually a lie, and praying that it might somehow buy her more time…"And you are one of the Five Claws?"

Lightning flared again within his eyes, and Chloe would have doubled over with the shock of pain through her head if she'd had the ability to move. Instead, she could only whimper and tremble as Uktena stood and stepped over her.

"You know of my name and the ways of the Old Ones— perhaps you are a witch as well as a queen," Uktena observed.

Chloe could feel the sweat dripping down her cheek as her stomach did somersaults. She feared her head might actually explode. "No!" she gasped. "I'm not a witch, and I won't be a queen after tonight! I'm just a sophomore in high school!"

The sky danced with electricity above them.

"I don't believe in witches," Chloe gasped. "I don't even believe in dragons!"

All in one swift motion, he released his assault on her mind, stepped back, and returned to the feline crouch before her. He watched her for a long moment with an unreadable gaze. "You speak the truth."

She shuddered with the lingering pulse through her temples and tried to focus through the pain on what she might say next. Her body was still locked in place with her legs stretched across the cold ground and her arms braced behind her. The muscles in her shoulders were starting to scream with lactic burn, and she felt a cold dampness seeping through her dress from the earth below.

"Then how did you summon me?" Uktena challenged with an air of threat returned.

"I...I didn't summon you," she stammered.

Uktena's eyes narrowed, and Chloe was overcome by the disturbing sensation that a serpent had coiled around her body and was beginning to squeeze the air from her lungs. Her eyes bulged, and her breath began to draw shallow as the swell of panic threatened to consume her...But in another blink, the infiltration over mind and body left her completely, and she fell back with a yelp before scrambling against the unforgiving leg of the lightning tower.

Uktena turned his gaze toward the sky, as if to read something in the darkness and clouds. "I was not meant to rise for another two cycles of the moon," he observed. The press of his attention swung back to her. "Yet I heard the echo of your thoughts in my dreams, called back from a thousand years of slumber by your pondering."

Again Chloe glimpsed the flicker of lightning in his eyes, and her shoulders suddenly felt as if they'd been pinned back to the steel beam.

"How can this be?" demanded the monster in man form.

"I'm sorry! I don't know. I didn't mean to bother you! I didn't know you were there," she spluttered. "I...I don't believe that you're real. It defies science. I...I mean, how can you be real?"

The press of his will lessened, and Chloe's shoulders fell into a quivering slouch.

He glanced back to the smooth sheen of the pond and was mesmerized for a moment by the reflection of the clouds in its surface. "The world is far older than humankind remembers," he finally said. "Your people forget that in your arrogance and greed."

She considered running, but she was too terrified to move.

"Your kind believes that the planet needs you to survive, but you will soon find that it is the other way around." His ancient eyes followed the lines of the metal tower up to its red-blinking tip. "The age of man will be forgotten by time like all those before it." His gaze turned back on her.

Chloe could feel his attention hovering in her thoughts. She had to keep him talking or risk losing herself completely to the strength of his presence. "Then why did you save me from the lightning and again at the quarry?" she asked.

This seemed to stump Uktena for a moment. He slowly tilted his head without breaking the intensity of his gaze. "Perhaps I have absorbed a bit of your curiosity," he speculated. "It was *you* that summoned *me*...I needed to know why before the end."

"The end of what?" she asked.

The dragon watched her closely without answering, and Chloe forced herself to look back—both of them were still and silent with a building hum of energy between them. Stan broke the tension with a satisfied murmur in his sleep.

"What did you do to my friend?" she asked, with a hand checking for a heartbeat on Stan's chest. She felt it thumping contentedly beneath her fingers.

"He will wake soon and remember nothing," the dragon answered. "Though I am not sure yet what I will do with you."

Chloe started to shiver with a combination of rattled nerves and the cold.

Uktena studied her closely. "I wonder—which of the three males will you choose as mate?"

"What?"

"The dark-skinned king who smells of the earth, the sad boy who longs for the ocean, or this one," he turned his eyes on

Stan, "who breathes smoke and dreams of flying?"

"Have you been following me?" Chloe asked.

"I have been watching and listening," he answered without hesitation. "I heard you as you came to this place throughout the last turning of the world."

He looked with disdain at the torn earth and waiting machines before his eyes turned back to the looming tower. The words "DAEDALUS GROUP" and the angel's wing logo of the company were stamped into the steel just above Chloe's head.

His eyes flashed again with latent threat, but in that moment, Uktena seemed sad to Chloe—lonely and lost beneath the veneer of strength. "They destroyed your home; I'm sorry," she offered. "I loved this place."

Uktena's gaze ticked back toward her with a terse little head movement that looked like that of a bird. "They will pay, like all the rest."

"What's going to happen in another two cycles of the moon?" she asked.

But before he had a chance to answer, headlights burned through the trees on the road below. Chloe could hear the crunch and roll of tires and the grumble of an engine.

"The inevitable," Uktena finally answered as a black SUV pulled up on the grass beside the station wagon.

"You better go," she warned just as she turned back to see a dark mass launch upward, accompanied by a blinding electrical flash and an earsplitting clap. She fell back against the ground beside Stan with what felt like a live current passing through her body as a buffeting rush of air came down over the hill around her. Her hair stood on end, and she squinted into the darkness. A terrible scream of wrenching metal sounded above.

Her vision cleared in time to see the blinking red lights snuffed out, and she watched in disbelief as the upper reach of the tower was carried away, dangling and sparking into the clouds. An abrupt wind brushed across the tops of the trees before the night returned to relative silence. Only then did she remember to breathe again.

Beside her, Stan began to stir with a wet snuffle and a little cough. He sat up and opened his heavy lids just as a powerful spotlight switched on at the side of the SUV below and swiveled its blinding beam toward the tower.

"Oh, crap," said Stan as the beam climbed the steel girders from the tower's base to the missing cap. He tilted his head back and followed the path of the light to the jagged and twisted spikes of metal high above. "What the...?"

Chloe was still dazed and tingling. Her breath locked in her throat again as the beam swung back down to blaze across the place where they sat on the hill. She winced and shielded her eyes with her arm, but not before streaks of light had burned across her retinas once more, pulsing in her head along with a quickly growing migraine. The last image she'd seen of the dragon-gouged earth remained pulsing on the inside of her lids.

A car door opened and then slammed shut, but when she tried to squint to see what was coming, she was forced to retreat again from the stab of brightness.

"Uh, Chloe, what's happening?" asked Stan, groggy and frightened beside her.

"I don't know. Just let me do the talking," Chloe whispered as she blindly scooted forward in the hope of filling the most prominent claw marks in the ground with her skirt. A dark figure climbed the hill, surrounded by light, with a long, gangly shadow stretching all the way up the slope toward her.

"Stay where you are," commanded a familiar male voice that Chloe couldn't quite place.

She heard the static and button press of a walkie-talkie before the man spoke again. "This is Car 4—checking in at Tower 1," a burst of static again, and then the button punch to silence it. "Repeat—Car 4 at Tower 1—I have a problem."

Another voice cut through the static in response. "Car 4—go for report."

"Uh—I've got two kids trespassing at Tower 1," static, "And the top of the tower seems to be—missing—over," he said.

There was a long moment of silence as Chloe tried to make out the features of the square-headed man before her.

"Repeat that, Car 4—did you say the top of the tower is

missing?" the voice asked over the walkie-talkie.

"Affirmative," answered Car 4. "It looks like the top section has been ripped off or something—there's no sign of it in the immediate vicinity."

Another long pause as Chloe fought to swallow. "Stay put, Car 4, and keep them there." Static. "We're sending a team out to meet you—over."

"Copy that," said Car 4 as his hand and the walkie-talkie lowered to his side..."Chloe, is that you?"

Chloe eyes bulged as Brent Meeks stepped closer, sporting a freshly trimmed crew cut and a hard scowl. He'd traded in the crisp police department uniform for a black tactical outfit, complete with a many-pocketed vest and what looked like a submachine gun slung across his chest.

"Officer Meeks," Chloe stammered.

"I'm not a police officer anymore, Chloe," he answered stonily. "It's just Brent."

Chloe saw the name "B. Meeks" printed across the breast pocket of his vest. "What are you doing here?" she asked.

"I work security for the Daedalus Group now," he answered with officious pride. "The question is what are you doing here? And what happened to the tower?"

Chloe wasn't sure why, but she felt like she had to protect the dragon. She owed him her life, and she tried not to shake as she forced herself to shrug. "What do you mean? We've just been hanging out...I didn't know anything was wrong with the tower."

Brent removed a little LED flashlight from his belt, and with a click of a button sent a brilliant blue beam up the side of the steel girders. Chloe and Stan both followed his gaze to the torn claws of metal that jutted from the structure some twenty feet below where the tower had previously ended.

Chloe fought against the brewing headache as her mind raced. "Wow, what happened there?" she asked with a bit of forced awe in her voice. "Is that not what it's supposed to look like?"

Brent turned the harsh beam on her without warning,

sending another streak of wincing pain through her head. "I'm pretty sure I saw red blinking lights when I came down the road. Are you telling me you didn't see any blinking lights up there?"

"Uh, I saw a pretty close lightning flash just now," Chloe offered. "Is that what you mean?"

Brent clicked off the flashlight, and though Chloe could barely make out his face amid the glare, she could feel his stare boring into her. "Why don't you two come with me down to the car and get warm," he suggested. "This is going to take a while."

CHAPTER 16
THE DAEDALUS GROUP

Chloe and Stan huddled in the center of the expansive back seat of the black Chevy Suburban that was known as Car 4 to the Daedalus Group security team. Brent Meeks paced back and forth in front of the windshield, occasionally responding to brief bursts of information over the walkie-talkie. The side-mounted spotlight had been retrained on the jagged end of Tower 1, and Chloe's gaze returned often to the brightly lit destruction highlighted there.

Stan's leg had started shaking as soon as Brent had left them alone, and it continued to bounce at a rapid clip with no sign of stopping. "Are we under arrest?"

"I don't think so," Chloe answered. "Brent isn't a cop anymore." She still felt the remnants of the surge that had gone through her throbbing in her temples and tingling in her fingers and toes. She tried to focus on the immediate predicament.

"But you know him?" Stan asked hopefully.

"Yeah, he's the guy I busted for cheating on my mom."

"Huh," said Stan with wild eyes and a slightly crazed smirk. "That's probably not ideal, is it?" He, too, looked back toward the newly missing section of tower. "What happened, Chloe?" asked Stan with an uncharacteristically serious expression. "And don't bullshit me; I'm high, not stupid. I saw the blinking red lights when we got here. I remember sitting beside you on the hill and looking up. Then…"

"I don't know what happened," Chloe started before stopping herself. She didn't know how to explain the dragon in human form, but there was no refuting the destroyed tower. *I'm not crazy!* She took a deep breath. "Okay, something came out of the pond. Like a giant snake...with horns...and legs...and wings." She forced herself to meet Stan's bloodshot gaze. "It came out of the water and took the top of the tower and flew into the clouds."

"A giant snake with horns, legs, and wings?" Stan repeated with a flat voice and deadpan face. "You mean like a dragon?"

Chloe shrugged. "Yeah, it looked pretty much like a dragon...and to be totally honest, I've kind of seen it around a few times before."

"You've seen a giant flying snake hanging around Charlottesville before?" Stan wasn't sure if he should smile or frown. "Why haven't you mentioned this?"

"I've been having trouble with my memory since the lightning strike, and I wasn't sure if I was going crazy or not." Chloe pointed at the decimated tower with a conflicted sense of relief. "But I'm pretty sure that that's real."

Headlights quickly approached along the road behind them. When Stan spoke again, he felt the subconscious need to whisper. "You were right, that's pretty weird." Two other black Suburbans pulled up on either side of Car 4 with tactical precision. Then a black Lincoln Town Car with tinted windows came to a gentle halt directly behind them with its brights blasting through the windows.

"Is it just me, or does this level of security seem a little weird, too?" Chloe asked as two men with outfits and haircuts like Brent emerged from their respective vehicles and converged in front of Car 4. The Town Car just idled menacingly.

"What was that tower for?" whispered Stan as the men looked to the highlighted damage and then turned their hard stares toward Car 4.

"I don't know, but I'm going to find out," Chloe declared.

Her courage faltered as she spied a low-flying light approaching over the trees.

"What's that?" asked Stan as a rhythmic THWOP started to echo about the clearing.

Chloe watched for a long moment as the sleek, black

helicopter tore overhead violently shaking the trees and circling with a spotlight held on the broken tower. "Trouble," she answered as the back door of the Town Car opened and a disheveled man with a coat slung over his pajamas stepped out and walked by Car 4 with his intense gaze squinting into the artificial wind. She recognized him as the same man from the library photos at Paul Markson's party a few weeks back.

"That's Dr. Markson," Stan confirmed as the pajama-clad man and the security team walked further into the clearing with stooped heads.

The helicopter lowered onto the level terrain at the base of the hill, and Chloe could see the Daedalus Group insignia blazoned in white on the tail. She also recognized the jowly scowl of Mr. Roberts as he stepped from the helicopter door, wearing a light grey three-piece suit. He moved to meet his partner as the spinning rotors wound down.

The two captains of industry nodded in greeting before moving their eyes back to the tower. Chloe watched as they shared a few terse words and then turned their formidable combined focus on former officer Brent Meeks. The two traded off, grilling him with curt questions that he responded to with short answers and a bowed head. Then all eyes swiveled back toward Car 4. Despite the tinted windows, distance, and darkness, Chloe and Stan both ducked.

Chloe peered from behind the headrest as Brent spoke briefly into the walkie-talkie. She hadn't noticed that the driver's side door of the Lincoln had opened behind her, and she jumped with an embarrassing yelp as another square-jawed security man tapped on the car window with the butt of a flashlight.

"Step out of the car, please," he said without emotion.

Chloe and Stan glanced to each other for silent moral support before taking deep breaths and opening the doors.

"Come with me, please," said the stone-faced man as he motioned them toward the waiting group in the field.

Chloe stood and felt the damp squish of the naked earth between her toes, remembering only then that she'd left her shoes on the hill. Her previously perfect dress was now grass-stained and soiled, and her hair was tangled and frizzy. Still, she walked with righteous conviction as she focused on the men who had desecrated her sacred glen. Stan followed at her heels with wide eyes and a nervous little smirk.

With the sound of the helicopter quieted, the clearing returned to a pregnant hush. Chloe was oddly aware of the padding of her own footfalls through the grass.

"I believe we've met before," stated Mr. Roberts before she'd come to a halt.

She looked up to meet his gaze and forced herself to stand her ground as she had with the dragon. "Yes, sir."

"And is this the spot of your lightning encounter?"

She nodded and looked to the mangled steel at the top of the hill.

"Had that tower stood there at the time, you never would have been affected," he noted. "The upper dome was shielded against conductivity to the ground."

"What is it for?" Chloe asked.

Mr. Roberts looked to Dr. Markson, who barely broke his gaze from the hill to give an assenting nod before he marched off toward the site.

Mr. Roberts turned to his forced audience. "Have you ever heard of antimatter?"

Chloe nodded and Stan shrugged.

"Scientists have been trying to locate and harness the nature of antimatter for decades. You see, when it collides with matter, its annihilation produces a hundred percent efficient clean energy with no byproducts—the perfect power source." He smiled coldly as his grey eyes moved back and forth between Chloe and Stan. "There's even an experimental antimatter trap traveling on a satellite toward the center of our galaxy right now. It should be able to reach and sample from a huge cache of suspected antimatter positrons in about thirty years' time."

Stan coughed nervously, but Mr. Roberts didn't seem to notice.

"But it turns out that particles of positron antimatter are also released every time a bolt of electricity is unleashed from the clouds." He stared up at the grey blanket above for effect. "These particles float up into the atmosphere and travel along magnetic lines that circle the globe, spinning away right over our heads for all these years without us even knowing it." He brought his gaze back down to Chloe. "But now the Daedalus Group has its own satellite, and if we can guess where lightning might strike, we can put our own positron trap along the path of the magnetic currents and snatch the antimatter right out of space."

Chloe began to grasp the enormity of what he was proposing. "How much antimatter could you collect?"

"That depends on how much lightning we can predict, now doesn't it?" Mr. Roberts turned back toward the broken tower with all hint of warmth stripped from his face. "Mr. Meeks tells me that he found you sitting on the hill just below the tower and that he saw the aircraft warning lights blinking as he drove up through the trees." He crossed his hands at his back and cleared his throat. "Yet you insist that you never noticed the lights in the time that you were here?"

Chloe swallowed hard. "That's right."

Mr. Roberts turned toward Stan, who had been looking at his own feet the whole time. "And you, Mr. Strakowski? Dr. Markson tells me that he knows your family quite well, that you've attended functions at his house...Is that how *you* recall the evening?"

"Uh, yes, sir," Stan stammered.

"I see." Mr. Roberts frowned. "So you're calling Mr. Meeks a liar?"

"It wouldn't be the first time," Chloe muttered with a quick glance to Brent as he scanned the woods and feigned disinterest.

"Ah," said Mr. Roberts. "Mr. Meeks mentioned that he'd had some dealings with you before. He vouched for your character, Miss McClellan, though it seems you do not share his kind regard...Tell me, what time did you arrive at the hill tonight?"

Chloe shrugged, "I'm not sure, maybe ten thirty...or so?"

"Hmm," said Mr. Roberts with a furrowed brow. "It's strange, then, that we were getting readings from the tower right up until 10:58 and twenty-six seconds, almost exactly the same moment that Mr. Meeks radioed in to announce his scheduled check of the site."

"That is strange," admitted Chloe without much conviction. She watched as Dr. Markson reached the top of the hill, surrounded by the glare of the spotlight. He was standing just a couple steps away from the clawed imprint from the dragon's launch into the air. Chloe held her breath and willed him to not look down.

"So you're telling me that while you lounged on the cold, damp hill in the middle of the night, twenty or thirty tons of steel, cabling, and research equipment was ripped away from over your heads without you seeing or hearing anything?" Mr. Roberts' flat little eyes locked on Chloe.

"I'd really like to help you if I could, but I'm not sure what to say. I guess we must have fallen asleep or something," Chloe said.

Mr. Roberts turned on Stan.

"Yeah, I totally passed out," blurted Stan with a little bolster of confidence. "When I woke up, the spotlight was on us. The last thing I remembered was getting sleepy while talking to Chloe."

Mr. Roberts frowned. "That is most unfortunate; it seems you were in a unique position to shed some light on a rather perplexing mystery—millions of dollars of equipment lost, just as it was about to become operational. Your help could have been worth a great deal to our company."

"I'm sorry," Chloe gulped, just as the three walkie-talkies crackled to life.

"This is Air 2—repeat—Air 2, with a visual on the missing tower—over," said the voice over the walkie.

"Copy that, Air 2—go for coordinates—over," answered the square-jawed security man who had come out of the Lincoln.

"I have pieces of it scattered around an old quarry located 6.4 miles southwest of Tower 1—some of the support beams are sticking out of the water—no indication as to how it got here—over."

Mr. Roberts held up a hand, and the security man delayed his response. For an instant, Brent shot Chloe what might have been a look of warning before the other guards stepped closer. *What was that?*

"Well, then, I suppose it is time for you to leave," interjected Mr. Roberts with cold dismissal. "The team will see you back to your car, and Mr. Meeks will follow you out."

They began to usher Chloe and Stan back toward the cars, but Chloe brushed past the arms of one of the guards and took a step toward Mr. Roberts. "Why here?" she blurted. "Why did you have to build the tower here?"

Mr. Roberts looked over his shoulder with a humorless smile. "I would think you, if anyone, would know the answer to that. This clearing is struck by lightning more than any other spot in Virginia. Perhaps you would be wise to steer clear of it from now on."

Firm hands grasped Chloe by the shoulders and directed her away. But before she let them push her back to Stan's wagon, she spied Dr. Markson up on the hill, crouched in the dragon's tracks with his hand pressed to the torn ground.

CHAPTER 17
I Am the Lightning

That night, Chloe dreamed of flying. Not as a bird or like the one time she'd ridden in a plane when she was five—in the dream, she soared over Charlottesville on the dragon's back, with the giant wings rising and falling on either side of her. She gripped a bony ridge at the base of his neck and squeezed tightly with her legs. She was oddly secure in her seat, as if it was meant for her alone. Despite the ponderous beats, the darkened buildings and trees below flashed by at a dizzying pace.

"Faster!" she screamed into the wind as the luffed sails rose before catching the current again.

As Uktena flapped, Chloe felt the surge beneath her, and she hunched lower. The dragon angled his head to glance back as a ripple of electricity lit his gaze.

"Faster!" she called again, and the dark clouds ahead answered with a flash and a rumble. With one last powerful beat, Uktena carried them higher before dropping his wings back and diving toward the thunderhead. Chloe shut her eyes and hugged closer. She found herself laughing as they rocketed through the night. But in seconds, the speed made laughter and breath impossible as a static charge gathered within and around her. They were vibrating at the same frequency, faster than Chloe could comprehend. It felt like the molecules of her body might come unglued and drift away, even mingle with those of the monster below her.

Still she wanted to scream out, "Faster!"

In that instant, she and Uktena streaked forward with a brilliant burst of light, traveling miles in a blink, not as beast and rider, but as raw energy.

It crackled in and around them as they arrived amid a dark cloud with a shockwave of sound emanating from that point. No longer was the dragon beneath her, and Chloe was no longer herself. They were free and inseparable. The wind gathered and heavy droplets of rain began to fall. They breathed in the storm, becoming one with the air and water. And they exhaled new life to both, spurring them on, telling them—why be a cloud when you can be a tornado? Why just rain when you could be a flood?

The whole world was vibrating, everything and everyone moving at its own speed. It was they who could turn up the frequency. They called to the riled molecules of the storm and dropped their attention below. With a spark, they were born anew, firing down to the ground with a blinding lash that was hotter than the sun.

In an instant, they met wood and soil, fusing with the earth just as they'd been one with the storm. And the dance of their twin vibrations gave birth to flame as the searing stroke bore down into the heart of the old oak beside the pond.

Chloe heard her own voice again as she called out to her brothers and sisters—air, water, earth, and flame. She was the spirit who'd come to wake them and bind them. She was the spark that would set the world on fire.

. . .

Chloe woke the next morning with the pressure of a migraine waiting to break free and wash over her. A few minutes later, it did. She'd wanted to talk with Dr. Liou again, knowing that she needed to act fast in case her memory started to slip once more, but by lunchtime, the worst headache of her life had settled in. By seven o'clock that evening, she'd sunk into such an emotional and physical mess that Audrey had been forced to take off the late shift at Pete's and then the following morning at her office job in order to stay home and tend to her sallow and quivering daughter. That Monday would be the second school absence that Chloe had taken in years.

For those twenty-four hours of torture, when Chloe's eyes were open, the light seared through her temples like an electric current. But in the darkness, when she clenched her lids tightly against the throbbing, she saw the deep, lightning-filled eyes of the dragon staring back. Finally, after countless trips to face the toilet and a sheet-clenching, sweat-drenched night, the onslaught relented and she found sleep again.

When she woke on Monday afternoon to find her life as she had left it, she wept in a way that she hadn't since she'd been a little girl. Not with a sense of relief or because of the pain she had felt, but because of the profound loss of connectedness to the greater world that she'd known when traveling through the elements as living lightning. The absence of that freedom left her hollowed out and stripped bare. Audrey had rocked her and whispered soothing words, but Chloe knew that her mom could never understand why.

Audrey left for the evening shift at Pete's with her brow creased with worry as Chloe slouched into the sofa with a bowl of chicken soup balanced on her stomach. It was the first food other than five Saltines and a Pedialyte popsicle that she'd eaten since Stan had taken her out to dinner with his father's money before the dance.

The TV flashed terrifying images from Berlin, where a massive car bomb had gone off in city center earlier in the day. The news channels replayed pictures of screaming, bloody people and burning buildings as the "BREAKING NEWS" logo pulsed in bright yellow across the bottom left quadrant of the screen: NOW 416 CONFIRMED DEAD IN WORST TERRORIST ATTACK ON EUROPEAN SOIL.

The smoke and ash cloud that was billowing out of Mt. Kilimanjaro was so last week, though nothing had been done to move the half a million refugees that were encamped in its shadow. The news flavor of the moment had swung back to humanity's amazing affinity for killing itself. Like the rest of the world, Chloe felt numb.

But this time, she would not forget what she'd seen; she could not. The dragon had said that he was not supposed to wake for another two cycles of the moon.

Only two months until "the inevitable." Chloe had to find out what that meant. She had to find Uktena.

. . .

Maintaining the daily appearance of normalcy was another challenge. Since their run-in with the Daedalus Group, Stan had sent more than thirty texts looking for answers that she didn't have to give. And since Homecoming, any semblance of anonymity in school had become impossible. It had been one thing when there'd been a small undercurrent of fascination with the notorious Lightning Girl, but now everyone knew Chloe McClellan by name and sight—as if her secret identity had become more popular than the superhero persona she'd been hiding behind.

She was relieved to have Stan in on her new, and most bizarre, obsession to date, but she hadn't felt right about divulging the full extent of her interaction with Uktena. Perhaps it was the inescapable fear of being labeled as "CRAZY" like her father, or perhaps it was due to the lingering connection she'd known with the dragon in her lightning dream...Regardless, she still couldn't bring herself to mention the lengthy conversation she'd had with the creature, preferring to keep her late-night research into the history of horned serpents in Native American lore to herself for now.

And then there was everything else: Ezra still being his obnoxious, charming self, Kendra still plotting to kill her, and above all, the fact that Kirin was possibly interested, though still grounded and almost entirely unavailable...

After a few days, she wasn't sure if she needed the trials of adolescence to help her forget about the insanity of monsters and evil corporations or if perhaps it was the other way around. On Saturday, after another victorious cross-country race, her mom took the long way home, and they drove past the Daedalus Group turnoff to the pond. Now the dirt road was barred by a keypad gate, and the "NO TRESSPASSING" sign had doubled in size.

"What the hell are they up to now? Probably cutting down the forest and poisoning the ground water for their bottom line!" Audrey snapped angrily before driving on with a heavy foot on the gas. Chloe remained silent. But the following Sunday morning, when she found herself with an extended amount of free time and a total lack of adult supervision, she put on her black running sweats, laced up her shoes, and locked the door behind her.

She paused at the side of the old barn and pushed against the weathered boards of the wall to stretch her hamstrings. Muted red paint flaked off beneath her fingers, and the half-rotten wood creaked as she bent low into the stretch with one leg and then the other.

She caught the sickly sweet reek of a dead animal and broke the stretch to cover her nose. Shipwreck had taken to leaving dead mice, squirrels, and birds rotting within. The half-eaten remains could get really gross, but at least it was better than the year the cat had experimented with carrying his fresh kills into the house—and once, to his near demise, onto the kitchen counter. It had since fallen on Chloe to occasionally venture into the derelict building to clear out the putrid carcasses. She wasn't sure she had such a mission in her today.

This one smelled like a big one, too, and she shuddered at the thought of having to shovel a mangled possum or raccoon into a trash bag. She stood on her tiptoes and peered through the filthy window, but thankfully saw nothing past the dirt and gloom to demand her immediate response. *It's not like it's going to get any deader.*

She took off at a gentle lope that carried her across the street and toward the mouth of the Red Hill Trail Loop. This would be what her coach referred to as a "day-after wind-down run," meant to be a short, leisurely paced jog to ease her postrace legs back into a fresh week of training. She, of course, had ulterior motives, and half a mile later, she turned from the winding path and charged into the woods at a good clip.

She'd come in third in the race against Jefferson Academy the day before, and though she was happy enough to come in behind her teammate, Angela, who was potentially the fastest girl in the state, she didn't like losing to a private school girl as well. She pushed herself past the same forked tree that she always passed and started to travel more naturally over the leaves and through the woods. Even though she was only a sophomore, Chloe would bet real money that there wasn't a girl in the state who could beat her in a race from her house to the pond.

The wind brushed her cheeks as dappled autumn light filtered through the leaves. She remembered years when the leaves would have completely turned by mid-October, but now, only a couple days away from Halloween, there was barely even a yellowing to the lush canopy above. Her feet found just the right places to step as she wound her way through the trunks. She moved with such assurance that the birds in the trees didn't even bother to bolt as she passed below.

She streaked by the stump from which she'd once given Liz an impromptu speech about the profound ecological importance of trees, and she adjusted her pace to the gradual incline that led to the lightning hill. Running up hills was Chloe's specialty, and she'd learned quickly that attacking the slopes was the best way for her to go from tenth to second or third place in a competitive race.

Chloe climbed, pretending that every tree she passed was another struggling runner. She embraced the pain in her thighs, as every little victory pushed her harder toward the next. She imagined that she was long, sinewy, and sleek, gliding through the forest with ethereal grace—both master and servant of the elements. For a moment, she was lost in the deep, resonant thundering of her own heart, beating in union with the land and filled with a seemingly bottomless pool of vitality and hunger...

She snapped out of it as her feet instinctively reversed into a frantic, scrabbling attempt to stop. She lost traction on the groundcover, and found herself skidding on her hip and elbow into the new twelve-foot-high chain link fence that blocked her way. The links were not forgiving, and she crumbled into a heap with a loud rattling that traveled along the weave of metal in both directions.

Slowly she shook off the weird runner's high and gazed up at the spiraling barbed-wire that capped the length of the barrier. She used the fence to pull herself to unsteady feet, thankful in that moment that it hadn't also been electrified. Fifty yards further on the other side, repair work had begun on the destroyed lightning tower. Already the bent and torn steel had been cut away, and two sections of fresh beams had been riveted in place on the existing foundation. As she watched, a crane swung another ten-foot girder toward a team of men who were strung about the scaffolding that surrounded the structure.

Chloe ducked and scampered behind a tree. Her elbow throbbed where she'd clipped a root midslide, and she rubbed it for a moment as she caught her breath before peering back around. Two men with hard hats and an open map were moving in her direction. One of them made a sweeping motion across the woods, but their eyes remained focused on the paper stretched between them.

Chloe darted along the fence at a bent shuffle, looking for a spot with a view of the pond itself. A hundred yards later, she crouched behind the trunk of a large elm. She peeked out from behind a bony knob of the tree, and her gaze was drawn to the swarm of activity around the water.

A platform boat was anchored at the center of the pond with a cluster of people in white bio-hazard suits on board. One of them was probing the pond with a long, thin rod. Another was dangling some sort of device into the water as the figure beside him stared at a handheld contraption. A woman sat at a desk on the platform, watching a trio of monitors with unwavering attention. Her gloved hands gripped a pair of joysticks as a spool of cable ran out from the humming computer and disappeared into the water over the edge.

Then Chloe spied Dr. Markson, pacing along the pond's perimeter. He'd forgone the bio-suit for an outdoorsman outfit that looked straight from the pages of L.L. Bean: crisply ironed khakis, duck boots, and a charcoal grey explorer blazer. As he paced, he spoke occasionally into a headset with a fixed gaze that looked past the world around him.

He knows something. Should I tell him what I know? But there was something off about the Daedalus Group; everything they touched seemed wrong. Chloe's mom did not hate easily, but she'd openly worn her contempt for Mr. Roberts and his people for as long as Chloe could remember. Though she'd only been five or six at the time, Chloe even recalled her father's anger when he'd come across the Daedalus Group recruitment campaigns in the local paper. He had a knack for the fire-and-brimstone talk in those days, and nothing set him off like corporate greed and industrial waste. Chloe remembered how Audrey's smile froze when he really got going.

A scuba diver surfaced at the pond's edge and held something up toward Dr. Markson. It was about the size of a dinner plate and reflected the sunlight with a milky sheen that resembled mother of pearl. Dr. Markson shuffled over with obvious excitement and snatched the oblong disk with both hands before inspecting it closely.

Chloe stepped out to try to get a better look but dropped to the ground an instant later. She held her breath as a man emerged from the trees along the fence, heading toward her. She slithered around the trunk with her back against the rough bark and peeked around the other side. Former officer Brent Meeks's footsteps crunched past as he continued to scan the perimeter with a determined crinkle of his brow.

Chloe exhaled slowly as Brent moved on. *This is getting too real...I need to talk to Dr. Liou.*

. . .

After a sprint, a quick shower, and more than an hour of waiting for and riding various buses, Chloe bounded up the steps of the Brooks Hall Anthropology Building at UVA. She needed to tell someone about Uktena, and only a student of myth and history like Dr. Edward Liou might be made to understand the lunacy she had witnessed. But she was also wearing the least practical outfit she'd worn since the dance, hoping that Kirin might still be there on lockdown.

She felt a little naked with the freedom of bare legs beneath the long, flowing skirt her mom had always encouraged her to wear as a jeans alternative. But she was hoping to find an opportunity to take off her jacket and display the formfitting tank top that Audrey insisted made her arms and shoulders look "awesome."

Of course, Chet the TA was there to greet her with a pretentious glare. He tapped his pen on the sign-in book and tracked her approach. "Well, if it isn't community outreach day."

"I need to see Dr. Liou. Is he in?"

"Sorry, he's busy and his office hours are over. You'll have to come back next week," he said as if he thought he were a judge passing verdict.

Chloe ignored his ruling and sidled up to the desk, taking off the jacket. She took the pen with a flex in her arm and watched as his gaze moved to her skin and widened just a little. Her eyes flitted to his ringless finger and then down to the book.

CHET SWANBURG: #123637 9:06 A.M.

"You have a girlfriend, Chet?" she asked.

He swallowed and sat up a little straighter. "No," he said warily.

"Surprising," she offered with a coy smile that could have been taken either way. She looked back to the book.

DR. EDWARD LIOU: #288362 10:00 A.M.

No +1; Kirin's not here. The smile faltered, but her front of joy vanished completely as she saw the third entry on the list.

RICHARD ROBERTS: #GUEST 12:30 PM.

"What the?" she blurted.

"What?" asked Chet with a raised eyebrow.

Chloe pointed at the name with a shaky finger. "What is he doing here?"

"Oh," said Chet, snapping out of his daze. "He's kind of a big deal, actually. Dr. Liou sees lots of important people."

Chloe stared at the name and tamped down the impulse to bolt. The clock on the wall behind Chet read 12:46 p.m. Her heart was beating as if she was back at the run, but she had to know what Mr. Roberts wanted. "Well, he's expecting me, too. So is it all right if I wait?" she asked with the play of sweetness returned…

"I guess you can wait over there if you want," he acquiesced with a point to a wooden bench framed by a couple ferns.

"Cool. Can you tell me where the bathroom is?" She flashed him the cutest smile she could muster.

Chet eyed her closely as she scribbled a deliberately illegible name in the book. "Top of the stairs on the right," he answered.

"Thanks." She flew up the steps two at a time.

At the top of the stairs, she heard Mr. Roberts's pompous voice echoing into the hallway through the open office door. It was joined by a flutter of laughter from Dr. Liou that reminded her of Kirin. Chloe ducked through the squeaking door of the coed bathroom and closed it sharply behind her. *I seem to be making a habit of hiding in bathrooms.*

The room had five weathered but clean stalls on one side and a row of matching sinks beneath the spotted mirror on the other. Cool air whistled through the cracked window with a tinny echo off the vaulted ceiling. Chloe ducked low to check the stalls for legs and then turned back to press her ear to the door. All she could hear was the muffled huff of her own breathing.

She pulled on the tarnished knob just enough to peek out. The hall was still empty, and Mr. Roberts's voice had started in again. She strained to listen, but could only make out a few strings of his words:

"…trying to take a greater interest in the university's resources…want to show our support of a wide array of disciplines throughout the academic community…"

Chloe opened the door wider and leaned her head out into the hallway.

"…My partner in particular, Dr. William Markson, smartest man I've ever met, has taken a real interest in local mythology," he chuckled. "You know, Indian stories and folk legends and such, particularly as they pertain to fantastic beasts and cattle mutilations—things like that. Everyone we asked said you were the man to talk to. Wilkie even tracked down and read your paper on these dragons of yours; I swear he doesn't sleep.

Long story short, he'd be interested in funding your research and hearing everything you know on the subject, if that would work for you?"

Chloe could picture his insidious smile despite the distance and walls between them.

"I…I don't know what to say," said Dr. Liou. "This is all so unexpected."

"Yes, well, the best things in life often are," answered Mr. Roberts with a cold little laugh. "If you're interested, we'd even be able to look into making arrangements for you to go take a look at this old cauldron firsthand."

"I would love to, but I'm afraid it's in a very private collection in Hong Kong—"

"Oh, we can be very persuasive, Dr. Liou," cut in Mr. Roberts. "With the Daedalus Group behind you, you'll find that doors open up to you that you didn't even know were there."

Chloe heard the abrupt scooting of a chair and she ducked back further into the bathroom.

"I'm at a loss for words," Dr. Liou admitted. "Thank you, this is an amazing offer."

"Well, you don't have to answer now; I have a few more stops today. We can finalize everything later this week."

"Yes, yes, of course," stammered Dr. Liou.

"And I'm sure Dr. Markson will want to stop by and talk to you in person before long, so get your notes ready; he can be an intense student." Mr. Roberts chuckled again as Chloe retreated behind the door. The sound of Mr. Roberts's phony attempt at mirth sent an unpleasant tingling down her spine.

"I look forward to it," offered Dr. Liou. "There's nothing I like more than talking about my obsessions with a challenging and attentive audience."

"Very good," replied Mr. Roberts with a tone of finality. "I'll let him know, and I'll have my secretary phone you in a couple days."

Chloe listened as their footsteps moved past the door, and she breathed a slow sigh of relief. Her breath seized when she heard the steps pause at the top of the stairs.

"I'm going to make a quick stop before I'm on my way," sounded Mr. Roberts as the footsteps reversed course.

"Of course, thank you again," offered Dr. Liou as Chloe darted away from the door, scanning for an escape. There was no janitor's closet and no way out the window. As the footsteps drew closer, she frantically ducked into the third stall and latched the door behind her.

The door swung open with a shrill creak, and Mr. Roberts cleared his throat. As quietly as she could, Chloe rose to an unsteady balance with her feet on the rim of the toilet bowl. The fringe of her skirt slipped into the water below, and she yanked it back out with an echoing drip of water as Mr. Roberts opened the first stall and unzipped his pants.

Her breath locked in her throat as he started to pee... *Come on!* After what seemed like an eternity, he zipped up and walked to the sinks, where Chloe glimpsed his reflection for a moment through the seams of the stall. He ran his hands under the faucet for a few obligatory seconds before turning around to peer at the stalls behind him. Chloe hunched into a ball and froze. *Don't see me! Don't see me!*

She only allowed herself to look up again when she heard the dialing of a cell phone. Mr. Roberts moved over toward the window before he spoke.

"Wilkie, it's me," he announced. "The paleontologist and the anthropologist are in, though one or both of them may very well be crackpots...Yes, I'll get them to sign the nondisclosure agreement later this week, and then we can find out what they know and keep them quiet."

Chloe was a statue.

"Really?" cut in Mr. Roberts. "Where did you find that? Does it match the scale we found at the cow farm?"

"...Well, that sounds like something this paleo-guy might help with." There was an edge of impatience in his voice. "I don't see how; *he's* writing a book about dragons...Wilkie, more importantly, where are we with getting Tower 1 back up and operational? These guys are breathing down my neck for actionable results, and apparently the Chinese aren't as far behind as we thought…I'm not asking you to forget about it; I'm as curious as you are, but we need hard data on the positron trap last month, and we don't have time right now for another of your wild goose chases…"

Even from across the room, Chloe could hear the muffled anger of Dr. Markson on the other end of the call.

"And where would you have had me find the funding for this? You think some private investor is just going to throw half a billion at your theory?" countered Mr. Roberts with his own anger on the rise. "This is half a billion dollars we're talking about here. I don't think there's a name for whatever branch of government these guys are from, and they don't care if you disapprove of their money; they expect a return on that investment soon…Yes, but if we can give it to them, and we both know that we can, then we'll make twenty times that amount, win the Nobel Prize, and solve the world's energy crisis by the end of next year."

Chloe's leg muscles started to tremble.

"I understand your position on this, Wilkie, really I do, and after this one, we can finally afford to be idealists. Whatever you think of the circumstances, this will change the world for the better! History needs to know your name, and this is the one to make it happen!"

Despite the chill in the room, a bead of sweat rolled down from Chloe's scalp.

"Yes, I told Dr. Liou that you'd come and talk to him this week, and I have people looking into getting access to this old cauldron if we can't just buy it outright…"

Chloe's foot slipped and almost wound up in the water. She froze again with wide eyes and her hands pressed against the walls of the stall. For a long moment, all she could hear was the sound of the wind sailing through the window and the sporadic ticking of the radiator.

"The girl doesn't know anything. She's in high school, for God's sake…Yes, I knew her father. He was a nut-job and a troublemaker, and I had to get rid of him. If it comes to it, I'll take care of this girl and the mom the same way—trust me, these people are totally unconnected and poor as dirt. For now, you just worry about getting the tower operational and the data flowing in. Everything relating to this Loch Ness Monster, or whatever it is, can wait…"

What did he do to my father? What could he do to mom? Now Chloe's arms were shaking, too.

"Honestly, I'd say we only have a month or so before Mr. Allen shows. I've stalled for as long as I can…All right, I'll set it up, but I need that tower up and running again next week."

Chloe's nose started to itch terribly.

"I know it's impossible; that's why I have you." Chloe heard the hang-up beep of the cell phone.

Please leave! Please leave! But as the footsteps moved back toward the door, she heard him start to dial again…

"Have Mr. Duncan bring the car around and get me Mr. Allen on the phone as soon as possible," The door's hinges screamed in protest again and Chloe all but collapsed onto the tile floor.

She put her back against the stall and tried to still the trembling throughout her body. She didn't care about the wet spot on her skirt clinging to her leg or the stink of lemon-scented ammonia that surrounded her. Chloe was deeply rattled. *I have to protect mom. I'm only fifteen. Curiosity did not reward the cat…I have homework to do.*

And with that, she picked herself up and fled.

CHAPTER 18
THE GAUNTLET

Chloe tried to force the jagged-edged shape of her life back down into the neat little hole of high school. Before, she'd struggled to hold on to every nuance of her encounters with the dragon only to have them stripped away in her sleep. Now, her failed attempt to suppress those same memories left her sullen and irritable. She'd worn the mask of scholarly focus for a few days without incident, but today was Halloween and her attempt at assimilation was derailed before she even got through the senior parking lot to her homeroom class.

First Ezra came bounding toward her wearing the white-sheet toga and golden oak leaf crown of a Caesar. "You can't ignore me forever, Lightning," he bellowed from twenty paces out.

Chloe scrunched lower as more than one pair of eyes swung to watch her response. She forced a weak smile. "Don't count on it, Your Highness." She'd managed to steer clear of him for the better part of a couple weeks, and a public confrontation was the last thing she needed right now. She headed for the side entrance to the school, knowing before she'd taken two steps that her evasive tactics were futile.

He drew his cardboard legionnaire's sword and blocked her path. "What are you supposed to be?" he asked.

She grabbed the fake sword by the blade and pushed it aside. "I'm an angry high school student." She eyed him up and down and kept walking. "Let me guess, you're a premature frat boy with a weakness for jailbait."

He looped around and fell into an exaggerated step beside

her. "What, you plan to avoid me until I graduate?"

"I hadn't really given it much thought," she muttered without looking at him. "How about you? You plan on robbing the cradle until June?"

"Chloe, come on!" he shouted, stopping her in her tracks.

She flinched and turned to look up at him.

He looked at her in a way that made it seem like they were the only two people there, despite all the eyes and ears that had turned their way. "What's really your problem with me?" he challenged. "You're the one who's in love with that surfer dude and always running around with the stoner doofus!"

Chloe shriveled as her gaze danced between multiple sets of watching eyes. "Why are you shouting at me?" she asked in a harsh whisper.

"'Cause you're too damn thick to listen otherwise," he answered in a more reasonable decibel. "I've gone out with your presumed enemy a couple times—so what? She's actually pretty cool and hilariously sarcastic once you get to know her, but despite popular belief, I'm not actually all that sleazy," he proclaimed. "I'm not pretending or hiding anything. I'm just having fun when I can, and I don't apologize for that…But YOU are my homegirl, Chloe. I'd move the earth for you."

That was when Kendra zipped into the parking lot in her brand-new sweet sixteen BMW. Sleek and fire red, it slid into an open space a few cars ahead. She emerged with a cackle and pranced into Chloe's line of sight with a wicked grin. She was wearing a hospital gown and booties, and her hair was clumped with artfully placed twigs and leaves beneath a golden makeshift crown. She wore makeup that made her face look dirty and pale, but still she couldn't keep from looking beautiful. Her wild eyes met Chloe's in open challenge. "Look at me, everybody; I'm the Lightning Girl!"

Chloe shot a hard look back at Ezra. His face had gone slack. "Right, good speech," she said before moving on toward the door as steadily as she could.

"Christ!" Ezra muttered behind her. He gave Kendra a disgusted look and stormed off in the other direction.

Chloe kept walking. She could feel her blood starting to boil as she got closer, but she didn't even glance over as she stepped past Kendra's theatrical display of hostility.

"Stay away from him, freak!" Kendra hissed at her back.

Okay, bitch, that's it! Chloe stopped and turned slowly. "Happy birthday, Kendra. Looks like Daddy bought you a good one." Her calculating eyes moved to the license plate: HAWT-16. She burst out with a cold laugh. "Wow, congratulations! Now you're one big moving advertisement for pedophilia."

Kendra snorted. "Better than being a walking billboard for Paxil."

Touché! Chloe hadn't expected that. She stopped laughing and dropped her death gaze to scan the costume. Kendra had used an impressive attention to detail: complete with fake abrasions and bloody bandages on her hands and knees. "I like your costume."

"Yours sucks," Kendra retorted. Without warning, she held up her phone and snapped another surprise picture of Chloe. "You dress like a fifth-grade boy." She bent her wild-haired head to examine her digital work and grinned.

"Gee, maybe you could take me shopping with Daddy's credit sometime?" spat Chloe.

"Yeah, that'd be so cute, just like an after-school special. Except, as we're leaving from the big clothes spree with tons of bags, I suddenly push you in front of an oncoming bus and we learn that the moral of the story is 'don't fuck with Kendra!'"

Chloe couldn't tell if she was furious, embarrassed, or impressed. Part of her wanted to burst out laughing, and the other was on the cusp of lunging across the distance and tearing into Kendra's throat. Instead, she just stood there mutely.

Kendra waved the picture in front of Chloe and then dismissed her. "Run along and have a good day. I got your number from Ezra; I'll totally CC you this time."

Chloe turned her back on the scarlet nightmare and kept walking as Kendra's victorious cackle rang out across the parking lot. Chloe cinched her backpack straps tighter and picked up the pace. She felt the press of eyes on her from all directions and sank her head into her shoulders. The rumble of thunder sounded in her inner ears.

She didn't even hear Stan calling out to her until he caught her at the side door. Still she latched on to the handle with a death grip and swung the door open with enough force to smack it into the brick wall with a loud echo down the hallway.

"Stupid door!" shouted Stan with an angry point. He was wearing a hooked bird beak over his nose, and his eyes were already bloodshot.

"I hate this place!" shouted Chloe with steam trailing behind every word. "This is all a monumental waste of time!"

"Happy Halloween to you, too," answered Stan with an undaunted grin.

She turned on him and narrowed her eyes. "Are you high already?"

He shrugged.

"That's really sad."

"I have no sound argument to dispute that," he said with a nod. "But dude," he continued with a dramatic hush to his voice, "did you hear about the missing livestock?"

Chloe shook her head.

"It's been all over the local news today—more than ten cows, a few goats, and a pig have all gone missing over the course of the last couple months with only a few specks of blood to show for it." Stan flared his eyes for dramatic effect. "They finally gave the culprit a name…The Charlottesville Cow Thief. It's gonna be bigger than the Chupacabras!" He was nodding his head with a knowing look. "Police say there's no sign of entry or struggle at any of the sites; it's like the animals were plucked from the ground and carried off into thin air." He winked. "Sound like anything to you?"

Chloe felt like she'd been slapped back into reality, or perhaps back out of it. "Really?"

"Dude, Google it."

Chloe stared off through the wall, trying to decide what she thought of this information. Self-preservation told her to forget the whole thing, but to do so would be against her nature. Her eyes drifted back to Stan's waiting grin. "You believe me?"

Stan shrugged. "You're real moody and pretty weird, but I'm fairly certain you're not crazy...If you say you've seen a giant flying reptile hanging around and now a whole bunch of animals have gone missing, then it seems to check out, right?"

"Thanks, Stan."

He leaned closer. "So what are we going to do?" he whispered with conspiratorial glee.

All the drama of the parking lot was a distant memory. Chloe's eyes thinned and a smirk crept closer. "We have to find it before anyone else does."

.   .   .

But even though she should have been focused on the renewed hunt for the improbable beast, all the petty pains of high school returned when Kirin didn't show up again for homeroom. Chloe hadn't really talked to him since he'd given her the ride before the dance, and she began to fear that he might graduate before she got a moment alone with him again. She pondered the possibility of having to slog through the rest of the semester without his active presence in her life. *What if Ezra is right? What if I do love Kirin?*

She stared at the back of Liz's head while she expertly thumbed yet another text exchange with Paul Markson from under her desk. Somehow, even with her back turned and head down, Liz seemed to radiate bubbly joy. It had been a full month since Liz had entered this constant euphoric state, and in her lower moments, Chloe had actually started to hide from her sight in the hallway.

Though she wouldn't admit it, Chloe was jealous. Not of being with Paul Markson—who had on occasion proven to be as much of a dullard as his father was brilliant—but more of Liz's simple ability to embrace happiness.

Mr. Jacobson waxed on with his back turned and his mind on his next cigarette. Chloe turned her gaze to Kirin's empty desk as her fingers thrummed quietly on her textbook. A few other students about the room were also mid-text, and two boys in the back were blatantly watching some hyper-violent Japanese cartoon with shared earphones and a high-def tablet screen between them. Just when Chloe was about to start an internal diatribe against the wrongs of modern communication, her own pocket started to vibrate. She tried not to smile as she fished her three-year-old flip phone from her jeans and slid it into her lap. *Please be Kirin. Please be Kirin.*

The text was from an unrecognized number, and it took a moment for the picture to render. Kendra was true to her word—there was Chloe, looking angry and ridiculous in the middle of the parking lot with a bold-faced message beneath.

BREAKING NEWS: Local Homecoming Queen and lightning enthusiast ALSO suspected Cow Thief! Keep the animals in the barn and your man locked up tight...Have a happy AND SAFE Halloween from KR.

Chloe glanced around and saw the picture popping up on multiple little screens around her. A boy near the front snickered and looked over his shoulder. Directly ahead, she heard a sudden gasp before Liz turned around with wide, angry eyes.

"I'm going to kill her," Liz whispered.

Chloe dropped her gaze back to the unflattering picture in her grip as the phone started to get hot. She felt light-headed and her fingers tingled. Her hand began to shake as the picture on the screen wavered with bands of static. The phone sparked with a loud POP! A whiff of smoke climbed from the ear hole. Chloe gasped and dropped it to clatter across the floor as all eyes in the room spun around to find her.

"Everything okay, Ms. McClellan?" asked Mr. Jacobson amid an undercurrent of stifled laughter throughout the class.

Chloe leaned over and cautiously picked up her dead phone as the scent of burnt plastic filled the room. It was totally fried, and everyone was still looking at her. She held it up for all to see and forced a little smirk. "Sorry, my phone blew up...must have been a bad text."

The class erupted into a joint guffaw that Liz quickly steered into an infectious cheer. After twenty disruptive seconds, Chloe took a little bow, which only added to the problem. Mr. Jacobson couldn't get the noise under control for a full minute, and the story had spread throughout the school before class had even ended.

. . .

Throughout the rest of the day, random students yelled "Cow Thief" whenever Chloe walked down the hall. Some people openly laughed or cringed away with a snicker as she made her way through the cafeteria. Kirin wasn't waiting for her at the table in the back as she'd secretly hoped.

Chloe couldn't explain what had happened with her phone; there wasn't a reasonable explanation for much of anything that had happened to her lately. So she faced the wall and kept her attention on her peanut butter and honey sandwich. Stan slid into Kirin's seat across the table with his eyes even more bloodshot than they'd been that morning. Instantly the high school spell was broken again, and the two sank toward each other with a flurry of whispers and a plan to meet up later that night. Chloe had a race the next morning, but Halloween still carried some cache in the McClellan household, and Audrey would be working the late shift until about eleven thirty anyway.

"I'll get the family wagon and pick you up at eight," said Stan.

Chloe nodded. "We'll need costumes—unrecognizable."

"Yup," Stan agreed. "What's the plan? We can't go back to the pond and neither can it."

Chloe thought about it for a long moment. "You have a video camera?"

Stan's smile grew. "My dad is the IT manager at a pretty big law firm. He's a total tech geek—I've got a camera, dude."

"Okay…bring it tonight…with a tripod," Chloe was thinking out loud now.

"What are we gonna shoot?" asked Stan.

"You said he's taking cows most every night?" Chloe asked. Stan nodded but raised an eyebrow. "He?"

"Or it, whatever—it's taking cows?" Chloe knew just the spot, a pull-off on a rarely traveled country road that overlooked the finest herd of free-range cattle that money could buy in the whole county, which was, of course, owned by none other than local business wizard Richard Roberts. "We need to get the dragon on video."

Stan started to chuckle. After looking around for eavesdroppers that weren't there, Chloe leaned over until the lip of the table dug into her belly. She told him about what she'd seen at the pond on Sunday. Then she added the story of her near encounter with Mr. Roberts in the bathroom, though again she neglected to mention the Tipping Point Prophecy or the extended conversation she'd had with the man/monster on the night of the dance...But she did make it very clear that NO ONE else was to know about the dragon or the Daedalus Group, especially not Brian and the big-mouthed, stoner posse!

Stan's hand sprang up by his head. "Mum's the word, dude, scout's honor," he whispered. "I'll back up whatever footage we get on multiple hard drives and a cloud-based server just in case. I can totally get you your own law-firm-branded thumb drive with the footage on it by tomorrow morning. That way, we can both have some insurance and a bargaining chip if one of us gets taken."

"Maybe you watch too much television?" Chloe suggested.

"That's entirely possible, but I'm gonna do it anyway," he admitted. "You can never be too careful with these things."

"I don't think the dragon means us any harm. I think it's just confused and scared," Chloe offered as she recalled the sadness she'd seen behind Uktena's gaze.

"Dude, I'm not worried about the dragon; I'm scared of the Daedalus Group!" Stan announced. "Hell, if I get to see an actual dragon, I wouldn't even care if it eats me!"

.   .   .

Chloe remained steely and above it all for the rest of the day. She was unfazed by the barbs that followed her throughout gym as Kendra and the hive enjoyed every moment of close proximity. And her mind was blissfully empty during practice that afternoon as the team ran six miles in a cohesive line while the runner in the rear had to sprint to the front at regular intervals. But she was not prepared for what awaited her return to the senior parking lot after practice.

Angela, the cross-country girls' team captain, had started to give Chloe rides home most days, even though it was pretty far out of her way. As always, she and Chloe made their trek across the now mostly empty span of asphalt and concrete to the sea-green Dodge that Angela had inherited the year she'd moved in with her aunt after a harrowing immigration process from Ethiopia. Angela didn't talk about it much, except to say that she'd literally run away from her homeland and that she'd spent much of her youth within the fenced-off structure of varying refugee camps.

It seemed that every time Chloe rode in the car, something else would fall apart, but Angela would laugh and repair it with makeshift love every time. The bumper was held on by artful spirals of coat hangers, and the interior was a comical patchwork of mismatched fabrics and multicolored strips of duct tape. One of the doors was a muted maroon color, having been appropriated from another car in the junk yard, and the fabric of the roof had been replaced with an old quilt that made the backseat feel like the inside of a gypsy's tent. The car didn't like the cold or the wet, and it produced an unseemly roar whenever it switched gears to climb a hill—Chloe dreamed of one day having a car just like it.

She admired the crooked line of the roof while she waited for Angela to get in and unlock the door, but failed to notice the Grand Wagoneer that was parked in the adjacent space until Kirin spoke behind her.

"Hey, Cow Thief, could I give you a ride home?" he asked from the open window at her back.

"Oh!" she jumped, but tried to play it off. "Hey, where were you today?"

"It's kind of a long story," he said, motioning to the passenger seat. "Get in."

Chloe looked across the dented green hood, where the antenna was held on by tin foil and electric tape. Angela nodded. "Chloe would be happy for the ride," she announced without room for dissent. "See you tomorrow, Chloe," she added.

Chloe shot Angela a wide-eyed look before spinning back around with a smile. She rounded the Jeep as both cars revved to sputtering and roaring life respectively. She hopped in and slammed the heavy door behind her before casting a sideways glance at her unexpected chauffer. "Please don't tell me that you're grounded again?"

Kirin chuckled. "No, not this time; my dad took me to D.C. this morning to get an expedited travel visa to China...I'm leaving tomorrow."

Leaving? Again! I give up. "Really? That's amazing!" Chloe forced a grin.

"Yeah," he added with a sigh as they pulled out of the parking lot and headed for the hills. "We were trying to work out a way for my uncle to bring my grandmother over, but my dad got some grant to go there for that cauldron paper he's writing. We're flying to Hong Kong to see the cauldron and then making our way to Shanghai to meet up with my uncle and grandmother. I don't think I've ever seen my dad so excited in my life," he added with a roll of his eyes.

"That's great news, Kirin, and a fantastic opportunity," Chloe admitted as she wondered if she'd ever make it off of the East Coast. "I wish I could go to China."

"You could go in my place. I'm sure my dad would love it," said Kirin with a hint of anger behind his smirk. "I'd kill for some time to myself, without Dad watching my every move like a damned hawk. I feel like I've been in prison since school started, and this seems like it's just going to be an inmate field trip with the warden."

"How long?" asked Chloe.

"A little over a week," he answered. "My dad's already

gotten the teachers to give him all the assignments, and he's worked out a deal where I won't be counted absent if I e-mail them in every day." He winked. "There's a pop quiz in American Civ next Wednesday."

He turned away from the main road and started to head upslope as the engine switched gears with a subtle lurch. "I wanted to see you before I go."

Then why have you been avoiding me for the last two weeks? The silence stretched on between them.

"Not sure if you've seen it yet, but the same company that gave my dad the grant has kind of moved in on your pond." There was genuine sadness in his voice.

"Yeah, I know. Stan and I kind of got busted trespassing there the night of the dance," she admitted. "I was trying to follow your advice and get back there, but it didn't really work out so well."

Kirin tensed noticeably beside her. "So you and Stan are hanging out a lot?"

"We're just friends," she blurted a little too quickly. "He's actually really cool and hilariously sarcastic once you get to know him," she added, only realizing after she'd spoken that she had echoed Ezra's defense of Kendra earlier that day almost verbatim.

"And what about Ezra?" Kirin asked, as if reading her mind.

"He's a friend, too, though I'm not sure I'd even call him that since he started dating Kendra." She glanced to Kirin before letting her gaze drift nonchalantly out the window. "Why?"

Kirin shrugged. "Just wondering...First you're the Lightning Girl, then a track star, then the Homecoming Queen, and now on top of it all, you've been outed as the Cow Thief," he said with a chuckle. "I felt like I had to get a few minutes in with you before I leave, or by the time I get back from China, you'll be too famous to remember who I am."

"That's true," said Chloe. "I suppose I could give you an autograph now—it'll probably be worth some real money by the time you graduate."

"Rather than an autograph, I was actually wondering if you

were free tonight to hang out?" Kirin asked. "I thought maybe we could go to the Halloween parade if you didn't already have plans."

Oh! Chloe choked on her own spit. She went from thrilled to terrified to confused in rapid-fire succession. She had, in a sense, been waiting for this moment for her entire life, though a public outing with much of her school in attendance was far from the venue she'd had in mind for her first official self-sanctioned date. And she didn't know what to do about her plans with Stan...

"No, I don't have any plans," she lied. "But I'm not so sure the Halloween parade is the least conspicuous place for the Cow Thief to go."

Kirin laughed. "That's why you wear a costume; it's the one day you get to be inconspicuous and conspicuous at the same time."

Chloe put her hand out the window and let it cut through the cool air the way she'd used to do as a kid. She remembered the look of her father's profile from the backseat and the smell of the cigarettes he always had hanging out the window.

She caught the descending deep orange glow of the sun in the rearview mirror as it dipped below the tree-lined horizon, and for a moment, the forest looked like it was ablaze in the little picture in the mirror. It was going to be a perfect autumn night.

"I'm warning you, it can get pretty crowded at the parade." She could already feel the terror of such a public outing diminish with Kirin's smile.

"Good, I'll pick you up at eight."

CHAPTER 19
MASKED REVEALS

And so by 8:30 that night, rather than doing her part to avert the "end of the world" with the one person in her life who had fully embraced her lunacy, Chloe found herself at Kirin's side in the thick of the town's most crowded celebration.

Chloe was again thrust into the role of tour guide as she took Kirin by the hand and led him into the fray. Beneath the cover of a black ski mask, she felt strangely empowered as they slipped down Main Street. A huge crowd had turned out for the Halloween parade. All the local schools had elaborate floats and marching bands, and every year the numerous UVA fraternities and collegiate groups competed for the most outlandish display to roll through town.

Every year, Mayor Marty O'Neil came out to wave to the masses along the parade route, sitting in the back of a white Cadillac convertible beside his pill- and Botox-filled wife and his increasingly unfortunate looking daughter. Chloe caught a glimpse of young Meghan O'Neil, sitting sullenly in the backseat with her hands locked at her sides as if in stubborn protest of the expectation for her to wave. She'd picked up a case of bad acne that no amount of cover-up could conceal. As always, Chloe felt bad for her.

But the normal cascade of doubt and anxiety that typically squelched Chloe's every happy moment couldn't take hold as she turned back to see Kirin's smirk through the mouth hole in the foam and cardboard shark's head mask he was wearing. He'd made it that afternoon with supplies he'd scrounged from his garage, complete with a swiveling jaw attached by a couple of brass fasteners and an oversized dorsal fin that regularly clipped passersby.

It was brilliant, artful, and hilarious, and it made Chloe like Kirin all the more. Her unrelenting smile was visible only in her eyes as she gave his fingers an extra squeeze and led him into an even thicker swarm of masked revelers. She pulled him past a cluster of drunken zombie frat boys and turned her back on a coven of cackling vampiresses as they went by. Beneath the ski mask she was dressed in a stereotypical black-and-white striped robber's shirt over black jeans and black Chucks. In her other hand she carried a burlap sack with the cardboard cutout of a big, juicy steak taped on.

Everyone under the age of thirty from the surrounding twenty-mile radius was packed within the two-block perimeter that surrounded West Main Street. Most of them had decided to embrace this opportunity to put on absurd outfits and behave poorly in public. Chloe was blind and deaf to them all, free at last with her anonymity returned. Her whole focus locked on the beautiful boy who was inexplicably ready to follow her every move. *This is awesome!*

Chloe felt as if she and Kirin were somehow jointly shielded from the jostle and cacophony of the surrounding horde. She felt invisible and invincible as she pulled him to a halt beside a cluster of drama kids she recognized from school. She took a moment to catch her breath and pretended to be interested in the parade as Kirin adjusted his shark helmet beside her.

"Ugh, Check out that O'Neil girl," said a hyper-skinny boy who was dressed like a hipster Sherlock Holmes and spoke with overwrought disgust.

"She looks like Shrek," snickered a pig-nosed, self-styled stage queen, whose costume consisted of little more than bangs and bosoms.

Chloe and Kirin exchanged a quick glance; she decided it was time to keep moving in the Ezra Richardson School of Crowd Negotiation. Without asking, she weaved her fingers back into Kirin's willing grip, lowered her shoulder, and charged. She clipped Sherlock in the kidney as she passed, and Kirin followed up with an accidental fin swipe that swatted him across the bridge of his nose and knocked his prop pipe to the sidewalk.

"Watch it, dick," Sherlock hissed a moment later, just loud enough to make sure that his friends heard him and the offending party did not.

Chloe slid through the crowd like a serpent lacing through the grass. Kirin never missed a step behind her, sticking just at arm's reach without fail or question as their joint movement began to feel like a choreographed waltz. They traveled away from the sidewalk and through the town square, where the collegiate crowd thinned and the younger locals held dominance around the fountain. Chloe spotted Brian and some others moving away quickly as a film of suds began to collect on the water's surface. She felt a pang of guilt as she looked for Stan among them, but the fleeing culprits were lost in the chaos.

Earlier that evening, she'd floundered and waffled on the phone with Stan, making up some unnecessary story about her mom not letting her go out rather than telling the truth about Kirin…She wasn't sure if she felt more guilty because she'd cancelled plans after having gone so long without having any friends to plan with, or if maybe she felt like she was betraying her universally ordained obligation to pursue the dragon above all else.

"Operation Bovine Justice," as Stan had started to call it, had been amicably postponed until Saturday. *What's wrong with wanting to take a shot at one night of enjoyment before the world ends?* Though the Daedalus Group was unlikely to take off any days for high school or Halloween…

Chloe's drifting thoughts returned to the present as other kids began to whoop and cheer around the fountain. The soapy froth gathered and spread as the water jets churned the detergent spike that Brian had left behind. After only a couple minutes more, the rise of bubbles threatened to spill over the sides.

Chloe spotted Liz and Paul kissing sloppily at the rim of the fountain, oblivious to it all. Liz was dressed in a green leotard that left little to the imagination and left Chloe feeling a little inadequate. Around her neckline Liz had stitched bright yellow daffodil petals, rimmed with armature wire, which completed her remarkably convincing costume and overall demeanor as a "beautiful flower." Chloe kept her eyes straight ahead as she led Kirin past with a quick step.

"Some of the kids from school soap the fountain a few times a year during these sorts of events," Chloe said over her shoulder. "Supposedly it costs the city more than a thousand dollars to clean it every time."

With Liz and Paul behind them, Kirin steered Chloe toward the fountain's edge. He grazed his hand over the water and came away with a thick tuft of soapy foam in his palm…"That's kind of a dumbass thing to do," he said.

"I completely agree with you!" Chloe blurted. "It's terrible for the environment and a total waste of water and money. It's like no one has a conscience or gives a crap about the world anymore. Before long, all of our arrogance and neglect will be the end of us," Chloe winced beneath the mask. *Wow, that was uplifting! Maybe less talk, genius?*

Kirin's eyes were still locked on the spectacle of bubbles beside them. Despite the news of his grandmother's safety and the goofy teeth that framed his face, he still carried the burden of sadness within his gaze. Perhaps it was his sadness that Chloe was so strongly attracted to.

"You could be right," he finally answered. "Have you been watching the news? My dad watches a lot of news at night, and so recently, so do I…Things are getting crazy."

Chloe wasn't sure if he was referring to the nature of the news itself or what was being reported. She looked down at his soapy hand and thought about reaching out to grab it again. Against the backdrop of the punch-drunk crowd, she couldn't quell the niggling itch to second-guess her every move without the security of his touch.

"Wasn't Mayan Armageddon supposed to happen a few years ago?" He gave an unconvincing smile. "December 21st, 2012—sometimes I wonder if maybe they just miscalculated by a handful of years."

Chloe chuckled nervously. "December 21st is my birthday."

Kirin turned on her with big eyes, and his open warmth returned. "That's awesome! How old are you?"

Chloe looked away and considered not answering the question. He was still waiting for a response…"Fifteen," she mumbled.

His eyes went wider. "Really? You're still a baby."

There it is! I suppose I could probably drown myself in these bubbles.

Instead he grabbed her hand again without asking and gave it a playful squeeze. "So where to, baby?" he asked without judgment or expectation.

Chloe thought she might explode with joy. She shrugged with a big, hidden grin. "I don't know, I was thinking we could get milkshakes," she suggested.

"Yes," answered Kirin with a comical nod of his helmet. "I could go for a black and white."

Without a moment more of hesitation, she led him away from the fountain and through a section of the square rimmed by hedges. Kid-packed benches were scattered throughout, each seat offering its own fleeting story as they passed. The first held a trio of nerdy private school kids passing around a couple cigarettes in a duel to look cool. All sides seemed to be failing. "It's not too harsh," one of them said as he exhaled the smoke out of his nose in an attempt to impress.

At the next, an obscenely drunk girl was draped precariously across the bench with her legs in the air and a sloppy cackle spilling out of her upside-down head. Her friend was beside her, wrestling with her arm in an uproarious attempt to keep them both from spilling onto the slate.

Chloe and Kirin kept moving toward a set of stairs at the other end of the square that would take them down a less traveled street to Positive Pete's. Chloe stopped short of the last bench as she spied Kendra and Ezra sitting just a few strides away.

Ezra was wearing a long, blonde, scraggily wig that hung across his face. He had tinfoil and spike-covered football shoulder pads over his bare chest and pants that looked to be made of mock animal hide and fur. Chloe wasn't sure if he was supposed to be a professional wrestler or some sort of black

Viking, but she couldn't help but notice his body beneath all the silliness. She also did not fail to register the fact that his arms were locked at his sides and his scowl was pointed at his feet.

Beside him, Kendra was dressed like she'd stepped from a background role in a hell-themed porn movie: she was covered in red skintight Lycra with little devil horns and a plastic pitchfork. She also looked to be close to tears as she struggled to claim Ezra's attention.

Emboldened by the ski mask, Chloe slowed her step and drifted closer to the unaware couple. She released Kirin's grip with a wink and pretended to tie her shoes against the stone basin of a nearby topiary. Kirin lingered with his hands in the pockets of his jeans.

"Do you plan on ignoring me all night?" Kendra asked.

Ezra didn't turn or respond.

"Hey, my dad's about to disown me for dating a black guy, the least you can do is make eye contact," she joked with a desperate little tug on his arm.

He glared at his fur-coated boots.

"Please stop being mad at me," she said. "I'm sorry I was mean to her; I'm kind of a bitch sometimes—I can't help myself!"

"I don't really buy that," he mumbled.

"I'm serious," she said. "My shrink says I have a borderline personality disorder or something. It's not my fault; it's just chemicals and stuff."

Ezra turned on her with hurt eyes, framed by the stringy blonde strands of the stupid wig. "Why *her*?" he challenged.

"I don't know, something about her just bothers me...I had a dream about her the other night where she grabs my arm and I burst into flames! It was totally freaky! She's like a psychotic child!" She thinned her eyes. "And I might ask you the same question—why her?"

"You don't even know her," he answered bitterly. "She's cool...and she's real."

"Well, if you're so in love with her, then why don't you date her instead?" Kendra snapped as she started to get up. Her red-rimmed eyes drifted over to where Chloe was taking too long to tie her shoe.

Ezra grabbed Kendra's wrist—somehow both fast and gentle at once—and eased her back down to the bench. "It's not like that. She's my friend. She keeps me grounded, and because of you, she won't talk to me."

"I don't get it," Kendra whined. "I mean, what's so special about her?"

Chloe was transfixed, unable to move, despite the fact that her shoe had been successfully double-knotted for more than a minute. *Yes, what is so special about me?*

Before she could hear the answer, Kirin took her by the shoulders and marched her away toward the stairs. "Hey, remember me?" he whispered in her ear.

The hair sprang up along her neck as a delightful little shiver traveled down from the spot where his lips grazed the fabric against her earlobe. "I'm, uh, sorry," she sputtered, suddenly feeling a little exposed despite the mask. "That was kind of hard to walk away from."

Kirin smiled. "He's right, you know; you are real…I'd say you're more authentically yourself than pretty much anyone else I've ever met."

"I am?" She wasn't totally sure that she even knew what that meant. "I usually feel like a fraud," she muttered under her breath.

"See, there it is again." He took her hand again and stepped into the lead as they skipped down the stairs. "So where are we gonna find these milkshakes?"

Chloe relaxed into the surprising warmth of his grip and met his eyes. Instantly her burdened thinking washed away. It was true that Ezra helped to keep her grounded and sane, just as he claimed she did for him, but with Kirin she felt loose and unstoppable, as if anything was possible if she simply allowed herself to go with the flow. She never wanted this night to end.

"Follow me," she said, retaking the lead.

.   .   .

Chloe and Kirin sat at the Positive Pete's counter and slurped greedily at a couple of black-and-white shakes. Chloe had lifted her mask just long enough to surprise Audrey and order "the usual," but she'd lowered it again as a handful of kids she recognized from school clustered into one of the tables behind her.

Kirin rolled his eyes at her presumed need for anonymity and joined her close watch of the diner through the mirror above the coffeemaker. With the harsh jangle of the little bell above the door, a quartet of super preppy boys strolled in like they owned the place. The one in the lead looked like he thought he was God's gift to women and the world as he scanned the restaurant with his cocksure gaze. His eyes didn't even hesitate on Chloe and Kirin, locking instead on Audrey as she walked by with a tray of drinks. Chloe watched as he dropped his gaze to her mom's behind and made a 'look at that' nod to his idiot friends. *Men are disgusting!*

She considered walking over and "accidentally" spilling her entire milkshake down the front of his pants...

"I bet you that the greatest story of that guy's life will come out of his time as the captain of his high school lacrosse team... And one day, he'll have a wife that's going to cheat on him," cut in Kirin.

Chloe burst out laughing with an unseemly spray of milkshake.

"I bet his name is Brock," he added.

Chloe wiped shake from the edges of the mouth hole in her mask. "He probably drives a Hummer and has a really small penis." *Christ! Did I just say that?*

"I don't know, I drive a Grand Wagoneer, but I'm HUGE," Kirin stated with an exaggerated smirk.

Chloe laughed again, this time with a little involuntary snort. Kirin looked very proud of himself as Chloe glanced up to catch his eyebrow pump in the mirror. Both their gazes moved back to the door as the lacrosse boys were led to their table and a trio of glassy-eyed college kids ambled in.

The two guys were dressed up like a tinfoil robot and a

convenience store pirate. They flanked a tall, borderline sloppy girl wearing a Little-Bo-Peep-gone-bad costume, complete with a shepherd's crook and a skirt so short that Chloe could almost see her underwear.

"What about them?" Chloe asked.

Kirin gave them a hard look. "The pirate and the robot are best friends, but the friendship is going to end tonight when one of them winds up with Bo Peep there...They've both had a thing for her for a while, but neither has ever had the guts to do anything about it."

Chloe watched as Bo Peep walked ahead, ignoring them both as she drunkenly scanned the crowd. "Yeah, but Bo Peep is playing them off each other. She thinks they're both losers and is just using their fawning attention to attract a third option."

Kirin gave Chloe an appreciative nod. "Well played, Miss McClellan."

Chloe sipped at her shake and tried to subdue the building urge in her gut to giggle joyously.

"How about this guy," said Kirin. "The one getting out of the black SUV...President of the Chuck Norris fan club?" he suggested as former officer Brent Meeks removed his mirror shades and stepped into the diner.

He was wearing his black-on-black tough guy ensemble and quickly picked Audrey out of the bustle on the other side of the restaurant.

"I know him," hissed Chloe.

Brent marched over to the bar without waiting to be seated and took the stool beside Chloe. He took out a toothpick and started chewing on the tip as he waited for Audrey to notice him. Despite his outfit, he looked nervous and unsure of himself as his eyes tracked her progression toward the kitchen window.

Chloe hunched her shoulders and tensed as her mom approached. Audrey's lips went very thin as she saw who was there. She walked over deliberately, sharing a quick glance with Chloe as she passed.

"What are you doing here?" she whispered to Brent. "You know Loraine isn't working today."

"I'm here to see you," said Brent.

"Why?" Audrey challenged with a frown.

Brent chewed a little more intently on the toothpick. "I got a new job, for a lot more money and really good benefits," he said lamely.

"Yeah, I heard," snapped Audrey. "So?"

"So…I could help you. I mean, I miss you…and now I have more of a future and stuff," he stammered.

"Wow," said Audrey. "Did you rehearse that?"

"Come on, Audrey, I'm sorry," he flared. "I'm just saying, you could really use the help, and you could do a lot worse than me."

"Gee, Brent, that's really sweet," she said icily. "You always knew just what to say to the ladies, didn't you?"

"Dammit, Audrey, what are you going to do when Chloe goes to college, huh?" Brent was breathing hard now. "How are you gonna pay for it? You gonna get a third job on your day off, or are you just gonna cut out sleeping altogether?"

Audrey glanced back to Chloe, whose eyes were still locked on the shake. "I don't need your help, Brent. Now please just drop it and go," she said before turning to leave.

"Do you even know what Chloe is up to while you're off at work all the time? Do you know where she goes? Did you know that I caught her trespassing on private property a couple weeks ago?" said Brent, freezing Audrey in her tracks. "She was making out with some stoner kid on the same hill where she got struck by lightning, and there was some pretty serious vandalism done to some expensive equipment on-site."

Audrey slowly spun back around with her furious gaze passing across Chloe's deer-in-the-headlights response. Audrey leveled her gaze on Brent, like a mother bear readying to charge. "If you'd been paying any attention at all while we were together, you'd know the one thing you *never* do with me is try to come between me and my daughter."

Brent leaned back from the bar and actually looked a little scared. "I'm not trying to come between you," he stammered defensively. "I care about Chloe, too; I'm just trying to look out for her, you know, when you're not around." He put his hands up as if he was readying to ward off an assault.

She took a step closer and snatched away the menu that sat on the counter in front of him. "Thanks for that, but you're gonna have to go now. And I'd appreciate it if you didn't come back when I'm on shift, you understand me?"

He could only nod and swallow his pride in silence before getting up, putting his mirror shades back on and storming out the door.

Audrey walked over to the kitchen window and handed over her most recent ticket before glancing back to Chloe. "We'll talk later tonight," she said curtly before heading back out to the floor.

Chloe was a little shell-shocked as she turned back to see Kirin's raised eyebrows.

"I didn't make out with any stoner kid," she finally offered in her defense.

"Uh-huh," he said with a skeptical little smile.

"I swear," stammered Chloe. "Stan is…a friend."

Kirin scratched the side of his nose. "At least this time while *you're* grounded, I'll be away in China anyway."

Chloe leaned in to fill her scowl with shake, but all that came out was the hollow slurp of an empty glass. *Maybe wearing a mask isn't so helpful after all.*

·   ·   ·

A heavy plume of smoke billowed out from under the hooked beak that covered Stan's nose. He sat in the shadows on the front porch with a mostly empty bowl of candy at his feet—no longer open for business. The butt-end of a joint hung from his lips as half-closed eyes trailed the last few costumed kids that skittered away down the street.

Mr. and Mrs. Strakowski were out for the night at a law firm Halloween function. After Chloe cancelled, Stan had opted to stay home and greet trick-or-treaters rather than attempt to chase down Brian and the crew. The van was still sitting untouched since the accident in the back lot of an auto body shop run by his older sister's ex-boyfriend, Tad. The deal had been a bag of weed and carte blanche to make whatever alterations Tad felt inspired to make, for an otherwise pro bono fix-up and an open-ended work schedule. Stan would be lucky to have his ride back by Christmas.

Without the wheels, and now that Brian was dating Rosalie, Stan found himself stranded at home more and more often. But he didn't care about that anymore. Now he just wanted to hang out with Chloe. There was something about her that made him feel at home in his skin for the first time in his life—more than just the fact that she was the only one who knew his secret. She'd even started to show up in his dreams, which had begun to get increasingly…strange.

With his eyes closed, Stan could still feel the sensation of traveling above Charlottesville as the wind itself. It was the most spectacular feeling he'd ever had, and he wanted more. Soaring above the trees in whipping bursts as Chloe's wild laughter crackled and sparked around and within him—it had come every night for the past week, getting more vivid every time.

His lids opened back to half-mast, and he took a last unnecessary toke from the joint. It burned the tips of his fingers as he inhaled before he leaned over to tamp out the dregs against the side of the brick stoop. The lazy spill of smoke rose from his beak once more, and for a second, it climbed into the cool air in what looked like the ethereal form of a winged serpent. Stan smiled, and his gaze drifted up to the watching moon. Something in the dark hemisphere held his attention. After a moment, he almost expected to see a pair of glowing eyes staring back from the shadow there as a disconcerting tickle crept up his spine.

He shook off the creepy feeling when the headlights of a car streaked by as it rounded the corner. He couldn't tell if it was a station wagon past the glare. *Don't be my parents. Don't be my parents.* It was a hatchback, and it kept going.

Still, they could return any minute now. He checked his ironically cool calculator watch: 11:19 p.m.—the sanctuary of his bedroom was calling. He reached into the plastic pumpkin bowl and plucked a last mini box of grape Nerds for the road.

Even in his lucid moments—this not being one of them—Stan couldn't explain why the idea of a dragon living in Charlottesville seemed right to him. Something about the alleged monster, and Chloe, and the dreams—all strangely believable, all connected, like how it felt in the dream.

Despite the sugar overload, he yawned hard and turned toward the door. He'd be flying again before long... *Dude, Chloe's hiding something. I'm gonna find out what it is.*

CHAPTER 20
THE BIG STINK

Chloe did not race well on Saturday afternoon. It was a regional away meet against two other schools, one of which was likely to be a strong competitor for the state title. She came in seventh place overall. Angela won it, as always, but four of the Richmond Raiders girls came in before Chloe. Worse still, another rising young sophomore at Monticello High had crept by her at the end as well. Charlottesville got second place at the meet, and Chloe felt like she'd let the team down.

The mood was jovial on the bus ride home, but Chloe imagined an undercurrent of disappointment around her. At one point in the race, she'd actually tuned out to the degree that she ran ten long strides in the wrong direction. She probably would have kept going if not for one of the opposing girls who'd screamed for her to turn around in a further humbling act of sportsmanship. After that, Chloe hadn't been able to recover before the final hill, and she'd had nothing left for the sprint toward the finish.

Chloe's head hadn't been in the race; there was no one to blame but herself...Audrey had come home the night before ready to fight, and Chloe had been foolishly willing to oblige. Chloe couldn't remember ever seeing her mom that pissed before.

She wasn't mad about her daughter allegedly making out with a stoner on a hill; Stan had set off Audrey's fairly reliable gaydar both times she'd met him. BUT she was furious that Chloe had betrayed the hard-fought sense of trust between them. In fact, according to Audrey, Chloe had betrayed that trust twice—

once when she'd returned to the banned site of her electrical mishap and again when she'd demonstrated a "complete lack of judgment" when she hadn't told her mom about the latest incident that had occurred there. Breaking the often flexible rules was one thing if you owned up to it, but keeping secrets and lying to cover it up was something else altogether.

In what had become a rare act of emotional weakness since the year after Ray McClellan had left, Audrey had actually started to cry as she was expressing her disappointment. Chloe had, in turn, started to cry as she acknowledged her mother's side of it and asked for forgiveness, and before long, the two of them were wrapped in a prolonged hug while laughing and weeping at once…Of course, Chloe still didn't mention the ongoing interaction she was having with the giant mythological beast. She figured that there was only so much honesty her mother could take in one night.

Despite it all, Chloe still couldn't get her mind off Kirin. She wouldn't see or speak to him for eight more days, and just as he'd predicted, she would be grounded for all of them.

It was already dark by the time Audrey picked her up from the bus at the school parking lot, and as the rest of the team said their good-byes and waved, Chloe got in the CR-V with a hangdog expression. They drove in silence for a while.

"That good, huh?" Audrey finally asked.

Chloe shrugged. "I came in seventh and the team got second."

"Is that bad?" Audrey asked. "Sounds pretty good to me."

"I could have done better," Chloe muttered, looking at the flutter of dark trees out the window.

The engine lurched into a higher gear and started to groan as they climbed the winding hill toward the Daedalus Group turnoff to Chloe's pond. *I guess it was the dragon's pond all along.* Then she remembered the way Kirin had looked, sun-drenched and shirtless as he'd pulled himself out of the water…

"Is there something else bothering you?" Audrey asked with a quick glance to her daughter. "Anything you want to talk about?"

Chloe shrugged and pressed her lips together.

"Didn't Kirin leave for China today?" Audrey pressed.

Chloe deflated. "Mom, I'm not supposed to feel like this!" she blurted. "I can't stop thinking about him. This sort of thing doesn't happen to me!"

"You're only fifteen! You have no idea what sort of things are going to happen to you," Audrey cut in. "But you need to learn to be open to whatever comes because life is going to throw you some curve balls, and not all of them are going to be as easy as a cute boy who likes you."

"How do I even know if he likes me?" Chloe asked. "I'm basically just holding my breath and waiting for him to lose interest and stop talking to me altogether."

"Not all men are like your dad, Chloe," said Audrey.

Just the mention of Ray McClellan rendered them both temporarily frozen. "Sorry, but that's a little hard to believe coming from you," Chloe mumbled.

"Hey, I'm not pretending I have all the answers or that I've found my soulmate, but I'm still out there trying, despite all the duds that have come in and gone back out the door," said Audrey with a sad little smile. "But from what I've seen and what you've said, Kirin, Ezra Richardson, and even Stan seem like pretty solid guys to me."

"Ezra's an egomaniacal man whore, and Stan's gay and has a bit of a drug problem," Chloe admitted.

Audrey shot her daughter a hard look but then eased it back into a shrug. "I know, but they're good people, and I think they really value you as a friend."

Chloe suddenly felt a swell of guilt as she realized how lame she'd been toward them this week. She groaned and buried her face in her hands. "Yeah, but what if I'm not a good person?" she asked through the muffle of her fingers.

"Don't be ridiculous, Chloe, you're one of the best people! You're my favorite person, and outside of my own failed romances, I think I'm a pretty good judge of character," she said with her eyes locked on the road. "People are drawn to you without you even trying...You're like your father that way—a natural-born leader."

Chloe looked up just in time to see the headlights pass over the Daedalus Group sign as her mother shot a glare that way. "Mom, what happened with Dad and the Daedalus Group?" Chloe asked hesitantly.

Audrey looked at her through the dark and then back to the road. "He worked for them about nine years ago; I guess it was about a year and a half before he left," she said quietly. "Your dad was a pretty impressive talker when he wanted to be. I used to joke that he could sell ice to an Eskimo if he put his mind to it…Well, Richard Roberts recognized his talent right off and hired him to work in the PR department at the new company headquarters, trying to build a corporate brand image for the community."

"I'm guessing that didn't work out so well," Chloe muttered.

"No. Your dad had started to get pretty heavily into religion around that same time. You remember the way he used to talk in the kitchen?"

Chloe nodded.

"He didn't think too highly of some of the Group's experimentations and policies regarding bioengineering and stuff like that, and he became increasingly contentious the more he learned about what was going on over there…until they finally accused him of leaking some of the classified documents he'd been hired to whitewash to the *Washington Post*. They could never prove it was him, but he was fired for breach of his nondisclosure agreement and threatened with some pretty serious legal repercussions if he kept at it. I always suspected that Richard Roberts might have had something to do with his leaving."

The car rounded the bend toward home and pulled into the driveway beside the barn with the familiar crunch of gravel beneath the tires. The headlights caught the shine of Shipwreck's eyes, watching from the bushes, before Audrey switched off the engine and returned the yard to the dark of a cool autumn night.

"Did he do it?" Chloe asked.

"I don't know, probably," Audrey answered.

"Was he right?"

Audrey sighed as if measuring an answer to a question she had long pondered. "You know I'm no fan of what that company is doing to this community for a profit, and despite all of his failures as a husband and a father, your dad was nothing if not passionate about what he believed in. I always respected him for that; it's a big part of why I fell in love with him in the first place. But you were still pretty young then and may not remember it so well. He got pretty out there by the end—talking all the time about Judgment Day and how the Daedalus Group was going to accidentally destroy the world and all kinds of mumbo jumbo like that," she admitted painfully.

Despite the calm quiet of the car, Chloe's heart was thundering in her chest. She had never heard that story before, and she wasn't sure what to think about it. *What if he was right? What if it's happening now?* "You think Dad was crazy?"

"I don't know, honey. He was a good man, underneath it all, but I think he'd have to be pretty nuts to leave you. And it seems to me that the world is getting on just fine here without him," she said as she opened her door and flooded the cab with the light from the overhead. "But I do know that it's time for dinner."

Chloe forced herself to smile, though her stomach was doing somersaults. It didn't help that when she stepped from the car, she was immediately hit by a nauseating waft of rotten death from the barn. Audrey's hand went to her nose, and Chloe winced and coughed.

"Good God, Shipwreck has outdone himself this time! That's awful!" Audrey proclaimed with a nasally twang.

They started running toward the house in an attempt to escape the reek, and it quickly turned into a race as they jostled to be the first to get through the door amid a flurry of laughs and squeals. Shipwreck darted in behind them and disappeared upstairs before they slammed the door. Chloe knew what was coming. Audrey ruffled through one of the shopping bags and removed a brand-new box of thirty-gallon trash bags.

"I'm gonna need you to clean that out tomorrow morning before I get home." She handed the box to Chloe with a cross between a grimace and a smile.

"Mom!" Chloe whined.

"Sorry, honey, he's your cat." She headed toward the kitchen with a little chuckle. "Consider it part of your grounding."

.   .   .

Chloe rummaged through the cabinet beneath the sink and came away with a pair of yellow rubber dishwashing gloves and the bulk jug of industrial cleaner her mom had swiped from the restaurant. A year later and the jug was still half-full; it smelled like someone had crossbred a lemon tree with a Douglas fir and then sent the whole thing through a wood chipper.

The unopened box of trash bags still waited for her on the counter where she'd left it the night before. Audrey had added a Post-it that said, *"Do a good job cleaning the barn and I'll see about getting you a new phone this afternoon. GOOD LUCK!"*

Chloe unceremoniously shoved a piece of wadded-up tissue into each nostril before tying a red bandanna over her nose. She pulled on the rubber gloves like a surgeon preparing to operate. The bags and cleaner went into the bucket at her feet. She snatched its rusted handle and walked toward the back door while trying to concentrate on breathing through her mouth. Shipwreck eyed her warily from the top of the stairs as she came to the door and peered back at him.

"Thanks a lot, buddy!" she yelled just as he took off down the hallway.

She eyed the dilapidated structure of the barn through the storm door. The once beautiful, fireman-red building had been reduced to two stories of junk-filled storage in a rotten paint-chipped shell.

Chloe exhaled deeply and shouldered the back door open to a beautiful fall morning. Even from the porch she could catch the acrid stench of death in the air, and she wondered again why they hadn't bulldozed the barn a long time ago. She and Audrey didn't need the reminder of what the barn had become in that final year before Ray McClellan had left—hours spent within, pacing, tinkering, and ranting to himself.

She stepped from the porch and walked the length of the unkempt hedges behind the house. A large spool of garden hose sat dormant at the corner with four lengths of connected hose and a high-powered spray-gun head. She pushed aside the hedge and leaned over to turn the valve with a hiss and a rattle as the hose swelled with expectation.

Chloe grabbed the spray gun with her free hand and started walking the fifty paces to the barn as the hose wheel unspooled behind her with a reoccurring squeak. For half the length of the yard, she pretended that she was a gunslinger heading to a duel, but then it was too hard to imagine anything past the stink.

Shipwreck hadn't killed anything bigger than a squirrel in a couple years, but Chloe was still traumatized by the unfortunate family of possum carcasses that the cat had left in the upper floor of the barn three summers back. Audrey had only found them after they'd ripened for more than a week of ninety-plus degree days. It was a mother and three young: ambushed and murdered in their den. That was the day that Audrey had decreed that she would never go into the barn again. Chloe shuddered when she thought about it.

The cooler weather was working in her favor this time, but the advance assault on her nose spoke of another potentially soul-scarring discovery. She kept walking with the rhythmic squeak of the uncurling hose behind her, unable to believe that this was how she was spending her Sunday morning.

She dropped the hose and bucket at the door to pull out a couple of the heavy plastic bags from the fresh box. Reluctantly she raised her shiny yellow fingers to the iron latch, and as the creaking door swung open, a blast of warm, fetid air punched her in the gut. She had to stop herself from the impulse to drop everything and sprint back to the house.

It took a moment for her eyes to adjust to the darkness beyond the pool of sunlight that burned through the open door. Most of the windows were greased over with neglect or blocked by piles of her father's discarded crap. One wall was stacked to Chloe's head with buckets of dried-up red and white paint, left behind from her dad's half-finished plans to renovate ten years prior.

The opposite wall was lined with a collection of farm equipment that, to Chloe's memory, her father had never once put to use. There was a tractor, an old VW Bug that hadn't run since before Chloe was born, and a refrigerator that Audrey had inherited when she was still in high school herself…but nothing to indicate how a smell this awful could also be housed within.

Chloe reached around the lip of the door and felt along the wall for the flashlight long kept on a hook for the rare occasions when one of the McClellan women ventured into the cavernous and creepy space beyond. Chloe remembered this approach as a confused eight year old girl—wanting desperately to be with the warm, patient, and inspiring father of her youth, but also a little scared of the volatile and distant stranger who had begun to take his place.

She hoped that the light wouldn't be there—*or maybe the batteries will be dead*—anything to justify putting off the task, even if only for the time it took to return inside to find fresh AAs.

Instead, her rubber fingers found the weatherproof plastic cylinder, and she clicked the red button to find a dull but steady beam of light at her feet. *Crap!*

Chloe pointed the light into the barn, but the weak orange glow only showed her fifteen feet of old, trampled hay and the still-functioning push mower that she occasionally used to cut the grass. She saw no animal parts and still hadn't heard the buzzing flies normally present at such occasions, but the stink seemed to increase with every step.

She cupped her hand over her face and took a deep inhale through her mouth before holding her breath. *Let's see how long these cross-country lungs can hold out.* She clenched the trash bags tightly and stepped on.

The barn was big, nasty, and beyond hope. The air was unpleasantly humid compared to the crisp breeze outside, and most every surface was covered with old bat poop and cobwebs. The front hood of the Volkswagen had so many little black dots scattered across it that, on a first look, it almost seemed that the car might have originally been painted grey rather than white.

No bugs, birds, or beasts so much as stirred throughout the gloom as Chloe scrutinized every lump and surface she could reach with the light. She continued moving toward the open and less used space at the far end, passing by stacks of her Dad's now-browned and warped *National Geographic* magazines. She stepped around a wood-paneled, antenna TV with its screen smashed in, and then navigated an unintended obstacle course of a large collection of rakes, hoes, and shovels.

Even with her breath held, the stink of death seeped into her pores and kept her on the cusp of a gag. *There's no way that Shipwreck could have done this.*

The flashlight caught something ahead, glistening and red, and Chloe stopped advancing. She held the beam on it as the reality of what she was seeing sunk in. She gasped.

There was a large brown cow lying on its side with its stomach ripped out and half its guts on display. Chloe might have screamed if she hadn't been too stunned to react. The increasingly shaky beam of light scanned to another lump beside it, this one comprised of a half-eaten bull that had been left to rot for weeks. Nearby she spotted a pinkish mound of what may have been pigs and another large pile of discarded bones, hooves, and horns, almost entirely stripped of meat.

A giant shadow in the corner of the barn began to uncoil and take shape. Its form filled the entirety of the space that had once been used to winter sheep; as it shifted, Chloe could see a silvery sheen within the gloom. Without thinking, she swung the flashlight toward it and caught the horned head of the dragon in her sickly orange light.

Steaming drool fell from Uktena's long crocodile jaws, and his blue eyes flared with electricity as he slithered closer. Chloe tried to bolt, but as before, she found her body locked in place by his will. She fought to break free as a surprisingly feral noise emerged from her belly and the tingle of electricity gathered in her extremities.

Uktena's head swayed slightly and seemed to tremble as more sizzling drool fell to the hay. His previously shining scales had taken on a waxy, clouded cast, and his muzzle and neck were splattered unceremoniously with layers of dried gore. The electric current in his eyes began to fade and then dimmed completely, just as his head visibly drooped…Chloe found that she was able to move again.

She forgot that she'd meant to scream as the dragon's head fell to the ground with a barn-rattling thump. Chloe stumbled back and tripped on a rake, winding up on her butt in the hay with her back against a stack of tractor tires. Her body surged with panic, but everything began to slow again as the dragon emitted a long, wheezing sigh and closed his eyes, almost as if he were ashamed to have her see him this way. They stayed motionless for a few seconds—silent, save for the pounding of Chloe's heart and the rasp of the dragon's labored breaths.

In that moment, the threat of the Daedalus Group and the warnings of the Tipping Point Prophecy became immaterial. "You're sick," she said with a quivering voice. "Maybe I can help?"

His unnaturally blue gaze snapped open again, and the black slits in the center thinned to focus on her as the spiny ridge down his neck bristled. "I am the Fifth Claw of Typhon's talon, the Lord of Lightning and Great Worm of the West—I need no help from humans!" he growled.

His deep, gravelly voice echoed through Chloe's mind with the power of an avalanche, but his eyes were red-rimmed and sunken, and his focus could not maintain the ferocity for long. In some spots along his neck, the scales had begun to look translucent, and the diamond shape across his brow held no trace of the internal light that had been there before. The spines along his back dropped back down as he huffed out another labored breath that devolved into a series of hacking coughs. Uktena winced with obvious pain.

Chloe could hear the fluid rattling in his lungs as still more of the steaming bile dribbled from between his teeth to singe the hay below. She yanked the bandanna from her face and sat up. With all the adrenaline coursing through her blood, she'd somehow forgotten about the stink. *I nursed Shipwreck back from*

251

the brink of death. How different can this be?

"It's the pond, isn't it?" Chloe suggested. "You woke too soon, and now you can't go back there since the Daedalus Group took it."

Uktena studied her closely as his body rose and fell with the ponderous work of his lungs. Finally he answered, "Those men meddle with forces beyond their comprehension. Now they plague my rest and poison my den with their presence."

"Have you been here since the night you destroyed the tower?" she asked, awed that a hundred-foot-long monster could have been living in her backyard for almost a month without her noticing.

Uktena did not answer as he began to lick his blood-caked claws with a long, purplish serpentine tongue. He averted his eyes and seemed in that moment to be self-conscious of his messy appearance.

"Is that why you're so weak?" she asked. "Because you can't sleep?"

The dragon looked as if he might protest, only to find that he lacked the strength to do so. His eyes glanced to the freshly killed cow nearby. "I have awoken with a great hunger to fill, but I cannot eat," he admitted. "Something is wrong with the meat. It is unclean like the water and air, corrupted by toxins— unnatural like all that you *humans* touch."

He said the word *humans* with such vitriol that Chloe began to shake as she pressed painfully into the tires at her back. But she swallowed through a dry mouth and rebelled against every fiber in her body that told her to run, forcing herself instead to shuffle forward toward the bloody mess of a cow. She swung the beam to the cow's haunches and illuminated the angel wing Daedalus Group insignia branded there.

"These cows have been pumped full of hormones and steroids to make them bigger and more valuable," Chloe said, remembering her mother's many rants on the evils of the Daedalus Group's industrial food production. "You're sick because you've been eating the wrong cows."

"And you would know where I could find clean meat?" The dragon hissed and leveled his gaze on Chloe, and for an instant, the electricity flashed within his eyes again.

She felt the probe of his will through her mind for an instant, and then it was gone as his jaws slumped back to the ground. She was close enough to feel the hot, stale air of his breath against her face, but she held fast. He looked too weak to leave the barn, let alone snatch a four-hundred-pound steer from the wing.

"If this smell doesn't go away by tonight, my mom is going to come looking in this barn, and neither one of us wants that to happen," she said, thinking while she spoke. "If you can somehow clean up this mess, I'll promise to bring you clean meat until you get your strength back…How did you get in here anyway?"

Uktena motioned with his eyes toward the upper story, where the fifteen-foot-tall sliding door for loading and unloading hay was cracked open with a bright slash of light burning through.

"Right," she nodded, trying to play it off like all this was business as usual. "Do we have a deal?" she asked.

"Why would you help me?" he asked, seeming in that moment more like a tired old man than an ancient monster.

"You saved my life twice; it's the least I can do," she stated, not knowing how to voice the deeper connection she'd felt to him since the lightning dream. "Plus, we seem to have a common enemy," she said with a nod back to the Daedalus Group's poison cow. "And I'll tell you what," she added with the hint of a mischievous smile, "when you can fly again, I'll show you where to find some of the finest meat you've ever tasted."

CHAPTER 21
THE COW THIEVES

Perhaps the only thing that could have taken Chloe's attention away from pining over Kirin the following week was attempting to secretly nurse a dragon back to health. She came to understand rather quickly that dragons ate a tremendous amount, and her grand declaration that she would provide for one of their god-kings in her mother's barn had already proven to be a bit rash by Sunday night.

Luckily Audrey, in her wonderfully thrifty way, had gotten into the habit of flash freezing large amounts of locally raised, grass-fed organic beef a few times a year. She'd just made her usual winter meat purchase the week before when the beef supplier for Positive Pete's had showed up with some discount overstocked cuts and a fondness for flirting. Audrey knew how to capitalize on a good thing.

Chloe tried not to eat beef that often, but her mom had a borderline unhealthy appetite for "the good stuff" and would have eaten steak every day if Chloe let her. This time, Audrey had come home with twenty or so pounds of NY strip, another ten of filets, and a bag full of pork tenderloins with some homemade sausage on top. With Audrey's appetite, it was meant to last until spring…

By Tuesday, Chloe had stolen it all and she hadn't even put a dent in Uktena's hunger. Still, the dragon began to improve noticeably by midweek. He spent most of his time in a state of torpor, and the dam of silence between them held back the endless flood of questions that Chloe was waiting to ask. The dragon even seemed to eat in a weird sleep state as Chloe tossed hunks of semifrozen meat into his open, stinking jaws before they snapped shut with a loud CLACK.

Chloe wanted to keep the process as clinical and scientific as she could, needing to bury her thoughts in a practical approach to the undertaking rather than get swept away by the impossibility or implications of it all. She noted changes in his appearance and tracked the feeding schedule on a piece of graph paper; she pretended it was just research for yet another 'A' report in science class. But more than once, she'd found herself walking the length of the unresponsive beast, tempted to reach out and touch it again.

On Wednesday night, as she stood beside the dragon and monitored the improvement in his breathing, she closed her eyes to listen as a shiver ran through her, and for a moment, she envisioned herself climbing up to straddle Uktena's wide neck. She was stunned to find that she'd taken an involuntary step in that direction before opening her eyes again. A dragon breath later and she'd fled back toward the relative safety of her room.

By Thursday morning, the reek of death was gone, though the smell of dragon had permeated the barn in its place. It reminded Chloe of the reptile house at the zoo—not unpleasant, just off-putting and alien. She was glad to discover, however, that Uktena was not by nature grizzly and gore-strewn in his personal hygiene. He had cleaned up quite nicely, the silvery shine to his scales returned, and any trace of filmy translucence changed back to an almost metallic solidity.

In an attempt to divert Audrey's lingering curiosity surrounding the big stink, Chloe had supplied a dramatic cringeworthy story of finding an entire squirrel colony that had come under Shipwreck's bloody claw. For the remainder of that week, she felt pangs of guilt every time Audrey shot the cat angry looks or swatted his butt off the counter with a little extra judgment. All the while, Shipwreck kept his distance from Chloe, watching her with what seemed like a knowing sense of betrayal, or perhaps fear.

After Audrey had gone to bed on Thursday night, Chloe rose from the couch and put down her book. She'd read the same paragraph four times before finally succumbing to the insuppressible impulse to go see the dragon again...as if to prove to herself, once again, that it really was there.

She slid into the kitchen and removed a tightly wrapped paper package from beneath the lettuce in the bottom of the vegetable drawer. Clutching it to her side, she stepped lightly across the creaking living room floor and put on her running shoes.

She opened the back door as quietly as she could and slipped out before gently easing it closed on creaking hinges. There was a dusting of fallen leaves about the yard, and her steps across the lawn seemed to crunch much louder at night than they had during the day. As she approached the barn, she looked back to check her mom's bedroom window—still shuttered and dark.

Despite the tight schedule after practice, Chloe had been making dinners all week to keep Audrey from sniffing around the meat freezer in the basement. Earlier that night, she'd even cooked a couple of fine steaks that she'd blown her own saved money on in hopes of both passing it off as the farm-raised original and sating her mom's meat craving for the week. She had no idea what excuse she would give when Audrey finally noticed the theft, and after their recent heart-to-heart, she knew it was only a matter of time before she would have to tell... the truth?

She'd bought four hormone- and antibiotic-free steaks in total, hoping that the measly offering of the remaining two might keep the dragon satisfied with their arrangement for another night.

She slid into the barn and shut the door behind her, remaining in total darkness until she found the flashlight by the door. She clicked on the freshly battery-powered beam and waved it in a slow arc around her. She still wasn't sure how the sickly dragon had done it, but Uktena had held up his end of the bargain and had continued to clean and straighten as the week had progressed. The barn was cleaner than it had been in Chloe's lifetime, with all the junk in neatly arranged stacks, rows, and piles and no trace of the gore that had temporarily infested the back corner.

The paint cans were tightly arranged to block the nearest window, and the farm tools were leaning against the opposite window in a straight line. It was the work of someone with a fastidious attention to detail, and the anal-retentiveness of it all made Chloe almost as uncomfortable as knowing who/what was responsible for it. She realized, as the light flashed across the dragon's handiwork, that there was no way Audrey would ever believe that she had done this. The sense of order that had been imposed on the space was in its way more conspicuous than the dead cows that had been there in the first place.

Chloe started to unwrap the meat as she moved to the back, noticing how the dragon had constructed a wall from the tire towers and a couple giant spools of moldy hay so there was no direct line of sight to where he slept until she was practically on top of him. She forced a little cough to announce her arrival before swinging her foot past the barricade. She froze as the light in her hand danced around the space with jerky ticks... Uktena wasn't there.

For a moment, she panicked. *What if he's left for good? What if someone else has found him?* But then she reassured herself that he wouldn't have bothered with the wall if he wasn't looking to stay. She stepped further into the clearing and continued the search for some sign of his recent activities.

Even the blood stains had been cleaned from the floor, and aside from the odd, animal undertones to the musk of the barn, there was no indication that a giant, winged monster might be residing there. In the back corner, where she'd first found him blended among the shadows, there was now a little pyramid of antlers and horns. It was stacked deliberately—like the rock cairns that Chloe had sometimes found along the Appalachian Trail—though this small monument was clearly meant for no one but the builder: a homey touch comprised of the trophies from recent kills.

A shiver ran down Chloe's spine as she sensed someone behind her. She spun around, and the flashlight caught the silver-white hair of Uktena in man form a few paces away. He was standing utterly still as he watched her with rapt interest.

"I went to hunt," he said without emotion. "It seemed safer to consume my meat where none would find the remains."

Chloe noticed that he held another, even larger, set of antlers in his hand. He stepped past her and reverently placed them on top of the pile before turning back to face her hushed stare.

"I honor those who have died for my hunger," he explained. He sniffed the air, and his eyes moved down to the half-wrapped steaks in Chloe's hand.

Chloe suddenly felt insecure. "I wasn't sure if you were getting enough. Sorry, I couldn't afford much," she shrugged. "I guess you've probably had your fill—"

"No," Uktena cut in. "Deer meat is too salty and stringy for my taste; I much prefer the flavor of the cow you have brought me."

"Oh, good," said Chloe with a little smile. "This might not be as fine as the stuff before, but it isn't frozen." She held up the meat as a bit of blood dripped from the paper.

Uktena's gaze tracked the droplet as it fell to the hay at Chloe's feet. Now it was the dragon-man's turn to look uncomfortable. "I cannot feed in this form, and I still lack the strength to maintain it for long," he said, as if trying to formulate what he would next say. "I must ask you to look away as I change."

Chloe was momentarily confused about what he was asking; his clothes looked like they were knit from the deep grey of the surrounding shadows. Then her eyes went wide and she turned around. "Of course," she called back as she stepped across the open space that had previously been scattered with carcasses.

Behind her there was a sound of indistinct movement followed by the heavy creaking of floorboards. She wanted to peek, but willed herself to remain still. *How the hell does a man change into a hundred-foot-long winged creature? It defies the laws of physics!*

The voice that answered was that of the beast. "My kind was born to this universe long before the age of your science," he said at Chloe's ear.

She whipped back around with a yelp, but the dragon's horned head moved out from the shadows, still in the far corner.

"There are truths of the natural world still well beyond human grasp," Uktena added as his front claws scraped across the floor and drew the powerful mass of body from the darkness behind it.

Still, she had to check her impulse to bolt. *Do not run. Do not run.*

The head came closer as the slits in his eyes focused again on the meat in her hand. "I would taste that meat now if you still offer it?"

Chloe raised the bloody handful a bit too eagerly as the monstrous jaws scissored open before her. She tossed the first steak with sloppy haste, and the jaws moved at a speed Chloe could barely register before clamping together with an echoing clack over the place where the meat had been. The gust of wind from the movement whipped against her face, and she stumbled back a step with shaky knees.

Uktena tilted his head back and swallowed the steak the way a pelican would swallow a fish. His expectant gaze settled back on Chloe, and the fang-lined mouth opened again. The long, forked serpent's tongue curled away from his teeth; Chloe gripped the butcher's paper and tossed the second steak straight in.

This time, his bite closed more gently around it, and he cocked his head to the side and started sawing on the meat with the ridged teeth at the back of his maw. As he worked the mouthful, a dribble of blood slipped out and fell to the hay, and a contented grumble climbed from the back of his throat.

The deep, gravelly hum sounded to Chloe a little like Shipwreck's purring.

Finally he swallowed with a little jerk of his head, and for a moment afterward, it almost looked like he was smiling. "For all of humanity's clever gadgets and bold invention, it is the cultivation of flavors such as this that must be your greatest addition to the world."

Chloe fumbled a folded piece of paper from her pocket and opened it before him. On it was a rough, pencil-drawn map of streets and pictorial landmarks that she'd sketched in homeroom class that morning. It showed the path, as she remembered it, to finding Richard Roberts's private herd of five-time, County-Fair-winning, grass-fed cattle. "I told you I would show you where to find some of the best meat you'd ever tasted," she stammered. "Well, if you follow the dotted line west from the barn, it will lead you to a pasture with the best cows in the state."

Uktena came closer until his head hovered only a foot away from the upheld paper. One of his powerful five-clawed hands rose to pluck the map from Chloe with two of his sword-length talons skewering the top corner in a surprisingly delicate grip.

It looked to Chloe the way a stereotypical British royal might hold a teacup, though in this case it was a hooked ebony talon rather than a pinky that was extended for balance. The dragon studied the drawing a moment longer before lowering the paper to the hay.

"But if you don't want to be spotted by anyone else, there are rules you'll need to follow," Chloe added nervously, hoping she didn't overstep her bounds. "You should only take one at a time, and don't go too many days in a row...The Daedalus Group suspects something weird already, and I think that some of them are looking for you."

The dragon's smile faded, and the electricity flashed again within his gaze. "In ages past, some of your kind sought me out in the high or deep places of the world, warriors looking to test their manhood or shamans looking for forbidden wisdom."

Chloe straightened. "How did that turn out for them?"

"Most became trophies for my pile," he gestured back to the cairn of antlers and bone. "But some few found what they were searching for."

Chloe felt the tickle of his will at the edge of her mind, but he restrained from entering. No longer was there an air of threat at the forefront of their interaction. Instead, there was a current through the air between them, and the diamond plate on his forehead began to pulse again with an internal radiance. Chloe's gaze was drawn to the mesmerizing rhythm of it as if with a magnetic pull.

"What are you searching for, Chloe McClellan?" he asked. "You who talk to the world, are a witch without intending it, and were queen for a night—what knowledge would you ask for if any answer could be yours?"

Chloe shrugged. "I don't know."

The dragon's head slithered closer. "Do you seek the key to riches or the riddle of power?" Uktena slowly circled as the diamond began to pulse brighter. "Would you ask for fame, or the secret of immortality, or perhaps the return of a loved one cruelly taken from you?"

Chloe felt a tremble in her legs, but she refused to react as the rows of teeth slid behind her.

"I could gift you the love from any and all who you desire and punish those who seek to tear you down or stand in your way."

His words crawled through Chloe's thoughts, insidious and impossible to resist. She closed her eyes and tried to block them out, but imagined instead what it would be like to have Kirin as her own and know that he loved her. Then she fantasized about breaking Kendra and leaving her in whimpering public humiliation.

Chloe shook the tempting images from her head and opened her eyes. "No, I would only ask you if the Tipping Point Prophecy is true," she said. "What is going to happen to the world when the others wake up? You called it the day of the Ascension; I would ask what I can do to stop it."

Suddenly one of the dragon's giant blue eyes was beside her, and the black slit thinned as the internal spark flared again. "You could have anything you desire, and you would ask instead what you can do for your world?" he asked in challenge.

Chloe swallowed hard. A part of her longed to reach out and touch the glow of the diamond—needed it—but she kept her arms locked at her side. "If the prophecy is true and the world ends soon, what good would anything else I wished for be then?"

Uktena's neck retracted back toward the shadows that still obscured the bulk of his form, and the diamond light in his forehead dimmed and went out. For a long moment, he stared at Chloe with a mixture of confusion and fascination. "Some knowledge proves to be a curse to those who grasp it—wisdom that leaves no room for happiness."

"Is there even such a thing as happiness in high school?" Chloe mumbled. "I just want to understand what all of this means," she said. "I need to know what will happen. What am I supposed to do?"

"None can truly know what will happen," the dragon answered, "or fully understand what their role is in life until after it has passed." He sunk back further into the darkened corner as his voice took on a melancholy tone. "Even I am too small to change the events that direct the world…Perhaps the greatest gift I could give you is the continued security of ignorance."

"Wait," protested Chloe. "You said—"

"Leave me, Chloe McClellan. I am weary," Uktena cut her off and turned away. Somehow, as he tucked his head under his wing, his massive form all but vanished into the gloom of the barn. "Sleep and dream of the pond in the summer sunlight," his muffled voice grumbled from the shadows. "Wake tomorrow and live your day with all the spirit you have to give it."

Chloe turned around and marched out of the barn in a huff, wondering why the thousand-year-old dragon was starting to sound more and more like her mother.

.   .   .

That was it! Chloe couldn't keep this secret to herself any longer. She did not have pretty dreams of summer days or wake with a newfound zest for life. She was tormented instead by hazy nightmares of riding on Uktena's back though smoke-filled air over a dying planet. She woke with a pit in her stomach and a hunger to fight.

Plans were solidified during Friday's lunch period for her and Stan to finally put Operation Bovine Justice into practice. Chloe reminded Stan that NO ONE else could know about what they were up to. The following Saturday night, Chloe's latest grounding would be over, and they would convene for the video stakeout at the original site she had suggested—but now with the unspoken insurance that the Cow Thief would actually show up, as if on cue.

Chloe figured that if she could prove to Stan that the dragon was real, then she could ease him into the rest of her secret and elicit his help with how best to proceed. If Uktena wasn't giving her answers and signs continued to point to some sort of looming apocalypse, she was damned sure not going to sit back and pretend everything was life as normal.

It didn't matter that Kirin had gone the full week without so much as a text or an e-mail to her or that her friendship with Ezra had all but evaporated since Kendra had gotten her poisoned claws into him. The pitfalls and failures of her adolescent social life were meaningless in the face of a pending global crisis and a possible extinction level event for the human race. At least that's what she repeatedly told herself right up until her phone rang at 5 p.m. on Saturday afternoon.

"Chloe, it's Kirin," he said as if no time had passed since their last conversation.

She couldn't keep her voice from spiking. "Oh! Hi, welcome back...Was China cool?" *God! What a stupid thing to say!*

"Eye-opening," he answered, holding something back. "I can't tell if I'm supposed to be getting ready for dinner or breakfast, but I've been told to try and reacclimate to Eastern Standard Time and stay up until I would normally go to bed."

Chloe could hear what sounded like a yawn over the phone.

"I was wondering if you were around tonight to hang out or something—help keep me awake for a few more hours?" he asked. "I could tell you all about the trip."

Chloe was about to blurt "YES" before she caught herself. *I can't do this to Stan again!* "I would love to hear about the trip, but I kind of already have plans...with Stan," she said weakly.

There was a hushed pause on the other side of the line. "Stan, huh?"

"Yeah, but maybe you could come with us?" she found herself suggesting.

"I don't know. What are you doing?" asked Kirin skeptically.

Oh boy. "It's kind of a funny story, actually. You know how sometimes an absurd idea can get so much talk that it kind of steamrolls out of control until you wind up following through with it?" *What am I talking about?*

"What are you talking about?" he echoed over the phone.

"Good question," she said with a glance out to the barn through her bedroom window. "We're going on a video stakeout of a secluded cattle farm to try to catch the Cow Thief on camera," she said rapid-fire. She shut her eyes for the moment of silence that followed.

"Huh," replied Kirin. "That's pretty cool...If you're serious about me coming along, I would totally do that."

"Really? I mean, excellent! Yes, I'm absolutely serious." *Stan is not going to like this.* "We're meeting over at my house at eight."

"Cool. Should I bring anything?"

"It's gonna be a proper stakeout, you know, so bring snacks and maybe some cards or something," she answered with the butterflies in her stomach taking flight. "And you should wear black," she added.

"And you're sure it's okay that I'm crashing your thing with Stan?" he asked.

"Absolutely!" she replied too emphatically. "I think you'll really like Stan; he's hilarious, you'll see."

"Okay, I'll see you at eight," he said before hanging up.

Chloe was rocking jauntily on the heels of her feet as she lowered the phone from her ear. There was no movement in the barn, and she hadn't seen Uktena for more than twenty-four hours. As she turned away from the watch, she caught her reflection in the mirror on the back of the closet door. She was not impressed by what she saw.

Her hair was unwashed, and she was still wearing her pajama pants and a tattered old T-shirt. She wiped the smirk from her face and squared off with the judgmental gaze that looked back.

"What?" she challenged. "If it's the end of the world, I'm going to need all the help I can get."

. . .

And so it was that at a quarter to nine on the first Saturday night of November, Chloe found herself perched on a hill beside an unlit stretch of road with her secretly gay and increasingly stoned friend on one side and her increasingly exhausted semisecret crush on the other. A small HD camera with a night-vision setting sat atop a tripod before them. The wide-angle lens was pointed at the vast stretch of cow pasture beyond the wooden fence that spanned half a mile in each direction and contained the impressive herd of resting cattle below.

There had been no mention on the Saturday evening local news about the award-winning cow that had vanished from this same field the night before, and Chloe was hoping that no one had yet noticed the missing piece of Mr. Roberts's bovine collector's set. She searched the woods and hills before her and scanned the surrounding skies for movement—lost for a quiet moment in the way the moon's light reflected off the grass along the crests of gentle hills.

Kirin was staring at her out of the corner of his eye. "You really are the Cow Thief, aren't you?" he whispered.

She was dressed in head-to-toe black with her red-cheeked face shadowed within the recess of her hoodie. Still her smile showed through the dark. "As I see it, we're all Cow Thieves now; you fools are complicit." She hoped to bridge the frosty gap between the two boys with humor. So far, it wasn't working.

Stan was doing his best to ignore them both as another skunky waft of white smoke drifted toward the field. His typical flow of banter had gone stagnant with Kirin's unexpected inclusion in the evening. Chloe needed the return of his easygoing wit to fill the numerous awkward silences that passed between the unlikely trio—which was pretty much the only reason why she wasn't vehemently opposing his passive-aggressive drug protest.

He turned toward them with the curl of his grin starting to re-form. "You guys sure you don't want some?"

Kirin and Chloe both shook their heads.

"More for me," Stan shrugged and took another long pull

of the joint.

Chloe watched the orange flare at the tip and pictured the glowing pulse of the diamond shape in Uktena's head instead.

"So your big plan is to just sit here until the Cow Thief, whatever *it* is, shows up to take a cow?" chuckled Kirin.

"Yeah, kind of," said Chloe, realizing how weak a plan it would be without the insider tip of a relative time and place for the next strike.

"Or until bedtime," added Stan unhelpfully. "My curfew is eleven thirty."

Kirin laughed. "Wow, you two are a couple of detectives; this is like CSI Charlottesville. The Cow Thief doesn't stand a chance."

"Okay, how would you suggest we proceed, Mr. Genius Sleuth?" she challenged.

"Well, first off, I don't believe in aliens, and I think the whole thing is a bunch of nonsense with a strange but perfectly mundane explanation for why cows are vanishing."

"I never said aliens," Chloe retorted. "But let's just pretend, for the sake of argument then, that there is some*thing* taking them," she suggested. "Then what would you do?"

Kirin chewed his lip and thought about it. "What do you know about it?"

"We know that it hunts at night and has come to this spot most recently," Chloe stated, realizing only after she'd said it that half her statement had no public evidence to back it up.

"Really?" chimed in Stan. "I hadn't heard about any new cows for more than a week."

"My friend Liz got a text from Kendra about a prize-winning cow going missing from here last night," she lied. "This herd belongs to Kendra's father."

"And does the thief typically hit the same spot a few times in a row?" Kirin continued.

"Nope," interjected Stan, as if determined to highlight their strategic failings. "I've charted it out according to news stories, and it's been pretty random so far."

"Okay, is that all you have?" Kirin dug into a bag of pretzels.

Chloe could only nod.

"We know it can fly and that it's big enough to snatch a cow from the wing," added Stan while holding in another hit.

Chloe shot him a warning look.

"Err…probably." He slipped into a barrage of hacking coughs.

"That sounds to me like aliens again," said Kirin with a shake of his head.

"Call it whatever you want," Chloe cut in. "The facts are that livestock have been removed from open fields or pens without any tracks or witnesses…how many times now, Stan?"

"Eleven separate confirmed incidents," Stan answered.

"Eleven times," Chloe repeated, "and no trace at all of any chase or struggle except a few drops of blood from one of the sites." She had a smug expression of her own to counter Kirin's. "That sounds like aerial removal to me, and it would have to be pretty big to take a four-hundred-pound cow without landing."

"And in one of the earlier incidents, there is some speculation that two cows may have been snatched at once," Stan offered.

Kirin fished another handful of pretzel rods from the bag and yawned. "Yeah, I'm still not buying it."

"Now you're just being difficult," Chloe protested with a playful edge.

Stan tamped out the joint on the bottom of his shoe and rose abruptly. "Well, I'm going to take a piss and let you two figure it all out," he declared as he sauntered down the hill toward the fence.

Chloe and Kirin were left alone. They volleyed casual glances back and forth across the pronounced silence.

"You still haven't told me about your trip," Chloe said. "Did your grandmother make it back with you okay?"

Kirin nodded, suddenly more serious. "She's moving into the guest apartment above the garage, but she's still shaken up by what she went through. There's nothing left from her seventy-five years in China."

"I can't imagine how hard that must be," Chloe admitted.

Kirin put the pretzels down. "We went to Xining to try to recover her photo albums and letters," he said quietly. "I never would have believed how bad it was...There was nothing but bodies and rubble. It didn't even look like a city had ever been there except by the sheer number of the dead."

Chloe didn't know what to say.

"TV can't really do justice to that level of misery," he added with a hollow gaze. "Makes me wonder if the world really is coming to an end soon."

"If you knew that it was, what would you do differently?" Chloe murmured.

Kirin turned to find her stare within the recess of the hood. His own perpetually glassy eyes were filled again with the sadness that he'd carried at their first meeting, but there was something else in the look besides. "I think maybe I'd ask Stan to leave."

Chloe started to feel like she was vibrating. *Please. Please. Please.*

Then the sound of Stan hocking a loogie and zipping up his fly carried up the hill from the fence line.

Kirin broke the gaze between them and looked off toward the noise. "But I think the world is going to keep on spinning, and I don't want to be a jerk to your friend," he whispered hoarsely as the intensity in his eyes faded.

"He's kind of not representing himself very well tonight," Chloe whispered.

Stan shuffled back beside Chloe and dropped in a gangly heap. "If I was a giant aerial hunter, I'd totally grab that big, black bull down there on that first little ridge," he blurted with a follow-up point to the field, where the prominent curving horns of the bull stood out in contrast to the dark surroundings. "Think about it," he challenged. "From the sky, if you could, wouldn't you just have to swoop down and latch a claw around those horns?"

Kirin hoisted himself up with an impossible-to-read chuckle. "My turn," he said before heading up the hill in the opposite direction.

Chloe watched him walk away before catching Stan's study

of her from the corner of his bloodshot eyes. She gave him a scowl in return and sank deeper into the shadows of her hood. *Maybe the end of the world wouldn't be such a bad thing.*

"Did I interrupt something?" asked Stan.

Chloe hugged her knees to her chest. "No."

"I think he's into you, dude, congratulations," he said with an edge.

"Please shut up," she hissed. "And since we're on the topic, what's gotten into you? I don't know if you think this is some sort of drug smoking competition, but just so you know, you're the only one competing."

"Hey, sorry, I'm just trying to tune out and leave you two to your big night," he said.

"I'm sorry I invited him without asking! I know I'm kind of a hypocrite, but I couldn't help it!" Chloe said in her defense. "But at this rate, you're not going to be able to walk, let alone drive home."

Stan winked. "Don't worry, I'll manage; lots of practice driving home alone as my friends run off with their lovers."

Chloe considered kicking him in the leg but refrained. "You can be a real manipulative jerk, in a slightly cute, underhanded way."

"Oh, I'm just getting warmed up," Stan grinned. "And just so you know, YOU can be a little judgmental and self-indulgent, but I still love you."

As they turned back toward the field, a massive dark shadow swooped down from above. Its bat-like wingspan reached almost two hundred feet, but it slid through the sky with little more sound than a stirring of air. The black bull didn't even look up before the dragon's down-stretched back claw latched around its head and ripped it from the ground. The snap of the bull's spine sounded across the field. And then, just as swiftly and silently as it had come, the dragon and cow both disappeared back into the whispy clouds without a single flap of its wings.

Chloe and Stan were rendered temporarily speechless.

"Did you see that?" she finally asked.

Stan nodded.

"Did you get it on video?"

They both turned to the camera sitting idly on the tripod before them. There was no blinking red light and no REC indicator on the open view screen.

"Hmmm," said Stan.

Chloe felt the bottom drop out of her stomach. "You didn't press record, did you?"

He got on his knees and hovered over the camera with a sigh. "Nope...doesn't look like it."

Just then, Kirin strolled back down the hill. "So did I miss the aliens?"

Stan burst out laughing and flopped to his back with a flurry of little leg kicks. Chloe buried her face in her hands and groaned.

Kirin looked back and forth between them and raised an eyebrow. "What's so funny?"

Chloe pointed to the empty grass-covered hillock where the black bull had been. "Just now; it came."

Kirin looked at the hill and then back to Chloe. She slid the hood from her head and gave him her most convincing nod. "It took the black bull and flew into the clouds."

"It...what it?" he asked.

There's no turning back now. "A dragon, like on your dad's cauldron. It's why I went to talk to him," she offered.

Stan just kept on cackling like an idiot.

Kirin wasn't sure if they were having a laugh at his expense or not, but he didn't like it either way. "Uh-huh, let me see the video," he demanded.

Chloe winced. "It seems that someone was too stoned to press record."

This only made Stan laugh harder.

"What is this, take advantage of the severely jet-lagged kid?"

Chloe popped to her feet. "No, Kirin, I swear! There's a giant flying creature hunting livestock in Charlottesville! I've seen it before, and we saw it again just now!"

He raised an eyebrow. "What are you doing?"

"Kirin, I'm not messing with you!" she insisted.

"Okay, so if I jumped the fence and walked over to that hill, I wouldn't see the bull hanging out on the other side?" he challenged.

"Trust me, you wouldn't," she said before kicking Stan in the leg. "Tell him!"

Stan had tears on his cheeks and a look of pure glee on his face. "Holy shit, dude! I saw a real-life dragon!"

Without another word, Kirin marched past them down the hill and vaulted the fence with a single hand on the top rung.

"Kirin, don't!" Chloe yelled at his back as he continued to stride across the grass toward the hill. A few other cows turned to look at his advance from the next ridge over.

"That was the most amazing thing I've ever seen!" blurted Stan.

But Chloe kept her eyes locked on Kirin as he bounded up the slope and stood in the place where the bull had been. He looked over the other side, scanning the dark for the animal that wasn't there, but Chloe knew it wouldn't be enough to convince him of the truth. "What would make him believe me?" she begged the sky.

At first she didn't notice the building reverberation that was coming toward them...It wasn't until Stan stopped laughing and Kirin looked up that she broke from her inner angst spiral and noticed the bright light growing above the tree line. *Huh?*

Kirin shielded his eyes as a helicopter tore over the field and a spotlight swung its blinding beam upon him. The echoing report of the rotors was disorienting, and he stumbled back from the buffeting wind as it circled.

An amplified voice commanded from above, "Stay where you are!"

Stan scrambled to his feet and started toward his car, but two black SUVs and a Lincoln Town Car pulled up to block the street. Another spotlight burned out from the lead SUV and settled on Stan and Chloe as multiple car doors opened and familiar square-jawed men stepped out. Brent Meeks was frowning as he approached in the lead.

Instinctively Stan and Chloe put their hands in the air.

"I don't know," Stan whispered from the corner of his mouth, "this might do it."

CHAPTER 22
THREATS AND WARNINGS

Chloe cringed as the beam of a tactical LED flashlight shined in her face. The light moved on to wither the gaze of Kirin and then Stan, lined up with their backs against the SUV beside her.

"What are you doing here tonight?" demanded an emotionless Daedalus security goon standing wide-legged before them.

Kirin and Stan had nothing to volunteer.

For a moment, Chloe's attention lingered on their stone-faced interrogator's blonde buzz cut. His gaze was buried beneath a thick brow, and there was something weasely about his eyes—colorless and too close together. She scanned his waistline for a gun, but for the moment his weapon of choice was the flashlight, though she got the impression that a choice of firearms wasn't too far away. "We came out here to try to catch the Cow Thief on video," she answered.

The painful glare swung back to her. "What did you see?"

"Nothing much before you guys showed up," she answered flatly. "A bunch of cows and a lot of grass." She felt Stan's and Kirin's eyes on her for a split second before they focused back on the ground.

A walkie-talkie crackled to life from Brent's belt nearby. "This is Air 1—we've got the signal heading west toward the quarry—still no visual."

"Could you please stop shining that light in our faces?" Chloe asked.

The weasel-eyed man seemed not to hear her as he swung the beam over to illuminate Stan's toothy grimace.

"Is that how you remember it, long hair?" the goon pressed. "You didn't see anything going on with the cows either?"

"No, dude," said Stan, bringing a hand in front of his eyes. "And aren't we totally on public property right now? You're not exactly cops?"

Stan flinched as weasel-eyes stepped toward him to take a deep sniff. Stan reeked of marijuana. "Actually, it's private property all the way up to the road, if you wish to check public records," he answered with a self-satisfied expression. "But if you'd like me to call the police, I'm happy to make that happen… if that's what you think would be best for you?"

"That's enough, Mr. Fitz," said Richard Roberts as he and his chief of security, Mr. Duncan, walked up the hill holding Stan's camera. Mr. Fitz lowered the flashlight and took a step back. Richard Roberts was wearing a bespoke hunting vest and a cashmere outdoorsman cap. He walked by Chloe and Stan to stop before Kirin.

"You're Professor Liou's boy, aren't you?" he asked. "Kirin, isn't it?"

Kirin nodded and met his chilly gaze without faltering.

"Did you enjoy your trip to China?"

"I did, thank you," Kirin answered, giving him nothing.

Mr. Roberts smiled. "I wonder, do you have the same passion for myth and monsters as your father?"

"No, not particularly," Kirin admitted.

"And yet here you are, out searching for flying monsters on a Saturday night with a couple of underclassmen," Mr. Roberts pushed.

Kirin gave Chloe a quick glance, and their eyes met across Stan for only a moment. He looked back to Roberts. "Flying monsters?" Kirin raised an eyebrow. "I'm here to get a video of ALIENS stealing cattle."

Chloe couldn't wholly suppress the pesky smirk that tugged at the corners of her lips. *I think I'm in love.*

Mr. Roberts motioned to the camera beside him. "Mr. Duncan here says that there's nothing on the tape but a woman's forty-fifth birthday party."

"That would be Mother," Stan spoke up with his hand shooting into the air. "I hung up the streamers myself," he declared proudly.

The walkie-talkie crackled again. "This is Air 1—the signal is holding steady at the quarry—we're moving in."

Mr. Roberts and Mr. Duncan exchanged a look before Mr. Roberts turned back toward Chloe. "We keep meeting like this, Miss McClellan...I wonder, why did you think to come to *this* field tonight?"

Chloe swallowed hard. "My mom always said that you had the best cows in the state; I figured it was only a matter of time before the Cow Thief came for them." She forced all the fake excitement she could muster into her voice. "Do you mean that a cow was actually taken here?"

Mr. Roberts frowned at her. "It would seem that the finest bull in the state is missing."

The walkie-talkie chimed again. "This is Air 1—I've got a visual on the signal."

The whole security team straightened as Roberts snapped his fingers at Brent. "This is Car 4—go for description," said Brent.

Chloe's heart was pounding in her chest as the static continued for a long moment. *Come on, Uktena, get out of there!*

Stan's leg was shaking nervously.

"This is Air 1—I've got the back half of the cow perched on the edge of the quarry—no sign of what took it."

Roberts walked over and motioned frenetically for the walkie-talkie as Brent handed it over and stepped back. "Go again, Air 1—you've got what of the cow?"

"It's just the back half, sir—its legs, tail, and haunches—the rest of it is gone," responded the tinny voice.

Even through the darkness, Chloe could see that Mr. Roberts's normally red face was getting significantly redder. "What do you mean, 'gone'?"

There was a pause before the response. "Richard, it's me," said the voice of Dr. Markson over the walkie-talkie. "It's the damndest thing I've ever seen—it looks like your bull has been bitten clean in half with one bite."

"And where did you implant the tracking devices?" Roberts asked stonily.

"In its back right haunches—it's still here transmitting," said Markson with a hint of reverence.

Chloe choked back a laugh and wondered if the dragon really could hear her thoughts. *Nicely done, Uktena! Now keep out of sight until these helicopters give up and turn around.* She immediately received a sensory rush of contentment, and for a moment, she tasted the oddly pleasing flavor of blood in her mouth. But just as abruptly as it had come over her, the agreeable alien presence dissipated with a shudder, and she found herself unmoved from her own continuing predicament.

Mr. Roberts paced angrily. Mr. Fitz was licking his lips. Brent was playing at being a statue. Chloe risked another glance at Kirin as he motioned with his head toward his car.

Chloe nodded and cleared her throat. "I'm really sorry about your cow. I wish that we could've helped out with our video, but we really have to be getting home now," she suggested to all.

Mr. Roberts clutched the walkie-talkie like he was trying to break it and turned his chilly attention on her. He regarded her the way a lion in a zoo looks at little kids that taunt it from the other side of the glass. But he regained his humorless smile as he walked back toward them and his predatory gaze refocused on Kirin. "Be sure to mention to your father that you ran into me, would you?" he said. "And remind him that we'll expect to see his presentation on the cauldron by the end of the week."

He motioned toward Kirin's Jeep with a dismissive wave and then turned his gaze on Stan. "And you should make sure to drive safely, Mr. Strakowski. I'll have Dr. Markson check in with your father later just to make sure you got home okay."

Stan dropped his shoulders, frowned, and nodded, and this time Richard Roberts smiled in earnest. He focused back on Chloe. "Speaking of fathers, how is your father doing, Miss McClellan? I feel like I haven't seen him for years."

Chloe was trembling as she met his cold stare.

"You're starting to remind me of him, you know," he baited.

"What do you know about my father?" she hissed.

"I know that he liked to start trouble." He leaned in close to whisper, "And I know that he isn't around to cause trouble anymore."

A tear fell down Chloe's cheek as the scream she tried to unleash caught in her throat. Mr. Roberts turned his back on her and stepped away to hand the walkie-talkie back to Brent with a nod. "Mr. Meeks, make sure the young lady gets home safely, and let her mother know that we're becoming increasingly concerned about her daughter's propensity for trespassing on private property with…questionable chaperones and worrisome motives." He flashed his artificially whitened teeth. "I believe you know where she lives, don't you?"

Brent nodded.

Kirin took a step forward. "I'll drive her home," he declared, giving voice where Chloe could not.

Mr. Roberts looked over his shoulder and shook his head. "No, no, that's quite all right. You must be exhausted from all your travels, and I'm sure you're going to want to rise early to help your grandmother settle into her new home."

Somehow the simple mention of Kirin's grandmother seemed like a veiled threat. Kirin recoiled with nothing more to say as Mr. Roberts and his security team loaded back into their vehicles. Doors slammed and engines revved a moment later, leaving only Brent Meeks standing before the three high school kids with an expectant look on his infuriating face.

"This is Air 1—nothing else on the sweep of the area— bring in the documentation and clean-up teams—Dr. Markson wants saliva samples." Brent met Chloe's furious gaze and scrambled to turn down the volume on his walkie-talkie. He was clearly as uncomfortable with his boss's orders as Chloe was. He sighed and waved her over. "Come on, Chloe, let's go."

Chloe bit her bottom lip in a failed attempt to keep it from trembling.

But Kirin stepped in front of Brent as if he wasn't even there and touched Chloe's shoulder with an instantly calming effect. "Are you all right?" he asked.

He made her want to be strong. "Yeah, I'm okay," she lied.

"Are you really gonna go with him, or do you need me to make a stink? Cause I'll go big if you want me to!" he said with absolute conviction.

"No, there's no reason for both of us to get re-grounded... again," whispered Chloe with an appreciative smile. "Thanks for coming out and playing along."

Kirin had to fight back a yawn. "Are you kidding me? I don't think there's another person alive who could have kept me up this late."

"Hey, they took the tape!" hollered Stan, ruining the moment. The video camera tape slot was open and empty in his hand.

Brent straightened and tried to look official. "Sorry for the inconvenience. It will be mailed back to you on Monday," he stated like he was reading from a cue card.

"You can't just take peoples' stuff," Stan protested meekly.

Brent sized him up and turned back to Chloe. "Let's go."

She gave a nod to Stan that spoke of unfinished business, and he flashed the biggest, toothiest grin she'd ever seen in response. Then she turned to Kirin and tried to think of something cool to say. "Thank you...and sorry," was all she came up with.

Kirin just looked at her with an odd intensity behind his tired gaze. As she turned to begin her slow perp walk to the black SUV, he reached out without warning and pulled her back. She looked down at the firm grip on her wrist just as he stepped into her with a deep kiss. The tang of his faintly salty lips found hers as she shut her eyes and leaned into him—he tasted like a summer at the beach, like the ocean and lip balm. He reminded her of vacations at the Delaware shore when she was younger, when her father had still been there and her mother had laughed all the time. She felt like she was vibrating as his tongue rubbed against hers, and she wished in that moment that it would never stop.

But he pulled apart from her gently and gave her a sheepish smile. "I didn't plan to do that," he admitted.

Chloe was still trembling. "I don't mind."

He leaned in close again to whisper in her ear, and she felt the warmth of his breath on her neck. "I don't know what you're up to here tonight, but I want to know more."

"Okay...but I have to warn you, it could get pretty weird," she whispered back.

He let her wrist go and stepped away as his easy smile returned for the first time that night. "I'm counting on it."

Brent coughed behind them, and Chloe remembered only then that they weren't alone. She glanced over to Stan, who was still smiling like an idiot. He gave her the thumbs-up, and this time Chloe bit her lip to keep from squealing with glee.

She turned toward Brent and the waiting SUV to keep herself from doing something truly embarrassing. As she started to walk again, she prayed for some excuse to turn back around and start kissing Kirin again. *Keep it together! Don't freak out!*

"I'll call you tomorrow," said Kirin to her back with an unfortunate sense of finality.

She turned around with the best cool smile she could muster. "I hope I'll still have a phone to answer."

. . .

Neither Chloe nor Brent had said a word since they'd gotten in the car. Chloe was content to ride out the rest of the journey staring out the window in silence. The fences, trees, and fields flashed by in a blur, but she kept her eyes on the sky, searching for movement as her mind vacillated between anger and elation.

She replayed the kiss over and over—the feeling of his body pressing against her and the undeniable rightness of his lips. It felt like a litter of rambunctious mice were alternately roughhousing and fighting in her stomach. She'd spent the last seven years trying to manage every aspect of her life, but Kirin made her want to lose control.

She wanted to roll down the window and scream out at the night, but she caught Brent's smug expression in the rearview mirror and stifled the impulse. Her high spirits plummeted in an instant as Mr. Roberts's cruel words came back to her. The angry mice took over.

Chloe wanted revenge. She would make them pay for what they'd done to her pond, and she would make them tell her whatever it was that they'd done to her father. She never really believed that Ray McClellan had gone insane. Chloe had always held out hope that maybe her father had left for a very good reason...

She stared at the rectangle of Brent's stupid face in the mirror and imagined what he'd look like if Uktena swooped down from the clouds and plucked the SUV from the road: his eyes wide and his mouth agape in a noiseless scream as he tried to squeeze himself onto the floor beneath the steering wheel.

What would that power feel like? She fantasized about landing on the roof of the Daedalus Group headquarters, firing bolts of lightning from her gaping, fanged mouth and crushing brick and steel with heavy curving claws. It felt like there was an open current of electricity in her belly, and she wanted to release its potential for destruction. *How dare these wicked men drive me from my home and hunt me across the skies. They will break beneath my fury!*

Chloe shivered, and again it was only the reflection of a pouting little girl staring back at her in the window.

"I know you don't like me, Chloe," said Brent as he met her gaze in the mirror for a moment. "But I really care about your mother."

"Cheating on her with a married woman was kind of a funny way to show it."

He focused on the road for a long moment. "I messed up; I know that," he admitted. "But when you get older, you'll see that things aren't as cut-and-dry as they are in high school."

Chloe laughed cruelly. *What I wouldn't give for cut-and-dry!* She willed lasers to shoot out of her eyes at the back of his head... nothing. "My mom deserves a whole lot better than that."

Brent held his gaze on the road.

"Yes, she does," he muttered as he started to look a little red in the face. "And I wish I could be the one to give it to her," he added with the hint of glassy sheen in his eyes.

Chloe hadn't been prepared to discover that Brent was

capable of real emotion, and she couldn't think of her normal biting response.

He filled the silence. "But even if I can't be that guy for her, I can still do what I can to keep her from getting hurt." He looked up, and this time it was Chloe who had to look away. "All she really cares about is you, you know, and if anything happened to you, it would destroy her. So I'm telling you now, as a friend—whatever it is you're up to, you need to stop messing with the Daedalus Group."

Chloe hadn't been expecting that either.

Brent slowed the vehicle along a flat stretch of road and edged into the grass on the side before coming to a full stop. He turned around and commanded her attention. "These guys are in big business with some very serious people, and they don't play nice. You need to stay out of their way or they can make your and your mother's life very difficult."

Chloe shrank back in her seat. "What did they do to my father?"

Brent turned back around and eased the car back onto the road. "I don't know, and I don't want to know. I've only been there for two months, but it's a really great job for me, and I don't get paid to ask questions," he said defensively. "And you shouldn't either!"

"I'm a fifteen-year-old girl; what can they do?"

"This isn't some game, Chloe. I'm talking government contracts and huge sums of money. That guy I work for, Mr. Duncan—he used to be special forces. And another guy in my group was some kind of mercenary in Iraq, and all of them seem to be scared of the money man who's coming from D.C. in a couple weeks…I'm telling you, you and your friends need to stay out of this!"

Chloe had been rendered mute as the black SUV pulled into the McClellan family driveway and came to a stop beside the barn. Chloe could see her mom through the living room window as she moved through the kitchen with a teapot. Brent couldn't take his eyes off her as Audrey noticed the bright headlights in the driveway. Chloe put her hand on the door handle to leave, but stopped herself before she opened it.

"If they're so bad, then why do you work for them?" she challenged.

"It's like I said: nothing is cut-and-dry anymore."

"Whatever," she blurted as she opened the door and flooded the car's interior with light just as Audrey came to the window and squinted out at them.

"You don't like me and that's okay," called Brent. "Honestly, I don't particularly like you either," he admitted. "But I still love Audrey, and I don't want anything to happen to you for her sake."

Even from a hundred feet off, she could tell that her mom wasn't happy.

"Do us all a favor and focus on your schoolwork like you used to," he said as he switched the SUV into reverse.

"If only life could be that simple," she muttered before slamming the door. His infuriating face was finally blocked out behind tinted windows as the SUV reversed out of the driveway and sped off down the road toward the pond. The red glow of the taillights dipped over the rise of the hill, like two fiery eyes retreating through the darkness.

Chloe turned and glared at the side of the barn, listening for some sign of the creature that lurked within. It was utterly quiet, not even the creaking of old boards or the scurry of mice. But then, as she closed her eyes, it almost seemed like the barn itself was breathing…Chloe was filled with the feeling of contented slumber, and in that moment, her eyelids became heavy. She yawned just as Audrey opened the screen door with the squeak of hinges.

She held the door open with her heel and crossed her arms, waiting with the telltale pursing of her lips that Chloe knew so well. "Why did Brent just drop you off at 11 p.m. in a Daedalus Group car?"

Chloe chose not to answer as she started to shuffle toward the maternal fury with her head down.

"And where is all of my meat?" Audrey added.

Please, just let me keep my phone! Please, let Kirin call me tomorrow!

CHAPTER 23
TWO WEEKS OF TOMORROWS

The morning frost crunched beneath Ezra's boots as he strode across the field carrying a bushel of hay and a hoe on his back. They'd left the horses in the barn overnight; he was the first one to cross the dried grass and hardened soil that morning. At 5 a.m., it was just him and the land and the coming sun, the way he liked it. His body ached from football and manual labor, but he loved the immediacy of that dull pain, the twinge in his muscles and the slow loosening of his joints. It made him feel present.

Ezra tossed the hay to the center of the field and took it apart with the hoe and his boot before turning back toward the barn. The darkened ridge of the distant hills claimed his attention, and a dream from earlier that morning came back all at once. In it, he'd stood in this field, just as he was, while lightning flashed in those hills up by Chloe's house. It had been colder, full winter, with a thin layer of snow clinging to the hard earth, and he'd been carrying something heavier than hay over his shoulder…

The sound of thunder rolls out seconds later, and somehow he hears Chloe's voice calling to him in the far off rumble. It's like she's saying his name from right beside him, or all around him, or maybe even from within—and then the call is answered from below. At first, it's just a gentle trembling in the soil. But the murmur gathers, as if reaching up to reply to the grumbled challenge that carried through the air moments before. The ground begins to shake as Ezra fights for balance.

But he is not scared and he does not run; he just steps back from the center of the field as a fissure cracks open before him. A cloud of dust and steam rises from beneath the surface, and buried within the wrenching groan of the land is what sounds like a bestial growl. Ezra moves toward the fracture and heaves a giant saddle from his shoulder to his feet.

Only then does he realize that the hand-stitched seat of leather and brass is maybe five times the size of a normal saddle—far too big for a horse, too big for an elephant even. And he knows then that he's made it himself and that it's for riding whatever is climbing up from below…

With a chuckle, he shook off the clinging remnants of the dream and turned back toward the barn and the hungry, waiting horses within. Ezra was not one for interpreting dreams or giving weight to strange portents in the wind. He believed in things he could touch with his hands and the solid earth beneath his feet. His boots crunched back along the same path that he'd come, and he tried instead to remember the nuances of the Kendra sex dream that he'd woken with only a few minutes earlier.

Still, it was the impression of Chloe McClellan that lingered as he slid open the heavy wooden door and heard the excited whinny of the horses. As he marched toward the first stall, he glanced to the worn leather and dangling stirrups that hung on the post beside it and saw again the design of the oversized saddle he had crafted in his dream.

·   ·   ·

Kirin didn't call on Sunday morning. And though Chloe was just as grounded as expected, she hadn't been prepared for the level of fury that her mother had reached after Chloe had refused to give a suitable excuse for the two hundred dollars of missing meat. It did not make matters calmer that Chloe had also been caught trespassing again on the private property of the company that had helped to ruin Audrey's husband. Brent being the one to bring her home didn't help either.

After Chloe had shut her mouth and hung her head, Audrey had become apoplectic for the remainder of the night. She was red-faced and trembling as she stormed about the kitchen, slamming drawers and banging pots under the pretense of putting away the dishes. Chloe woke the next morning expecting to have her new Radio Shack flip phone taken away, but her mom's temper had settled into an even scarier cold indifference. Audrey let Chloe keep her electronic contact with the outside world in what at first seemed like an act of kindness, but only proved to magnify her daughter's pain throughout the following weeks of purgatory.

That afternoon, Chloe was instructed to rake the yard and cart the leaves out to the compost pile a hundred feet into the woods off the side of the house. She was an experienced raker with years of practice, but since Ray McClellan had left, the first big raking of the fall had always been a mother/daughter joint effort...until now. Chloe estimated that to clear the yard it would take her about twenty trips with a large sheet's worth of leaves dragged behind her.

While she worked, she could feel her mother's stern glances from the kitchen window as Audrey prepared her winter supply of chicken soup stock within. Even from outside, Chloe could smell the layered waft of onions, seasonings, and chicken broth simmering in the giant vat on the stove. Normally that smell filled her with a sense of contentment and belonging, but now she was afraid that she'd forever associate it with her mother's boiling rage. The smell would linger in the house for days.

Chloe was only on her second load of leaves when she heard the crunch of tires on the gravel driveway. Her legs cleared the distance to the side of the house as if with a mind of their own. *Please be him! Please be him!*

She did not expect to see the beat-up white Ford Focus come to a squeaky stop at the end of the driveway or know how to react as Ezra climbed out and spotted her. He smiled and waved before starting his long strides toward her. Chloe glanced to the window, but didn't see her mom watching. She moved to intercept him with her rake dragging behind.

Ezra was wearing a black-and-orange sweatshirt with a charging black knight insignia on the front, and he was cradling a football in his right arm. Without warning, he took a lateral stutter step and threw the ball toward her in a perfect spiral. She didn't have time to think as she dropped the rake and brought her hands up to catch the pass before it buried into her stomach.

"Jesus! Are you trying to kill me?" she yelled.

Ezra clapped. "Nope, I knew you'd catch it," he hollered. He stopped before her with a flash of his pearly whites and held out his hands for the ball.

She scowled and tossed it back before reclaiming her rake from among the leaves. "Maybe I should hurl a rake at you and see if *you* can catch *it*?" she challenged.

He smiled and turned to look back at his car across the yard, gauging the distance to the rolled down passenger side window. The football twirled in his palm before he latched on with his long fingers. He wound up and rocketed a perfect bullet of a spiral into the back of the seat from thirty paces and then spun back around with a sly wink as he reached for the rake.

That's amazing! Chloe tried to play it cool as she handed it over. "Looks like you're ready for the state championship game."

"I better be; it's next Saturday." He started to rake up long paths of leaves toward the sheet. He covered twice the distance that Chloe could with every sweep.

She watched him for a long moment, temporarily struck by how his every move was strong and confident. It was as if the leaves moved ahead of his every stroke with the rake, governed by his commanding will just like all the kids at school. To anyone else, it would seem that he lacked the capacity for doubt or worry, but Chloe knew better.

"Is there another rake?" he asked without slowing. "I'm not doing this whole yard by myself."

Chloe smiled. She'd leaned her mom's rake against the old oak in the failed hope of enticing Audrey to join in. She claimed it for herself and looked back to the kitchen window. Audrey still wasn't there.

"Is your mom home?" asked Ezra, as if reading her mind.

"Yup," answered Chloe. "I'm grounded again and on a short leash."

Ezra chuckled. "For such a goody-goody, you sure do like to get into trouble," he observed. "What was it this time?"

"Let's see: trespassing, lying, and stealing."

Ezra stopped raking and shot her a disapproving look. "That doesn't seem like you."

"The trespassing was debatable; I didn't actually lie, so much as plead the fifth; and the stealing was for a good cause," she said in her defense.

Ezra shook his head and continued raking. "How long are you down for this time?"

"This one could last awhile," Chloe replied over her shoulder as she tackled the leaf-infested shrubs beside the house. The silence between them stretched on as the rhythm of the work took over—just the sound of the shaky metal teeth as they ripped through the grass and pushed waves of brown leaves and acorns before them. With two, the work went quickly, and in only a few minutes, they had the second full sheet ready for the dumping ground.

"That's too bad," Ezra said, like no time had passed since her last words. "I was hoping you could maybe come to the game in Richmond and cheer me on next Saturday. It'd do me good to look up and see you in the crowd."

"Yeah, I'm afraid that's not looking too likely," Chloe muttered, swallowing the urge to make a petty comment about Kendra.

Without needing any direction, he dropped the rake and gathered the four corners of the sheet into an overstuffed sack that he flung over his shoulder. "Where to?"

Chloe wanted to tell him how much she'd missed him, but her thoughts lingered on Kendra and her mouth stayed shut. She pointed to the worn path into the woods. "Compost pile, about fifty paces that way."

Without another word, Ezra went, and Chloe couldn't help but track his graceful strides across the yard until he slipped into the shadows of the trees. She waited for a moment and then checked her cell phone for any new calls or texts. *Still nothing?*

Chloe slipped the phone back into her pocket, feeling the weight of someone's attention on her again. She glanced to the barn for any sign of the dragon before looking over her shoulder to catch her mom's gaze from the window. Audrey looked down into the sink and tried to play it off.

Ezra was whistling something classical and dramatic on his return down the path. He emerged with the empty sheet dragging behind him and broke off from his tune with a big smile and a wave to Audrey.

Audrey waved back with a bright yellow dishwashing glove on her hand and a fling of soapy water.

"Now that's what I call domestic bliss," Ezra whispered for Chloe's benefit as he laid the sheet back down for the third load.

She leveled her stare. "You're already on my shit list, remember?"

Ezra turned the smile on her. "Yeah, how much longer are you gonna keep that up, anyway?"

Chloe sighed; her presumed anger was already starting to falter. She remembered the way Ezra had defended her on Halloween and the surprising vulnerability she'd seen hiding behind Kendra's veneer of perfection. "Until you dump Kendra, or until the end of the world…whichever comes first," she offered.

He thought about it for a moment and then nodded. "Cool, I can wait it out; according to the news, the end of the world will be, like, any day now."

Despite her building fears that his statement may have held more than just a kernel of truth, Chloe found herself laughing. Though Kirin made her want to experience life and know the world, and Stan kept her rolling her eyes at all the pitfalls and perplexities the world presented, only Ezra could keep her grounded and focused on the here and now. He made her want to meet whatever challenges lay ahead with courage and grace.

Maybe he's the one to help me figure out what to do? She considered walking him into the barn then and there, but she doubted his levelheaded brain would ever be able to accept the insanity of what lay within.

"I'm sorry I can't come to the game," she said. "I'm sure you'll be amazing as always. But even if I wasn't grounded, how am I supposed to get back and forth to Richmond on a

Saturday night?"

"I don't know; you're a resourceful girl." He shot her a reserved smile. "I kind of figured you could get a ride with Kirin."

Despite her initial impulse to deny and evade, Chloe found herself unable to respond to the unexpected utterance of his name.

"So how are things going with the So-Cal lover boy anyway?" he pressed.

Chloe could feel the blood rise in her cheeks. "What?" she said lamely.

Ezra started to chuckle. "Ah, I guess it's going pretty well," he said before turning away and starting to rake again. "Hey, good for you," he added with a bit of an edge and his back turned. "I hope he's everything you'd hoped for."

Chloe snapped out of the deer-in-headlights routine and leveled her gaze. "First you say you don't want me hanging out with Stan, and now you're giving me attitude about Kirin. And all the while you're spending your time with the underage bitch-slut from hell!" She wasn't sure why she'd raised her voice. "Why do you even care what I do or who I do it with anyway?"

Chloe planted her feet and held her ground as Ezra spun around in a fury and stepped close. He towered over her with his finger leveled toward her nose. "She's not a slut; it's just an act!" he shouted back. "And I care about what you do and who you do it with because I'm jealous, all right?!"

Chloe stared up into the intensity of his brown eyes and searched for some sign of the punchline to follow. But there wasn't one.

Ezra looked away. "I still think you're too young for me, and you don't have a clue how to let loose and have fun, but no one else gets me the way you do," he admitted quietly. "I miss you, Chloe. I just need you to be a part of my life."

"I miss you, too. I'm sorry I've been such a jerk," she said just as Ezra enveloped her in a huge hug. She nestled into him, smelling the earthy undertones of the farm on his sweatshirt and holding tight to the strength in his back. She shut her eyes and squeezed tighter, feeling more secure in that moment than she remembered feeling for years.

She barely even noticed that her feet weren't touching the ground as Ezra stood upright with her still clutched in his arms. He nuzzled his face into her neck and kissed her tenderly under her ear. "Mmmm, you smell good," he said with a hint of his old lasciviousness returned.

Chloe felt flushed and confused. She pulled her head back with a nervous smirk. "You really are incorrigible!"

His cocky smile returned before he eased her gently back to the ground. "What? I love women; is that so wrong?"

Chloe laughed it off as she reclaimed her rake and tried to ignore the electric thrill that jangled through her body. "I just hope this doesn't mean that you're not going to help me finish the yard."

He took up his rake as well. "I told you, I'm a gentleman; I don't just kiss and run."

They bantered and played and continued the work, and this time Chloe refrained from checking her phone for almost ten minutes…

.   .   .

…Kirin lowered his own phone and dropped it in the empty passenger seat beside him as Chloe marched away with another load of leaves. He watched as Ezra tracked her progression across the yard with his eyes blatantly locked on her butt. Kirin had seen enough. He turned the key in the ignition and started the Jeep with a roar that sent a few birds fluttering into the air from the trees above.

He'd wanted to surprise Chloe, hoping that if he showed up at her house, her mom couldn't so easily turn him away. He needed to ask her a hundred questions about what had happened the night before and what she knew about the Cow Thief. He'd planned on telling her about all that he'd been through in China and the feeling that something bad was coming.

Above all, he had to let her know about the dream—the same spot just beyond the break as always, but this time it was *Chloe* who sat on the surfboard as *he* circled and nudged at her feet. It was as if he'd been called up from the depths by her presence. And as the dream continued, he realized that he wasn't the shark, but something else, far bigger and older—a long, sinuous form and yet somehow also a part of the water itself. He swayed and swelled with the pull of the moon, and Chloe was his moon…It was magnificent!

It had taken him almost three months to find someone that he was ready to let in and less than fifteen minutes of watching from his car to convince him that he'd been a fool for thinking it. Kirin had been burned by girls plenty of times back in Santa Cruz, but it was the betrayal of his mother's cruel death that came back now…Watching Chloe with Ezra, he felt the belonging of the dream stripped away—left empty-handed and abandoned once more.

He reversed the car along the gravel pull-off on the road and did a U-turn. He had to get home to help his grandmother. He had to make sure that he could ace his midterms to get his father off his back. As he rolled down the winding, wooded street, his thoughts stayed with the ocean—the calming rock of the waves and the sun glistening across the water—where his real life had been left behind.

.   .   .

Kirin didn't call or text the rest of the week either, and his short exchanges with Chloe in homeroom and lunch were subdued and even a little awkward. *Maybe he's just disturbed by what he saw in China? Maybe he regrets the kiss and wants me to leave him alone?* By the end of the week, he'd begun to speak more softly and less often, and though his easy smile persisted, Chloe didn't always see the warmth behind it.

She could tell that he was in pain, but there was never an opportunity for her to get him alone to talk about it, and he seemed to go out of his way to avoid her whenever she made the attempt. She had Audrey drop her off at school half an hour earlier every morning before first period, but Kirin had begun to shuffle into class late every day. When she tried to isolate him at lunch, she found it impossible to get an extended moment away from either Stan or Cynthia, or both. The last two calls and three texts she'd sent him had either been ignored or answered with truncated deflections.

Outwardly Kirin remained focused on his studies and the effort to make his grandmother feel at home. But still, as far as Chloe was concerned, this lack of post-kiss communication was getting to be ridiculous…maybe even borderline malicious?

Even with all that there was for Chloe to think about—a dragon in the backyard, the increasingly mysterious disappearance of her father, the evil corporation that was haunting her every move, or the end-of-days prophecy that she may have inadvertently begun—all she could think about was kissing Kirin and if she would ever get the chance to do it again.

Stan could offer her no solace or support. As threatened, Dr. Markson had taken the time that Sunday to call Mr. Strakowski and notify him of his son's two counts of trespassing and suspected drug use. Stan had been on hard-core lockdown ever since. He would remain without car, phone, or Internet privileges for three weeks as he was shepherded back and forth to school every day by his scowling mother.

Ezra was too focused on football leading up to the state championship game to give Chloe more than a cursory "hello" and a high five in the hallway. Even after he'd led the team to a squeaker of a victory with a scrambling quarterback touchdown in overtime, he was too caught up with Kendra and his hordes of adoring fans to break from the King Ezra persona at all.

To add insult to injury, Uktena had also managed to be out the few times throughout the week that Chloe had escaped from her mother's watchful eye to go looking for him in the barn. The dragon's trophy cairn of antlers was growing steadily, however, and Chloe left a note sticking to the uppermost horn that strictly forbade him from returning to Richard Roberts's bovine collection. Uktena had managed to stay out of the papers and blogosphere with his further hunts, and Chloe was determined to keep it that way for as long as possible. Still, his absence and the unanswered questions that surrounded his existence only amplified Chloe's growing sense of isolation and helplessness.

In an effort to hide from her life, she tried to retreat back to the pursuits of personal excellence, focusing as much as she could on pending midterms and the quickly approaching cross-country state championships. But even with those mental and physical distractions, she found her mind wandering back to the beautiful boy from California and the perpetually baffling sway of his moods.

.   .   .

Audrey wasn't really sure what to do with the bizarre stand-in for her daughter. Every morning, and then again when she returned home after practice, Chloe had taken to moping about the house like a zombie. She barely touched whatever food was put in front of her and had started to speak in one-word sentences. Chloe's hand remained perpetually wrapped around the unresponsive cell phone, and Audrey had spied her more than once with the same vacant, unblinking gaze that she'd seen before on her ex-husband.

By the second week, Audrey's rage had been replaced by worry, and she started to turn down the night shift at Pete's in an effort to break through Chloe's wall of melancholia. Aside from regularly coming home filthy and generally making a mess, Chloe had never really done anything wrong before the lightning incident. But now that she was keeping secrets, becoming increasingly reckless with the law, and stealing large quantities of meat without reason, Audrey wasn't sure what to think.

This grounding would remain open-ended until Chloe came clean about her reasons for stealing the meat. The close supervision was alien to both mother and daughter alike. Audrey decided to finally make a stand at Thanksgiving dinner, hoping to break through before the monthly headaches kicked in.

"Chloe, have some of the broccoli," she urged, trying to catch Chloe's eye from across the heavily laden table. "I made it with the melted parmesan the way you like it."

Without looking up, Chloe stabbed her fork into one of the broccoli spears and dragged it toward her mouth with a crumbling of baked cheese across the tablecloth. She took a tiny bite from the stalk and plopped the rest down on the plate beside the untouched turkey and mashed sweet potatoes.

"I take it that all of this has something to do with boy trouble?" Audrey suggested hopefully, finally putting aside her own anger to command Chloe's attention.

"What?" Chloe croaked.

Audrey had decided to take a new tactic to get her daughter to open up. "You're still pouting a week and a half later, so I'm assuming it's got something to do with Kirin?" She took a bite of turkey slathered in cranberry sauce and waited for her daughter to come to terms with the conversation she was proposing. "'Cause as far as I can see, the only one between us who has any reason to be angry or sullen is me."

A small bite of potato hovered on the tip of Chloe's fork. She put it back down and took a sip of water instead.

"I'm just saying that if you want to talk about it, I promise to listen without getting mad this time," Audrey offered. Chloe shrugged, but Audrey could tell that she'd gotten her attention.

"He kissed me the other night," Chloe mumbled. "But he hasn't called or mentioned anything since…It's been like two weeks. It's like that whole night never happened."

"Oh, is that all?" Audrey had to play down the rush of relief that swelled through her, as she put away the worst-case scenarios that had been lingering in the back of her mind. "That's just the way boys are sometimes, honey," she said with a dismissive wave. "Their whole existence, especially in high school, is pretty much just to flail about, be confusing, and make girls' lives miserable. But it sounds pretty clear to me that he likes you!"

Chloe looked up with a momentary glimmer of hope, but it faded again as the weight of the world bent her shoulders once more. "I guess," she muttered with an inadvertent hand on her cell phone. "I'm just tired of waiting for something to happen; it's like I'm being held captive by my own life…I'm waiting to look the same age as everyone else, waiting to be normal and happy, waiting to understand how I fit in."

"Well, then stop waiting and do something about it!" Audrey interrupted. "What happened to the Chloe who can outrun or outsmart anybody and doesn't care what people think?" Audrey challenged. "That's the girl that Kirin kissed, and that's the girl that got elected Homecoming Queen as a sophomore! You have to stop putting all these unnecessary expectations on life for whatever you think is supposed to happen. It's not going to happen the way you want it to. You could spend your whole life waiting by the phone for someone to call with all the answers to your problems, but it's never going to come."

Audrey sliced off another bite of turkey and watched as her daughter put the cell phone on the table with a crestfallen pout.

"If you want something, you have to go out and take it. If you want Kirin, you have to make sure he knows it," Audrey said.

"Is it all right if I go to the anthropology building at UVA on Sunday morning?" Chloe asked hopefully.

"Are you ready to tell me why you took all of the meat out of the freezer?"

Chloe wanted to explain all that had happened, but still saw no way to confide in her mother. She opened her mouth to answer and then closed it without a word.

"Well, I've got all the time in the world, and you're going to be grounded until you tell me the truth," snapped Audrey with the heat of her anger rekindling in an instant.

"Mom, I want to...but I can't." Chloe dropped her eyes again to the table.

Audrey abruptly stood to clear her plate and walked over to snatch Chloe's phone from beside the broccoli. She slipped it into her pocket. "Then I hope you can solve all your problems between the hours of eight and three next week."

CHAPTER 24
THE DRAGON RUN

Chloe walked through what had been the lush forest surrounding her home—now turned to a vast field of scorched earth, pierced by a maze of blackened spikes that had once been trees. Some of the charred trunks were little more than ash, waiting to be felled by a strong wind, but others were loosely held shells for millions of jagged little splinters.

Chloe had found people stumbling blind with a hundred tiny wood shards in their eyes after getting caught without goggles in one of the freak storms. Others had been torn and skewered by falling branches. Sometimes their screams kept her awake at night.

She passed by a particularly large tree spike and noticed the pockmarks that covered its entirety. All the trees and even the ash-grey earth were littered with the little divots. Chloe glanced warily at the dark clouds advancing across the red sky overhead. Gone were the days of blue skies and pleasant afternoon showers. The acid rain was getting stronger, more concentrated. She moved on in a hurry.

Every footfall sent up little dust clouds as she climbed a rise in the land, leaning on an old ski pole as she went, knowing she couldn't trust the trees to help her. At the top, she looked down into the next little valley, where a spiderweb of cracks had split the ground. At the widest point, the rip in the floor was open fifteen feet or more, and a similar break had been estimated to drop a quarter of a mile down. Dr. Markson referred to them as stress fractures across the earth's crust, and they, too, were increasing in number.

Chloe would have to go around. She checked her watch; it was getting close to dusk, feeding time. She cinched the straps of her backpack as tightly as they would go and started to jog; the sound of her breath echoed back within the confines of her face mask. At first, she had found it hard to breathe through the rubber and plastic filters, but she'd gotten more used to it than she had ever thought possible. Given enough time, the human animal could come to terms with any level of suffering.

Her feet carried her back down the hill, having also grown accustomed to running in thickly soled boots as opposed to the running shoes of her earlier days. But as she rounded the lowest fork of the crack, she heard the alarm sound from the hidden encampment below—high-pitched and piercing as it carried through the deathly still air. Almost instantly her eye caught the movement of a dark shape sweeping through the sky above.

She jumped over a fissure in the ground and started to sprint as she heard a heavy wing flap behind her. Two strides later, a hot tail wind blew in, and the dust spiraled into little dervishes. She heard the massive leathery wings flap again, and she pushed her legs as hard and fast as they would go...But as fast as she was, she wasn't fast enough. Trees crumbled apart on either side of her, and she felt a sharp pain in her thigh as a little avalanche of black shards tumbled down the slope toward her.

The heavy flap sounded again, and a dark shadow came over her path. Still Chloe ran harder. She started to scream amid the sound of a slow, deep inhale of breath from above.

"NO!" she screamed herself awake and was instantly slammed silent by the pain in her head. *I'm dreaming! It's only a dream.* Chloe forced her eyes open to look up at the ceiling. She traced the familiar cracks in the paint, seeing for a moment longer the splintering rend in the earth from her nightmare. After a few more pulsing throbs in her temples and a threatening churn of her gut, her worries switched to more immediate concerns. *Do I try to make it to the bathroom or go with the trash can?*

She breathed through her nose and stilled the urge to wretch, noticing only then how cold the room had become since she'd fallen asleep. She clenched her eyes and shivered, pulling the blanket up to her chin. One of her arms slipped free and reached blindly for the hot washcloth by her bed, but it had long since gone cold and clammy.

With a slow breath, she forced herself to sit up and slip the rag back into the tepid water basin. The insulting sound of Shipwreck's purring carried through the silence from the other side of the room. She glanced to her desk chair, readying to chastise the insolent beast, but her words caught in her throat.

Uktena sat in the chair in his human guise, watching her. Shipwreck nestled contentedly in his lap. "The cat did not like me, but I have finally won him over," Uktena said as he stroked Shipwreck behind the ears.

"How did you get in here?" Chloe blurted with a rush of adrenaline.

Uktena glanced to the open window in answer before his attention returned to the surprisingly tender treatment of the cat. Shipwreck shut his eyes and arched his neck for more.

"You can't be here! My mom will come to check on me soon!" Chloe hissed as another wave of nausea and pain washed over her.

"Your mother will not wake until dawn," answered Uktena with certainty. "I wished to speak with you. The torment of your dreams woke me from my slumber."

Chloe sat up and held her head in her hands for a moment as the pain edged back from the threshold.

"Your anguish clouds my thoughts day and night; I cannot escape it," he said with an undercurrent of anger. "This boy who longs for the sea…why do you not just claim him and be done with it?"

This took Chloe by surprise. "What?"

"All of this pining and indecision is insufferable. The human life is far too fleeting for such wasted time," said Uktena. "All you need do is touch my head and ask; I shall charm the boy and give him to you."

"No!" Chloe blurted with an extra throb behind her eyes. "I don't want him charmed…And why do you even care? I thought humans were insignificant to you!"

"You are," Uktena responded almost defensively. "But you have shown me kindness, and I would see it returned to you before…" he trailed off.

"Before what?" Chloe pressed. "What's going to happen?" She couldn't understand how she continually allowed herself to forget about the prophecy. "Do these dreams show what's coming?"

"I do not know the future," the dragon deflected. "If what you dream comes to pass, that gift is yours, not mine."

"No more riddles!" Chloe shouted, surprising herself. "No more forgetting!" Shipwreck unseated from Uktena's lap and darted out of the room. "Before, on the hillside, you mentioned the Ascension." She was trembling and tears started to gather in her eyes as she remembered the suffering of the nightmare world. "Tell me what's supposed to happen next month."

For an instant, the dragon-man's gaze flared with a spark of electricity, but then his face settled back into sad acceptance. "Soon others of my kind will return to the world of men—earth, air, fire, and water made flesh—called back from distant sleep to usher in a new age and erase that which has come before."

Chloe fought to catch her breath, feeling for a long moment like she was suffocating before the air finally came to her in a wheezing gasp. Uktena watched with a look of regret overlaying his normal cold curiosity.

"I am sorry to tell you this," he said with a slight dip of his head. "You have reminded me that not all of your kind is lost, but there can be no new beginning for our planet without first facing an end. Too much of the land's blood has been leached out by your people. The coming cataclysm will refill the well again."

She struggled to gather her racing thoughts into words. "But you said that you didn't know the future. How do you know what will happen?"

"A series of events have begun, which I do not believe can be undone," he answered solemnly. He closed his eyes. "Already I can hear the stirrings of my brethren as the time draws near."

"What can I do?" Chloe pleaded with a quivering voice. "How can I stop it?"

Uktena opened his eyes again. "You can run and hide for a time, but no one can run fast enough to escape their fate for long."

He inhaled slowly, and Chloe heard the echo of her pending demise from the dream. She shuddered with a feverish tingle along her scalp.

"I have come to realize that I am but the catalyst of what is to come, the forerunner to the doom of man. Just as it is your role to act as witness to my oracle." As he exhaled, he suddenly looked old and tired. "I cannot outpace my part any more than you."

Chloe started to shiver uncontrollably, and it felt like her skull might burst. "No...no," she found herself saying as she built toward a defiant shout. "No...NO! There has to be something!"

Uktena stood, and the lightning stroke of his gaze flashed out to silence her instantly. She fell back to her pillow in limp unconsciousness as the dragon came to stand by her bed. He reached out gently and placed his pale hand on her brow, quieting the anguish within with a feeling of warmth he did not know was possible toward one of her species. "Run, Chloe McClellan. Run as fast as you can. That is all there is left to do."

.   .   .

Chloe ran up the muddy hill, flinging clumps of dirt with every footfall. Her shins and thighs were already splattered with the spray from the other girls who jostled and heaved around her, and they were only a few hundred yards out of the starting gate. She'd led out fast as Coach Barnes had instructed, keeping on Angela's heels, but not pushing it so hard that they'd spend all their energy too early. Plenty of girls were ahead of them, carried further along the path with a reckless use of adrenaline, but they would pick them off one by one over the next three miles. According to the coach, the real attack would come from the Richmond Raiders and two Northern Virginia teams called T.C. Williams and Lake Braddock. For now, they were all staying back and biding their time.

The course was covered in a cool mist, and the ground was still wet from the rain the night before. Every leaf Chloe brushed made her skimpy black uniform wetter and heavier. The tank tops were mesh, see-through, and flimsy, and the shorts were little more than sturdy bikini bottoms. It was even worse than the uniform at gym, and the only consolation for Chloe was that everyone around her was dressed the same way.

Deceptively deep puddles dotted the course along the muddy tracks left behind by the truck that had been used to mark the way earlier that morning. Chloe saw a girl stumble and fall with a splash of brown water about ten strides ahead of her. She leapt over the girl's splayed arms and kept going.

She loved the minimalist soles of her new racing flats—it felt like there was nothing between her feet and the soil. She vaulted, almost weightless for an instant, as if she might fly if she were to only close her eyes and forget to hit the ground. But when she did land, she dug in and kept going, reveling in the traction of the screw-in metal spikes that grabbed the earth like little claws.

The crowd of cheering spectators was left behind as the runners came over the rise and were funneled into a densely wooded path. Girls collided and elbowed for position as they came together. Angela passed them going wide up a root ledge, and Chloe followed.

It was then that the first two runners from T.C. Williams, clad in a patriotic uniform of red, white, and blue, passed on their left and kept going like they weren't planning to slow down. Two Lake Braddock girls, dressed in purple and gold, followed a moment later, but already they were breathing hard and running toward the wall. Chloe instinctively picked up the pace to go after them, but Angela stayed her with a quick glance. Her cool eyes flicked back behind Chloe, where two more T.C. runners were sitting on their heels. One of them met Chloe's gaze with the hint of a smile.

Behind them, four of the Richmond Raiders, in green and gold, were closing in, but the third runner from Charlottesville was coming with them. Chloe turned back to the path ahead and focused on the rhythm of Angela's strides. Her breathing settled, and she found her place of calm, competitive strength. It felt like a live spark sizzling in her belly, just waiting to explode into a full-blown electrical storm.

Other girls who had led out too quickly were steadily

overtaken by the newly forming pack. Minutes ticked by as the group worked their way through the woods, swallowing and spitting out runners with the relentless pace set by Angela. As they stampeded out of the woods and into a rolling section of open field, the crowds appeared on both sides.

The sound of the collective cheer was intoxicating, and Chloe felt the group surge as they stormed down a gentle slope toward the large clock that stood at the side of the mile point. 5:18 – 5:19 – 5:20 – 5:21 – 5:22 was the last count Chloe saw before she went past.

"That's a fast first mile, ladies! Pace yourselves!" Coach Barnes shouted as they approached. "You know what to do, Angela! Stay on her heels, Chloe!" she bellowed into Chloe's ear as they sped by.

The lead T.C. Williams girls came into view about forty yards further along the field, but Chloe's eyes were drawn to the place on the side of the course where Liz was lunging up and down with a poster in the air while screaming like a crazy person. The bright yellow words were painted on a black background in jagged lightning bolt script: *BEWARE THE LIGHTNING GIRL!* Paul Markson stood beside her with his hands cupped in front of his mouth. "Come on, Charlottesville, give 'em hell!"

Chloe saw her mom off to the side a few strides later, and Audrey released an indistinguishable scream of raw encouragement as Chloe streaked past. She felt recklessly bolstered by the support, but needed to restrain herself from getting carried away and making an ill-timed spectacle of her efforts. Angela responded by easing the pace back, and Chloe stayed on her heels as instructed, even when the four Richmond Raiders girls moved up. All four of them passed at once, two on either side, in what was clearly an orchestrated move meant to break the morale of the other teams. But Chloe could see from the blotchy red face of one and the wheezing breath of another that Angela's brutal first mile pace had taken its toll.

As the pack moved across the rolling fields through the second mile, one of the two T.C. front-runners fell back and was left behind. Chloe was also starting to feel the heaviness in her thighs, and her breath didn't flow as easily as before. Her focus slipped even further when she looked past her runners' blinders once more and saw the radiance of wavy red hair at the side of the path ahead.

Ezra was there, too, shouting at her through a rolled magazine. "Long and strong, ladies! You got this, Chloe; stay with Angela!"

But all Chloe could see and hear in that moment was Kendra Roberts's predictably shrill but oddly genuine words of support. "Lookin' good, Chloe! You're a monster!" she shouted while bouncing up and down on the balls of her feet.

Did that really just happen? Chloe wondered, taking her mind off the race for a moment longer. That was when the smiling T.C. girl behind them streaked by on Chloe's right and moved in front of the Richmond foursome before Angela had time to register. Angela gave Chloe a little nod before taking off as the real race for first place began.

At that moment, Chloe had neither the stamina nor the hunger to go with her. She watched with a mixture of helplessness and guilt as Angela's black ponytail bobbed ahead to pass the Richmond girls and lock in beside the challenger. The two-mile marker came into view after a few more labored strides. That was when the sophomore from Monticello High who'd beaten Chloe at regionals passed and locked in on the Richmond foursome ahead of her.

Chloe's legs and spirit started to wilt. Despite the cool air, her head felt swollen and hot, and a white film began to creep at the corners of her vision. As she crossed the two-mile clock at 11:04, heaving and straining with every step, Coach Barnes appeared again with her bullhorn. "Dig deep and stay with 'em, Chloe! You can't let them go!"

But Chloe's feet had started to feel like they were glued to the mud with every stride, and she couldn't keep her focus in check. *I'm losing this…I'm letting everyone down…The world is dying, and there's nothing I can do about it!* The lead pack was pulling away, and the path ahead climbed a long incline back into the wooded highlands. The last mile would snake across a spectator-free ridge before descending to the fields for a last, cruelly steep hill and then the open field sprint to the finish. Chloe's breath was already coming hard and ragged.

That was when she saw Kirin through her tunneling vision. He was the last person before the climb, standing at the end of the wall of spectators behind the neon orange tape that held back the cheering swarm. A wrinkled and bent old woman who could only have been his grandmother stood beside him, watching Chloe's approach with the same beautiful, sad eyes as her grandson.

Kirin was clapping vigorously and shouting something, though Chloe couldn't make out his words through the pounding of the blood in her ears. As she got closer, she actually tried to smile, but her lips stuck to her teeth and her eyes were bugging crazily. She approached, looking something more like an unhinged goblin than a schoolgirl in love.

"Chloe!" he shouted. "Be the water, not the rock!"

That's an odd thing to say, she thought as she passed.

"You are the Lightning Girl!" he asserted to her back.

His words sunk in, sparking the current in her belly again. Just like that, Chloe started to run faster. She noticed the traction of the spikes on her shoes once more, and felt the wind's current pushing her forward. Her legs lost the weight of pain and doubt, and she slipped back into the flow of the pace.

The others were about thirty feet ahead of her now, but Sarah, the third girl from Charlottesville, came up beside her, winded and weary. Chloe gave her a defiant look over her shoulder. "Follow me," she commanded with a newfound sense of purpose. Sarah nodded and matched Chloe's pace as they hit the slope. It started to drizzle, and the grass on the hill became slick and precarious.

Ahead, one of the Richmond girls lost her footing and tumbled to the side of the course as the others left her behind. But Chloe was used to these conditions; this was her domain. She dug in with the metal fangs on the balls of her feet and surged to make up the lost ground. Chloe had no fear of the water—she was the water; it had come at her bidding. She could still feel Kirin's encouraging gaze on her back as she strode past the struggling girl a few short seconds later with Sarah hitched at her heels.

By the time the path leveled out, the course was densely lined with vegetation on both sides, and the leaves were dancing with the steady patter of rain. Chloe's uniform was wet and heavy, but she relished the feel of abandon, to be covered in water, mud, and sweat. It reminded her of her runs home from the pond throughout the summer, the feeling of absolute freedom in nature—she belonged to the terrain, more at home in these woods than she'd ever felt anywhere else. These other girls, from the suburbs outside of D.C. and their fancy schools in Richmond, they did not belong here as she did. They were intruders, and it was up to her to defend the turf.

Chloe spied the jaunty bob of hair on the sophomore from Monticello High as an invigorating tingle of energy traveled throughout her limbs. She actually growled as she lunged ahead. She carried Sarah with her across the gap to reach the tail of the lead group, and they held there for a moment to catch their bearings.

Angela and the smiling girl in red, white, and blue had dislodged from the front of the pack as the other runners began to wither from the surprisingly merciless tempo of the race thus far…all but Chloe.

I am the Lightning Girl. I am the queen who summoned the dragon. She pushed on, coming up beside the sophomore who'd beaten her at regionals. Her young nemesis was red-faced and panting, and her spirit wilted further as Chloe and Sarah moved by. They streamed by the third-place runner from T.C. Williams as well, and Sarah latched onto the tail of the remaining three Richmond Raiders. Chloe hovered for a moment, gauging her own will to continue before her legs spurred forward as if with a mind of their own.

She was riding the dragon again, flying over roots and through the trees. She worked her way to the front of the remaining pack as her sights shifted ahead. Twenty paces further, Angela and the smiling girl disappeared around a bend as the path curved down toward the three-mile mark and the final battleground beyond. For an instant, Chloe had seen Angela's dancing ponytail again. *I can get there! I can cross the distance!*

Chloe moved a stride ahead, bolstered by the approaching roar of the crowd as Angela broke from the woods below. Soon that roar would be for Chloe. *Soon Kirin and all the others will see what I'm capable of.*

The rain started down with more conviction, and Chloe's breath was coming hard and fast as her feet flung mud into the girls behind her. As if in answer, two girls from the Richmond trio came up on either side with jostling elbows and even harder breaths. They attacked, trying to pass on the left, then right; but every time Chloe saw someone creep into her peripheral vision, she pushed a little harder to stay out front.

The path slanted down through the gloom of dense woods, but beyond a branch archway, the course returned to the comparative glow of the open field. Chloe's thighs screamed, and her knees pounded with every footfall as the grand noise of the crowd grew. She started to pull away as the urge to giggle swam in her belly—just as a sharp pain stabbed into her calf from behind. All of a sudden, she found herself falling face forward down the hill.

She barely had time to register the bizarre change of motion before her chin slammed into the mud and she tumbled into a sloppy heap. The rest of the pack streamed around and over her as she tried to shake away the ringing in her ears.

"Chloe!" Sarah yelled with muffled desperation as she ran by with the others. Chloe managed to wave her on, too light-headed and dazed to meet her concerned eye and too focused on getting up to think about what was happening. She looked down to see three bleeding, spike-sized holes in the back of her calf, and her hand came away from her chin smeared brown and red. She stood on unsteady feet as the secondary pack, approached from behind...Against all judgment, Chloe got up and started to run again.

A feral yell tore out of her throat as her battered legs began to thunder down the hill once more. Mud fell off her jersey in clumps, and her calf throbbed with every footfall. *I am the Lightning Girl! I am the queen who summoned the dragon!*

As she emerged from the trees, the sky flashed far off on her left, and the crowd along the path gasped at the sight of her. Six long strides later and the low grumble followed. Despite all the pain, Chloe would have cackled if she'd had the energy. She heard Uktena's roar in her head and felt the strength of his fury. The rhythm of his deep, ponderous heartbeat filled her; his blood shot through her veins like a stroke of lightning. She did not ride the dragon; she was the dragon. The laws of physics were hers to bend. She took off like a madwoman. It was way too far from the finish line, but Chloe started to sprint.

This time Liz was screaming so wildly that her voice cracked. "Go! Go! Go! Go!" Paul pumped his fist as Chloe tore across the field, swallowing the distance between her and the pack. She could feel their strength waning with every step as her own grew.

Before long, she came up on the Monticello girl's heels again as Kendra tracked her progress with her iPhone from the sideline. Ezra jumped high into the air with his booming voice carrying above everyone else. "YES! YES! YES! YES!"

Chloe passed the Monticello girl and then one of the Richmond Raiders soon after. She snaked around Sarah and moved past the third T.C. runner without a glance. She crossed the three-mile marker without even looking at her time and did not notice as Coach Barnes ran alongside the course with her bullhorn blaring. "You can do this, Chloe! You're doing this!"

Chloe streaked by another runner in gold and green and advanced on the remaining two girls in the pack as everyone started to give all they had left to the final stretch. Ahead, the path fed straight into Suicide Hill—fifty yards of a steep climb—before the flatland finish. Chloe tackled it with an involuntary scream as she climbed past the others and set her sights on the dance of Angela's ponytail above.

Audrey had taken up residence on the hillside as per Chloe's request, but Chloe couldn't see her mother's expression of shock and worry as she streaked by, looking like she'd been run over by a truck. Her legs were numb but kept on pumping, and she lowered her arms to gather more momentum with every swing. Angela was starting to pull away from her competition, but Chloe was gaining on them both.

She crested the top of the notorious climb like she was claiming the high ground in King of the Mountain, and did not hesitate. She flew, leaving a trail of sweat, blood, and mud across the field behind her.

Angela had gained ten strides on her challenger and wasn't looking back, but Chloe kept coming, with her wild eyes locked on Angela's ponytail as if the smiling girl from T.C. wasn't even there between them. Chloe couldn't feel her body as she floated toward the finish; there was no earth or gravity to hold her down. She hurtled alongside her nameless enemy as both surged with a further pull on energy that didn't exist. Their heads tilted back with open, distorted mouths while every swing of their arms jerked them forward like a punch. Chloe felt the will of the smiling girl break beside her as the primordial roar echoed in her mind, and she lunged toward the line.

She stumbled over the finish only a few seconds behind Angela and staggered down the ribbon-lined corral that led toward the results table. The muffled howl of the crowd blended with the dragon rage in her thoughts, and her eyes were stuck in an unfocused gaze, as if she'd forgotten how to blink. Someone helped to prop her up from the other side of the ribbon, but she couldn't see who beyond the white haze that clouded her sight. She wanted to say "thanks," but instead she stooped over and gagged with an unseemly array of dry heaves.

Whoever was supporting her rubbed her back gently and guided her woozy motion further down the chute as a barrage of cameras flashed on either side of her. Chloe wasn't even sure what had happened. Angela was ahead, gasping for air with a disjointed saunter on wobbly legs. The girl from T.C. Williams was whimpering in her coach's arms behind her.

As Chloe turned back and tried to catch her bearings, Angela enveloped her with a hug that almost knocked them both to the grass. She felt the hand slip away from her back as she held onto Angela with lifeless arms.

"That was amazing, Chloe! You did it!" she gasped in Chloe's ear above the din of the cheering audience.

"What happened? You won, right?" Chloe asked in breathy confusion.

"Yeah, and you got second! You're a sophomore, and you just beat every other girl in the state!" Angela shouted. "Charlottesville might actually win the team competition!"

Chloe looked back at the remains of the stretched-out pack as they charged across the field toward them. Through the tunnel of white, Chloe could see Sarah's black-and-orange uniform holding with the second of two remaining Richmond Raiders, just where she needed to be. Her gaze swung limply over to the smiling girl who wasn't smiling anymore. Their bugged and teary eyes met.

"Where did you come from?" said the girl, disengaging from her coach to stagger toward Chloe with a post-battle sense of camaraderie.

Chloe met her with a sweaty embrace. "That was awful," she mumbled in her ear.

The girl barked a laugh. "Yeah, but a great race," she added. "You deserve it."

Chloe swung back toward Angela with a profound sense of love for every girl that was running. She wished that she had the strength to cheer for them, regardless of what team they were on. In that moment, she realized that she loved her school, and her town, and all the people in it. She loved Liz, and Paul, and Ezra, and Coach Barnes, and she wished she could individually thank all the people who'd come out in support. Hell, she even loved Kendra for her part, even though she was the epitome of everything that was wrong with teenage girls today.

That was when the tunnel of her sight passed over Kirin standing at the ribbon's edge with smears of her blood and mud wiped liberally across his jacket. He grinned, and she felt like she might dry heave again.

"Oh...that was kind of ugly," she mumbled in her defense.

"Chloe, that was probably the most beautiful thing I've ever seen!" he countered.

She swayed toward him as other girls stumbled into the chute behind her. She had to move with the press, and he moved alongside her, pushing other spectators out of the way. His gaze held her with a mixture of guilt and adoration.

"Where have you been?" she asked, with tears leaking from her eyes and a hint of anger. "I've been waiting for you to ca—"

"I'm sorry," he cut her off. "I was stupid and confused, but I'm here now, if it's not too late?"

The emotional weight of all that was happening was too much for her to bear. She glanced from Kirin to the cluster of photographers around him as flashes went off in her face. Bright splotches dotted her sight, and through it she could vaguely make out the rapid, jubilant approach of Coach Barnes and her mom. In her mind, she still felt the lurking presence of Uktena, but now a vague sense of approval came with it.

She turned back to Kirin as her head started to spin. "I'm not going to let this world die," she announced with a thick tongue. Then her legs gave out, and she slipped back toward the mud and the sweet embrace of unconsciousness.

CHAPTER 25
HOME INVASION

It turned out that Angela had run the fastest 5K in Virginia AAA high school girls' history. Chloe and the girl from T.C. had also beaten the old record by more than twenty seconds. Even the fourth through eighth place finishers crossed the line within seconds of the historic best, and it was considered to be the most competitive team totals race in memory. Charlottesville High came in second overall, losing out to T.C. Williams by only four points from the total standings of the top seven girls from each school. The Richmond Raiders came in a close third.

But it was Chloe's heroic sprint that was highlighted again and again on local TV stations. Angela and Sarah had both been interviewed on camera, and Coach Barnes was smiling so big that it looked like her face might split open on the Channel 5 Evening News. Of course, Chloe had missed all the hoopla, having instead spent those moments in the back of an ambulance on her way to her favorite hospital.

She'd woken in Kirin's arms, slumped unflatteringly in the middle of the chute less than a minute after she'd gone down. But the race officials and on-site medical team had squirreled her away from the crowd just as quickly, and she'd lost sight of his reassuring smile in her mother's smothering hug.

She wound up with five stitches on her leg and a big bandage on her chin before they let her go, and by then she felt like she really had been hit by a truck. Chloe didn't remember much of what had happened, though in truth she'd been in a relative fog of distraction and forgetfulness since her headaches the week before. She saw the first footage of her final, grimacing, mud-caked sprint on Channel 7, but it was some of the other stations that really focused on all the fanfare and adulation that apparently followed. Luckily they had refrained from putting the images of her least dignified moments of dry heaving and unconsciousness on air…

But, of course, Kendra had gotten the whole thing on an iPhone video. By 8 p.m., she'd been nice enough to e-mail it to Chloe, along with EVERYONE else, so that Chloe might relive it again and again and again. The red-headed hag had gotten there just in time to catch Chloe's eyes rolling into the back of her head and Kirin's lunge across the ribbon to catch her before her face hit the dirt. The attached message said, "**Only Love Can Tame the Wild Beauty of Lightning!**"

As always, Kendra's work had been put together with a good eye for composition, but her first foray into Chloe-based mockumentary video showed a keen understanding of slow motion and graphics as well. Audrey had tried not to laugh when Chloe had shown it to her, but she was so relieved by the time they'd gotten home from the hospital that she was laughing at pretty much everything she saw.

Chloe could tell that her mom was deeply proud of her and more than a little thankful that she was all right, but she suspected that Audrey was particularly happy after Coach Barnes had called to check in and casually mentioned that Chloe could have probably procured a full-ride agreement from UVA before she'd left the field. Audrey was practically bouncing off the walls and had stopped to give Chloe unsolicited hugs at least five times that night. Chloe, for her part, just wanted to sleep. She never even made it off the sofa.

She woke the next morning with a blanket tucked in lovingly around her, a little puddle of drool on the pillow, and Shipwreck eyeing her closely from the armrest. She'd slept for eleven hours without moving. Audrey was already in the kitchen, whipping up blueberry pancakes and fresh-squeezed orange juice. Chloe's phone was waiting for her on the kitchen counter along with a note: *Kirin called twice last night and you have 14 unchecked texts.* With that, her grounding was over.

Her mom had left for work later that morning with the unspoken understanding between them that Chloe would still be expected to come clean about her reasons for the theft and stonewalling, but that she would be trusted to bring it to light when she was ready. Chloe could barely walk on her abused legs, though she still managed to hobble into the next room and call Kirin within seconds of her mom's departure.

He answered on the third ring. "Hey, how are you feeling? I was trying to get a hold of you all night."

Chloe was bouncing, though her calves screamed every time her heels left the floor. "My mom just gave me back my phone. I'm pretty sore," she answered. "Is this too early?" she added in a hurry, realizing that it was only 8:45 in the morning.

"Nope," he said with the hint of a yawn. "Are you still grounded?"

"Nope," she replied with a smile.

"Hmmm…how 'bout I pick you up at noon?" he asked. "I want you to meet someone, and we could have lunch."

Chloe was beaming. "Okay."

"Okay then," he said with finality. "I'll see you in three hours."

. . .

Chloe spent that time in a joy-tinged anxiety spiral as she tried to make herself look effortlessly pretty. She changed her outfit at least ten times and still ended up feeling unprepared when the knock sounded from below at 11:43. *He's early!* She peeked out the window of her room, but didn't see the Jeep in the driveway. Still, she went to answer with a sudden upswing of nervous energy.

At the end of the upstairs hallway she caught sight of her winning outfit in the mirror on the closet door: a pair of jeans and a zip-up sweatshirt over an arguably "cool" T-shirt that depicted a T. rex with an AK-47 and sunglasses. *Ugh!* She contemplated going back to her room to try again, but the knock returned softly from below. Despite the prescribed half of a Tylenol 3 she'd taken with her orange juice at breakfast, she limped down the stairs with a wince on every step.

She brushed a strand of hair from her face and unceremoniously flung open the back door with her best casual smile. No one was there. Then the knock sounded again at the front door, this time with a little more conviction. *Come on, Kirin, no one uses the front!*

Shipwreck leapt from the sofa and slid around the banister to retreat up the stairs as Chloe shambled along the downstairs hallway, past the questionably valuable wall hangings that Audrey had inherited from Ray's mother. There was a framed mint of old Chinese coins and a collection of regal-looking mid-nineteenth century miniatures painted on ivory of the last Punjab dynasty. She'd only ever known it as the Court of Lahore, and it, along with the rest of her dad's leave-behinds, had always made Chloe want to go out and explore the world—find the places where these coins and interesting people had come from.

The front door was perpetually locked, and Chloe fumbled through the steps of undoing the dead bolt and then turning the key that her mom left in the doorknob. "Just a second," she called. It seemed to take forever as her stomach fluttered with butterfly aerobatics.

Finally the door creaked open with a visible sprinkling of dust. Chloe pulled it back to reveal the startlingly non-Kirin smile of Dr. Markson. Her own smile dropped as she unlatched and cracked open the storm door suspiciously.

Dr. Markson's grey hair was unintentionally messy, but the pronounced crow's-feet behind his glasses made him look dignified nonetheless. He was an attractive man, like his son, but with an obvious intelligence in his eyes that Paul didn't possess. An unmarked brown paper bag with a folded top sat on the stoop beside his foot. "Sorry to bother you on a Sunday," he said with convincing sincerity. "I'm Dr. William Markson. I was hoping to speak with you and your mom, if you had a moment?"

Chloe opened the door a little wider and looked out to the black Lincoln Town Car, idling at the side of the street, then back to her visitor. Echoes from her nightmare the week before came back to her: *Dr. Markson referred to them as stress fractures across the earth's crust, and they, too, were increasing in number.* She hadn't been able to focus on that night since… *Had Uktena been in my room when I woke up?*

Dr. Markson's smile seemed genuine, but Chloe could tell that he was a little unsure of himself. "My mother isn't home."

"Actually, I'm more interested in talking with you," he admitted. "Just for a moment, here on the porch if you'd like— it's important."

Chloe stepped out and zipped up the sweatshirt to cover the suddenly NOT cool T-shirt. She closed the door gently and leaned against the iron railing. *Kirin, please come now!*

"I'm sorry we haven't actually spoken before," he said with a sheepish nod. "I tend to let my partner do most of the talking."

Chloe nodded back. "I've heard a lot about you."

"I've been hearing a lot about you as well," he acknowledged. "I saw you on the news last night; very impressive." His calculating hazel eyes scanned her face and narrowed ever so slightly. "And before that, I'd heard your name spoken on a few occasions. You were at the pond when you were struck by lightning, and then again when the tower was destroyed. Then you were videotaping when the cow was taken, and Dr. Liou even mentioned your recent interest when he was talking about his work." He spoke as if he was pontificating out loud rather than engaged in a conversation.

He seemed to notice Chloe again and the smile returned. "Chloe, I was wondering what you knew about, for lack of a better word, dragons?" He watched her closely, gauging her response.

She raised an eyebrow with a skeptic's smirk, but she wasn't sure if it was convincing. "Dragons?" she repeated.

Dr. Markson nodded. "Yes, like the myths that Dr. Liou writes about."

"I've always been more into science than fantasy," she countered.

"Then why seek out Dr. Liou to ask him about mythological monsters and doomsday prophecies?" he probed with a wry turn at the corner of his lips.

I opened myself up for that one. "It was for a term paper," she said, not even buying it herself. She recovered with a well-timed blush. "And I'm kind of more interested in Dr. Liou's son than his studies."

Dr. Markson furrowed his untamed eyebrows. "Yes, Kirin was with you the night of the cow snatching, wasn't he?"

"Yes. Actually, he's on his way to pick me up right now…so—"

"Damn it!" he said with a sudden burst of frustration that took Chloe by surprise.

She shut her mouth and took an involuntary step toward the door.

"I'm sorry, Chloe, I don't have time for games," he stammered. "I need to know if you've seen something strange recently."

"Like what?" Chloe forced the words, but could hear the futility of her continued deflection.

Dr. Markson reached down and opened the paper bag at his feet. He removed the pair of Audrey's flattened green dress shoes that Chloe had left on the hillside after Homecoming. "I believe these belong to you," he said, handing them over. "I found them buried in a five-clawed footprint the size of a car…I know that you know what I'm talking about, Chloe. I need to know what it is and how to find it."

"Why?" she demanded. "Whatever it is you think I've seen, why do *you* need to find it?"

Dr. Markson settled down and leaned back against the opposite railing as he ran his hand through his hair. "You say you're interested in science, well, so am I. I've devoted my life to it, and now I am on the cusp of doing something that could change everything." He glanced back toward the waiting car, and when he spoke again, his voice was quieter. "I can't believe that it's just coincidence that some…*thing* that seemingly defies the laws of physics and evolution would appear at the same time and place where I'm about to prove that mankind can harness the true power of lightning."

"Like how Oppenheimer harnessed the true power of nuclear energy?" Chloe challenged.

Dr. Markson met her gaze. "Ah, so you're a student of history as well," he observed. "No—nuclear energy is messy and volatile, and Oppenheimer was naive. This, this is clean and elegant and three times more potent. It would replace rocket fuel, get us farther and faster into space than we've yet thought possible. It could end our dependency on fossil fuels entirely."

He started to gesticulate passionately as he spoke, as if he had too much energy for words alone to demonstrate. "The towers themselves don't just attract lightning; they summon it! Two oppositely revolving shield walls laced with amber and iridium to produce a powerful static charge of its own. The lightning can't stay away, and when it strikes, it acts as a wholly independent self-perpetuating power source." He pointed his finger to the sky. "But the real prize is the antimatter that rises from the clouds above, flowing right where we want it to toward the positron traps on our satellites."

Now he spoke with the intensity of a zealot. "Once the one tower is proven, we'll go global with tower fields on lands already purchased in Venezuela, Florida, and the African plains. We're not the bad guys, Chloe; the Daedalus Group can help to save this world before it's too late."

Chloe remembered—Uktena had told her what was coming...next month! *How much time do we have left?* It was as if the urgency and gravity of the Tipping Point Prophecy had somehow gone dormant again until now..."You heard Dr. Liou's theory on that cauldron," she said. "What if the world is ending sooner than you think?" Chloe wished she could take the question back as soon as it spilled out of her mouth.

"Yes, Dr. Liou's story of the five dragons that will bring about the end of days for mankind." His focus suddenly switched from that of a hummingbird to a hawk. "The fifth claw was called Uktena by the Eastern Cherokee. A giant winged serpent shrouded in lightning." Dr. Markson followed Chloe's involuntary glance toward the barn, and the intensity of his gaze settled on the flaking red door.

"I don't believe in dragons," he said, almost as if to himself. "And I don't think that the world is coming to a quick end either." His eyes returned to the flattened shoes in Chloe's hands. She leaned over and dropped them by the door.

"But I also know that there are an estimated two million native species on this planet that we have yet to discover," he continued. "Most of them are microscopic, and most of the rest are minor variants on known species, extremely isolated and small. But a couple big species might have slipped through the cracks as well…or maybe just one very old, rare, and large species at the top of the food chain, capable of hibernating for centuries at a time…Scientifically, it is possible."

Should I tell him? Maybe he would know what to do? "That sounds kind of crazy," Chloe announced instead with her heart thundering and the pain flaring in her jittery legs.

Dr. Markson reached back down into the paper bag and removed a plate-sized scale with a pearly-grey sheen. "We've found nine of them now buried in the sediment at the bottom of the pond." He handed it to Chloe, and she did not have to pretend to be momentarily mesmerized by the smooth feel of it. It was oddly warm to the touch, despite the brisk autumn air. "Brent Meeks tells me that you spent your whole summer break at that pond…Do you know where *it* is, Chloe?"

YES! "No," she answered flatly. That was when she heard the gravel crunch of her savior's arrival in the driveway. She peered over her shoulder to see the woody siding of the Grand Wagoneer and turned back around, trying to hold in a relieved grin. "I'm sorry I couldn't be of help, Dr. Markson, but I really have to go."

He nodded coolly and reached out to take the scale back. Without thinking, Chloe jerked it away from his approaching fingers, suddenly feeling a possessive urge swell over her.

Dr. Markson eyed her closely and waited.

She handed it over. "Sorry," she said. "It's really cool, whatever it is."

He returned the scale to the brown paper bag and took it with him as he stepped down the stairs. The car revved to life street side, but he turned back just as Chloe grabbed the handle of the storm door for a quick retreat. "You know, I'm not going to be in charge of this project after today," he admitted sadly. "You would be wise to steer clear of this whole matter from now on."

"Is that a threat?" she asked.

"It's a warning," he stated. "A lot of people you care about could face some serious difficulties if they get caught up in this: Stan Strakowski, Kirin, your mom…Dr. Liou signed a detailed funding agreement. If they find out he knows more than he told us, he could be bankrupted and possibly even jailed under breach of contract. The people who are coming are not known for their kindness, and they own everything we do."

Dr. Markson truly meant it as a warning, and Chloe nodded in thanks. "Do you ever worry that your work is being used to help the wrong people?" she asked quietly.

Dr. Markson stared at her for a long moment and then walked away toward the waiting car without another glance back.

The wind seeped out of her, and the tremble that had been threatening shot through her body. She had to brace against the rail to keep her legs from giving out. As Kirin stepped from the car and waved, Chloe breathed in again…Already her legs felt a little stronger.

. . .

Chloe was shaken by the tense encounter with the head engineer of the Daedalus Group and even more so by the newfound memory of Uktena's words about the fast-approaching dragon apocalypse. She wanted to tell Kirin everything, but wasn't sure which would be worse: him thinking she was bonkers or him believing her and getting on the wrong side of the most powerful people in town and the shadowy government agency that backed them?

"Dr. Markson wanted to know if I knew anything else about the Cow Thief," she finally answered.

"Do you?" he asked.

Chloe nodded begrudgingly. "Yes…it's kind of why I've been meaning to talk to your father again, but I didn't want to get him into any trouble."

Kirin glanced from the road to her face. "My dad isn't home today, but you can tell me if you want."

Chloe returned the glance from the corner of her eye. "I thought you didn't buy into my whole Cow Thief theory, and I know how you feel about your dad's research."

Kirin shrugged. "I know something's going on, and I like to think that I can keep an open mind," he countered as he pulled into the crushed shell driveway beside a dark-stained arts and crafts house with a wraparound porch.

"I haven't really been able to tell anyone about this yet," Chloe admitted.

"Not even Stan?" Kirin probed.

Chloe shook her head. "Only a little; it's kind of hard to explain."

The Jeep came to a stop before the matching two-car garage behind the house. Kirin turned toward her with his hands still on the wheel and his eyebrows raised expectantly. The tinny clanks and ticks of the cooling engine were the only sound to fill the silence. Chloe didn't know how to begin, unable to bring herself to finally put voice to all of the doubt and confusion that had been plaguing her for months. She opened her mouth to speak, but then closed it again.

"You need to talk to my grandmother," Kirin declared abruptly before hopping out with a loud metallic screech of the door. "Come on."

Chloe followed slowly, hesitant to put weight on her legs as she stepped from the tall SUV. She winced but held in a groan as Kirin appeared beside her with an offered hand. She wasn't sure what to expect as he helped her up the flight of wooden stairs toward the door to the little apartment above the garage. A wind chime of hollow reeds and shells clacked above the door in the gentle breeze. Kirin gave her an encouraging smile as she limped her way to the top.

"Sorry to make you climb," he said, "but my Nai Nai wanted

to meet you after she saw your race yesterday, and it sounds like you might want to meet her as well."

"Nai Nai?" Chloe repeated.

"It's what we call her, but it just means 'grandmother' in Mandarin." He gave a gentle knock on the door.

Chloe anticipated a cracked voice summoning them to enter in Chinese or perhaps a long wait as the old woman she'd glimpsed on the field slowly made her way to the door. After only a couple seconds, the door swung open with surprising conviction, and Nai Nai stood smiling with a steaming kettle of water clutched in her hand. She was wrinkled, spotted, and small, but Chloe could tell instantly that there was nothing frail about the little woman who stood before her.

Nai Nai embraced Kirin with a one-armed hug before turning her sights on Chloe. The old woman looked her over for a moment and nodded in approval before waving her in and bustling back to the stove. There she poured the steaming spout of water into a waiting teapot that sat on a tray beside three fine teacups.

Kirin took Chloe by the hand again and led her to a little room with a sofa and some chairs around a low table. There was an array of finely tended orchids on display atop little pedestals in the corners: each stem was reinforced with wood and wire scaffolding, and every pot held at least six flowers in full bloom. "This was my dad's orchid greenhouse before Nai Nai moved in. It's another of his obsessions—he thinks they look like dragons."

Chloe peered closer at one of the white blossoms nearest her, but had trouble picturing the fanged and horned head of Uktena in its place. "They're beautiful," she offered as he pointed her to a seat on the sofa. She fell into it with a stab of pain in her thighs and a little grunt.

He plopped beside her. "Hope you drink tea, because you're about to."

"I love tea," Chloe answered. "Does your grandmother speak English?" she whispered as the old woman started toward them with the tray from the kitchen.

Kirin smiled.

"My husband went to university in England." Nai Nai spoke with a thick accent. "I have not had much opportunity to practice since he died, but it comes back quickly with Kirin's help." She placed the tray on the table and sat in a particularly plush chair that was clearly designated for her before pouring the greenish-brown brew through a strainer that she held over each of the teacups.

Then she presented the cups first to Chloe and then to Kirin before taking up her own. Kirin waited until Nai Nai had taken a sip before bringing his own cup to his lips. Chloe watched him closely and did the same. Again the old woman seemed to acknowledge Chloe with an approving nod.

The tea was both naturally sweet and a little bitter but with a toasted rice aftertaste that Chloe really liked. She sipped again and felt a calm settle over her jangled nerves as the hot liquid traveled down to her belly.

"I have heard Kirin talk so much about you these last weeks that I finally demanded he take me to see you race yesterday." She flashed her grandson a reproachful look. "I enjoyed watching you run. You have a strong heart and great..." she looked to Kirin. "What is it again?"

"Courage," he answered with a sheepish grin.

"Yes, courage," she repeated with a little shake of her fist. "When I was a girl, I was the youngest with three older brothers. I had to learn to run fast and be strong from an early age."

"It seems your strength has served you well in life," Chloe observed, wondering if it was appropriate to comment on the giant elephant in the room. "I can't imagine all of the adversity and loss you've had to face recently," she found herself saying. "Getting through that would take a courage I don't think I possess."

Nai Nai smiled. "That is the thing about courage: we cannot know if it is there until the time comes to show it." The smile faded as she stared for a long moment into her teacup. "But when the ground shakes and the skies darken, there is no room for courage, only terror and prayer, and those who are lucky enough to be alive after."

"Nai Nai thinks that mankind has grown complacent and that the world is readying to test our right to be here," Kirin interjected. "Her stories were how my dad first discovered his interest in dragon myths as a kid." He and Nai Nai shared a smirk. "You should hear some of the arguments they get into over dinner."

"Arguments about what?" Chloe pressed.

"About the nature of myth," Nai Nai answered. "Edward believes that myths are stories to help give insight into the past. I believe that the same stories can be guides for how to understand the present and prepare for the future."

Chloe let those words settle over her for a moment before glancing at Kirin. "What do you believe?" she asked.

"I'm on the fence," he answered with a diplomatic bob of his head.

Chloe turned back toward Nai Nai. "Do you believe in dragons?"

Nai Nai sipped her tea. "My mother believed there was truth to many of the old tales," she answered. "When I was little, she told me stories about how there were still dragons deep down in the hidden places of the world. My brothers went away to school and then to work, but I stayed home and learned to sew and cook by mother's side. She filled my head with legends and fables." She smiled, remembering. "I grew up believing in ghosts, faeries, dragons, and more."

"In the stories, could the dragons ever turn into humans?" Chloe asked quietly.

Nai Nai thought about it for a moment. "Most of the dragons could only be found in the wild, bound to the elements and only seen by the lucky few. But there were also stories of rare dragons with five claws, which could change form and enter the towns and cities to give wisdom to the worthy." Her eyes looked past them to another time. "The five-clawed dragons had great power over earth, water, fire, air, and spirit, and some could grant wishes to those who met their favor. It is said that it was they who gave us the gifts of speech and writing and they who will one day take it away again—just like on my son's cauldron."

Chloe's mouth felt like it was filled with cotton, but the words spilled out anyway. "What if it was happening now? What if the Tipping Point Prophecy was real?"

Nai Nai chuckled with her little frame shaking but her tea-holding hands remaining still. "My mother never told me that story; perhaps that one is yours to tell," she suggested.

"When she saw you finish the race yesterday, Nai Nai told me that you have the heart of a dragon," Kirin said. "I kind of mentioned that you might have seen one flying around Charlottesville," he added with a guilty grin.

Chloe shot Kirin a reproachful look before turning back to face Nai Nai's unreadable gaze. Her heartbeat went wild, and she felt the impulse toward fight or flight, but Kirin placed his hand on her wrist and nodded.

"It's cool. Tell her what you saw," he encouraged.

Chloe smiled nervously. "You'll think I'm crazy."

"No," answered Nai Nai.

But Dr. Markson's words of warning came back to her. She couldn't live with herself if she was the reason that this old woman was deported back to China or Kirin's dad was sent to jail.

"I'm not even sure what I saw," Chloe backpedaled. "It was like a big shadow with wings that swooped down to grab a cow from the field…But I was pretty sleep-deprived at the time," she added with a chuckle.

Nai Nai watched her closely as Kirin waited for her to continue. "And Stan saw it, too," he added, hoping to elicit more.

"Yeah, but he's kind of an unreliable witness," Chloe deflected.

Nai Nai smiled with a look that seemed to see right through Chloe's attempt at deception. She took a long sip of tea and closed her eyes for a moment. "One of my favorite stories that Mother used to tell was of a very special group of people called the xian." She looked to Kirin, "Do you know this one?"

He furrowed his brow and shook his head.

"Well, this is not Xian, like the city in China, but an older word in Taoism for enlightened people, who after years of focus and training became one with the elements. They lived beyond mortal constraints, having learned to harness the wind, earth, and rain for their purpose. It was said that some could fly, while others could swim like fish or weave fire in their hands." She took another sip of tea. "They were also called Dragon Riders, and my mother told of how they learned to summon and harness the dragons long ago. Maybe it was even the xian that sent the dragons away, imprisoning them far underground and beyond the wall of sleep when the age of legends came to an end..."

Chloe thought of her lightning dream and remembered the feel of riding on Uktena's back, traveling miles in a millisecond. Kirin remembered what it was to be one with the ocean, moving through it with long, supple strokes, flowing as living liquid, and yet bound also to the presence of the girl who sat beside him.

"I used to pretend that I was one of them, almost like your superheroes today," Nai Nai added. "For a time, when I was very young, I actually believed that one day it would be so." She smiled knowingly and placed her intense gaze back on Chloe. "Perhaps if the dragons return as you fear, the xian might return to save us once again?" she concluded just as the sound of a car crunched across the driveway outside. "I would love to talk more about this, but Edward has come to take me shopping for new glasses on his lunch break."

Chloe wasn't sure what to say. "It was wonderful to meet you. Thank you."

Nai Nai stood.

Chloe and Kirin started up as well, but the old woman waved them back down. "No, you two stay and finish your tea; I'm sure you have plenty to talk about," she encouraged before bustling toward the door to claim her jacket from the coat hanger. "It was very nice to finally meet you, too, Chloe," she said with a deep nod that almost looked like a bow from across the room. "Just to see a dragon is a sign of good fortune in Chinese lore." She opened the door to go, but hesitated before stepping out. "I have a feeling that you are meant for great things, and I am glad to know that Kirin will be there to help you achieve them." She left with a little smile. The door closed gently behind her.

"She's amazing," said Chloe to break the silence that followed.

"Yeah, but what was that?" Kirin countered. "You're not telling me something."

Chloe took another calming sip of the tea. "It's kind of hard to tell." She felt a swell of encouragement from the old woman's words. "But maybe I could just show you? Tomorrow after school, my mom will be working late. You can drive me home, and I promise once and for all to show you something hidden in my barn that will completely change your life." She put out her hand to shake on it.

"Hmmm, not really sure if you're going for aloof and mysterious again, or if this is all some bizarro, unnecessary ploy to get me alone in the hay," he said with an eyebrow pump as he took her hand and they shook. "Either way, I'm in."

The Feathered Serpent

The far side of the moon is permanently turned away from the shining brilliance of Earth, shielded from the unending clatter of radio waves that lance recklessly through space. There, amid the frozen wasteland of darkness and utter silence, at the bottom of an ancient crater from before the time of life in this galaxy, the ground stirred.

At first, the sediment danced in a series of sequential rings, as if with a tremor, but then slowly a form emerged from the dust with a shower of minute grains drifting lazily back to the surface. A massive serpentine form uncoiled from within the cloud and shook off a centuries of ice crystals and mineral deposit.

Quetzalcoatl flared the featherlike scales that covered his three-hundred-foot body, and a fluttering wave of brightly patterned rings emerged from the grey film that had long hidden his splendor. An undulating ripple of shifting rainbow colors traveled down his length. With a last rattling shake of his tail, his scaled plumage settled, and he unfurled the immense angelic wings that had for so long been folded at his back.

The old civilizations of Mesoamerica had worshipped him as a god of the sky, bringer of food and rain and the maker of kings. They carved his visage into the sides of their temples and sacrificed jaguars, birds, and their enemies to curry his favor. For millennia, he had bestowed his wisdom and guidance onto the worthy through the ritual smoke above their incense burners. Some still told tales of his pending return, passed on from generation to generation in an archaic tongue. Dates had been carved long ago into standing stones by those who had listened to his whispered command.

The Feathered Serpent flapped his powerful wings and lifted from the pockmarked landscape. He longed to feel the weight and pull of the earth's gravity once more, having spent too many years sleeping near the emptiness of the vacuum. He had awoken from restless dreams, where the humans looked again to the skies to behold his homecoming with prayers and lamentation as the winds of change followed in his wake.

He crossed the wide distance to the bright side of the moon with only three unhurried flaps of his outstretched wings. Tornadoes whipped through the dust beneath him as he went, tearing across the dead terrain before finally losing steam in the low pressure void. On Earth, these spiraling little storms would not be stilled so easily. Each would grow in the gravitational conditions that sustain life and would soon fuel the death he would bring.

The kaleidoscopic swirl in his primeval gaze locked onto the blue-and-green beacon of his home, and again he heard the chime, buzz, and chatter of the signals that the humans cast out toward the unknown reaches. He touched down again with a couple more flaps buffeting against the lunar highlands, and a minor hurricane of basalt and regolith spun out from the place where he landed.

Quetzalcoatl turned to look at the position of the sun and then the planets that circled in orbit. The galactic alignment was not right, though it would be soon. After so long asleep, the knowledge of what was to come filled him with unavoidable excitement, but also a great well of sadness. He turned back toward Earth and closed his heavy lids to listen to the last few breaths of mankind.

CHAPTER 26
G-MEN

Despite the looming prospect of calamity, Chloe sat beside Kirin in homeroom the next morning consumed with giddy excitement. Kirin had told her about his dream, and she had described her own, and the two of them had fantasized about becoming like the xian of old. It reminded Chloe of the unbridled enthusiasm she had shared with Liz summers back, at the start of each new obsession. As Mr. Jacobson rambled on in his emotionless tone about the role of the legislative body, she and Kirin shot each other meaningful glances in the back of class.

They'd spent the rest of the previous day talking—over lunch, then phone, and then text—until Dr. Liou had shut it down just before midnight. They'd shared stories about lost parents, secret fears, and grand hypotheses about the universe. Together they felt more like the individuals they'd always wanted to be. Now it was as if there was some sort of force field surrounding just them, making everything else outside it seem muffled and blurry. Within, life was vivid and full of potential.

Sitting in front of them, Liz could sense the difference, uncharacteristically keeping her eyes locked on the blackboard, though she wore an odd little smile that did not seem to fit the topic. The rest of the class was utterly oblivious, unable to conceive that the two quietest students in the far corner could somehow be bound to the struggle for the future of mankind or that they were gearing up to face so daunting a task with a disproportionate level of optimism.

Chloe knew that the whole thing was irrational, even ridiculous, having moved from the comfort of her beloved science into the realm of science fiction. But she was ready to be a part of something that truly mattered, and she couldn't ignore the inexplicable events that had brought her to this point. The weird connection with lightning, the dragon in the barn, the legend of the xian, and now Kirin beside her—it all just felt right.

She hadn't been able to sleep the night before, too worked up by all that was happening to still the rapid-fire thoughts that swam through her mind: *How does a dragon respond to unwanted visitors? Will Kirin know what to do? What if Uktena tries to eat him? When should I tell Stan and my mom what's going on?*

Uktena hadn't been there the night before when Chloe had used the excuse of taking out the trash to slip into the barn and propose the pending meet and greet. She'd had to leave another note, this time detailing her plan to bring Kirin over after last period on Monday to *"help determine how to avoid detection by the Daedalus Group."* She even proposed that maybe it would make sense to bring Stan into the initiated circle soon after so that Uktena might rely on a cohesive team to *"best look out for your continued interests and safety."* Now she could only pray that the dragon had been contentedly fed when he'd read it.

Chloe couldn't pay attention to the drone of her teacher and hadn't even done the reading that had facilitated this particularly long-winded recap of the text. Instead, her eyes held on Kirin's fingers, thrumming quietly on the edge of his desk. The nails looked to have been trimmed with his teeth, and the hand itself was tanned and calloused. They were good, practical hands, and she found herself mesmerized by the gentle rhythm of his long digits. They looked strong and weathered, and she wondered what he did to keep them looking so…ready.

She realized in that moment that there was still so much that she didn't know about him. *What kind of music does he like? What's his favorite color, or book, or movie? Please, just give me the time to find out!*

She caught his sideways gaze on her and quickly straightened her spine with a sheepish smile. Her hand instinctively went to her phone in her pocket before turning back for a pen instead.

She quickly scribbled across her notebook and angled the page for him to read: *Sorry!*

He raised an eyebrow and scribbled on his own notebook in answer: *For what?*

Staring. And dragging you into my weirdness, she scrawled in response.

This time, Kirin wrote for a while with a little smile creeping across his face as the gentle scratch of the pencil continued. Chloe's leg shook with anticipation. He angled his notebook with a wink: *Stare away, babe—I know I'm easy to look at!* Then he moved his hand to uncover the rest: *And your weirdness is the best thing that's happened since I moved to Virginia, so SHUT IT!*

If Chloe could have leaned over and kissed him without creating a shockwave of rumors and repercussions, she would have. Instead, she chewed her lip and wrote *"Thanks"* before turning to face the back of Liz's head. That was when she started to feel an uneasy quiver building in her stomach—like a deep, grumbling vibration…

She looked out the window at the parking lot but saw nothing strange there or in the overcast sky above. But the grumble grew like a warning inside her as cold sweat glazed across her scalp and her heart rate climbed.

Kirin leaned over from his desk. "What's wrong?" he whispered.

"Nothing," she answered unconvincingly as Mr. Jacobson shot her a brief glance over his shoulder before continuing on about the hazy limits of executive privilege. But then she heard Uktena's deafening roar tear through her, shaking in the marrow of her bones as she lurched in her desk and went delirious with a rush of rage and terror.

Liz and some of the other students turned around to look as the blood drained from Chloe's head. She'd gone deathly pale and a feverish tingling gathered in her extremities. She heard the muffled echoes of splintering wood and shouting, and she began to thrash in her chair as if she'd lost control over her own body.

"Chloe!" Kirin said beside her, no longer even trying to

whisper as the rest of the eyes in the class swung toward her and a wave of mockery and concern pressed from all sides.

"What is it this time, Ms. McClellan?" asked Mr. Jacobson from the front.

But she couldn't answer as she felt the scorching crackle of electricity erupt from her open mouth. Her own teeth were clenched shut and chattering, but she could sense the shock of searing heat passing between them all the same. Then she heard the shrieks of dying men around her and pressed her hands to her ears in a useless attempt to silence the horror.

A series of sharp twinges stabbed into her neck with what felt like hornet stings, and she instantly started to feel woozy and light-headed. One of her hands traveled from her ear to her throat, but there was nothing there but her own unbroken skin. She was only vaguely aware of the abrupt knock on the classroom door, and Mr. Jacobson's march to reveal Principal Harlow standing beside two men in dark suits beyond. She began to tremble uncontrollably and clenched the edges of the desk with white knuckles as the men conferred in hushed tones before turning back toward her with hard eyes.

"Chloe McClellan and Kirin Liou," called Principal Harlow, stepping into the room. "Please gather your things and come with me."

Kirin reached out to help, but before Chloe knew what she was doing, she reeled back from his touch and snarled at his outstretched fingers as if she was preparing to bite. His hand retracted suddenly, and his eyes went wide as tears began to stream out of Chloe's eyes. She staggered to her feet and knocked over her chair with a loud clatter.

"I'm sorry," she muttered, hearing her own slurred words echoing back in her mind as if from a great distance. Her vision clouded, and she could barely make out the two dark blurs that moved into the room past Principal Harlow.

"Ms. McClellan, we're going to need for you to come with us," one of them commanded.

"Hold on! Who are you and what's this about?" interjected Kirin as the men came closer.

"It would be better if we stepped outside, Mr. Liou," said the other dark shape with a gesture for Kirin to follow.

"I think she's sick," said Kirin. "I'm not sure if she can hear us right now."

Chloe's hands and feet tingled with such intensity that they felt like they were on fire. She wanted to scream, but instead a deep guttural moan emerged from her stomach and reverberated through her skull.

"Right now, Ms. McClellan! Gather your things and let's go," commanded the first voice again as his hand reached out toward Chloe's elbow. Now, when the urge to snarl and snap coursed through her, she found her appendages completely unresponsive, as if she were outside her own body.

Her head rolled on her rubbery neck as the man took her elbow in his grip. Instantly a shock of built-up energy passed into his hand and launched him across the room to crash into the vertical blinds. The window cracked, and he fell onto the radiator before flopping to the linoleum in an unconscious heap. Kids started to panic as everyone but Kirin stumbled and tripped in a frantic attempt to get away from her. Chloe just stood there on the edge of collapse, like a severed tree waiting to tip over.

That was when the second man fired two Taser darts into her stomach and started to pump the trigger...

.   .   .

Before she could see or hear, Chloe smelled industrial antiseptic and plastic. Then she slowly began to move her fingers and toes, but found that her ankles and wrists were strapped in place. Her lids fluttered open. She was lying on her back, staring into a bright light. There were people moving around her, and hushed voices fired back and forth from either side. The words started to make sense.

"There has been no indication since you brought her in that she could have the capacity to carry an electric charge," said a woman's voice that sounded like it had been worn down by a lifetime of smoking.

"Then how do you explain what happened to Mr. Wagner at the school?" a man countered with cold, clear enunciation.

"I really couldn't tell you," she responded curtly. "But as far as I can tell, your men have tased and abducted a perfectly normal teenage girl here."

The blurred face of the woman started to come into focus above her.

"She's awake." The woman leaned closer. She was wearing a surgical mask over her nose and mouth, but her magnified brown eyes peered through thick lenses and locked on Chloe. "You're okay. You'll be groggy and a bit woozy," she said with a gentle rasp that betrayed a southern upbringing. "You were sedated, but you're safe and in no danger," she reassured.

"That will be all for now, Dr. Cunningham," said the man dismissively. "I'll need to speak with her alone."

The brown eyes pulled away, but the woman's voice grew louder. "I don't agree with this at all!" she said. "I'm taking this to Dr. Markson, and I promise you he won't stand for it either." She started toward the door.

"Thank you for your opinion, Doctor, but this is a national security matter, and I'm really not concerned with whatever Dr. Markson will or will not stand for."

"We'll see," she challenged before slamming the door in punctuation.

Chloe tried to move her hands again, but they wouldn't budge, belted down tightly to the gurney below. She turned her head when she felt a fumbling at her right wrist, and the face of the man came in to focus. He didn't look to be any older than in his mid-thirties, with neat black hair and chiseled features that would have been handsome if they didn't also look a little cruel. His big smile looked a bit like a leer, and something about the twinkle in his eyes was artificial. He unstrapped the belt at her wrist and freed her hand.

"Hello, Chloe, my name is Mr. Allen." He moved down to unbind an ankle. "I'm sorry about all this, but we needed to restrain you until we were sure it was safe." His teeth were too white to be believed. "You gave us quite a scare back there;

one of my associates is just a couple rooms down with second-degree burns and a concussion."

"Where am I?" Chloe croaked.

"You're in the medical center at the Daedalus Group headquarters just a few miles away from your school." He moved to her other ankle. "Your mother has been notified of your whereabouts and is waiting for you in another part of the building. There's nothing to be concerned about. We just need you to answer a few questions."

"Who are you?" Chloe demanded.

"My name is Mr. Allen, like I said." He paused before releasing her left hand. "I'm a civilian contractor with the Department of Homeland Security. We're here working with the Daedalus Group in a cross-agency development initiative funded by the U.S. government." He smiled again. "We're the good guys."

"Where's Kirin?" Chloe demanded, trying to piece together the outlandish and horrifying chain of events that had occurred before waking up here.

"He's nearby in another room," said Mr. Allen, "as is Stan Strakowski."

Chloe clenched her eyes tightly. *Please let this be another bad dream!* "Why?" she asked with as calm a voice as she could muster. "They don't know anything."

"You know why, Chloe." He released her left wrist. "Because of the thing that you've been harboring in your barn, the thing that destroyed our twenty-million-dollar research tower and electrocuted two of our men."

"I don't know what you're talking about," she blurted, just as Mr. Allen took a piece of paper from his pocket and laid it across her legs. She pushed up on her elbows to get a better angle. It was the note that she'd left in the barn for Uktena—it detailed everything. Her head sunk into her chest. *I'm such an idiot!*

"You refer to it as Uktena and imply that not only does it read, but that you have spoken to it on a number of occasions." His gaze was unwavering. "I'm going to need for you to tell me everything you know about what it is and why it's here."

Chloe's heart was thundering in her throat. "I won't tell you anything until you let the others go," she declared in an unconvincing show of defiance.

Mr. Allen gave her an oily smile. "Have you heard of the Patriot Act, Chloe?"

She nodded.

"Well, among the tenets of that act are the details of the DHS's power to fulfill its job of protecting the territory of the United States from terrorist attacks and natural disasters. It also details our legal rights for the heightened needs of guarding our resources and energy infrastructure against any possible outbreak of dangerous illnesses or elements."

"Okay?" Chloe said, waiting for more.

He cleared his throat quietly. "The *creature* that you have been aiding has proven to be a direct threat to a brand-new and potentially world-changing source of energy. It also poses a major health risk for introduction of unknown toxins into our environment...As of now, and until we understand what we might be dealing with, it will be considered a terrorist threat to our way of life, and you and your friends will be charged with aiding and abetting an enemy of the state."

"You've got to be kidding me," she muttered under her breath.

"Have you been read your rights yet, Chloe?"

"No." Her eyes widened.

"That's right, and we can detain you without doing so for another—" Mr. Allen checked his watch, "seventy hours...But I don't want your friends to have to be here that long, do you? I'm not sure your mom will make it through the next three nights sleeping on that metal bench in the lobby."

"What did you do with the dragon?" Chloe demanded with a shaky voice.

Mr. Allen perused some notes on a clipboard. "Dragon, yes, this Uktena." He scanned a few lines. "A giant winged creature that breathes lightning like some monster straight from myth...I must admit that I never thought we would find something like that in the barn, despite all of Dr. Markson's outlandish claims... To tell you the truth, I think even he was a little shocked after we managed to bring it in. We had to pump it full of enough tranquilizers to down a whole herd of elephants."

Chloe said nothing. She stared at the note and tried to remember all that she'd written there.

Mr. Allen snatched it away from its perch on her knees and scanned it himself. "It seems that maybe we'll have to bring in this old lady and the college professor with his little story about the end of the world after all." He slipped the note into the pocket of his jacket. "He's the father of this boy, Kirin, who was supposed to come to your barn today to meet 'the dragon,' is that right?"

Chloe kept her mouth shut and her eyes down.

"Doesn't it seem odd that it's just one family of Chinese nationals and their acquaintances that happen to have foreknowledge of this...dragon? And all of this just happens to occur in the same rural town where our Daedalus Group development team is testing?" He shook his head and started to pace around her gurney like a circling shark. "It seems to be more likely that a group of recently transplanted deep-cover Chinese spies has relocated to the area because of its proximity to the project. And that they have brought with them some sort of fast-growing, bioengineered monstrosity that's designed to look like a beast from mythology."

Chloe shut her eyes and tried to reach out to Uktena in her mind. All she found was darkness. Her lids snapped open again. "That's the stupidest thing I've ever heard." Although her voice quavered, she forced herself to meet his cold gaze. "Don't you think that maybe the simplest explanation might be that, against all that we thought we knew about science and reason, maybe the prophecy on the cauldron is true? And unless we can do something about it, maybe the world really is going to end in a few weeks."

Mr. Allen stared at her for a long moment. "All the more reason to cut it open and see what's inside."

A rush of panic tore through her as she shot up and started

to yell. "You have to let him go! You have no idea what you're doing or what you might start!"

"Then why don't you tell us," he countered.

"I want to see my mother now! You can't just keep me here!"

Mr. Allen took a step toward her and raised a hand to silence her. "Your mother has no idea where you are or what's going on. She's frantic and quite frankly on the verge of a nervous breakdown, but she won't know anything more for days unless you play ball with me."

Tears welled in Chloe's eyes as she tried and failed to force herself awake from this nightmare.

Mr. Allen started toward the door. "I want to know everything you know about that thing and its involvement with the Liou family, and I want to know how you were able to shock one of my men unconscious." His hand rested on the doorknob for a moment as someone unlocked it from the other side. "You tell me that, and we'll see about letting your friends go and getting your mother in to see you."

He opened the door into a brightly lit hallway, but Chloe couldn't see anything beyond that. "If you don't talk to me, these next seventy hours are going to get pretty uncomfortable for you and a lot of people you care about." He stepped into the hall and closed the door behind him with a metallic bang. A trio of locks slid into place on the other side.

The only thing to fill the silence that followed was the sound of Chloe sobbing.

CHAPTER 27
THE END IS NIGH

Chloe wanted to be able to say that she'd remained strong in the long days that followed. She would have been proud to tell of how she'd done the right thing despite the suffering and threats, and that she'd held out against the tyranny of her oppressors—but that would have been a lie. Twelve hours after her initial meeting with Mr. Allen, Chloe cracked under the stress of it all. She told them everything. She couldn't stand to think that the Liou family and Stan were caught up in this mess of her making, that her mom was screaming and pulling her hair out before some stone-faced, agency goon nearby.

Amid the waves of blubbering and shaking, she told them what she could remember about her various encounters with Uktena. Months of pent-up fear and confusion spilled out of her in a disjointed rush as Mr. Allen and his flunkies recorded and inscribed every word she said before following up with a repetitive onslaught of nit-picking questions. Once she got started, she found herself wanting to get out every detail, but her connection to Uktena and all that had happened between them was still hazy and distant. More than once, she caught impatient looks flashing back and forth between her various interrogators.

They left her alone to wallow in shame and self-loathing, waiting for the door to open again so that she could leave or for the moment when her mother would rush in with a consoling hug. But the minutes, then hours, crept by, and there was no reprieve from the misery.

After she'd lost any concept of time, Mr. Allen returned to demand that she answer all the same questions again. And after another unbridled fit of screaming, she found herself, once again, recounting the secrets she'd sworn to keep to a room full of complete strangers. Blank faces watched her closely as she spoke. Others kept their compassionless eyes trained on a machine that scrawled lines on a spool of graph paper while straps with electrodes were connected to her arm.

When they'd opened the door to wheel out what she could only assume had been a polygraph machine, she'd heard Dr. Markson's voice yelling in the hallway, but the door had slammed shut and locked again before she could make out what he was saying. Sometime after that, they'd brought her some bland food and a bottle of water. Mr. Allen thanked her for her candor and told her to get some sleep with a casual wave to the bed, which was nothing more than a steel slab that was fixed to the wall and fitted with a blue polyester hospital pillow.

Chloe sipped the water and perched herself on the cold slab with her back to the wall. Her eyes locked on the ceiling above. Behind the tinted glass dome in the corner, she could see a camera lens tracking her every movement. She'd had to pee for hours, but couldn't bring herself to do so with an audience. When her legs were shaking and she couldn't take it anymore, she marched over to the bowl, hunkered low with the pillow across her lap and let go with a desperate rush of relief. After a blissful few seconds of listening to the metallic splatter, she looked directly into the camera with her middle finger held over her head.

Afterward she'd climbed back onto her perch and curled up with her sweatshirt stretched over her knees. She closed her eyes and tried to reach out to Uktena—searching for the deep rumble of his heartbeat, hoping to gain some sense of his presence—but there was nothing. *What if they killed him? What if his death is why the world will end—and it's all my fault?*

Finally the fatigue won out, silencing her spiral of fear and doubt as she moved to her side and dropped her head to the pillow. But just as she was starting to drift off, the door opened abruptly, and Mr. Allen and his team bustled into the room. This time a portly, shrew-faced woman with a syringe came with him.

"Sorry to interrupt your sleep, Chloe," he said with a conciliatory wave. "I know this must be starting to get a little uncomfortable for you," he smiled. "But my colleague, Dr. Hoyt here, is going to administer a shot, and then I've got a couple more questions to ask…"

. . .

After a while, Chloe couldn't tell if she was dreaming or awake or if she'd been there for hours or maybe days. It was Dr. Markson who finally ended it, opening the door early Wednesday morning with soothing words for Chloe and furious looks toward Mr. Allen and his team. But before Mr. Allen relinquished the room, he commanded Chloe's attention one last time. He put a finger to his lips. "Be careful who you talk to about any of this, Chloe," he warned. "I wouldn't want to have to bring anyone else in to answer these same questions."

Chloe couldn't stop trembling. She felt like she had hypothermia, though she suspected this chill was mostly in her head. Dr. Markson zipped up her jacket and draped a blanket over her shoulders with surprising tenderness before helping her to stand.

"I'm sorry, Chloe," Dr. Markson said quietly. "This never should have been allowed to happen. I haven't been able to gain access to you until now." He gave her a quick glance then looked away. "I'm ashamed this occurred on Daedalus Group property. I tried to warn you, but it was too late."

"How long have I been here?" Chloe's voice was hoarse from sobbing.

"Forty-six hours." He helped her toward the door, where Dr. Cunningham was waiting with a hot cup of tea.

"Drink this. You'll need a jolt of caffeine and something hot to get you home," she said. Her breath smelled like cigarettes and coffee. "You're a tough girl. That officious son of a bitch, Allen, is still convinced you're some kind of Chinese spy," she added with a bark of a laugh.

They watched her down the tea in a few desperate gulps

before ushering her out of the room and down a long hallway that was lined with morning-lit windows.

Audrey leapt up from the waiting area sofa and turned toward Chloe's shuffling approach. Chloe slipped a hand from the blanket and waved. In an instant, Audrey was running as fast as her daughter had ever managed. She enveloped Chloe in a hug with a sob of relief before stepping back to scan her daughter for injuries. "Honey, are you okay?" she begged. "What did they do to you?"

"I'm all right," Chloe forced, though she felt far from it. "They just asked me a lot of questions and didn't let me sleep."

Audrey took Chloe by the shoulder and held her close as her eyes locked on Dr. Markson. He wilted before the fury in her gaze.

"I'm sorry," was all that Dr. Markson could offer.

Audrey looked for a moment like she might actually attack. "Who the hell do you people think you are?" she snapped before starting to lead Chloe toward the door.

"I don't know anymore," answered Dr. Markson as his sad eyes met Chloe's weary glance. "But for what it's worth, Chloe, I believe everything you said…It's the most magnificent thing I've ever seen."

Chloe and her mom stopped and looked back. "It's a he, not a thing," Chloe mumbled. "You need to save him."

Dr. Markson gave her an intense look. "Maybe *you* do," he whispered with a nod that she did not understand.

Audrey stepped between them with the heat of her rage forcing Dr. Markson to step back. "Someday I'm going to get you for this," she hissed.

He nodded again, this time with resigned acceptance. "I hope we're all here long enough for you to get the chance."

.   .   .

Chloe woke up twenty hours later with a hacking cough and a throbbing in her temples. A flu-like ache had taken hold throughout her body, and waves of teeth-chattering chills kept her shivering beneath layers of blankets. After stumbling out of bed and shuffling her way downstairs, she'd fallen backward into the sofa just a little after five in the morning; she hadn't taken her eyes off the perverse ramblings of the cable news since.

The day's BREAKING NEWS was an unceasing bombardment of analysis and conjecture surrounding what they were calling the worst tornado disaster in recorded history. Entire towns had been sucked up and reduced to kindling, and thousands of people were dead or missing. Images of splintered homes and ruined lives played in repeat across every station. Chloe had seen the same footage of a filthy dog limping down a littered wasteland, which had been the suburban outskirts of Topeka, Kansas, at least forty times already. Apparently a series of what they were calling long-track F4 and F5 tornadoes had cut a swath from Wyoming to Louisiana, and the full extent of the carnage was still being pieced together.

Relegated to the ticker along the bottom was an endless streaming text:

> Continued volcanic activity at Kilimanjaro leads many to predict a big blast just days away. Still more than 1.2 million displaced refugees living in the possible blast radius…Another 6.1 earthquake rattles central China, further hampering ongoing aid efforts as starvation and cholera continue to spread…Lindsay Lohan arrested again for DUI and cocaine possession…

Chloe felt helpless and alone.

* * *

Audrey came downstairs at seven after a miserable night of nervous pacing and checking on Chloe again and again. She still had no idea what the hell was going on. Half of the barn had exploded across the yard on Monday morning, and by the time Brent called and she'd gotten home, the whole site had been cordoned off with caution tape. After she'd retrieved Chloe two days later, a black SUV had been permanently installed across the street, and people in plastic ponchos were digging around the wreckage and taking pictures. All that anyone had told her was that her daughter had been temporarily detained at the behest of the Department of Homeland Security.

Chloe had been barely coherent during the car ride home—both wired and asleep at once—as she mumbled in disjointed spurts about "the hubris of mankind" and how the planet was "getting ready to shake us off and start over."

Though Audrey was reluctant to admit it, she'd heard that sort of talk before, and it rattled her deeply to hear it again. With one weary look at her daughter splayed and shivering on the sofa, she decided to not even bother asking if Chloe was ready to go back to school. "How're you feeling?"

Chloe just shrugged, her vapid gaze locked on the television.

"Can I get you something to eat?" Audrey asked before noticing the dregs of a large bowl of cereal and a pulp-smeared juice glass discarded on the coffee table.

Chloe shook her head. "No, thanks."

Audrey approached the sofa and waved toward the slipper-tipped legs that were draped across the cushions. Chloe scooted back into the nook of the armrest to give her mother some room.

Audrey sat and put a reassuring hand on her daughter's fuzzy white foot before speaking again. "How are you, really?"

Chloe kept staring at the TV. "There was a whole string of giant tornadoes across the Midwest last night," she droned. "They think a couple thousand people might have been killed."

Anderson Cooper had a grave look on his face while another reporter on the scene tried to summarize the misery highlights in a minute and thirty seconds. "That's horrible," Audrey observed, mesmerized for a moment by the spectacle of disaster.

She turned her attention back to Chloe. "But I need you to turn off the TV and focus on me for right now."

After a moment of hesitation, Chloe picked up the remote and did as she was told. "I'm kind of tired of answering questions," Chloe sighed.

"I know you are, and I'm truly sorry to make you do it

again, but you have to anyway." Audrey inched closer. "You said a lot of pretty out-there stuff to me before you fell asleep, and I was up all night trying to make sense of it all."

Chloe met her mother's eyes. "I'm not crazy, Mom," she insisted. "I need you to believe me!"

"I do believe you, honey; I just don't understand," Audrey reassured. "I might be upset that you didn't feel the need to talk to me about whatever it is that's going on with you, but I want you to know that I still trust your reason and judgment over that of pretty much anybody else."

Chloe didn't think she could possibly have any tears left, but she was wrong. "I was worried you'd think I was...like Dad."

Audrey scooted closer and used her thumb to wipe away the drip from Chloe's cheek. "Chloe, your father was a kindhearted and loving man, and I thank God that you are like him in so many ways." She gently raised Chloe's head to claim her watery gaze. "I know you're not crazy. But it's my job to help you, and I can't do that if you won't let me in."

Without warning, Chloe lunged in for a hug and buried her face in her mom's neck. Audrey rocked her gently and squeezed her closer. It had been a long time.

"I'm sorry for everything," came Chloe's muffled words.

"Everything is kind of a lot to be sorry for," Audrey answered. "You don't have to shoulder all that."

Chloe pulled away, and her eyes seemed to state the contrary. "Yeah, I think that maybe I do."

"Chloe, what's going on?" Audrey pressed as Chloe crawled back into her cushion-lined nook. She seemed to consider her response for a long time before she answered.

"I saw something in the woods by the pond that they didn't want me to see, and now they're trying to make sure that I keep my mouth shut."

"What did you see?" Audrey pleaded.

Chloe met Audrey's gaze and shook her head slightly. "You said you trusted my reason and judgment, well, I need you to trust me now."

"I do trust you," said Audrey.

Now it was Chloe who reached out to put a hand on Audrey's knee. "I can't tell you what's happening, Mom. I don't want to go back there for more questions, and I don't want you there either," she stated. "I'm pretty sure that I'd still be in there if I hadn't been a minor."

"Chloe, what happened to the barn?" Audrey whispered. "I know you've been sneaking out there a lot recently, but I just thought you were going out to talk on the phone or write in your journal or something." Audrey held her daughter's gaze. "Chloe, the barn is gone, and they won't let me get within a hundred feet of the wreckage!"

Chloe shrugged unconvincingly. "Maybe it was a tornado?"

Audrey glared and waited.

"Mom, I'm sorry, but you're going to have to let it go for now!"

Audrey sat quietly for a long moment, trying to come to terms with "letting it go." Chloe's tone left no room for debate, and Audrey knew from experience that if she pushed now, she would hit her daughter's impassable wall of silence. But she could tell how scared Chloe was, and the fact that she couldn't fix it made her want to scream. She managed to breathe and hold her impulse to freak out at bay, recognizing, above all, that Chloe needed her now to be rational and calm. "What can I do to help you, honey? You have to give me something so that I don't feel totally useless here."

Chloe thought about it. "I have a birthday coming up."

"Yes, sweet sixteen, just two weeks away." Audrey thought for a moment of the brand-new microscope and refurbished iPhone that she'd saved up for.

"Well, I think I want a hand-crank radio, a high-powered flashlight with a lot of batteries, a year's supply of canned food, and some industrial-sized jugs of bottled water."

"That's what you want for your birthday?" Audrey was incredulous.

"Yes," Chloe answered with a decisive nod.

"Chloe, should I be scared right now? I have to tell you that all of this is scaring me."

Chloe sighed. "I'm not really sure, Mom…But yeah, I think maybe being at least a little bit scared is probably appropriate."

.   .   .

The fever didn't break for four days. Audrey and the family doctor thought it was just a standard flu, brought on by the extended stress and lack of sleep, but Chloe knew better. At least once a day, she woke from a nap with Uktena's low, melancholy growl vibrating as if from within her own throat. In quiet moments, she could still sense his muted fury and the deep well of sadness beneath it.

At least I know he's still alive, she told herself again and again as the ghost malady persisted. And though she wanted more than anything to be able to tell her mother what was happening, how could she explain that she was sick because of a sympathetic link to a tranquilized dragon across town? How could she voice the possibility that the end of the world could be only days away and there was nothing she or anyone else could do about it?

On Sunday, Chloe started to feel a bit more like herself again, though it brought her no comfort. She knew it was not because Uktena was also coming out of the darkness; he had sunk deeper into it, and the unexplained link that they'd shared was fading completely. Despite the continued texts and e-mails of support from Kirin, Stan, Ezra, and Liz, with the severed connection from the dragon, she felt lost and helpless…until she decided to venture outside for the first time to get a closer look at the barn late that afternoon.

She grabbed her jacket from the coat rack, where her mom had hung it days before, and slipped her weary arms into the sleeves. It had started to get cold outside, and she stuffed her head into a wool hat and wrapped a hand-knit scarf around her neck before burying her hands in her pockets to shoulder open the back door. That was when she felt the piece of paper and a hard, plastic rectangle in her right pocket.

Her hand came out with a handwritten note and a 64GB compact flash drive with the Daedalus Group logo blazoned on the side. She glanced out at the black SUV parked across the street and backed away from the windows. Despite the lingering pain in her stitched leg, she found herself bounding back up the stairs an instant later. She hurried down the hall and retreated to her room, quickly drawing the blinds before she finally allowed herself to open the note.

Chloe,

I'm sorry I can't do more. They're watching everything I do. "The dragon" is being kept heavily sedated as they run experiments. More so-called scientists arrived from Washington, and there's a lot of jurisdictional fighting over which department will own the tests. I've convinced them to keep it alive until I get to examine it myself after the Lightning Tower Project goes live on the 20th of this month. But I fear that it's already having a bad reaction to either the drugs or the food they're giving it.

On the afternoon and evening of December 20th, the experiments will be put on hold, and all hands will be on-site at the pond. There will be five or so hours of relatively low building security from 4 p.m.–9 p.m. that day.

I don't know what you might be able to do with this information, if anything, but there it is. It's the best I can do. It truly is the most magnificent creature to have ever existed, and I could not live with myself knowing that I didn't at least try to save it. From listening to your account, I can tell you feel the same way.

I don't believe the world will end, I can't, but then again, I don't believe in dragons either.

I'm sorry and good luck!

–Dr. Markson

Chloe read the note again and looked down at the flash drive in her hand. In a matter of seconds, she'd ripped the hat and scarf from her head and started booting up her computer. A second later, her printer beeped and whirred to life.

CHAPTER 28
HAREBRAINED

Chloe kept the hood of her sweatshirt up as she walked quickly through the lunchroom. Still she could hear people whispering about her as she passed. Now wherever she went in school, her classmates either wanted to inexplicably be her friend or they averted their eyes and quickly backed away from her approach. She had no time for any of it, striding with unwavering purpose as she rounded the fern planter into The Cave. She kept her head down as she passed the table where Cynthia and Brian were sitting; Stan and Kirin waited at the furthest table in the corner.

Both of them had received her latest text, and both nodded when they saw her. She'd been trying to prep them for this moment via e-mail and text since the mad plan had come to her the night before. She sat down across from them and scanned the surroundings for anyone in earshot before sliding a manila folder across the table. Kirin opened it just enough so that he and Stan could peer inside.

Stan's face split into a grin as Kirin's eyes went wide. He leaned in to get a closer look.

"He's being held by the Department of Homeland Security in the Daedalus Group headquarters," Chloe said quietly. "They have him in deep sedation as they run experiments, but there's going to be a five-hour window of opportunity to get him out on the evening of the twentieth."

Kirin turned to another laser-printed photograph of the unconscious dragon, this one showing a close-up of a heavily dilated blue eye and the diamond-ridged pattern on his forehead.

"Dude, are you saying that we're going to try to bust a

348

dragon out of a high-security government complex?" Stan whispered without taking his eyes from the picture.

Kirin flipped to the next print, this one showing a wide angle shot of the monster's full length, though Uktena's blade-tipped tail still stretched off the edge of the frame.

"Yes, that's what I'm saying," Chloe answered. That silenced them for half a minute as their eyes fixed on the unlikely series of images.

"How did you get these pictures?" asked Stan with a hint of awe.

"Someone in the Daedalus Group slipped a flash drive into my pocket before they let me go. I just found it last night along with a note."

Kirin was expressionless as he studied what he saw.

"Who gave it to you?" Stan pressed. "And why you?"

"I think that maybe the fewer people that know who is helping us, the better," Chloe stated. "And he gave it to me because I kind of know a lot more about the whole Cow Thief situation than I told you."

Kirin looked up and met her gaze. "It was living in your barn, wasn't it?"

"Yes," Chloe admitted. "And I'm sorry I didn't tell you both about him a long time ago, but I was scared of what might happen if I got you involved."

"Him?" Kirin repeated. "You've talked to him?"

Chloe nodded. "His name is Uktena, just like the fifth dragon on your father's cauldron." They both stared at her, waiting for more. "He's been alive for thousands of years but asleep for the last seven hundred or so...And he believes that he's woken up this time to usher in the end of mankind."

Their silence stretched on as the sound of Brian's raucous laugh carried from beyond the ferns. The trio was deaf to the outside world.

"Then why would we help him escape?" Stan finally blurted.

"He saved my life twice," she met Stan's wild eyes, "and yours once, too...I'm not totally sure about this whole end-of-the-world thing yet, but if it's true, I think that maybe he could help us stop it."

"The van," Stan said with awe. "I knew we went over the edge of the quarry."

Chloe nodded, glancing back to Kirin as she tried to gauge his response. "He told me that he's just the forerunner to the doom of man, the catalyst that sets it off. And the prophecy said that 'when the spirit of the land withers and dies,' the other dragons will return to claim dominion. Well, Uktena is the spirit dragon and he's dying now, but maybe if we can save him, then we can stop the others from waking up."

Kirin was looking down again as he turned to the final print, showing an overhead schematic of the Daedalus Group building with one little 'x' on a side door beside the loading dock and another big 'X' in the center of a large room at the heart of the complex.

"How do you intend to get him out of there?" Kirin asked while studying the map.

Chloe shrugged. "I have a couple ideas, but that's kind of where I was hoping for your help."

Kirin straightened the prints and closed the folder very deliberately before sitting up and meeting her gaze again.

Chloe's palms were sweating, and her leg was shaking below the table.

He cleared his throat and took a sip of his Vitamin Water, then nodded with the hint of a little grin. "First tell us everything you know."

·   ·   ·

By the second Friday in December, various elements of The Plan had already started to take shape. Stan had procured the video camera again and had managed to steal a ten-pound bag of espresso-strength, organic ground coffee from the office where his dad worked. Since his parents had implemented biweekly drug tests, he'd found that he was operating at a far more efficient level. But he also discovered that he was remembering things that he'd just as soon forget and dwelling on things that he'd previously been able to brush aside. The fact that he'd signed on to Chloe's potentially bleak view of the immediate future did not inspire confidence in his prospects at continued sobriety.

Kirin was still working on his assignments. Through a "college friend" of Cynthia Decareux's and a quick perusal of Craigslist, he'd managed to procure both a set of lock-picking tools and an authentic grappling hook. After a week of nightly online tutelage and steady practice on the locks around the house and at school, he'd become semiproficient at identifying and breaking an array of simple, standard locks. So far, with the grappling hook, he had only managed to break a couple tree limbs, partially remove a rain gutter, and badly bruise his shoulder bone.

Chloe was not doing as well with her list as either of the others. She'd tracked down the name of the organic meat farmer that sold to Positive Pete's, but he was out of town until the New Year and she didn't have any money anyway. She knew that to get Uktena strong again, she'd need a grossly large quantity of clean meat. Against all better judgment, she could think of only one other place to get it…

That Friday night, Kendra was having a smallish gathering at her house with only the coolest and most fortunate kids in attendance. Needless to say, Chloe, Kirin, and Stan were not invited. But Liz was still dating Paul Markson, and that got her past the twelve-foot-tall radio-operated gate.

Chloe approached Liz after school on Friday, and Liz's reasons for refusal were not able to withstand Chloe's onslaught of guilt and pleading. By 9:30 that night, Chloe, Kirin, and Stan were all hunched low in the Grand Wagoneer, parked across the street from a shadowed stretch of the stone wall that ringed the Roberts estate. They were all dressed in black—except for Stan's absurdly sky-blue sneakers. Kirin fidgeted nervously with the barbed prongs of the grappling hook in his lap, and Chloe's gaze danced back and forth between the street and her cell phone.

"I still don't think it's fair that so much of this plan relies on me and this grappling hook," Kirin muttered for the third time. "It's a lot harder to use than you'd think."

Stan's leg hadn't stopped bouncing for twenty minutes. "What are you complaining about, dude?" he whispered emphatically. "You get to stay by the wall with an escape rope. I've got to steal God knows how many pounds of raw meat and carry it through the woods without being seen!"

"It's all going to work," Chloe declared just before her phone lit up and vibrated with a new text. Everyone went silent as she grabbed it from the dashboard and opened the message from Liz: **Basement door off back patio. Txt when close.**

"It's on," Chloe announced. "The meat locker is in the basement. There's an outside entrance from the back patio." She closed the phone and started toward her pocket just as another text came in from Liz. She opened the phone back up as a pregnant hush returned to the car: **This is totally STUPID!** Chloe frowned and snapped the phone shut. "Let's go." She opened the passenger side door before the others had time to protest again.

She was at the wall with her back to the cold stone and her breath pluming before the others had even shut their car doors. They joined her in a crouch beside the designated entry point a few seconds later. Chloe gave Kirin a supportive nod.

He sighed deeply before rising to his feet with the coiled rope in one hand and the three-pronged hook in the other. "You might want to watch out," he whispered. "It's been known to come back down in a hurry." He wound up and hurled the black hook over the wall, where it swung down and smacked against the far side with a dull clang.

He took another slow breath before starting to haul it, scraping and bouncing, back up the rock face until it finally latched securely at the lip. He tugged again with a relieved smile as the rope went taut in his hands.

"See," said Chloe with a playful punch to his shoulder before she grabbed hold of the rope and scurried up the side of the wall. *I hope my butt looks good in these jeans* popped to mind before she swung a leg up and disappeared over the top.

Kirin and Stan were watching closely.

"She made that look pretty easy," whispered Stan before accepting the rope. But he, by contrast, ascended with a lot of fumbling and cursing under his breath. He made it over the top with banged knees and elbows and dropped down to the ivy on the other side with a grunt.

Kirin followed quickly, unhooking the prongs from the stone edge before leaping down gently into the woods beside the others. All three scanned the grounds before exhaling again. Through the woods, they eyed the side of the sprawling mansion a hundred yards away.

Chloe caught Kirin's sideways glance and smirked with a spark of excitement passing between them. "No sweat."

Kirin whipped out a small LED flashlight in one hand and his dad's binoculars in the other. Stan took the video camera from the bag and turned it on with a series of quiet beeps.

Chloe and Kirin watched as he pushed record and it beeped again. He'd covered the glow of the red REC light with a piece of black tape, and he switched the camera into NIGHT SHOOTING mode and aimed it at his two accomplices. "Cool."

"Stan, what are you doing?" Chloe asked.

"What do you mean? I want to get the full experience before we go next week." He zoomed in for a close-up on Chloe's face.

"It might not be such a good idea to videotape our grand larceny one week prior to breaking into a government facility," suggested Kirin.

Stan brought the camera away from his eye for only a moment. "Dude, if this is gonna be the end of the world, I want a record that we at least tried to stop it." He returned his eye to the viewfinder to better capture the moment of Kirin's response.

Kirin shrugged. "Sounds reasonable to me." He raised the binoculars and continued scanning the grounds. "It looks clear to the house."

Chloe took the coiled earbud from her pocket and attached it to the headphone jack on her cell. Kirin did the same with his iPhone before pressing the autodial. Chloe's screen lit up in her pocket a second later. She pressed the button to answer and then locked the keypad.

"Now I'm in your head," Kirin whispered in her ear, despite facing in the other direction.

"Nothing new there," she confessed.

Stan swung the camera smoothly between them. "Gee, maybe this could be a documentary about young love?"

Chloe gave the camera the finger and turned back toward the house. She took a ski mask from her pocket and pulled it on as the others did the same. They shared a last quick look.

"Good luck," Kirin offered.

Chloe nodded. "Okay, on three…One, two—" and before she knew it, she was running through the woods toward the brightly lit windows. Stan followed just a few strides behind, with the camera bag slapping against his back with every step. They moved along the tree line, passing window after window—no hint of activity within.

The house itself was a brick McMansion, clearly built in the last ten years, with class and style taking a back burner to the desire for overwhelming girth. Its multistory wings stretched across the property for what looked like twice the length of Uktena, and there must have been fifty or more rooms within.

Chloe and Stan slinked through the shadows toward the back as the sounds of laughter and conversation carried from around the corner.

"Looking good," whispered Kirin in Chloe's ear, sending a little thrill down her spine. "It's clear to the back, but I'll lose you around the corner."

They moved out from the shelter of the woods and scurried across the manicured lawn before sliding between the evergreen hedge and the wall of the one-story annex that ringed the back patio. Chloe put up her hand to stop at the corner; the sounds of roughhousing and banter were close by, and she could smell the drift of cigarette smoke clinging to the crisp air.

She turned back to face the dark woods and flashed her LED pocket light.

"I see you," said Kirin in her head.

"Me too," whispered Stan with the camera in her face.

Chloe took her phone from her pocket and unlocked the keypad again. "All right, I'm texting Liz now." She was wearing black fingerless gloves, and her thumbs worked quickly despite the cold: **I'm in place, but I hear people on the back patio?**

They waited for a long moment, staring at the phone. Then the screen lit up again: **Smokers. W8 a sec.** A minute later and the sound of talking receded and then a distinct slam of a door was followed by winter silence… **GO! Stairs down on right.**

Chloe nodded and they took off around the corner. The "back patio" was more like a theme park recreation of a Roman Villa, built by a flamboyant emperor. There were curving staircases and complex topiary designs that climbed up a multitiered garden toward a magnificently lit heated pool. Steam rose from the crystal blue water.

For a moment Chloe and Stan lost their focus amid the cherubic fountains and nude statues on pedestals. Their rushed scamper slowed to an unsure shuffle as Stan's camera swung around, trying to take it all in. Chloe snapped out of it after she stumbled through a flower bed and conked her head on a bird feeder that hung from a willow tree. She grabbed Stan by the shoulder and yanked him after her as they climbed up the slope of the yard past rings of hedges and waterfalls.

At the top tier, adjacent to the pool, Chloe spied an iron railing that led down a stairwell to a subterranean door. She motioned toward it and darted across the terrace, but before she reached the descent, someone opened the glass doors at the back of the house. She and Stan doubled back and ducked behind the sixteen-burner gas grill that was mounted into the wall of a barbeque piazza off to the side.

They held their breath as the sound of dance music blared from inside, but no one signaled the alarm. Then a girl let forth with a high-pitched yelp before a familiar, grating voice cut through the chill air. "It's friggen COLD!" Kendra announced. The patter of her bare feet across the patio was followed by a splash as she entered the pool.

"Damn," muttered Chloe under her breath.

"What's happening?" implored Kirin in her ear.

She peeked over the grill's lid to see Ezra approach the pool behind Kendra. Despite the cold, he wasn't wearing a shirt as he sauntered toward the water, carrying two cans of beer. Chloe was momentarily distracted by his molded perfection.

"Daaaaaamn," repeated Stan. The lens of the camera hovered over the grill beside her with Stan's face glued to the pop-out screen. Ezra dropped out of frame with a splash.

"We've got company in the pool," Chloe whispered into the dangling microphone cord of her earbud.

There was a long pause as Kirin considered the predicament from afar. "Could Liz create a diversion?" he suggested.

"Worth a try," said Chloe as she removed the phone from her pocket again. She wasn't skilled in all the shortcuts and emoticons of accepted text-speak, but her quick thumbs made up for it: People in the pool! I NEED help with a short diversion???

She waited a long moment for a response as Stan switched out of NIGHT SHOOTING MODE and zoomed in for a close-up on her phone's screen.

"Anything?" asked Kirin impatiently.

"Waiting," whispered Chloe just as the screen lit up with a returned text from Liz: Chloe U $ me 4 this!!! 1 sec.

Chloe and the camera peered back over the grill, unable to see what was causing the hysterical cackle of squeals and giggles in the pool. Stan artfully framed the ripples of light that played off the back of the house. Suddenly the lights went out.

The back terrace went dark as Kendra's laugh morphed into an angry yell. "Hey!"

Chloe scrambled to her feet and grabbed Stan by the elbow. "Come on!" she hissed as the two bolted toward the railing. Chloe glanced through the gloom as she ran, able to make out the two shapes in the pool that splashed toward the wall at the far end.

"Come on, turn the lights back on!" shouted Ezra toward the house as Stan and Chloe grasped the cold iron and slipped down the stairwell. Chloe grabbed the doorknob and turned it as quietly as she could; the door swung open without a creak. They slid inside with a soft click behind them just as the full array of lights returned to the terrace above. Chloe and Stan shared a joint exhale to cut the silence.

"We're in," said Chloe into the mic.

"Nice work," said Kirin.

"Dude, I've done a lot of stupid stuff when I was high, but this has got to be the dumbest thing I've ever tried!" Stan allowed himself only a moment to lower the lens and reflect on his predicament. He snapped it back up and did a 360-degree pan of their surroundings. "What now?"

The term basement didn't quite do justice to the sprawling maze of dark wood-paneled rooms that stretched out in three directions. To the left was a multilevel descending wine cellar. To the right was the entrance to an extended man cave, complete with pool, ping-pong, and poker tables beside a full bar with swiveling bar stools and a classic jukebox. The room they were in was lined with shelves laden with all manner of grilling tools and games. Tongs, knives, two-pronged forks, and grill brushes were next to the spices and sauce collection on one side; a high-end croquet set, horseshoes, and an assortment of other lawn sports were displayed on the other.

Directly ahead was a steel door with a plaque above it that said *"MEAT ME."*

Chloe rolled her eyes, but Stan zoomed in on the door. "Uh-oh," he said as Chloe followed his focus to the oversized combination padlock that Richard Roberts had kitschily, but very effectively, placed on the door's handle.

Stan panned from the lock back to Chloe's face. "Your pal Liz might have mentioned this part," he suggested.

Chloe shut her eyes and shook her head. "This isn't going as smoothly as I'd planned."

"What?" asked Kirin.

"There's a lock on the door." Chloe walked over to the door and tested it just to be sure. "It's a combination lock," she added, lifting it up to get a better look at the old-timey design with a big ring loop and a hundred-number wheel.

Kirin sighed over the phone. "Does it have a master-key hole at the bottom?" he asked with an audible wince.

Chloe swung it up higher and allowed herself a smirk. "Yes, it does."

"Okay," he said, thinking out loud…"Do you think there's

any way we could get Liz to make that diversion again?"

"Well, I suppose I could tr—" Chloe stopped talking abruptly and craned her head toward the wine cellar. Stan swung the camera in that direction as the sound of scuffing footsteps grew.

The two scrambled through the door to the Man Cave and darted toward the shelter of the pool table just as a girl's voice hissed Chloe's name in the foyer.

"Chloe!" Liz called out a little louder as Chloe got back to her feet and emerged from hiding.

"I'm here," she answered.

As Chloe stepped back into the foyer, Liz shrieked. Chloe remembered the ski mask and yanked it up from her face. "Liz, it's me."

Liz met her eye with a look of extreme disapproval. "This has got to be the worst idea you've ever had."

"No, I'm pretty sure that one's going down next week," she admitted. "But you didn't mention that the door was locked."

Liz noticed the lock for the first time as well. "Oh! It wasn't the last time I was here," she said in her defense. Then she noticed Stan, still in the ski mask, with a video camera trained on her. She raised an eyebrow and turned back on Chloe. "What's going on with you, Chloe? And why are you trying to steal Mr. Roberts's meat anyway?"

"It's a long story," Chloe deflected. "But I promise you that there's a really good reason for everything and that Mr. Roberts has it coming."

Liz tried to keep her frown, but Chloe could tell that she was softening. "You really are a crazy person, you know that?"

"Yes," Chloe accepted. "I've come to recognize as much in the past few months, but I still really need your help."

Liz shook her head and tried to summon the strength to say no. "I don't know the combination, and I have no way of getting it."

"I've got someone on my team who can pick the lock if they can get here," Chloe declared.

"I wouldn't be too sure of that," Kirin countered in her ear, though Chloe pretended to not hear him.

"What do you think the possibility is that you give it a couple minutes and then turn those lights off again?" Chloe put on her best pleading smile…

"You're kidding, right?" asked Liz with a snort.

Chloe shook her head as Stan zoomed in for dramatic effect.

"You're bonkers! We're all going to get caught for this," Liz whined, though Chloe's contagious enthusiasm for adventure had already infected her.

"I know it may not seem it, but this is important, Liz; the most important thing I've ever done," said Chloe.

"Uh-huh, like the Indian arrowhead project? Or maybe that time we had to spend a whole month looking for those little cube-shaped rocks up in the hills?"

"Devil's dice," Chloe muttered. "We were charting the geological spread pattern."

"Whatever, I don't want to know." Liz started back the way she'd come with an exasperated groan. She gave a last look over her shoulder. "If you get caught, I'm not involved."

Chloe held up Stan's scout's honor salute. "I don't even know who you are."

Liz walked away with a dramatic sigh echoing about the vaulted ceiling of the wine cellar as Chloe and Stan shared a look—*that was close!* She lifted the microphone to her lips. "Kirin, leave the grappling hook someplace easy to find and move to the back corner of the patio."

"Crap," was all he said in response, though Chloe could already hear the wind and heavy breathing of running.

Chloe and Stan returned their focus to the lock, as if jointly willing it to open. "This is going to work," Chloe added, just as the door to the patio swung open behind them and a wet and shivering Ezra burst through with an undersized towel clutched tightly around his shoulders.

Chloe and Stan froze as he slammed the door shut behind him. Then Ezra noticed the two masked figures lurking in the dark on the other side of the room. "What the hell is this?" His eyes met Chloe's deer-in-the-headlights gaze.

"Hey, Ezra," she answered lamely before fumbling the ski mask the rest of the way off her head. Stan didn't help any by hiding behind the camera as it continued to roll.

"Crap," repeated Kirin from afar as the sound of running stopped.

"Chloe, what are you doing here?" Ezra asked with a disturbing calm.

Chloe chuckled nervously. "It's kind of a long story."

"You ignore my texts and phone calls for a week and then break into my girlfriend's house during a party," accused Ezra.

"She's your girlfriend now?"

Ezra was seething beneath his composed mantle. "Everyone is talking about you, saying that you're crazy and a terrorist and that you attacked a cop in school and got taken away by the Department of Homeland Security. But I've defended you, every time, because I knew you wouldn't be involved in anything that stupid and reckless…But here you are, not one week later, with…" He locked eyes on Stan and looked for a moment like he might reach out and smash the camera. "That's Stan Strakowski beneath that mask, isn't it?" he said with a hard point.

"Hey, dude." Stan popped out from behind the camera with a little wave.

Ezra threw his hands in the air. "I give up!" he declared before striding to the wine cellar, where he claimed the first bottle he came to. He turned back toward the door. "You know what, Chloe, go right ahead and do whatever it is you came to do. I don't give a damn anymore."

"Ezra, please," Chloe said, stopping him with his hand on the doorknob. "I'm sorry I didn't tell you what's going on; I couldn't risk getting anyone else involved."

Ezra was listening.

"I'm kind of in a lot of trouble, and because of me, so are Stan and Kirin."

He turned back to face her, but his eyes swung over to the camera. "Why the hell are you filming this?"

Stan was getting ready to answer when Chloe cut in. "I asked him to do it."

"Well, not really," added Stan quietly, though Chloe just kept on talking.

"A friend of mine needs me, someone who doesn't have anybody else. I can't explain why, but to save him, I need a lot of organic meat that I can't afford on my own...So I'm taking it from the rich asshole who ruined my father and allowed me to be interrogated in a holding cell for two days on his property." Chloe's anger swelled. "And I'm sorry, but he's also a shitty father to your girlfriend, and unless she wises up to it, she's going to turn into an asshole, too!"

"Why are you telling me all of this now?" he asked quietly.

"Because I need you to not tell Kendra about this when you go back up to the pool, and I need to walk out of here with the meat behind that door without getting caught," she said.

Ezra glanced to the door and then back to Chloe. "How are you planning to get past the lock?"

"I have someone coming in who can pick it," Chloe stated just before Kirin started laughing in her ear.

"And how are you gonna get this mysterious someone in to do it?" Ezra pressed.

"A window?" she lied.

"They're all alarmed; the security system on this place is no joke," he countered.

"We have someone inside who can turn off the lights," Chloe admitted.

"Ah, right." Ezra nodded to her. "I guess you have it all figured out."

"No, not even close, but I have no choice," she locked her gaze on his and neither of them wavered. Stan kept rolling as the silence stretched on.

"10—17—1," Ezra finally said as he turned back toward the door.

"What?"

"10—17—1," he repeated. "It's the day Kendra was born and the combination to all the locks in the house." He returned his hand to the doorknob. "Tell your man not to bother, and use the lights-out for your getaway." The door opened quietly.

"Thanks, Ezra," she called out in a whisper.

"I hope you know what you're doing," he whispered back.

"Me too," she admitted before the door closed.

She slowly brought her hand back to the microphone. "Did you get all that?"

"Yup," Kirin answered stoically.

"We'll meet you at the back corner with the haul."

And by the time she turned around, Stan had already opened the lock. He was grinning like a fool as he swung the camera back to Chloe for the reaction shot.

. . .

On Monday night, the sky shimmered with bands of green and red light. Chloe had never seen an aurora before in real life, though she'd sought out videos online and had always dreamed of one day traveling to the far north to see it for herself. It was far more beautiful than the little screen on her computer could share.

She stood in her backyard and looked up through the leafless branches of the oak that lorded over the property. Another ripple of green danced across the stars. Her neck was beginning to ache, and her teeth were starting to get cold since her jaw had dropped minutes before.

The news said it was the globally visible effect of a strong solar flare, sending charged particles into the upper atmosphere to collide with oxygen and nitrogen molecules in a vibrant release of energy. Satellite transmissions had been intermittent throughout the day, and Chloe hadn't had cell phone service in hours. Even the cable feed had started to pick up bands of disruptive static.

But most striking was that for the first time in over a week, Chloe had started to feel the stirring of Uktena in her mind again. With her eyes closed, she thought that she could hear the ponderous flow of his breath, slow and gravelly, like the distant rolling of boulders. And earlier at school, as she was pretending to pay attention in English Lit, her leg had lashed out suddenly beneath her desk. Her toes had curled involuntarily in her shoe as she felt the dragon's back claw clench and retract. She'd looked up to realize that she'd moved her whole desk a few inches across the floor with a loud scrape. Wary eyes had swung to her from every direction, but most shriveled away to avoid her returned gaze.

She dropped her focus from the colorful sky to the Daedalus Group security goon in the black Suburban parked at the side of the road across the street. He was pretending not to notice her as he sat in the idling truck, looking at a magazine that hadn't had a page turned in ten minutes. Her gaze drifted past him to the dark woods on the other side; she couldn't see anyone there. *Good.*

Sinuous ripples of red drew her attention skyward again, followed by a dramatic burst of emerald green. As Chloe heard the automatic window of the Suburban sliding down, she turned away to walk toward the ruin of the barn and the taut line of caution tape that surrounded it. She scuffed down the driveway, kicking little pebbles that skittered across the frost-coated lawn as she followed the bright yellow tape toward her house. She glanced over her shoulder and caught the eye of her observer before they both looked away furtively. Just to be sure she had his attention, she bounced her hand along the plastic band every time she passed the word CAUTION. The whole line shook with every hit. With a last look over her shoulder, she stepped to the shadow of the oak and ducked under the barrier.

She started to count in her head, *one Mississippi, two Mississippi, three Mississippi*, as she traversed red splinters of barn and upended farm equipment. She heard the opening of the SUV's door on the count of *six Mississippi* and continued quickly toward the jagged opening where the barn door had been. She stopped for a moment at the threshold and raised her wrist with a button push and a beep. The stopwatch began counting on an old Casio watch that she'd found in the back of her mom's nightstand. The light of the aqua blue screen faded as the digital count reached 00.00.10.

Half of the doorframe still stood, and the flashlight was

still hanging by a nail on the side of the entrance. She grabbed it and switched it on as she stepped to what was left of the hay-strewn floor.

The piles of tires had been knocked over, and the old tractor had been thrown fifty feet past where the left wall had been. It rested now on its side against the little cherry tree that dropped pink petals across the yard every spring. Deep gouges had been torn in the trunk from the impact.

Swinging the beam back toward the barn, Chloe saw that her dad's old car looked as if it had been stepped on. The roof was completely caved in, and distinct claw holes pierced the hood. She swung the beam across one of the last remaining barn windows as she heard footsteps coming down the driveway.

She walked quickly toward the back corner, where Uktena had been sleeping, and noticed charred lines of hay across her path. A mound of ash and debris was all that was left of her dad's old magazine collection. For a moment, Chloe thought back to the summer after he'd left, when she'd read every issue in the failed attempt to keep him close, even if only for a little while longer. She moved on as the beam found the antler and bone cairn still standing in what had been the corner. One of the walls was gone, and the scatter of shattered boards and fallen roof formed a ten-foot-tall mound of impenetrable debris around it.

A maze of little numbered flags had been stuck into the ground, and two shapes had been drawn with bright yellow tape amid a particularly large burn scar on the floor. She stepped closer with morbid fascination and held the beam on the spot where the dead cows had been, now marked by the outline of two splayed humans with appendages bent in unnatural directions. Chloe shuddered and turned her gaze back to the beauty of the night sky as a green pulse shot across the place where the roof had been.

A man cleared his throat behind her. "You can't be in here," he stated with officious certainty and the hint of a nasally whine.

She spun around and played at being startled. "Oh my God!" she yelled. "You don't have to sneak up on me!"

The beam of his flashlight was much stronger than Chloe's,

and he took that moment to swing it to her face. "You need to leave the cordoned-off area at once," he added, as if he hadn't heard her speak at all.

She decided to go with a different approach and squared off to face right into the light just to spite him. She'd seen him before at the pond when Uktena had destroyed the tower and again when he'd interrogated her the night of the Cow Thief—she thought his name was Mr. Fitz. "This is my property," she countered. "So I'm actually going to have to ask you to leave, if you don't mind."

"*Actually*, this is a crime scene under the jurisdiction of the United States government. If you don't leave the premises after two warnings, then I'm authorized to physically assist in your removal and detain you if you become combative." He almost smiled. "This is your second warning—you need to exit the cordoned-off area immediately."

He dropped his light to his feet, and Chloe could see that he was wearing a can of pepper spray on one hip and a holstered pistol on the other. She started walking back to the exit as slowly as she could manage without shaking.

"You don't even work for the United States government," she said as she passed him.

He fell in step behind her. "I'm a fully authorized civilian contractor employed by a development partner of the government and operating with a writ of authority on their behalf."

"I'm pretty sure this isn't constitutional," she added over her shoulder.

"You'd be surprised." He nudged her in her back with the butt of his flashlight.

Despite the alarm bells going off in her head, Chloe stopped at the half-standing doorjamb, slowly turned off her light, and returned it to the nail by the door. She could sense his brewing impatience behind her.

"Are you going to make me use force?" He stepped uncomfortably close.

Chloe skittered out the door with a few quick strides before hazarding a look back at him. Mr. Fitz remained in the doorway, looking at her with those blank, creepy eyes. He reached up to the McClellan family flashlight and unscrewed the bottom to let the four AA batteries drop out into his palm.

"You're going to owe us for those batteries," Chloe hollered while walking backward.

He tossed them into the debris pile and pointed toward the vague place where they landed. "Your batteries are just over there," he said, with a threat behind the cold surface.

This is a man who likes to hurt people… Chloe turned and started walking faster toward the house as she felt his eyes following. She glanced at the watch again: 00:04:37. *That has to be enough time!*

She ducked back under the caution tape at the end of the barn blast zone, but hazarded a last look back at Mr. Fitz from the other side. He stood leering at her with one hand resting on what was left of the doorjamb.

"I guess your jurisdiction ends here," she called out in challenge.

"Yeah," he answered, "but I'll be watching." He nodded toward the second-story window to her room and wet his lips in a way that made Chloe's skin crawl.

She turned and scurried the rest of the way back to her house before a quick slam of the door and a resolute throwing of the deadbolt. She charged up the stairs and down the hall, leaving Shipwreck in a moment of indecision by the bathroom door as he debated whether to sprint past her or return the way he'd come. Chloe slapped on the overheads in her room and walked straight to the window.

Mr. Fitz was still there, watching from the shadows. But Chloe's eyes drifted past him to the SUV and then to the darkness of the woods beyond. She saw the brief pulse of a flashlight deep within the gloom and resisted the urge to smile.

Instead, she forced herself to remain unaffected and in plain view of the bad man below. Operation Radio Control was a success. *Now I just have to stand here and give Kirin a little more time to get through the woods, get to the car, and get away.* A wave of red tumbled above the trees and drew her attention back up; it looked like an ocean of flame was crashing across the sky.

A hot, heavy breath swelled up from Chloe's gut before she heard the echoing rumble of the dragon's digestion in her mind. For a moment, she actually felt the buzzing of a live spark in her mouth. She opened her jaws and felt the static discharge toward the window. *Hold on, Uktena, just a few more days.*

CHAPTER 29
BREAKING IN

Chloe hadn't been able to sit down since her mom had left for the dinner shift at Pete's an hour before. She stood again at her bedroom window, this time with the lights off, as she stared out at the street. The black SUV was there as always—Mr. Fitz was not on duty tonight—but Chloe's eyes held instead on the bend in the road where she had first spoken to the dragon.

A pair of headlights approached, intermittently flashing through the winter-stripped trees. Moments later, Ezra's car came into view and slowed toward the entrance to the driveway. As his headlights swept across the SUV, the face of the watching guard was visible behind the tinted windows. The battered Ford came to a squeaky break at the end of the driveway and honked twice.

Chloe gave a last long sigh and then looked at her watch: 5:02 p.m. She snatched the backpack off the bed and fastened it tightly into position as she strode down the hallway. Beneath it she wore an uncharacteristically fashionable powder-blue coat that she'd borrowed from her mother's closet. It was the most noticeable warm jacket she could find, and Chloe had to admit that under different circumstances, she could have really enjoyed the knee-length cut and the Audrey Hepburn styling. For now, it was useful only for its colorful covering of the all-black garb and the array of tactical equipment she had strapped across her body.

She bounded down the stairs, and her black Chucks skidded to a stop by the large duffel bag by the back door. Within the army-green bag was eighty-some pounds of Mr. Roberts's still-frozen prime rib. Chloe had left a quarter of the haul in her mom's meat fridge to replenish what she'd previously taken, plus a little extra to prepare for the possibility of a coming apocalypse…The remainder was still way too much for Chloe to carry.

She grabbed the bag's straps and shouldered open the door before dragging the meat over the threshold to the back stoop. Ezra was already stepping out of the car to help before she'd turned to lock the door. He lifted the bag with one hand and raised an eyebrow.

"Please just tell me this isn't a dead body. I don't want to be an accessory to murder before I even get to college." He turned back toward the car with the meat bag dangling from his grip.

"Well, it's not a dead *human* body," Chloe answered. "And I wasn't the one to kill it, so you at least don't need to worry about the murder rap."

"Ah, yes, Mr. Roberts's meat, I almost forgot—so grand larceny then." He popped the trunk and heaved the bag into the back with a heavy thud. He shot Chloe a look over the hood of the car before they both slipped into their seats and banged the doors shut. "And why did you need me to transfer your stolen goods? Couldn't you get your druggie or surfer boy accomplices to do that?" He turned the key, and the tired little engine puttered back to life.

Chloe noticed that the windshield was still cracked from where the hailstone had clipped it a few months back. "No, and I'm truly sorry to involve you, but the Daedalus Group security team knows Stan and Kirin's cars, and they've been keeping occasional tabs on our movements this last week. I couldn't risk it."

The car backed out of the driveway as Chloe kept an eye on the SUV in the side mirror. "I needed someone I could trust with wheels who was also strong enough to lift that bag without making it look suspicious."

"Don't you think that you're being a little paranoid?" he suggested. "You sure you haven't been hitting your boy Stan's drug stash?" The car leveled out on the road and headed back the way it had come.

A moment later, Chloe felt the bump of the tires as they rolled over the claw marks in the pavement, and she looked back over her shoulder to make sure that the SUV's lights hadn't turned on to follow. There was no sign of pursuit before the SUV passed out of sight behind the trees. She breathed a little easier and turned her attention to Ezra. "Stan's actually been clean for almost a month, and I know this all sounds crazy, but I need you to believe me when I tell you that everything I'm doing is for a very good reason."

The two of them drove down the winding road in silence, heading out of the hills toward the meeting place: the parking lot behind Dunkin Donuts just a half a mile from the Daedalus Group headquarters. Chloe took her cell phone from her pocket and quickly texted Kirin that she was on the way. He was there already, monitoring the purloined Daedalus Group walkie-talkie for any indication of trouble. Moments later, his response arrived: **All's quiet. The whole gang is at the pond as planned. C U soon! ;)**

She snapped the phone shut and felt Ezra's attention on her, though his eyes were glued to the road. Despite it all, she found herself hoping that she looked good in her mom's coat.

"Do me a favor and reach under your seat there," he said, breaking the silence with the beginning of a little smile on his perfect lips.

Chloe did as was instructed and brought up a neatly wrapped package with a makeshift card taped to the front. She raised an eyebrow and handed it toward Ezra.

He shook his head. "Open it; it's for you."

Chloe opened the folded flap of wrapping paper for a card:

Happy Birthday, Lightning!
Here's a little something for the girl who can do anything.
Love, Ezra

Chloe looked over at his wry smile and felt her face getting hot. "How'd you know?"

"Liz told me. I figured I should give it to you today in case you end up in jail for your actual birthday tomorrow," he said with a little twinkle in his eye. "Open it."

She tore open the paper, and her fingers found the smooth surface of well-polished wood. She flipped it over in her hands, admiring the beauty and craftsmanship of the woodwork. It was carved from a single crosscut of a thick tree limb with the natural contours and grain of the wood left intact along the outside edge, but a perfectly cut double opening picture frame in the center.

"I made it in shop class," Ezra mentioned quietly. "Liz told me about the place where you were struck by lightning, and Kendra got me in past the gate. I cut it from a branch of that tree on the hill."

Chloe noticed the blackened scar of the lightning burn on the top edge, and her fingers traced the dark lines toward the two rectangular cuts in the center. "It's beautiful," she observed with a growing lump in her throat. Her attention settled on the two partitioned photos within.

On the left was a picture of her and Ezra on stage as the King and Queen of Homecoming. She was looking up, and he down, to meet each other's gaze in a perfectly captured moment of raw emotion. Between them was a blend of shock, embarrassment, elation, and undeniable affection. On the right was a photo of her dramatic sprint toward the finish line in the state championships. Despite all the pain and torture of that moment, the photographer had somehow managed to capture the ecstatic high and wild beauty in Chloe's face. A perfectly timed lightning bolt was tearing across the sky in the dark clouds behind her, framed almost as if it was an extension of the dark burn on the wood above it.

She had the beginning of tears in her eyes as she hazarded a look back to Ezra. "It's the nicest thing anyone has ever given me," she whispered.

He shrugged with a flash of his heart-stopping smile. "I was inspired by you." His eyes returned to the two pictures. "I know you said you'd never forgive me for Homecoming, but I just wanted you to see that you don't actually look too upset about it there…And I figured you could always use a picture of me to look at before you go to bed at night," he said with a smirk.

Chloe laughed and returned her gaze to the picture. She couldn't come up with an argument to the contrary on either count. *In fact, I look thrilled and you look gorgeous as always.*

"And the other one is the picture that I look at before I go to bed at night," he added. "It makes me remember that I can do anything I set my mind to when I wake up the next day."

"It's the only flattering picture I've seen of that run," Chloe admitted, feeling unworthy of such a gift or the neglected friendship that had given it to her.

Ezra smiled again and returned his attention to the road as they came out of the hills and stopped at a stoplight. "Kendra took it," he said. "Though she really didn't want to give me a copy of it."

"I have to say, she's got a good eye…And her taste in men isn't too shabby either. Thank you. I'll honestly cherish this as long as I live." *Whether it's for a couple more hours or a hundred more years.*

They drove in charged silence for almost a mile before Chloe saw the brightly lit Dunkin Donuts sign come into view a couple blocks ahead. She noticed only then that she'd been hugging the picture frame to her chest the whole way.

"I can't talk you out of whatever you're about to do, can I?" asked Ezra.

Chloe was starting to get scared, but she shook her head anyway. "Nope, just like you said, I've set my mind on this, and I'm going to see it through."

Ezra sighed as the squeaky breaks slowed the car to a halt at a red light. "Okay, then I guess I'm coming with you."

This caught Chloe off guard. "Wait, what? No, you're not!"

He nodded. "Yeah, I am. I've set my mind, too, and I'm pretty sure that you and your little disciples can't stop me."

"Ezra, you have no idea what we're even doing here! If you get caught, then you can kiss college and football good-bye," she counseled. "We're all still minors, but you've already turned eighteen. If you get mixed up in this, then you could spend the next four years in jail!"

"Do you plan to get caught?" Ezra countered.

"No, of course not, but no one plans to—"

"And you said it was important—the most important thing you've ever done," Ezra interrupted. "Well, none of you could even carry that bag of meat anyway, so now that's covered."

"Ezra, you don't understand, we've been planning this for weeks. We have masks and skills, and we're all wearing black!"

He zipped up his Black Knights sweatshirt and popped his hood over his head before reaching over to give her hand a reassuring squeeze. Despite Chloe's inclination to freak out, his touch instantly settled the jangle of her nerves, and she felt like everything might actually be okay. "Don't worry, Chloe. I'm part of your team."

The light turned green.

·   ·   ·

Kirin and Stan didn't know what to say when Ezra Richardson hopped out of the car behind the Dunkin Donuts and slung the meat bag over his shoulder with a twirl of his ever- present football. Without saying a word, he strolled over to Stan's newly renovated van and got in the back seat with a significant dip to the suspension. Chloe was left to deliver a whispered but impassioned argument on his behalf before everyone loaded up and the van roared to life a few awkward moments later.

It was the first time Stan had driven the van since its plummet over the quarry's cliff. It had supposedly passed inspection to be roadworthy, but Chloe could tell that the patchwork repair job was shoddy at best. More importantly, however, it was the one vehicle between the three, now four, of them that the Daedalus Group had not yet seen. And with the new "tough-black" paint job and "borrowed" license plates that came with the repairs, there would be no easy association between it and the Cow Thief quartet that would soon appear on camera in the Daedalus Group parking lot.

Sitting beside Chloe in the second row, Kirin glanced down to the woodcut picture frame that she'd lovingly placed on the seat between them. He shot a look over his shoulder and met Ezra's returned gaze. Neither blinked…until the stolen walkie-talkie in Kirin's grip buzzed to life with a burst of static: "This is Car 1—the Tower is preparing to go live in ten—perimeter status?" said the voice of the security chief that Mr. Roberts had identified as Mr. Duncan the night of the Cow Thief stakeout.

Kirin had found the security team's dialogue on channel 8 after a methodical search that had also stumbled across a far more scientifically minded exchange that was being directed by Dr. Markson's team on channel 4. Kirin and Chloe both stared expectantly at the walkie-talkie with a needlessly exaggerated hush between them, as if someone on the other end might be able to hear them listening in.

"This is Car 2—the gate is clear—over."

"This is Car 3—the nest is empty—beginning area sweep —over."

"This is Car 4—HQ is all clear—over," said the recognizable voice of Brent Meeks.

"This is Air 1—cloud cover is good—low-pressure system coming in from the west—over."

"This is Air 2—standing by at HQ—over."

Chloe's palms were sweaty, and her heart was already going a lot faster than necessary. *Oh my God, this is actually happening!*

"This is Foot 1—the package is secured and freshly sedated—over," said the distinctly bitter voice of Mr. Fitz with the tinny echo of a big room around him.

"This is Car 1—good status—make sure you keep that radio close, Foot 1—over and out," said Mr. Duncan with an edge of mockery.

Chloe and Kirin exchanged a nod in the dark as Stan sped down a more rural road past open fields. "So there's one guard in a car somewhere around the building, another driving around Charlottesville looking for us, and at least one of them on foot inside," Chloe summarized.

"Hey, so what's this all about?" Ezra asked casually

from the rear.

Chloe took the file from Dr. Markson out of her bag and handed it across the seatback. "It's about this. We're busting him out. If you still want in, then stay alert and keep up."

Ezra opened the folder. His brow lowered and he leaned in for a better look. "What the…"

"The dragon's totally drugged," added Stan from the front seat. "How are we gonna move him if we can't wake him up?"

Chloe didn't really have a good answer for that as they drove on in darkness with the sound of the photographs turning behind them. *He'll wake up.*

"Is this for real?" Ezra whispered.

"No one ever said that saving the world would be easy," Kirin declared, just as a bright glow of artificial light came into view across the field ahead. Chloe smiled with a swell of affection. Somehow the four of them together in that van felt right, maybe even powerful—like there was a shared energy ignited between them that was more potent than the sum of the parts. There was nothing more to explain as the van slowed to a crawl and Stan glanced nervously at her in the rearview mirror.

"Just keep going past it at the speed limit," she said quietly. "We'll loop around back by the service entrance, just like the map says."

Stan breathed slowly as the van picked up speed again. They came out of the gloom to a brightly lit stretch of road that took them past the building's main entrance. It was a massive sprawling corporate complex with an expansive employee parking lot off to the side. Only a handful of parked cars were left, clustered around the towering American flag-topped pole beside the walkway. A large, white marble statue of the company's angel wing insignia was bathed in light at the center of the visitor's drop off. A black Suburban with tinted windows was idling by the front.

Chloe instinctively slid lower in her seat. "That's got to be Car 4 with Brent Meeks in it," she whispered as they passed.

The building itself was so brightly lit and clean that it might have mistakenly appeared inviting to the casual observer. But looking past the veneer of polished steel and spotless glass, the whole complex screamed 'GO AWAY!' Cameras were mounted above the main entrance, and the outer façade itself seemed to hum with hidden alarms.

Stan continued at a steady thirty miles an hour, though his knuckles were wrapped around the steering wheel so tightly it looked like he might snap it off from the drive column. Chloe reached up and gave his shoulder a reassuring squeeze. "It's okay; they'll never even know we were here," she stated, though she wasn't sure she believed it herself. Despite her doubts, Stan seemed to relax immediately.

"It's cool, dude; I could just really use a little weed right now is all," Stan muttered as they left the expanse of mirrored windows and steel behind.

Looking back, Chloe could see a large windowless annex off the back with a helicopter sitting on a rooftop landing pad. She glanced down at the schematic of the building in her lap and focused on the place where Dr. Markson had put the big red 'X.' "That's got to be where they're keeping Uktena."

Stan came to a halt at a stop sign with no other cars in sight. Chloe turned around to claim Ezra's attention. "Now you see what we're doing. There's no time to explain more. This is your last chance to get out and hoof it back to Dunkin Donuts."

He closed the folder and gave the football a little twirl before smiling again. "No, I'm cool...Actually, things are starting to make a little more sense."

Chloe wasn't sure what that meant, but oddly she agreed. She returned the smile and turned back to Stan. "Just give it a little gas and take this left. The pull-in for the service entrance is just up the road a couple hundred yards."

Stan looked at her in the rearview. "Just tell me that this isn't completely insane, dude. Tell me it's all going to work out just like we planned."

Chloe swallowed the urge to cough. "I can't tell you that this isn't crazy. It's probably the craziest thing that any of us will ever do. But it's still going to work out just like we planned—it has to."

Stan watched her for a moment longer as the idling engine trembled in anticipation. "Okay." He sighed as the van lurched ahead and made the turn.

Chloe looked down to see Kirin's fingers link with her own on the torn vinyl seat cushion. She squeezed back and felt the swell of courage she needed in that moment to believe what she was saying. *This is all happening for a reason. This is meant to be.*

Stan turned left again, just after a sign that read "**Daedalus Group: Service Entrance and Deliveries.**"

Kirin pulled his hand away from Chloe's and grabbed the box of rubber surgical gloves that he'd lifted from AP Biology. "Gloves and masks," he announced before taking a pair and passing the box on. A moment later and he grinned through the mouth hole of his ski mask.

Chloe and Stan scrambled to follow suit, and when they rolled down the gradual decline toward the back lot, all three were decked out in ski masks and rubber. Ezra struggled with the last glove, unable to pull the stretchy plastic over his king-sized sweaty fingers until the third attempt. Chloe tossed him a black bandanna, and he fastened it around his face like a bandit before giving her a thumbs-up.

Aside from an empty eighteen-wheeler parked beside the dumpsters, there were no other vehicles in the service lot. The giant corrugated metal doors were closed at the four cargo bays, and security cameras were mounted above each one. Chloe looked to the schematic drawing in her lap and saw the spot where Dr. Markson had made a crude pencil drawing of a car. It was positioned directly in the center of a shaded V pattern in the line-of-sight gap between two camera angles.

She pointed past Stan's face. "Pull around wide and come to a stop just on the other side of that lamp post."

Stan did as he was told, and the van came to an abrupt halt before he hastily killed the headlights. They sat in silence for the better part of a minute as nothing happened. Ahead was a little stairwell that led up to an unadorned metal door. A fifth camera was mounted above it, but the corresponding camera on the map had been crossed off with a little 'x,' and the barely legible words "Enter here" were scrawled beside it.

"That's where we go in," said Chloe.

"This kind of seems like the point of no return," Stan mentioned.

"There may be no stopping what's coming whether we do this or not," Chloe countered. "At least this way we have a chance."

Stan removed the key from the ignition, and the van went totally quiet. All four of them stared at the door for a moment longer, trying to gather their courage and wits.

"All right then," said Kirin, breaking the tension. "Just like we planned: I'll get the meat bag, grappling hook, and lock picks, Stan takes the coffee and camera, and Chloe handles the radio and leads the way."

"I'll take the meat," Ezra interjected.

Chloe snapped out of her funk and slid into gear. "Right, Ezra's got the meat. We count to three and then go. Move in a straight line to the stairs and then up and in without hesitation."

"Hold on, dude." Stan unzipped the camera bag on the floor and took out the video camera, now equipped with an extra device with an antenna duct-taped to the bottom. He switched on the camera with a series of beeps and then powered the device beneath with a red light of its own.

"What's that?" Chloe asked, a little wary of added elements that weren't part of the agreed-upon plan.

"Well, I figured that shooting video wouldn't be much of an insurance policy if they could just confiscate the tape like before." He tapped the red blinking box, "So my dad helped me set up a wireless transmitter that streams the footage to a hard drive in my room." Stan smiled beneath his ski mask. "I figure if we get nabbed now, my dad will find the footage and there will at least be a record of what happened to us."

"That's brilliant!" Chloe exclaimed with a supportive punch to Stan's shoulder.

Stan winced. "Thanks."

"Okay, is everyone ready?" she prepped. The others secured backpacks and grabbed their assigned gear before nodding.

"Then we go on three…One, two, three—" All at once, doors opened and the team spilled out. Chloe led the way and they fell in line, scurrying across the pavement with eyes and camera swinging back and forth. Ezra wasn't even slowed up the steps with the eighty pounds of meat slung over his shoulder. At the top, Chloe wrapped her gloved fingers around the cold, metal handle of the door and yanked.

The darkness was flooded by the overlit fluorescent glow from within. The foursome scrambled in and closed the door behind them with an abrupt click that echoed down the empty white hallway. They froze, allowing themselves the luxury of a joint exhale as their eyes adjusted to the brightness. The path before them was lined with a series of closed doors marked only by numbers and letters corresponding to the layout of rooms on the schematic diagram.

Chloe clipped the walkie-talkie to the belt at her hip and affixed the earphone jack to her head with a bendy microphone that protruded annoyingly in front of her face. She curled it away, foreseeing no good reason to broadcast her voice to the entire Daedalus Group security team. From over her shoulder, she met Kirin's and Ezra's wide-eyed gazes with a nod, and then she caught her own reflection in the lens of Stan's camera. Her freaked-out eyes stared back at her from within the eyeholes of her mask, and telltale strands of brown hair jutted out of the neckline in a way that made it seem obvious that she was just a little girl far out of her element.

She thought for a moment about all of the tragic stories she always heard about on the news, where reckless kids got themselves, or each other, killed in profound acts of brazen stupidity. But she brushed that aside, and after her best imitation of a hand motion for 'tactical advance,' they moved forward down the hallway.

A series of arrows had been drawn on the map, intended to lead them on a circuitous route to the red 'X' in the center of the warehouse-sized room. There was a much more direct path from the main freight entrance to get where they needed to go, but little camera icons dotted that way at every turn. Instead, when they reached the intersection, she paused to listen and then looked both ways before leading them to the right and away from their goal. Chloe wondered if maybe Dr. Markson had himself walked this path in a test run a few weeks prior.

"This is Car 1—the Tower is going live now—over," came the voice of the security chief in Chloe's ear.

"Copy that—Air 1 is picking up increased electromagnetic field currents across the area—be advised, they're saying it may cause intermittent disturbances with our camera and radio feeds—over."

"Copy that, Air 1—all units on standby—over and out."

Chloe heard the distant rumble of thunder, followed by the distinct impression of Uktena stirring nearby. She stopped at the next intersection to check the map and give Ezra a moment to rest. He slid the bag off his shoulder and leaned against the wall with a deft twirl of the football.

"You brought the football?" Chloe whispered.

"It helps me think," he answered from behind the bandanna.

She shrugged and addressed the team. "The tower is going operational now. That should give us some time. We take a left here and another left at the end of the hall, and then we should be close...Let's get ready to move out." A part of her had to admit that she was really enjoying this.

She peeked around the corner, just as Kirin grabbed her by the shoulder and pulled her back. He pointed toward the ceiling, and both Chloe's eyes and Stan's lens followed his finger to the camera above them as it swiveled back and forth between the two hallways. They watched as it slowly swung back in the other direction before it began its gradual return to the stretch they had to clear.

"Dude, maybe someone else should carry the map," Stan suggested with a nervous chuckle.

Chloe glanced down to the corresponding intersection and saw no sign of a camera there. "This camera isn't on the map," she said in her defense.

"They must have added more security ahead of the test," Kirin observed.

Stan's quiet chuckle took on a desperate edge. "Or, I don't know, it might have something to do with the hundred-foot-long monster hanging out a few rooms over."

Chloe tracked the camera's movement, waiting for the instant it swiveled away from the target hallway. *One, two, three, four, five, six, seven, eight.* She met Ezra's gaze. "Do you think you can clear this hallway in about eight seconds?"

Ezra waited for the camera to turn again before poking his head out. "With an extra eighty pounds…it'll be close," he admitted.

Chloe nodded in agreement and turned back to the camera. This time, she counted out loud—getting the timing down. "One, two, three, four, five, six, seven, eight." And then again, "One, two, three," the others joined in, "four, five, six, seven, eight."

"Got it?" she asked. They nodded. She looked to Ezra. "All right, when I say GO, you take off along the left wall and start counting." Her look shifted to Kirin and the watching lens, "Kirin, then Stan, you follow after and pass him on the right, but don't slow him down. I'll be on your heels, and when I go by," her eyes slid back to Ezra, "you lock on my pace for the rest of the way."

Ezra smiled. "I know that pace well."

"My queen, it will be done," whispered Stan with a grin and a salute.

Chloe grinned too. "Good, now shut up and get ready."

Ezra returned the straps to his shoulder and positioned the weight for the sprint; the football was in the crook of his arm, just like another day on the field. All four of them tracked the swivel of the security camera and counted in unison for two full passes.

"Ready?" said Chloe as they all braced for the starter's gun. "GO," she barked as Ezra shot around the corner and the world slipped into motion.

"One, two, three," Chloe was counting out loud as she tore down the hall behind the others. Ezra had gotten off well, but he was already starting to lurch. "Four, five, six," Kirin and Stan blew past him on the right and skidded around the corner ahead as Chloe locked into step just ahead of Ezra and picked up the pace. "Seven, EIGHT," they lunged around the corner together and banged into the far wall before coming to a heaving stop.

Ezra dropped the bag and put his hands on his knees as Chloe gave him a pat on the shoulder. "I think we made it," she whispered.

Kirin smirked. "You're kind of a badass, huh?"

Stan's camera was zoomed in on the end of the new hallway. "Uh, guys?"

Chloe followed his focus and saw another identical security camera swinging their way. A jolt of panic fired through her, and without knowing what she was doing, she reached toward the ceiling as her hand began to vibrate painfully. She recalled the frequency from her lightning dream, the feeling that the molecules of her fingers might come apart or burn away—and in that instant, a deafening crack answered from above. The hall went dark.

Everything was pitch black for a moment before red emergency lights flickered on every ten feet along the hallway. The security camera had stopped moving. They all just stood there, dumbfounded.

Stan lowered his camera. "Holy shit!" he yelped without any attempt at caution.

Chloe was light-headed as a deep, resonant grumble rose from her belly to echo the thunderclap that rolled out from above. Just then voices started to clamor in her ear.

"This is Foot 1—we've had a direct lightning hit on HQ—I think we fried a transformer, and we've lost the camera feed—standby," said Mr. Fitz in an exasperated voice.

"This is Car 1 to Foot 1—let me know when the back-up generator kicks in." Mr. Duncan's tone was unflappable.

"Copy that," answered Mr. Fitz.

"We've got to move," Kirin announced as he grabbed Chloe's shoulders and pushed her down the darkened passage. The others followed without question as the voices continued to banter in Chloe's ear.

"This is Car 1 to Air 2—status?"

"My whole body is tingling, but I'm okay, I think," said Air 2, with a shake in his voice. "That wasn't more than fifty feet from me!"

Chloe shook it off and scanned the map midrun. Dr. Markson's next penciled arrow passed through a rectangular icon in the wall that corresponded to the imposing metal door that loomed ahead. They came to a panicky halt before it as all eyes fell to the perfectly polished knob and the brand-new ten-digit keypad on the wall beside it.

"Kirin?" Chloe pleaded.

"What?" he said, taking his reassuring hands from her shoulders and leaning in to the keypad. There was no keyhole. "I got nothing for that!"

"Maybe it's Kendra's birthday again?" said Stan hopefully.

Chloe actually reached her gloved fingers out and tried: 10—17—1. She half expected the little status light above the numbers to start flashing red just before the alarm went off, or maybe nets would shoot down from the ceiling. But nothing happened at all, just the continued low hum of the red emergency fluorescents and the sound of Ezra's heavy breathing at her shoulder.

"This is Foot 1—the backup generator will be up in ten seconds—over."

"What do we do?" she asked desperately.

"The grappling hook!" barked Stan. "We climb up to the ceiling and go in through the ventilation system like in the movies!"

Kirin didn't seem to hear either of them. He turned his furrowed brow away from the stagnant camera above and reached out to the doorknob. It opened without resistance, revealing a continuation of darkened space with hazy pockets of the bloodred glow within. "How about that?"

"Go," barked Chloe as she pushed them through the door and quickly latched it again behind her. The main lights clicked back on a second later, and all four of them cringed beneath the comparatively blinding onslaught. Before she could even fully see, Chloe found that her arms had wrapped around Kirin in a bear hug as they jumped up and down.

"That was ridiculous!" exclaimed Stan, with the full spread of his horse grin returned for the first time in weeks. "That's got to be less likely than winning the lottery."

"Maybe it was the dragon," said Kirin. "Nai Nai always said that to be in a dragon's favor is to be blessed by great fortune."

"No, man, I saw what happened," Ezra said, stepping closer to Chloe. "You put your hand up to the sky; I could feel the charge coming off you...You called that lightning, didn't you?"

Chloe shrugged. "I don't know, maybe?" The others waited for more. "I've been having weird dreams about turning into living electricity, and this was kind of like how it felt in the dream. In the moment, it just made sense."

The others were silent, until Stan spoke up from behind the camera. "Dude, I've been having strange dreams about flying and becoming a tornado."

"I've been dreaming about water—actually being the ocean itself—and in one, I become a tidal wave," said Kirin.

Ezra was still skeptical, but he was nodding. "Yeah, me too, but mine is about an earthquake, and I'm making something to harness whatever is coming up from below."

Realization struck Chloe. "It's the dragons, the Five Claws."

"And it's just like Nai Nai's story about the xian," Kirin added.

"Hey guys, check it out," said Stan.

They were in what appeared to be an observation deck with a full wall of windows that overlooked a massive two-story room that stretched below. There was an impressive array of cameras on tripods spread out along the window. Each had a long lens pointed down and a thick bundle of cables that snaked out to feed the various monitor banks on the opposite wall. It looked like a lot of money had been spent here very recently. As they watched, the cameras and monitors clicked to life as the full electrical feed came back online.

But the fancy AV equipment didn't do justice to the subject below. In unison, the team moved to the window and looked down at the huge shape sprawled across the stone floor. None of them said a word as they took in the sight of the dragon. The boys were stunned by the sheer majesty of the creature before them, but Chloe was shocked to silence by the sickly grey color and waxy sheen that had come over him.

Uktena was smaller than she remembered, shriveled and old compared to the way he'd looked when he'd first emerged from the pond. His back rose and fell with the ponderous effort of every breath, and his once bright, piercing eyes had been reduced to half-closed slits that held none of the vitality or intelligence that she'd last seen there.

Ezra was speechless.

Stan scratched his knit-covered head. "Duuude."

"He's magnificent," Kirin added.

"He's dying," Chloe countered. "We need to get down there."

"Chloe," Kirin said gently with a cautionary hand on her arm. "There are bound to be people watching those camera feeds. How do we get close without setting off every alarm in the building?"

Chloe didn't know, but stalling any longer wasn't an option. Her eyes scanned the room, looking for an idea. They settled on the coat rack by the door that led to the stairwell down. Every hook was fitted with a white, full-body hazmat suit…

CHAPTER 30
BUSTING OUT

Mr. Derek Fitz sat within the curved bank of video monitors in the security epicenter of the building, but his eyes were glued to the newly downloaded porn playing silently on his laptop instead. He was tuned out to the constant chatter of the science geeks jabbering away on channel 4 in one ear, while waiting for the next officious announcement from that blowhard Mr. Duncan in the other. He was sick of it.

In his early twenties, Mr. Fitz had been a guard at the maximum-security wing of Sing Sing Prison. Once he'd dropped two men with a rifle from a hundred yards as they'd tried to escape under a fence, and another time he'd gone in hard with nothing but a plastic shield and a baton to stop a riot in progress, and he'd liked it.

In his early thirties, he'd joined Blackwater Securities and done two tours in Iraq, running protection for dignitaries and securing trucking convoys through the worst parts of Baghdad. He'd been with a team of real heavy hitters then, South African mercs and ex-Soviet commandos who loved to use knives. That had been the best job of his life, right up until some pantywaist in the Army turned him and the boys in for giving a family of terrorists exactly what they deserved.

Now he was here, stuck in Podunk, Virginia, on a team of tough-guy-wannabes and sitting on the bench at that. He knew it was that little McClellan girl who'd taken his radio, and he dreamed of smacking that smug look off her cute little face and showing her who was boss. Maybe he could teach her unbelievably hot mom a thing or two while he was at it…

He looked up from his computer and scanned the monitors around him. The power was steady again, but he was keeping the backup generator online just in case. Aside from the occasional shuffling by of some office drone or tech nerd, the hallways and parking lots were empty tonight, but then his eyes flitted back to the hulking shape of the sleeping *thing*. Even now, weeks later, it still freaked him out. There was simply no way that such a creature, whatever the hell it might be, should be able to exist— it wasn't natural!

He didn't know why they hadn't killed it on day one and cut it open to see what made it tick. Instead, they made him sign the longest nondisclosure agreement he'd ever seen. And every day since, he'd watched as they fed it, washed it, and kept it drugged but alive. As he scanned the various close-up angles, another team of white-coat lab geeks stepped into the shot with a heaping cart of raw meat. He shuddered as the sleeping thing's jaws opened in anticipation with some unconscious response to the stink of flesh. As the first hunk of meat was thrown, the jaws snapped shut like a giant bear trap, and the little dork in white actually jumped back. Then the long rows of sharp teeth slowly opened again...The sight of it feeding turned his stomach every time.

Mr. Fitz glanced to the assault rifle leaning against the desk, and he had the impulse to walk down there and put a bullet square in the center of the thing's diamond-shaped head. But he knew that if he did that, he'd be stuck in nine tiers of legal hell for the rest of his damned life...If he didn't find a way to burn off some of this steam soon, he was going to get himself into trouble one way or another. With a last hateful glance, he swiveled his chair away and returned his eyes to the girls on the computer.

. . .

Stan tossed another hunk of semifrozen meat, and again the jaws snapped shut with enough force to blast a jet of hot air in his thankfully covered face. He shot Chloe a wide-eyed look over his shoulder, and she gave him a reassuring nod.

"Just keep it going, and remember to act like this is all part of the routine," she encouraged before wheeling a cart laden with unidentifiable electronic equipment past him. The front wheel wobbled and squeaked as she moved down the length of Uktena's splayed form. Up close, she could see that what had looked like a dull, mottled coloring to his scales from afar was really a patchy translucence that had spread across his hide. With every breath, she could hear the thick rattle of gunk in his lungs, like rocks grinding together. She wanted to put her hands against him, beg for him to wake, wondering if her desperate shouts might rouse him from the drug-induced torpor that had taken hold, but she knew that wouldn't help.

Instead, she tried to appear clinical and indifferent as she continued to push the cart toward Uktena's heavily chained back haunches. Kirin and Ezra walked behind her, both of them painfully aware of the many cameras trained on their backs and the likelihood that someone was probably watching them at that very moment. Using his back to shield his hands, Kirin slipped his lock-picking set from his waistline and palmed his largest torsion wrench and his luckiest pick for heavy-duty padlocks.

The head-sized lock that secured the thick, iron cuff around the dragon's ankle was bigger and far more impressive than anything he had previously tackled. The giant, obsidian-clawed foot that it held at bay was another concern altogether. Kirin's hands were shaking as they drew close. Chloe maneuvered the cart to block him and then made a show of turning the machine on and flipping an array of switches. It protested with a series of offended beeps before achieving a steady green line on a digital wavelength screen. She came around the back and handed Kirin a couple of protruding electrodes before motioning toward the lock.

"Good luck," she whispered with a helpful smile from behind the plastic of the mask. "And hurry up," she added with an unhelpful wink before turning to meet Ezra's close analysis of the dragon's spinal structure.

Ezra had purloined a clipboard with graph paper and had

drawn a surprisingly accurate depiction of Uktena's back. He seemed to be measuring the length from the floor to the bony ridge that Chloe had clung to in the dream.

"Anything of concern, Dr. Richardson?" she asked.

"Doesn't it seem like you could climb up and sit right there," he suggested with a point. "Almost like it was meant to be ridden?"

"Yes, it does," she answered with a meaningless notation on her own clipboard. "And just for the record, I'm really glad you came with us tonight."

"Me too," he answered with a nod. "I think I'm meant to be a part of it."

"Doctor," Stan called from the other end, bringing Chloe at a swift walk. He was almost done with the meat, but this time as the monstrous jaws opened, Stan thought that he saw a ripple of blue spark in the dark recess of its gullet. He swung the camera up with his other hand to catch it, but it was too late. He took a wary step back, noticing that one of its oddly blue lizard eyes had opened slightly, but there was a milky film across the surface and the black slit in the center remained unfocused.

"Any change?" Chloe asked as she came up beside him. She fought back the urge to glance at the wall of cameras facing her.

"I thought I saw something, but I'm not sure," muttered Stan. "Do you think I should give him the espresso bomb?"

Chloe looked into Uktena's sickly eye for a long moment without answering. "No, finish with the meat first and hopefully he'll respond...I'm not really sure what caffeine will do to him," she admitted with another deliberate but meaningless notation.

"Righto," Stan answered as the fanged maw scissored wide again.

The voices in Chloe's ear crackled to life. "This is Car 4—I've got an empty black van in the freight lot that wasn't here on my last pass—do you have it on camera, Foot 1?" asked Brent, trying to sound professional and not quite pulling it off.

Chloe's eyes bugged and her breath locked in her throat.

The weasely voice of Mr. Fitz came next. "That's a negative, Car 4—it doesn't show up on any of my angles."

Mr. Duncan chimed in. "Car 4, take a closer look and run the plates on the scanner."

"Copy that," answered Brent as Chloe snapped out of her temporary paralysis.

"We might need to speed this up." She tried to remain calm. "They've found the van."

Stan was sweating heavily and the visor of his hazmat helmet was fogging. He tried to think through any incriminating evidence in the car. "It's cool, dude," he reassured. "There's nothing there to give us away."

Chloe shut her eyes and gritted her teeth. *DAMN! DAMN! DAMN!* She could clearly imagine Brent leaning into the van's tinted windows just as the beam from his high-powered flashlight came to rest on the perfectly framed photos of her resting face up on the back seat...There was a long pause on the radio.

"Uh, Foot 1, this is Car 4—we may have a problem—do you have anything strange on any of your cameras?—over," asked Brent Meeks with a nervous edge.

"What am I looking for here?—over," pushed Mr. Fitz.

There was another long pause as Brent thought about how to answer. Chloe's heart pounded with almost enough vigor to break a rib.

"I'm not sure, Foot 1—anyone who isn't supposed to be there?—over."

We are totally screwed! "They're looking for us!" Chloe blurted out as Stan's head whipped around, and Kirin's masked face popped up from behind the machine.

Just then, another voice crackled across the line. "Hi, uh, security team?—This is Dr. Markson—we're right in the middle of this thing, and I'm picking up cross-chatter from you guys— I'm going to need you to switch to a different channel."

Dr. Markson is trying to buy us time. "Change of plan! Give him the espresso bomb now!" Chloe announced.

"Are they coming?" Kirin hissed from the other end of the dragon. His eyes remained calm, but the visor of his mask sucked in and out at a rapid clip.

"This is Car 1—I want a full team switch to channel 15

on three."

"Not yet, but it won't be long!" Chloe answered across the vast room with an unfortunate echo.

"One—two—three," said Mr. Duncan in her ear before the line went quiet.

Chloe watched Stan throw the last hunk of meat into Uktena's snapping jaws before she switched the walkie-talkie dial to channel 15.

"This is Car 1—Car 4, did you get an ID on the plates yet—copy?" said Mr. Duncan in her ear.

"Yes," answered Brent. "The plates were last registered to a Dodge Ram owned by a Milford Boone in 2003—but I think—"

"Car 4—I want you to try the doors," interrupted Mr. Duncan.

"Sir—is that legal?" asked Brent.

Chloe watched as Stan plucked the ten-pound sack of ground espresso from the lower level of the rolling cart and hesitated as the jaws cranked open again. "It's in a plastic bag. Do I just throw it all in there?" She could no longer see his face past the fog across his visor.

The chatter continued in Chloe's ear. "Car 4, this is Car 1—for the duration of this test, that car is on government property without permit—I want you to gain entry to the vehicle and perform a thorough search immediately—copy?"

"Copy that," said Brent with a nervous hitch in his voice.

"Just open one end and toss it in," Chloe urged as the scrape of metal on metal sounded from the dragon's rear leg.

"Damn," Kirin hissed from behind the continually flat-lining machine.

Stan yanked his hazmat helmet up to rest on his forehead and gulped fresh air.

"Stan, the cameras!" Chloe reminded.

"Dude, I can't see anything." He opened one end of the golden bag with the immediate release of a strong waft of coffee, and stepped closer to the bared fangs than he'd yet dared. With a delicate toss, the bag went in with the same snapping response. He quickly moved back beside Chloe as she made another fake notation on her clipboard.

"Sir—this is Car 4," Brent coughed before the line went silent a moment.

"Go Car 4?" pressed Mr. Duncan impatiently.

"Sir, I've searched the car—I have reason to believe that… someone may be illegally on the premises—over," said Brent, like he didn't want to admit it.

"Foot 1—do you have anything on the cameras?" Mr. Duncan asked, just as a loud, heaving grunt came from Uktena's throat and a fast-moving cloud of brown dust and hot wind enveloped Chloe and Stan.

Chloe's facemask went dark, but Stan's entire helmet flew off his head as he doubled over with his hands to his face. "Dude!"

Kirin and Ezra looked up to see that the white suits of their accomplices were now coated with a thick, brown layer of coffee dust and viscous goo. The dragon shut its mouth with a deep internal grumble before slumping back to its unresponsive state.

Chloe wiped gunk and grit from her visor as the voices in the earbud chimed again.

"This is Foot 1—yeah, I've got something weird going on by the package!" announced Mr. Fitz. "It just emitted some sort of ash cloud—and the lab techs that are in there feeding him are acting kind of strange—I'm switching cameras—over."

"This is Car 1—there is no scheduled feeding for this evening—Repeat—there is no authorized feeding tonight!—over!" declared Mr. Duncan.

"They've seen us!" Chloe blurted with an involuntary glance back to the wall of cameras. She could practically feel Mr. Fitz's eyes lock on to her via close-up.

"I think it's the McClellan girl!" spat Mr. Fitz over the line, ignoring protocol. "And she's got my radio!"

. . .

Uktena's mind stirred from deep within the drug-induced fog. He had tried and failed to reach outside of the prison of his form again and again—more alone in these last days before the

Ascension than he had ever been in the centuries of dreaming before it. From beneath the pond, his perception had wandered the cosmos without constraint; he had listened to the yearnings of animals, plants, and men, and had explored galaxy after galaxy filled with the dead planets beyond.

Over the passing of ages, he had learned of the terrors of the black rifts that moved invisibly through the universe, and he'd explored vast pockets of space with nothing but the darkness and cold to fill it. He had read the thoughts of killers and madmen, and he'd known what it was to be rabid and dying. But above all that, it was the recent silence of being locked away inside himself that terrified him most. The poison they'd put in his food and shot into his blood had kept him from action or escape. He had come to accept that it would be his own death that would soon mark the beginning of the end for mankind. That was what the prophecy had meant all those years ago. Finally the hubris of humanity would kill the spirit of the land—him.

But this time, as the boiling acid in his stomach leached the nutrients from his meal, he knew that something was different. He had not been able to stop his body from the mechanical act of eating, even when he'd known that the food he ingested would only hasten his demise. But now the food in his belly lacked the toxins that he'd come to expect. It was pure and natural, and it sent the hint of a spark through his gut. He felt the tickle of static collecting there as the heavy film that had hung over his perceptions began to thin. Though his eyes still wouldn't focus, his thoughts found the hazy presence of the Child Queen standing before him, and though he knew such thoughts were foolish, he felt an instinctive urge to survive.

He tried to raise his head to speak, but his body still wouldn't respond to his command. He tried to grasp her mind with his own, but still there was an infuriating distance he could not cross. Instead, he felt the gathering of energy from within as the tingling hum traveled up through his blood to focus on the diamond-shaped plate between his horns.

.   .   .

An alarm sounded throughout the building, and a red light had started to spin across the far wall. Chloe knew that at that moment people with guns were on their way toward her, but she stilled the urge to run, drawn instead to the glow of white light that pulsed within Uktena's forehead. She stepped closer and realized that the light was made by ripples of electricity flaring beneath the fine layering of scales that rose from the dragon's brow. For a moment, she was mesmerized by the current's dance.

Stan squinted through coffee-coated lashes at the red spiral on the wall. "Guys?"

No one answered. Kirin remained hunched over Uktena's back claw, continuing to scrape and mutter as he worked frantically on the unresponsive lock, while Ezra took off his helmet and palmed the football again—scanning the room for assets and exits. Chloe had gone completely deaf to the stern exchange that continued in her ear. The shining diamond beckoned to her as her feet brought her closer. *It's the only way.*

She couldn't sense Uktena in her thoughts as she ripped off the helmet and rubber gloves that came between them. She stepped close enough to feel the slump of his lower jaw against her knee. There was a sickly stale musk in the dragon's breath, and Chloe's fingers trembled as she reached toward the light. *It's not magic; it's just science we don't comprehend yet.*

"Guys, should we be running?" Stan asked.

Chloe touched the smooth, warm scales with just her fingertips at first, and then she pressed her whole palm against the diamond plate and felt the same sort of tingling as when she folded laundry fresh out of the dryer. She wasn't sure what she'd expected to happen…but nothing did.

.   .   .

Brent tried the handle of the outside door beside the loading dock, and it clicked open without resistance. He would have stopped to ponder how a couple of teenagers had gotten through one of the most advanced locks that corporate money could buy, but there wasn't time. He wasn't sure why he hadn't told Mr. Duncan that it was Chloe inside, but he knew that if Derek Fitz got to her first, something bad would happen.

"This is Car 1, en route to HQ—secure the package and contain all intruders—Mr. Roberts is coming in on Air 1—copy," said Mr. Duncan with the sound of a speeding engine behind him.

"This is Car 4—moving in on the package from the freight entrance—I'll be there in three minutes—over," Brent said, on the run.

"I'm at the door!" bellowed Mr. Fitz over the line with a loud banging as punctuation. "They've barricaded it with something!" he added furiously.

"Get in there NOW," commanded Mr. Duncan as Brent rounded another corner and started to sprint toward the enormous freight door that they'd brought the creature in through. Though he'd never realized it until now, he couldn't bear the thought of Chloe being hurt. She was annoying and had pretty much ruined everything, but Brent still loved Audrey McClellan, and loving her meant loving her daughter as well.

He'd even contemplated lying to Mr. Duncan at the van, saying the car was clean, and continuing on his way. But the pay-to-effort ratio of this job was astounding, and despite the fact that he kept screwing things up, at his core, Brent wanted to do the right thing. He just wasn't sure what was right anymore. For some reason, even though he'd done his job well, once again he felt like things were going all wrong.

He came to a halt before the thirty-foot-tall, corrugated metal door that had recently been fortified with all manners of backup security. He had no idea how to open it and doubted that he even had the security clearance to do so, but he had to get in there first. He had to help Chloe before that lunatic got to her.

* * *

There was a loud, repetitive banging coming from the camera room above. Ezra had had the brilliant idea of barricading the entrance with the heavy bank of video monitors before they'd descended the stairs in their white plastic suits. The whole array of built-in screens had been rolled away from the wall and tipped back onto its side. Chloe had worried then that this might seal them in when it came time to leave with Uktena. Now she was increasingly terrified that it wouldn't buy them enough time.

Her hand pulsed red with the bright light of the diamond burning through it, and she could feel the building vibration of the voltage just beneath her skin. But Uktena hadn't moved from his wilted and sickly state, and Chloe had run out of ideas.

"YES!" shouted Kirin triumphantly. There was a metallic click, and he bolted up at the other end of the dragon with the open lock brandished over his head. He lowered the prize as he heard the violent clanging above, and he tossed it unceremoniously to the floor when he saw the desperation on Chloe's face. "You have to make a wish!" he yelled. "Like the dragon said!"

Chloe leaned in toward the increasingly intense radiance before her. She was starting to get dizzy, and her whole body had begun to tingle as her hair stood on end. Now it felt the way it had when she'd once grabbed hold of an electric cow fence just to see how long she could hold on, but this time there was no jolt of pain with the odd floating sensation.

She clenched her eyes shut, but still the bright glare of the diamond's light seared through her lids.

"Dude, what's that light? I'm not getting this on camera," Stan mentioned.

But Chloe couldn't acknowledge the outside world. All that mattered was Uktena and the belief that somehow she could make a difference. "You can't let humanity die," she whispered.

The deafening report of semiautomatic gunfire erupted from the camera room above as bullets tore through the door and shredded the monitor bank behind it. Stan, Ezra, and Kirin dropped to the floor and covered their heads, but Chloe remained transfixed before the unmoving dragon.

"Please, I need you to help us!" she pleaded.

"WISH IT!" screamed Kirin from his hiding place.

"Uktena, I wish you would live...wake up and help us to save humanity," she said just as the door was wrenched open above and Mr. Fitz squeezed through with furious eyes and a smoking rifle.

Uktena's lids snapped open, and the black slits in his eyes thinned on Chloe. "MOVE!" boomed the deep grumble of his voice as his focus shifted over her shoulder.

Chloe looked back to see Mr. Fitz raise the rifle and take aim toward her. Just as she dove to the side, a blinding spear of lightning shot out from Uktena's jaws to connect with the glass façade above. The camera room imploded just as Mr. Fitz dropped behind the observational seating. Glass shards flew everywhere, seat cushions burst into flame, and the monitors were reduced to sparking hunks of circuit board and melted plastic.

Below, the sound of the blast was still ringing in their ears, louder than the gunshots by tenfold, which had only moments before seemed like the loudest thing that any of the boys had ever heard. Chloe, however, hadn't heard a thing. She remained on the floor with her body clenched with residual spasms of electricity coursing through her. She couldn't see past the blazing white streak that had burned across her corneas, and her ears were dead to the outer world...But in the surprising internal stillness of that protracted moment, her mind bloomed with a heightened sense of awareness that she'd never before dreamed possible.

All at once, she knew the thoughts and emotions of those around her:

Dude, I can't see shit! Stan thought as he crawled across the floor, searching for someplace to hide. *If we get out of this, I'm gonna get so high!* Then Chloe's attention drifted up and out of the building to find the distant approach of another vast consciousness high above. Something old and wise hurtled through the cold of space with the colorful beacon of Earth growing larger ahead, and the winds of change trailed behind it through the vacuum.

We need to make a break for that door! Ezra thought as he set his sights on an 'EXIT' sign at the top of a metal staircase against the far wall. *I can carry both Chloe and Stan up those stairs if I have to!* And as he moved to put his plan to action, Chloe's attention burrowed deep underground to the vantage of a hulking beast as it dug its way up through rock and magma from the center of the world. The phrase *I am the Iron King, I am the Iron King, I am the Iron King* was growled over and over with every earth-rending swipe of its colossal claws.

Then the repetition morphed into *Please let Chloe be okay! Please let Chloe be okay! Please let Chloe be okay!* as Kirin frantically scrambled toward her. She saw herself through Kirin's worried gaze—smoldering on the floor, with the walkie-talkie smoking at her hip and her lips turned almost the same blue as her eyes... Was she dead? But before he could get close enough to find out, her perception swam away, and she found herself instead in a bottomless well of anger. Something immense, ancient, and wicked stirred within the deepest cleft of the ocean floor, and the earth trembled with dread.

Then her perception jumped before a raging fire in an ornate fireplace. A familiar high-pitched voice sang along to an unfamiliar pop song blaring on a radio. *Baby, you know that I got what you like. Come a little closer, it's like riding a bike.* Just as the scene was coming into focus, Chloe was sucked into the flames. Her thoughts settled instead on the other side of the world— trapped within the hottest furnace of the land. There, a burning presence more powerful still lashed against the prison of stone that had long contained it. It listened to the terrified screams of thousands of human voices high above and found joy in their pain. In that dreadful moment, Chloe possessed both the exultation and horror of what would come.

YOU MUST RISE! commanded Uktena with a will that sliced through all the others and brought Chloe back into herself. She blinked and saw the room around her once more, just white and blurry at first, but then a giant blue eye came into focus above.

Her tongue felt too big for her mouth, and she was profoundly shaken by what she had seen. "They're coming."

A hot, heavy breath huffed out of the side of Uktena's jaws and tousled her hair. "Yes, you have begun to hear the thoughts of the others, just as I have long listened to your pondering," he answered in a voice that seemed to carry both a deep rumble and a soft whisper at the same time. "You carry the spirit of the land inside you, like the Elementalists of old who put me to sleep beneath the water and soil." He eyed her closely. "This is how you woke me before the Ascension. Now I see it."

Chloe didn't have a response for that. Her head was spinning as she tried to sit up, and then Kirin was suddenly beside her with his arm around her waist. "Are you okay?" he whispered in her ear.

Chloe nodded. "I think so." She looked back to the watching blue eye. "What can we do?"

"We must go," announced the dragon above them with his head cocked to listen. "The wicked men come with anger and fear. Their projectiles could pierce my hide in this weakened state."

Kirin tried to ignore the fact that a dragon had just spoken as he supported Chloe's weight and helped her to unsteady feet. "Can you stand on your own?" he asked, gently brushing aside the hair that clung to her forehead.

She nodded and he tentatively let her go. "He's looking at you expectantly," Kirin added as they both glanced up to meet the returned intensity in Uktena's gaze. The focus of that one glacial eye encompassed them both.

Chloe gave a last squeeze of Kirin's hand. "Help Stan," she suggested as she tried to shake off the residual fog of having multiple minds, both familiar and alien, sharing in her perception.

Kirin moved to take the coffee-coated camera from Stan while he blindly struggled to strip off his brown gloves. Chloe watched them for a second with a sense of understanding she'd not felt before—she was bound to these boys, had known their hearts from within. Was this how the dragon felt about her? And what of the exhilarating and terrible glimpse of the other dragons? Could they still be stopped? None of it would matter if they couldn't find a way out of this room.

There was a wide, corrugated metal wall designed to rise and slide across the ceiling, like an oversized garage door. But one look at the complex touch panel told her that there would be no easy clicker to open it. Her eyes shot up to the shattered observatory, and just then the overhead sprinkler system switched on with a spray of cold water raining down across the room. "How do we get out of here?" she asked Uktena.

But it was Ezra who stepped beside her with the answer. "Over there."

In the far corner of the room, a metal stairwell rose sharply to an exit for the roof. There was another touch-panel lock and a sign that read "HELIPAD" beside it.

"Sometimes they come and go through that door, from the bladed machines that land above," Uktena said.

"Can you change into your human form?" she suggested.

The dragon's head dipped with the hint of shame. "I am still too weak." Then he extended his long neck to examine the white featureless ceiling. "Go through the door and stand aside. I will break through here and join you above."

Kirin cleared his throat and spoke up. "I can tell from here that that door is locked, and there is honestly no way I can get through it in time."

Uktena peered at him for a second and then angled his head to regard Stan, who was staring up at him through squinty eyes with an enormous grin. Coffee was streaked across his face in brown lines. "Dude, are you getting this?" he whispered to Kirin while reaching for the camera.

The dragon turned back to the door with a resonant inhale. His chest and throat expanded rapidly before another brilliant stab of lightning blew the door outward off its hinges. The humans all flinched half a second later as the room shook with an extraordinary BANG!

GO! Uktena commanded directly into their minds, past the ringing in their ears. Ezra nudged Chloe ahead, and soon all four of them had started to run. They could hear a muffled thwopping from above as Chloe led the way up the steps two at a time. She glanced behind her to see Ezra following with calm determination while Kirin guided Stan stumbling up the stairs in the rear with his camera still held on the action behind him.

That was when Mr. Fitz popped up from beneath the shattered windowsill and opened fire. The dragon flinched as bullets smacked into him, and his accompanying roar made the whole room vibrate. He unfurled his leathery wings and ducked beneath while the bullets continued to tear through.

Kirin wasn't sure what was happening as his eyes glazed over and an intense pressure gathered in his inner ears. No longer could he sense his feet pounding up the stairs or his hand clinging to the metal railing. Instead, he felt that he was spread all across the room, gathering in puddles on the floor and falling through the air from the ceiling. He was underwater and yet somehow the water itself—every drop was a part of him, ready to answer his call. And at once, all of it, all of him, rushed toward the man with the gun.

Stan kept recording as an inexplicable rogue wave gathered from the floor and crashed through the shattered window of the observatory. Mr. Fitz was thrown back in a tumbling heap, and the remnants of the fires that had started there were instantly snuffed out.

With the momentary reprieve, Uktena extended the massive reach of his wingspan to fill the room before whipping the spiked outer strut of his right wing through the wall of the observation deck. The already-broken space was completely bisected as large chunks of the upper floor fell away and the steel eyebeam in the far wall was bent outward. The dragon wrenched the wing from the sparking heap, and a clutter of camera equipment and the wreckage of a sofa tumbled out with it. There was no sign of Mr. Fitz amid the ruin.

The dragon peered back to give Kirin a guarded look, just as the team topped the stairwell and hesitated in the blackened doorjamb. Kirin was pale and disoriented. "What just happened?"

The others didn't know how to answer. "Don't kill anyone!" Chloe yelled to Uktena, though the words still sounded distant in her own ears. The dragon ignored her, folding his wings again as he shifted his attention toward the ceiling. For a moment, he reminded Chloe of Shipwreck as his back legs took a series of little steps while he readied to jump.

"Hurry!" she shouted as they lunged through the smoldering hole to the rooftop, only to be immediately buffeted by the wind and cold beyond. It had started to snow, and the spinning rotor of the helicopter whipped the white drift into a little tornado as it gained speed toward takeoff.

Inside the cockpit, the pilot watched the instruments closely as he waited for the green light to pull back on the stick. He was surprised to see four wet and oddly dressed teenagers stumble out to the deck. The girl waved frantically, as if trying to get his attention, and then she shouted something that was inaudible beneath the pulse of the rotors. He started to worry in earnest as she scrambled after her cohorts in an alarming attempt to gain distance from his position.

Chloe had just made it over a low wall to the next section of rooftop when the floor below the helicopter erupted. Jagged slabs of concrete flew into the air, and the helicopter was thrown onto its side. The spinning blades clipped the landing pad and came apart in a violent pitch of flying shards. A large spike of metal buried into the wall just inches beyond Kirin before the vehicle tipped over the edge and fell with a loud crash onto the lower roof.

The kids watched with a mixture of awe and horror as the dragon climbed from the hole and let out a deep, bestial roar that pierced the winter night. In the darkened hills behind him, a quick string of lightning flashes touched down in the same spot. The tumble of thunder came a few seconds later, as if in answer to Uktena's call.

That man in the helicopter is probably dead! Chloe realized. *I'm responsible for that and for Mr. Fitz, too!* She was up and screaming a second later. "Uktena, you have to stop! You can't kill people!" The words still sounded mushy and dull in her ears.

He turned the fury of his sparking gaze on her and lashed his thoughts across her mind. *These are bad men! They will die for their insolence!*

Chloe stood her ground and stepped closer. "NO! Even if they're bad, these men you've hurt were just taking orders!" The pressure of a headache was building in her temples and along her brow.

Then I will wait here to kill the ones who gave the orders and any of their servants who try to stop me. Uktena's attention shifted to the sky, where a blinking light approached below the clouds.

"That's not what I meant!" Chloe fought to ignore the swell of nausea that was rising in her gut. Uktena acted like he didn't hear her.

Stan got to his knees and started to film again from behind the wall as Kirin fought to regain his composure. Ezra climbed over to join Chloe. "We need to go now," Ezra said with his hand on her arm.

"If they catch us after this, I'm not sure we'll ever be released again," added Stan.

Uktena continued to stare at the growing light in the sky as steam rose from his quickly heating scales. Already the silvery sheen had returned to his form, and he looked somehow much larger now that he was outside beneath the sky, compared to the sickly worm that had been chained and drugged beneath the fluorescents below. He still gave no indication that he'd heard the pleading of the human beside him.

"We risked everything to break you free!" Chloe's chin was trembling and her eyes were beginning to water. "You have to help us!"

The dragon met her desperate gaze, and for a moment the deep sadness returned to him. "I cannot help you."

"But I wished for you to live," protested Chloe. "You said it would be your death that brought the others! But you didn't die, so the prophecy can't be true!"

"It was a wasted wish," Uktena countered quietly. "The Ascension has already begun. My death was to be the spark that started it, but it was the pain of my slow dying that finally awoke my brethren." He lowered his head. "The tipping point has been reached. There is no stopping it now."

The sound of an approaching helicopter cut through the cold silence that followed. Chloe felt like she was on the verge of collapse, just as Kirin's rubberized fingers found hers and held her up. "That's not good enough," she whispered, just as Derek Fitz stumbled through the doorway and opened fire.

Ezra tackled Kirin and Chloe to the roof as bullets streamed overhead and slammed into Uktena. The dragon blinked and flinched away, though now the bullets burst against his scales without breaking through. Still, the crazed security guard was screaming his best battle cry as he braced and continued to pump round after round at Uktena's head.

The dragon's serpentine form retracted instantly and spiraled into motion. Stan kept filming as the fifty-foot-long tail whipped around in a wide arc to catch Mr. Fitz broadside. He folded in half the wrong way before he was flung pinwheeling a hundred yards across the roof like a rag doll. Thankfully the shattered body went down out of sight over the far side of the building, though they could still hear the meaty landing against the pavement. Stan dropped his eyes from the viewfinder just long enough to heave his dinner over the wall. The pulsing adrenaline in his system allowed him to recover quickly, and he shot to his feet a moment later with the camera lens swinging to catch the approach of the second helicopter.

The pilot of Air 1 was coming in fast and low. He pulled up short when he saw the giant winged monster perched above the smoking remains of Air 2. The rhythmic thump of the rotors bounced across the concrete lot with a disorienting echo.

Chloe sat up again with her head beginning to throb along with the concussive beat. "Uktena, no!" But the dragon growled and charged, taking chunks from the roof with every surging step. "No!" She shouted again below the din as the pilot pulled back on the stick and prepared to turn.

Another jet of lightning launched out of Uktena's throat and caught the evading helicopter midair. The pilot banked right and aimed for the grassy knoll in front of the building, but the upper blades sparked and faltered as the rear rotor burst into flames. It started to tilt and drop.

Without thinking, Stan dropped the camera and thrust his hands out. At once, a concentrated vibration moved through his palms, and his fingers became a stinging blur. He could feel the wild energy contained there transfer to the air as a wind whipped forward in a focused cone. He clenched his eyes and grimaced as the rush of supercharged particles shot out toward the listing helicopter. The living air wrapped around the doomed aircraft and thrust it into an abrupt spin that kept it aloft.

It hit the snowy grass right side up, though still with enough kick to knock the pilot unconscious as a choking plume of smoke rose from the fried controls. Uktena kept charging.

Stan fell to his butt, dazed and pale. "That was me," he muttered in shock. "I did that." His bluish lips and chattering teeth made it obvious that the buffering presence of the camera between him and these events had been the only thing enabling him to keep functioning. Now he was about to pop.

Uktena roared again, feral and bristling with destructive potential as Chloe shook her head, unable to fully grasp what she'd unleashed on the world. *What have I done?* "We need to get down there!" she shouted while searching for an external set of stairs or a fire escape. There was nothing. She looked to Ezra, hoping for some grounded direction or an encouraging word, but his shaken stare followed the enraged monster.

As her hope passed to Kirin, he held her frantic eyes with a nod. He extracted the grappling hook from his bag and pointed to the edge.

CHAPTER 31
THE GETAWAY

The cockpit of Air 1 was quickly filling with smoke, and Dr. Markson was coughing violently as he stepped around and yanked open the pilot's door. Bert Vilmes was one of the best helicopter pilots working in the private sector with more than ten years of combat experience in a Black Hawk and another ten in high-end commercial work. There was a bloody gash on his forehead where he'd smacked into the window; his unconscious slump was held up only by the four-point seatbelt strapped across his chest.

Dr. Markson didn't want to move him, given the risk of spinal injury, but the smoke would kill him in minutes if he didn't. He pulled the collar of his jacket across his nose and leaned in to unclick the buckle with his other hand. He was not a very strong man, but did his best to support Bert's weight while struggling to ease him down to the cold grass below.

Richard Roberts hunched nearby, red-faced and bellowing into a walkie-talkie between hacking fits that left trails of spit streaked across the front of his camel hair jacket. On the other side of the downed helicopter, Mr. Allen and one of his most intimidating thugs had handguns drawn and their smoke-burned eyes locked on the top of the building. All three of them would have let Bert Vilmes die of smoke inhalation before they'd stopped to think about it.

Things were happening a little too quickly for Dr. Markson, who was accustomed to the often glacial pace of science. First the success of his patented lightning tower design, and then the groundbreaking numbers that started streaming in from the positron trap on the satellite. The initial data had sent his longtime team of engineers into an eruption of congratulatory cheer, but he hadn't been able to enjoy the success, not while watching Mr. Allen's smug and dangerous smile grow bigger with every passing minute...And not while knowing that he'd sent a teenage girl, younger than his own son, on a suicide mission to attempt the rescue of what was probably the most dominant predator the world had ever known.

Dr. Markson couldn't even begin to process the fact that the same predator was now very much awake and loose, and that it had just spat what seemed to be a highly charged fork of electricity from its mouth. He watched as it crested the edge of the building with hooked black claws that sent the upper panels of the mirrored façade to shatter on the walkway below. He felt its will stab into his consciousness as it growled with a guttural rumble and looked down at them with shining reptilian eyes. That was when Mr. Allen and his henchman opened fire.

Dr. Markson dropped to his knees and took cover below the helicopter, but his gaze didn't waver from the remarkable specimen that loomed above. He watched with a mixture of terror and awe as it reared up a hundred feet onto its hind legs and inflated with a glowing ball that traveled up its long throat toward its open mouth.

.   .   .

Chloe let go of the rope and dropped the last eight feet to the ground. She sprinted toward the front of the building while screaming out to Uktena in her mind. *Please! Don't hurt anyone else!*

The night sky flashed brilliantly just before another sharp crack of thunder sounded ahead. She started to run faster, despite Kirin's pleading from the roof above.

"Chloe, WAIT!" he yelled to deaf ears.

They were supposed to head straight for the van and speed off without looking back, but Chloe couldn't let her actions, or inaction, lead to the death of still more people. She rounded the corner of the building and saw the smoking helicopter with

Dr. Markson and Richard Roberts cringing on one side and two burning bodies splayed carelessly on the ground on the other. The bodies were charred beyond recognition with parts of their extremities and clothes turned to ash.

Chloe kept moving with the impulse to scream and throw up at the same time. Then the hulking mass of Uktena landed in the drop-off loop before her with enough force to shake the earth. She lost her footing and stumbled into a face-plant in an evergreen hedge. Her palms were scraped bloody and mulch was ground into the wounds, but there wasn't time for pain. She sprang to her feet and hurdled a metal bench with her sights locked on the dragon's ridged back.

He seemed even bigger than he'd been only moments earlier on the roof, and now his scales reflected the building's lights with a metallic gleam as he circled the two heads of the Daedalus Group like a lion preparing to attack. Richard Roberts turned to make a run for it, but the immense serpentine form slid around to block any escape with preternatural grace. Roberts blubbered into a handheld radio and averted his eyes from the giant snarling head that extended toward him.

UKTENA! "UKTENA!" Chloe roared with her thoughts and voice at once.

The dragon flinched as if slapped, and his furious eyes turned on her. "You presume too much, human," he warned.

"No!" Chloe called defiantly as she stopped running and marched to where Dr. Markson was kneeling over a third man lying unconscious in the grass with a bloody gash in his forehead. She stood between them and Uktena's looming bite. "If you're here to kill everyone, then start with me!" she challenged.

Uktena shifted his attention to the whimpering of Mr. Roberts. His long jaws began to open mechanically, the same way they had to receive the chunks of tossed meat.

"You say your death was meant to spark the Ascension, but it was me who woke you up in the first place!" she yelled. "And it was me who saved you now from death…ME, US, this is all part of the prophecy then, too!" she realized. "What if this moment—your survival—this is what was meant to happen all along?"

The savage rows of hooked teeth snapped shut, and Uktena looked at Chloe with undulating waves of power held in his gaze. "I have seen into this man's heart," he said. "He is the one who poisons the water and meat—caring for nothing but his own wealth and power. He is the one who drove away your father and gave you all of your longing and anger. He does not deserve to witness the end of your kind."

Chloe moved beside Mr. Roberts and raised her open, bloody palms before the dragon. "He can change," she declared. "He can at least live long enough to say good-bye to his daughter... something that I never got to have from my father." With a quick glance to Mr. Roberts's red quivering face, she reached up to place her hands against Uktena's muzzle. Her blood smeared against his protruding teeth and his nostrils flared. "Humans can change if given the chance, and so can you."

The flash of lightning quieted in Uktena's eyes, and he stared at Chloe for a long moment. "I envy your human hope, Chloe McClellan...I am truly sorry that it will not be enough to save you," he finally said.

The pounding in her head was starting to make her vision tunnel, but still Chloe managed to stand tall. "Go," she commanded, just as Ezra and Kirin tore around the side of the building. At the same time, Brent Meeks slammed his way out of the front door with his wide eyes locked on the monster and his rifle shaking in his hands.

Uktena's focus flashed between them and then turned to face the screeching approach of Stan behind the wheel of the black van. The vehicle came to a skidding halt and shuddered in place at the far side of the turnaround.

Brent started to raise his weapon, but Dr. Markson stilled him with a cautionary shake of his head. Uktena turned away from them all as he unfurled his wings with the sound of opening sails. "I must leave this land soon, but I would speak with you again before I go. You know where to find me," he said to Chloe before launching into the sky with a wing beat that sent leaves, snow, and smoke spiraling into the night. With another flap, the glimmer of his form vanished into the clouds.

Chloe collapsed to her knees and shut her eyes. Kirin knelt to help her an instant later. The van sped up beside them, and the driver's side window rolled down in a hurry. "Dudes, get in!" Stan yelled as sirens approached in the distance.

Brent moved in, hoping for some sort of direction from Mr. Roberts, who continued to shake and whimper with averted eyes. Instead, it was Dr. Markson who spoke up. "Stand down, Mr. Meeks," he commanded. "Chloe and her friends will be leaving now, and as far as we are concerned, they were never here. Mr. Fitz was mistaken—the creature received no aid in its escape tonight. Is that clear?"

Brent nodded and stood aside as Kirin loaded Chloe through the sliding door at the side of the van and Ezra claimed shotgun. Dr. Markson returned to the injured pilot on the ground as Chloe sat up and called out weakly, "Thank you."

Dr. Markson nodded. "For what it's worth, our positron trap system works." He motioned toward the red blink of the tower over the trees in the distance. "Clean, endless energy with no more environmental side effects…It's real." Another claw of lightning touched down in punctuation.

"Everything has side effects," Chloe said amid the ensuing rumble.

Dr. Markson could only blink and swallow. "I still hope you're wrong about what's coming, but I'll be here, ready to help you if you're not."

Chloe nodded as Kirin moved to slide the door shut, but Brent's boot lodged in the track as he fumbled for a moment in his satchel. He handed over the framed pictures that Ezra had given her. "Take Route 128 North; the other roads are covered," he said with a chin thrust and an encouraging thump to the door of the van. Chloe gave him a grateful wave as Stan switched gears into 'D' and the van sped off with squealing tires.

Stan took a hard turn at high speed and tore up Route 128 as the black Suburbans and police came into view over the hill behind them. Ezra looked back and lowered his head with a hard grip on the football, just before a two-foot fracture split across the road with a resounding CRACK! A moment later, an intense shiver passed through him…"Chloe, what's happening to us?"

"I'm not sure yet," she admitted, unable to meet his expectant gaze. She clutched the picture frame to her chest and curled up on the backseat against Kirin as he gently brushed his hand through her hair…Stan finally broke the silence with a laugh, and after a few breaths, Kirin and Ezra both joined him in the giddy relief. They had done the impossible—freed a chained dragon from a high-security building and gotten away with it. But Chloe couldn't shake the reoccurring mantra from her pain-wracked mind. *I've failed. I've failed. I've failed.*

CHAPTER 32
THE BURNING HORIZON

Chloe hurried through the barren winter woods, following a faded path that she'd once walked with her father on Sunday afternoons. Leaves crunched under the soles of her running shoes. Looking down, she could see that one rogue lace had escaped from its knot, now trailing with every step. There wasn't time to stop and tie it now. There wasn't any more time for anything.

A haphazard formation of Canada geese tore overhead with a mad cacophony of trumpeting, heading south as they normally did, but this time with a frantic desperation to their cries. Chloe climbed faster, heading in the opposite direction toward the rocky outcropping on the upper hillside. When she was younger, it had been a place for sandwiches and Snickers Bars, heavy, satisfying pulls from a water bottle, and sitting quietly with her head rested on her dad's shoulder as they enjoyed the view. The cliff jutted out from among the tallest hills for a commanding view of the rolling Virginia countryside to the north.

But now, as her aching muscles fought against the elevation, she was terrified of what she might see from the familiar granite shelf. She exhaled with a last big step up to the lookout she'd once cherished, and immediately a surge of horror lodged in her throat.

The northern horizon glowed with a sickly orange light, and above that, a thick, black cloud gathered in the sky. Washington, D.C. was burning, an entire city engulfed in fire. Even from a hundred miles away, she could see the distant dance of flame. The wall of rising smoke threatened to block out the sun. All she could do was tremble and stare.

At first, it looked like a long tendril of the black smoke was approaching, as if with a mind of its own. But then it raced overhead in a blanket of mad chatter, and Chloe saw that the movement was comprised of many thousands of birds, all streaming south in a frantic attempt to escape the destruction. She sank to her knees and brought her hands to her face. She had caused this. Her actions had sparked this fire, and it was she who had failed to stop it!

She shut her eyes, trying to block out the madness or will it away. Instead, a hot wind cut through the cold to find her tear-streaked cheeks, and a hundred thousand voices sounded in her thoughts at once, all crying out in panic and pain…

Chloe woke up screaming. She was in her own bed, and daylight burned through the cracks in the shut drapes. She was drenched in sweat and shaking as her mother moved from the nearby chair to comfort her.

"Shhhh." Audrey held out a warm cup of tea and brushed a clinging strand of hair from Chloe's cheek. "You're okay, honey."

The dull ache still clung to her temples, but Chloe could tell that the worst of it was over. In fact, she felt oddly alive and alert considering all that had transpired—as if the pressure that had been slowly building in her head since the headaches first began had now, finally, been released for good. She sat up and took the tea with both hands, thankful for the warmth of the mug in her fingers and the reassuring sting of it against her Neosporin-covered palms. "What day is it?" she asked, bringing the steaming brew to her lips.

"It's your birthday, Chloe, a little after ten in the morning." Audrey smiled as she pointed to the chocolate cake waiting on the nightstand with a big "SWEET 16" blazoned across the top in yellow frosting. Audrey had heavy bags under her eyes and moved a hand to the painful knot in her neck.

Maybe it's okay; maybe I'm just crazy after all? Chloe took a sip, and it burned her tongue. "It's December 21 and everything is still normal?" Chloe reiterated hopefully.

Audrey's smile failed. "Well, no…not really."

.   .   .

The TV signal was intermittent again with heavy bands of static that interrupted service for sometimes twenty minutes at a time.

But between the breaks, Chloe could piece together enough of what was happening.

At 6:35 a.m. in Northern Tanzania, the tallest peak of Mount Kilimanjaro had broken off the mountaintop and tumbled down the Western Breach to kill thousands of unevacuated refugees and the remaining aid workers. The helicopter and cell phone footage was dodgy with static, but all seemed to show what appeared to be an eight-hundred-foot lizard climbing out of the explosion of magma and ash.

A few hours later, at 3:00 p.m., local time, in the Quinghai province of China, the ground broke with an earthquake that registered at more than twice the strength of any in recorded history. A fissure opened so wide in the earth that the largest lake in East Asia spiraled into an immense whirlpool that drained into an underground river of lava. The ensuing steam geyser was so great that it would raise the surface temperature across the entirety of the planet by two degrees in forty-eight hours. The ground shook with such ferocity that more than two million lives were snuffed out in minutes. Numerous surviving witnesses spoke of glimpsing a giant red serpent wreathed in flame amid the super heated cloud above.

Then, at 7:15 a.m., the unprecedented late-season, class 5 Hurricane Zamilla reached land along the eastern coast of Honduras with fast-moving floods and devastating winds that reached gusts of more than 225 miles per hour. No images or commentary got out from the strike zone, and the newscasters had nothing but the repeat satellite imaging of the cloud spiral to fill their stunned, awkward silences.

Finally, another close lightning strike knocked out power to the McClellan home just before lunchtime, and their link to the spreading global disaster went dark. Chloe and her mom sat close together on the sofa and watched the dead screen in silence for a long time before finally rising to share a cold cheese sandwich and tepid bowls of split pea soup. Even as they ate and bustled about the kitchen, they stopped to hold hands often or interrupted what they were doing to offer a reassuring squeeze or kiss to the top of the head…Words seemed meaningless now.

After lunch, Audrey presented Chloe with a secondhand iPhone 5s, but cell phone signals were down and Chloe didn't have the heart to turn it on to only see it fail. They were completely cut off from the outside world. As a consolation prize, Audrey led Chloe to the hallway closet, where she'd stashed multiple five-gallon jugs of water, lanterns and candles, batteries, a crank radio, and a wealth of industrial-sized canned food from the back pantry at Pete's. She showed off her survival supplies with a smile and a shrug.

Chloe buried her face in her mother's chest and wiped her tears away on her sweater. *She'd listened.* It was the best present that her mom had ever given her.

*   *   *

The effects of the migraine were completely gone by lunchtime, but the waves of nausea were replaced by the growing weight of anxiety in her gut. The house was filled with a charged stillness in the afternoon hours as Chloe sat by the window with Shipwreck in her lap. She listened for the frantic babble of birds overhead and shut her eyes, waiting for the collective scream of humanity's demise to reach her thoughts. Instead, as the early twilight stretched across the yard with long shadows and golden light, Uktena's will sounded in her mind. *COME*, he said with the word echoing.

She dressed warmly and put on her favorite running shoes— just like she'd worn in the latest nightmare—and she picked up one of her mom's new flashlights on the way to the door. With her hand on the knob, she looked back to meet Audrey's worried watch from the sofa.

"I have to go," Chloe said.

"Where?" Audrey asked, already knowing the answer.

"The pond," answered Chloe anyway, wondering if she should say more.

Audrey's nod said: *I trust you.* "Will you be back for dinner? We still have a cake to eat," Audrey reminded her with a crack in her voice.

Chloe swallowed and answered quietly. "I don't know; I think so...I love you, Mom," she added with more conviction.

Audrey smiled, and despite it all, her tired face was instantly radiant again. "I love you, too. You be careful, honey. I'll be here waiting when you get home."

Chloe left before her mother could see her tears—she could at least protect her from that. They started falling cold across her cheeks as she walked up the snow-covered driveway and crossed the street into the woods. She did not run—in no hurry to reach whatever waited for her ahead—and she wondered if she would ever run for something as simple as joy again?

The stark woods were baked orange, and Chloe's head cleared a little more with every inhale of the crisp winter air. She looked down at her feet as they crunched across the thin layer of snow over dried leaves, but unlike in her dream, her shoelaces remained in tight knots, and the fading glow hung on the horizon in the west, not to the north.

She climbed the last rise toward the place where the high chain link fence was supposed to be, but the entire length of posts and wire had been yanked roughly from the ground and carried away to an unknown destination. Ahead, she could see the lightning tower unmanned, but still standing and fully operational. As she passed underneath, she could hear the slow scraping sound of the outer conductivity shell, and her hair stood with the static charge.

Below, the observation platform had been removed from the pond's surface and tossed into the woods nearby. The remaining construction vehicles and a few black SUVs had been piled unceremoniously in a makeshift blockade on the road, and the uprooted fence was wrapped around them and stretched between the trees across the entrance. Chloe descended the hill to the pond as a collection of deer bolted away through the woods on the far side.

As she stepped to the familiar rocky edge, silvery movement glinted below the water. Uktena's giant horned crown emerged slowly from the center of the pool. The black slits in his eyes narrowed as his long serpentine neck rose up. He had grown since Chloe had last seen him. Now his hovering head was almost as long as a school bus, and she wondered how the rest of him could still fit within the confines of the little pond.

"It has begun," he said.

Water streamed from his scales in heavy rivulets, and Chloe had to squint as she looked up at him, shining now almost like a polished mirror as the last light of day reflected off him. "What happens now?" she asked.

"Soon Kadru, Queen of Serpents, will wake," Uktena declared with finality. "The four bulls will claim their kingdoms, and the Great Rut will begin as they compete for the right to mate with her...Her brood will bring about the final death of your world."

Uktena's gaze shifted as another figure emerged from the woods. Chloe turned to see Kirin approaching from the same spot where they'd entered while playing hooky on the second day of school. He waved with wary eyes locked on the dragon.

"Hey," he said, sounding almost casual. "I stopped by your house right after you'd left. Your mom told me where you'd gone."

"I'm glad." She took his hand, and he kissed her forehead as the slamming of car doors sounded from the other side of the barricade.

Chloe squeezed Kirin's hand tighter, but was relieved to see Stan picking his way through the debris soon after. She felt another little swell of gratitude as she caught sight of his big toothy grin from afar. Then Ezra Richardson's steadfast scowl followed a few seconds later, and he carried something large over his shoulder.

Uktena watched quietly as Stan raised his hand. "Hey, dudes. I ran into Ezra at the grocery store and he said a voice had commanded him to find you." Stan began to chuckle, "and I got to admit that I'd heard the same thing...So, here we are." Stan removed a half-smoked joint from his coat pocket and lit it with a heavy drag.

"Stan?" Chloe hissed.

He shrugged. "Whatever, dude; it's the end of the world."

Ezra stepped closer and heaved what appeared to be a giant riding saddle to the ground before Uktena. The dragon did not react. "You okay, Lightning?" Ezra asked.

"Yeah, I'm fine." With a closer examination, she noticed that the oversized saddle had been handcrafted with a close attention to detail, including stitched images of flying dragons through the leather edging. "What's that?"

"I've been working on it for a couple months now," Ezra admitted, "though I wasn't sure why until yesterday."

Chloe turned back to Uktena, who'd been watching intently. "Why did you call them here?"

"I did not call them. You are the spirit who summoned them and binds them together." Uktena studied the four kids, looking from Ezra, to Stan, to Kirin, and then back to Chloe. "Earth, air, water, and spirit—just like with the Five Claws of the dragon."

Chloe looked across the three men in her life and realized only then how true it was. "But what about fire?" she asked. The only answer was the approaching racket of loud pop music followed by the slam of another car door. Chloe turned, expecting or maybe hoping to see Liz appear. Instead, a shrill voice and a blaze of red hair cut through the fading daylight.

"Goddamn it, I broke a heel!" Kendra shouted before noticing the odd meeting before her. "What the hell are you all doing here?" she hollered before noticing the even odder creature that presided over them. "What the hell is that?" she shrieked.

Chloe ignored the escalating barrage of screams and profanity as Ezra moved to intercept Kendra's freak-out. She turned back to Uktena, who watched it all with an unreadable calm. "I don't understand," she said.

Ripples of lightning swam across the dragon's gaze once more, and Chloe felt an echoing tickle of electricity within. "Five Elementalists to match the five Elementals."

"Elementalists?"

"The Dragon Riders of old. They were the ones who imprisoned my kind long ago and foretold of our return on the Tianlong Cauldron…They have awoken again in you." His words echoed in Chloe's mind as if she had voiced them herself. "The prophecy spoke of Five Claws rising at the Ascension, not four, but it is only because of you that *I* live…Perhaps this is all part of the plan as you said."

The five teens came together for the first time. Kendra was on the cusp of a nervous breakdown with only Ezra able to hold her still, but all of them felt a stirring of joined power between them. The air and ground itself seemed to vibrate with anticipation.

Lightning flared in Uktena's gaze. "If we are to stop the Great Rut from happening, we will need to fight together."

Chloe felt an intense rush of euphoria and dread at the same time as her eyes followed Uktena's focus to the saddle waiting between them.

"It is time to ride," he said.

The Mother of Doom

The rumble rose from the deep. For more than fifteen hundred miles, the ocean floor trembled along the Mariana Trench, at first subtly, with barely enough force to make the sand dance on the lightless ocean floor, but gradually stronger as the sound of the wrenching earth grew. The whole Pacific shelf lurched as a massive fissure opened in the bed of what had previously been untouched ocean. Billions of tons of water were displaced in an instant.

The groan of the shifting fault that followed was staggering, audible all the way to Arizona in one direction and to India in the other. And yet somehow, what sounded like an animal roar rose above the tumult. From below the deepest point of all the oceans on earth climbed Kadru, Queen of Serpents, wriggling out of the pit like a newborn snake escaping from its shell. But Kadru had been called Tiamat by the Babylonians, and Illuyanka by the Hittites, and she was older than all the civilizations of man.

She fought her way into open water and started to swim up the five miles of cliff to reach the higher ocean floor. She'd grown larger during her slumber—stretching on for miles and more than a hundred feet thick at her widest point. She was covered from snout to tail in overlapping layers of supple black scales. In ages past, she had blocked out the sun when she'd reared up and opened her cobra's hood.

Even from 35,000 feet down, she could hear the screams and confusion of the humans—it made her swim faster. She hadn't fed in two thousand years, and she would need to eat her fill before she went into estrus again. Soon after the Ascension, the Great Rut would begin, and she longed for the battle that would see which of the four dragon bulls might win her favor. All of the cataclysm and death to come would be in her honor.

She would return upriver to the hot jungles of the eastern mainland to rebuild her nest, and once the humans had been broken and the five territories were established, the males would come for her. The brood that would spout from her womb would pick the earth clean of humanity and usher in the dawn of the next age.

In only a few minutes, her massive black form slipped over the lip of the trench and turned west, continuing toward the surface at a more gradual climb. The wave that preceded her would gather strength as it went. Before it found the islands of the South Pacific, it would reach speeds of more than five hundred miles per hour and have climbed ten stories into the air. Another wave rocketed in the opposite direction, toward the islands of Hawaii and the West Coast of the Americas. Soon, all around the Pacific, terrified faces would turn toward the water and offer their screams to the return of mighty Kadru.

Hundreds of millions of their jabbering, insufferable lives would be silenced in an instant, but that would be only the beginning.

ACKNOWLEDGMENTS

So much time is spent writing in a vacuum, that it's hard to imagine how much of so many is required to get a book into the world.

First there are the early readers who generously gave their time, notes, and ideas to make the messy pages cleaner and realer than what they'd been. Macon Blair, Jamie Falik, Peter Sharp, Meghan Groome, Sam Ware, Jennifer Phoenix, Rob Heffernan, and Joanna Wagner—you were all invaluable. Thank you!

Marilyn and Ben Sharp, who read this book more than once with a magnifying glass and a whole box of pencils on hand—I couldn't have done it or anything without you.

Allison Cohen, you gave a shot to a first timer in a climate where most first timers can't even get a rejection email. Thank you for believing, taking a gamble, and shepherding this book along.

Sarah Masterson Hally, Hannah Black, Brielle Benton, Mary Cummings, Scott Waxman, and the whole Diversion Books team. Thank you for giving this book a home, and for all the support, attention to detail, design work, and marketing love that enables a bloated Word.doc to become a thing I can hold in one hand and share with an audience.

To the audience, grow, spread the word, bang the drum; for a first timer with big dreams at a small publisher, YOU are everything. I love you.

To Chloe Ford and Charlottesville Virginia. Thank you both for your name and nature. To Scott Adkins and the Brooklyn Writers Space for giving me a place to write, and Joan Campbell for giving me the time to edit.

This book is dedicated to Alex for the daily inspiration, and to Lorna for your unending patience and support, your countless nights reading, discussing, and talking me down from the ledge. Without you none of this would have been possible.

And finally, to that nameless creative writing professor who once told me "not everyone needs to be a writer." You couldn't be more wrong. I hope you've found a better-suited profession by now and that others had the sense to ignore you.